Underlife

a prequel to

Adept

OMNIBUS EDITION

Robert Finn

snowbooks

ISBN13: 978-1905005-92-5

UNDERLIFE

Clipper spent a lot of time on the tube. It had a buzz he liked. And anything you could want was down there. Hurried people with too much money. Anonymity and good exit routes. Hot girls you'd never normally set eyes on – and they were stuck there for five minutes waiting for a train – no excuse for not talking to you. Sometimes Clipper would even help bewildered tourists. Of course if he was a little drunk or a little high, his help tended to really mess up their travel plans, but by and large he meant it well. Though lately he was cutting back on that – the getting high, as well as the freelance tourist advice. Gary had never let him get away with it anyway and somehow doing what Gary wanted seemed even more important now that he was gone.

So now Clipper's watchword was 'professionalism'. Though if he did happen to be a little high he'd try to avoid actually saying it out loud; all those syllables tended to trip your tongue up.

The problem was that he was by himself now and that messed everything up. For a start it meant he was having to make all his own plans, and that required concentration. Which was a problem. Whatever he tried, he just couldn't seem to motivate himself properly. His concentration slipped away from him the whole time and he found himself drifting, wasting time. And that was dangerous. It meant it was only a matter of time before he screwed up and got caught.

It was more than that too. When Gary disappeared, it didn't just leave a gap that needed to be filled, it changed things. Maybe for good.

If Clipper had had another way of earning a living he'd have been giving it some careful consideration at this point.

Today he was hanging round the Jubilee line, sort of goofing off despite his best intentions. Riding from Bond Street – where the best-looking shop assistants in the world worked – out to Canary Wharf – where you'd get these career girls in their suits, with their amazing hair that looked so natural because they'd spent a mint getting it that way. Great looking and they were all brokers or traders or bankers – if you could have girl bankers.

Brainy and in charge. He always liked that. And he always wished he'd been able to get somewhere with one of them. It was probably as much to see what their lives looked like as anything. He imagined they all lived in loft apartments – wood floors and little twinkly halogen lights – with gyms in the basement. And their boyfriends were Swiss ski instructors or else they were really old blokes with big, big amounts of cash – like from owning oil tankers or some copper mines. And it didn't matter that the blokes were like sixty or something because that was exactly the point about having stacks of cash.

Those thoughts had been vaguely in the back of his mind as he'd been eyeing up this one girl, trying not to let her notice he was paying attention. He was glancing at her, and letting his imagination wander, when really he knew he should have been working on the next grab.

They were outside, above ground, in what the signs called a 'plaza' by the entrance to Canary Wharf tube. A needling wind was skipping round Clipper's ankles, making him wish he'd brought that big old gangsta puffa jacket of his. Nearby the girl was talking on the phone, oblivious to him, tucking hair the colour of maple syrup behind her delicate ear and cutting up rough in what he thought was probably German. And yet she wasn't German because every now and then she'd swear or say 'get used to it' in English, only with an American accent. How hot was that? She was tearing a strip off some bloke in German and then dissing him in English, like rubbing his nose in how it wasn't even her first language that she was clobbering him in.

He reckoned she might be Californian. As he liked to remind people, he'd lived there for a few years himself – though he tended not to get very specific, because the truth was he'd been at high-school there for a few years and that probably didn't sound as impressive as whatever story people might come up with for themselves if he kept fairly quiet about the details. Relocating out there to be with his dad and then pulling up roots and coming back again had badly messed with his half-hearted attempts to get an education – not to mention how it had mongrelised the slang he used – but it had also left him with just enough of an accent, and maybe a bit of added mystery, so he wasn't complaining.

The girl had finished her first call and was dialling another. She took a deep breath before putting the phone to her ear and he could tell it wasn't a conversation she was looking forward to.

He really should get going, but there was something about this girl, besides her looks – and he found himself unable to look away. He watched her getting her nerve up before speaking and he couldn't help feel a bit sorry for whatever she was going through.

For a moment he thought about nicking her phone, a Blackberry (natch), but he couldn't get very excited about the idea, even if there'd been an easy way to make it happen.

Without thinking, he stepped in a little closer to her, careful to keep his eyes up ahead like he didn't see her. He was sort of hoping to catch a hint of whatever perfume she was wearing. He wasn't, you know, a pervert or anything – it was just that these girls always smelled amazing.

Afterwards, if he was looking back on that day and trying to choose a particular moment, he'd have to say that right then, as he stepped forwards, was probably when things started to unravel. It was about the last thing to happen that day that really made any sort of sense. Everything after that point was like a really unpleasant episode from someone else's life spliced into his, not to mention that most of it took place in fast-forward. Even the bits that weren't a speeded-up nightmare were still like something out of a dream, though at least it was one of his own.

The girl had made her difficult call. Clipper had stuck around, trying not to look conspicuous, but still watching her face, somehow captivated.

Then she'd hung up, and so softly you'd hardly notice, she'd begun to cry. From then on, that whole day just rocketed past him, one insane event after another, all seemingly unstoppable.

The girl had begun to cry and it had hurt him – it had physically hurt him – watching her face. A pain just under his ribs, like something sharp was pressing into a soft part of him, had forced him into motion. One minute he was detached, keeping out of her eye line, just a spectator; the next he was moving quickly forwards, asking gently, "Are you OK?" He could hear the compassion in his voice and knew that he meant it – though he had no explanation for it. But then it didn't seem to need explaining. She was upset; he wanted to help. It didn't require any more thought than if she'd stumbled and he'd caught her.

He was confused at his own behaviour and it seemed to have caught her off guard too. She should have glared at him, because he was a stranger intruding on a private moment, or at least she should have lied like normal people do and said, "I'm fine." But instead she told him exactly why she was crying.

And then they'd just talked.

It had been unlike any conversation he'd ever had. She said her name and he told her his: his real name. And it was… perfect.

Really, it was just about too good to be true. Of course as soon as he thought that, the world slid back into focus around him and he realised what he'd just told her – said right out, to a total stranger – and he felt panic. A panic that took on a different dimension when, out of the corner of his eye, he clocked a black shape moving towards him. Something about it held his attention. He looked round and was instantly annoyed with himself. This was what happened when you let your mind wander away from the business in hand.

The shape he'd seen was a black car, some sort of expensive 4x4, and it had stopped at the top of the steps behind him. It was probably the way the car had pulled up that had caught his eye. You couldn't park there – not even for a minute. He didn't know what it meant, but it sparked a little flash of adrenaline inside him.

The car – which was maybe an X5, that slick BMW SUV – spat out a couple of fast-moving geezers in black, who were dressed like coppers, but sort of tougher. Some sort of tactical group maybe.

His rising sense of anxiety over the arrival of a police car was starting to push away the acute shame he felt after his chat with the girl. He'd told her... well, he'd blurted out all sorts of things and he felt embarrassed and kind of exposed now. He'd made an idiot of himself and he just wanted to get away from her before she could point that fact out. The sense that the cops were bearing down on him magnified his agitation until he could hardly hold still. He needed to move. "Gotta go," he said to her, even as he skipped away.

He did what he called his 'fade'. He matched speed with a couple of secretaries who were click-clacking past, and shifted from his usual walk, which was kind of a chin-forwards swagger, to more of a rapid shuffle – what he thought of as his office-boy walk. Hassled and downtrodden. And today he was in the right clothes to pull it off. A month back he'd got a dark blue suit from Moss Bros – forty quid because it had glue or something on one of the trouser legs and a snag on the right lapel. He'd added a white shirt and a silver tie he'd stolen from Next: so freaked to be in there that he'd pocketed it on instinct. Looking at the other shoppers, he'd had a sudden glimpse of what his life could be like if he was a trainee estate agent or, you know, maybe working in credit control for a car leasing firm or something, and he'd bolted, forgetting his original plan to actually pay for the thing. Black shoes, which were bashed to bits, and his hair like he usually had it. Short all round with a sort of teased mop on top. It wasn't an office haircut, but then he was always seeing these junior types dressed just like that: creased-up office clothes and mad club hairstyles. Suits that looked like they slept in them. Maybe when you had a crap job on crap pay you got to have your hair how you wanted it.

Clipper felt better for being on the move. He was now angling towards the archway at the top of the escalator, the one that led down into the tube station, and thinking it was time to get out of the cold. The girl was forgotten – or at any rate he was working on it – and there was no denying that it was, as his granddad used to say, perishin' outside. He'd leave the coppers to their business.

But he risked a glance in their direction anyway, because he had a thing for any sort of cool-sounding elite police stuff, ever since he was a kid. They seemed to be heading in the same direction he was. So he began to turn away, so as not to put himself in their sights.

Speaking of which, he was hoping they'd be carrying guns. But they weren't. They'd got everything else though. The whole outfit screamed weapons training. Altberg Defender boots, ballistic flak tunics, lots of webbing and everything in black. The bulky flak tunics sort of ended at the shoulder, like a cap-sleeve t-shirt. If you happened to have ripped deltoids – which these guys did, you could see them bunching under their tight nylon sleeves – then you weren't going to have any problems looking serious in that get-up. He'd hoped for SWAT-style helmets, but they had on tight knitted caps instead. Very SAS. He took in as many of these details as he could, thinking how he'd google it all later. Both men were white and Clipper had more stubble on his chin than either of them had on what he could see of their heads. SO19 maybe? The Met's Armed Response group. Or maybe something lower profile?

Clipper was more than a little bit torn now. Part of him, the part he was doing his best to ignore, wanted to rush back to the girl, to ask her, "What just happened between us?" But he wasn't planning to act on that particular impulse. The rest of his brain was trying to decide how to react to these coppers. If there was any chance that they could be after him, or if the area was about to be sealed off, he needed to scarper. But these blokes had to be some sort of anti-terrorism outfit, which let him off the hook, didn't it? Besides which he just ate up that stuff. He wanted to know why they were here, what they were planning to do. Maybe something was going on.

Gary would have dragged him away, of course – he was all for the low-key, better part of valour stuff – but Gary was gone. And Clipper thought he'd like to get a *slightly* better look at what they were up to. With that in mind, he peeled off from the city gent he was now following, and began to loop slowly around so that the SWAT-looking guys could lead the way. If he got behind them instead of letting them bear down on him, he'd feel a lot happier about sticking around.

While he split off to the side, pretending he wanted to take a quick look at the quayside, he watched them out of the corner of his eye. They didn't talk, didn't use their radios, didn't even glance towards each other, but they moved together in a way that made Clipper *yearn* to be part of some organisation like that. Watching them walk, it was like a Tarantino thing, only they weren't in slow motion.

It reminded him of a daydream he had where he was recruited as an undercover member of some tactical unit like that. In the daydream they'd been watching him for a while, could see he was a bright guy and they were prepared to clean his record if he'd come and work for them... undercover. Which he didn't consider completely farfetched. Clipper knew what was what and boxed a little and liked to think he was in shape; all he'd need to get him ready for some special forces job was a little specialist training. Mind you, these lads in front of him looked like they'd had more than a *little* training. They were just about the toughest pair he'd ever seen. Try as he might, he couldn't see himself getting in their way for a second. Couldn't picture it.

Fascinated, he let them get on the down escalator, hung back as a stream of ordinary punters stepped on behind them and then, some distance back, he followed them down into the cavern of the station and the relative warmth below.

Every day, Clipper's first job was always to boost a travelcard and he had one in his pocket right now, but the spook-force guys were stalled up ahead, flashing badges and saying something to the trog on the ticket barriers ('trog' was what Gary called the underground staff) so Clipper busied himself with a ticket machine for a minute to make sure he didn't end up ahead of them again.

The transport bloke was looking very unhappy to see them, like they'd just offered to demonstrate some of their excellent specialist training on him. Right away the man was sweating. He was shaking his head and holding up his hands too, which they obviously didn't care for. Then one of the badge-flashing coppers took a step towards him. Simultaneously his partner laid a finger on his arm, halting him, but the transport bloke looked like he was about to lose some sphincter control. He fumbled a gate open for them and they pushed through leaving the trog standing there, looking all around for guidance, clearly not sure what he was supposed to do next.

Whatever this was about, Clipper was lapping it up. It was a treat to see a trog sweating for a change. They were always recognising him, making his life difficult, throwing their weight around. Now one of them was on the receiving end for once. *Yeah*, thought Clipper, looking at the rattled transport bloke and revelling in the way he'd been brushed aside, *back off*.

Moving through the gates and onto the escalator, leaving the flustered trog behind, Clipper lost sight of the cops for a minute. Maybe they'd double-timed it on ahead. Clipper thought about running to catch up, but he knew Gary would have had a fit at the thought if he'd been there. Sprinting after coppers being perhaps the stupidest idea ever. The whole point of working the underground was that it made you anonymous, impossible to remember, one of ten million faceless faces. What you didn't do – what you didn't *ever* do – was stand out. Because not only did it mess up whatever angle you were working at that moment, it risked messing up the next one and so on down the line. Pretty soon they'd be spotting your face on CCTV and passing out your photo and everyone knew what happened next. And in Gary's case what had happened next was prison. This was before Clipper had met him and it had only been an eighteen month sentence, which never sounded that bad to Clipper, but he tended to keep his mouth shut on that point on account of how Gary knew his real name was Matthew and he had a mum living in Bromley who liked to make him beans on toast on the rare occasions he dropped in and he'd never been 'inside' or even in a cell overnight and so any view he might have on prison would be based on sitting in a nice cosy flat eating his tea and watching it on telly.

Clipper tried to cut off that line of thought because the truth was that he was thinking about Gary the whole time. He missed him. Not only did Gary keep him out of trouble, and dispense these little gems of wisdom the whole time, but he was the one who made the whole thing fun. Without him it wasn't an adventure any more; it was just stealing things and trying not to get caught.

Gary, who'd read a lot of books – especially inside – was always making genius stuff up, like how he and Clipper were the Marxist Vanguard. Clipper never really knew what that meant, but Gary would quote the phrase 'all property is theft', which Clipper really liked, and it had become like a catchphrase for them both.

Sometimes when Clipper thought about Gary's disappearance, an unwelcome thought crept into his head; he worried that Gary had disappeared on purpose.

The first few times Gary had gone on errands for the mysterious Warren, and left Clipper to fend for himself, it had seemed like the beginning of the end. Whatever Warren had Gary doing, it was obviously a lot more fun than dipping for wallets and phones and such on the tube. Clipper had the sense that Gary was moving up in the world without him, like some sort of underworld promotion that Clipper had been passed over for.

That hadn't lasted long though. After the third job – and Gary would never say what the jobs actually involved – his mood had changed and it no longer seemed like Gary was off having fun. He was very subdued and he said even less about what he did for Warren, but Clipper got the distinct impression it wasn't for the fainthearted.

Clipper had seen Warren a few times, always from a distance. And the last time had also been the last time he'd seen Gary.

He and Gary had gone to a club that was supposedly part-owned by Warren. It really wasn't Gary's scene, though Clipper was quite into it, being a few years younger and a little less awkward when it came to being around loud music and girls dancing.

Gary had left Clipper talking to a couple of nurses from Hatfield and gone back behind the bar with a flunky who'd come to fetch him, saying that Warren was ready to see him now. Clipper kept up a bit of patter with the nurses, doing his best not to get distracted, but all the time he was watching out for any glimpse of Gary returning.

Because Clipper was with Gary, and Gary was with Warren, the bar was comping their drinks. So when Clipper finally did get a glimpse of Gary an hour or so later, it was after several more bottles of very tasty imported beer and he was no longer at his most lucid – over-refreshed was how he liked to think of it. The nurses were packing up, Clipper having got a little too Mr Grabby with one of them, when he saw Gary at the back of the club near one of the exits. Gary was nodding to an imposing looking bloke with a scarred face who stood nearby. Gary looked like he was trying to reassure him he was on the case. Clipper was pretty sure it was the same man he'd glimpsed before, and there was clearly a boss/employee vibe involved, so it had to be Warren. Clipper tried to get a proper look at the man, but the club lighting didn't help with that. Warren was dressed pretty sharply, though he wore some sort of tight skull-cap. It was difficult to tell whether it was the latest Hollywood fad or some religious thing. Despite looking pretty weird, it also looked sort of natural too. So much so that Clipper wondered about getting one too.

Gary had given a final nod, this one meaning goodbye, and strode away towards one of the exits without even a glance towards Clipper. Then out of nowhere, a Slavic looking guy was stepping up behind Warren and smacking him across the back of the head with an empty beer bottle.

Fragments of green glass sprayed across the nearest table, hitting some girl in the face, and triggering a scream that Clipper could hear from across the room. It cut through the pounding of a Sasha remix like a gunshot at a funeral.

Warren didn't go down though, he twisted round to place one hand over the spot where the bottle had hit, and then everything went peculiar.

What Clipper thought he saw was the Slavic guy ramming the shattered bottle in a twisting motion towards Warren's throat and the glass teeth grinding themselves to pieces all by themselves. For an eerie second he appeared to be holding the bottle steady a foot or so from Warren's throat. But at the same time, it seemed like he was leaning into it. It wasn't an image that made a lot of sense.

Then Warren straightened and pushed out with his palm, like an open-hand punch, which to Clipper never seemed to connect, but the Slavic guy went down with a snap, almost like a convulsion, as though he'd been bitten by the world's deadliest snake.

That done, Warren snatched a fresh cloth from the bar, pressed it to his bleeding head and leaned across to say something in the ear of a bouncer who'd rushed over. He didn't appear to be bothered by the damage done to his scalp or to notice the blood running out from under his skull-cap and down the back of his neck. A moment later, two other bouncers were carrying the fallen man into a back room and Warren was staring at the girl with the cut face, coldly assessing her, while one of the bar girls tried to stop her crying.

Gary was nowhere to be seen. Numb – both with shock and effects of the beer – Clipper did his best to get out of there quickly. He hunted up and down the street without success, and finally caught up with Gary at a cab place about five minutes later. For a moment he couldn't think what to say.

"Who is he?" he asked in the end.

Gary looked distracted, wrapped up in his own weary thoughts, and only half aware of Clipper standing there. "They're all..." he said and tapered off. His eyes weren't even focussed on Clipper. They were set on the middle-distance, where presumably he could play out and review whatever thoughts were bothering him.

A cab pulled up at the kerb and the dispatcher tapped on the scratched window, caught Gary's eye, and pointed to it. In something of a daze, Gary wandered towards the idling vehicle.

"Gary?" Clipper said sharply, trying to get his attention.

Gary turned to look at him, finally fixing on his face. "You can't hurt them," he said absently and then he was getting into a cab, leaving Clipper standing on the pavement in a shiny shirt that was glued to his back with sweat that got colder every second and did nothing to dispel the feeling that something good had ended.

And that was the last time Clipper had seen Gary. No one knew where he'd gone, but a lot people had suggested it was somewhere unpleasant and permanent. Clipper's guts knotted at the thought. But at the same time he somehow didn't like the idea that Gary was alive and well any better – that maybe he'd made a few bob on that last job for Warren and then decided he was better off without Clipper, that he didn't need him any more. It was a toss-up as to which idea upset him more.

Now, riding down on the escalator, Clipper tried for the millionth time to stop thinking about Gary and what had happened to him. He tried to focus on the present as he stepped off onto the platform, which at Canary Wharf was a great concrete cathedral of hollowed-out space. He looked around, realising with a little jolt that he couldn't see the spook-force coppers anywhere.

Instinctively he checked out the security cameras. He knew where they all were, but Gary had schooled him to do it anyway in case something changed or he remembered wrong. These days, without even thinking, he was able to face away from their gaze or seek out their blind spots.

Something about the closest camera immediately caught his eye, though it took him a moment to decide what it was. Partly that was on account of how you should never let your gaze stop when you looked at cameras: the staff who watched the monitors picked up on that. The first time Gary had caught Clipper looking right into a camera he'd given him a right bollocking and then asked him if he'd got a watch. "Don't need it. I use my phone," Clipper had said.

The next day, Gary had handed him a watch. Nothing too flash because (remember, remember) you didn't want to stand out, but nice all the same. Gary explained that a watch was like a manacle and you wore one to show that you were one of the workers, a slave to the system, and therefore beneath notice. Then he asked Clipper whether he knew what a 'manacle' was. Clipper had felt like a right plum for saying he thought it was like a big sea-lion or something.

Gary explained, "If you find you've been staring at a camera, look at your watch like this," he made a little surprised face, "and get moving. Or if you want to change direction, 'cos maybe you've spotted someone you want to avoid, look at your watch first. The drones look at their watches constantly because their time belongs to someone else. Do the same and it's like camouflage: they won't see you."

'Drones' was another Gary-word; it referred to ordinary working punters. Clipper reckoned it probably came from the way they whined on endlessly about their jobs.

Clipper glanced at his watch now – it was almost a compulsive tic by this point – and then he let his gaze roam as though he was maybe putting together some talking points for the next budget meeting or something. This time as his eyes swept across the camera he realised what was weird. The cable that should run to the back of it ended about ten inches from the case. Had it been like that this morning when he came through? Had he just not noticed before?

He drifted down the platform, looking for the coppers, and interested to see if the other cameras were hooked up properly. If there was some refit going on and there was no surveillance at the moment it was a golden opportunity to get a little bit of a nicking spree going.

One minute now until the next train. From the times of the other trains it looked like the tube network was running slow today. No problem for him, of course, but it meant you had to plan your getaways a little more carefully.

Clipper reached the next camera just as he saw one of the coppers tucked behind a pillar up ahead of him, almost as though he was hiding.

The camera down this end was even more obviously out of action. Well, 'obvious' if you bothered to look, which no one ever did. There was a crack across the lens that Clipper could see from thirty feet away.

Gary claimed he'd once paid two kids fifty quid to bust all the cameras in Old Street tube using catapults and ball bearings. And then while the staff chased them round the station, Gary had lifted some designer's courier bag which contained a Mac laptop, one of the metal-skinned ones with all the extras on it, a PDA, a video iPod stacked with tunes and a touch-screen phone from Japan. Clipper suspected that the haul might have grown a little in the retelling, but still it was a sweet score. He looked around now for any signs that someone was working a similar scam. He didn't see any little Dennis the Menace types with catapults.

Clipper was also looking for the other copper and was momentarily troubled to see that he'd unknowingly walked past him, because he too was tucked away like the first one. Clipper was now sandwiched between them, which he didn't like, and what was worse was that the copper in front of him was looking right at him now.

Could they be here for him? Why had they split up and flanked him like that? And why was this first copper staring at him?

The familiar sound of an incoming train grew louder and Clipper tried not to meet the copper's gaze; he tried to look nonchalant, but it was difficult. He could hardly pretend he hadn't noticed a bloke in full SWAT regalia eyeballing him. Despite himself he found himself locking eyes with the man.

And a realisation stole over him like a hot flush. He looked totally different without hair. And in bulky tactical gear instead of a Paul Smith suit. And Clipper would have sworn he had a big, angry scar underneath one eye before which was gone now, but it was clearly the same bloke. The bloke he'd seen Gary getting his orders from. Warren. And he hadn't been a copper then, according to the few snippets Gary had let slip about him. Not unless coppers drove Aston Martins, spoke Chinese on the phone and paid other people to break the law for them. Which sort of suggested, to Clipper's rapidly whirring brain, if he hadn't been a copper before then he probably wasn't one now. Because there was being undercover, and then there was just out and out being a crook who owned a police uniform. Which did sort of beg the question of what was going on here and whether Clipper might be any part of it.

And at that moment the train came rumbling into the station and the men either side of Clipper started to close in on him.

***

Clipper remembered the first time he'd seen Gary in action. It was nine-thirty in the morning and the trains were still packed – all sorts of hold-ups earlier meant lots of people were still on their way to work. A scrum was pressing toward the open door of a stuffed train that had no more room for them inside. Gary was in the thick of it and Clipper saw him take a step back, because he didn't actually want to board the train, but he tipped his head back with a 'tut' as though it was someone else's fault, like he'd been elbowed aside.

"Can you all move along inside please," Gary called out, in a firm, pleasant voice that Clipper didn't recognise. Was there a Gary in some alternative universe somewhere who talked like that all the time? A teacher maybe.

The announcement came: "Stand clear of the doors please. Stand clear of the closing doors. This train is about to depart."

Gary did it again, allowed himself to be pushed back and let the annoyance register on his face. It was clear that no one else was going to get on board and most of the other punters were pulling back now, positioning themselves for the next train. Gary was still apparently optimistic though, attempting to insert a shoulder into the compressed mass of bodies. But it wasn't going to work.

The doors began to close and Gary retreated just enough to get out of their way. Then the train started to move and Clipper noticed the expression of one of the blank faces squashed up against the window changing to a look of alarm. And as the carriage moved past him, Clipper saw that something was caught in the rubber seal of the doors. It was about ten inches of thin white cable with a shiny plug at the end.

He looked towards Gary, who raised his eyebrows with a little expression of triumph and let Clipper see the iPod he was concealing in his palm. It was about the sweetest lift Clipper had ever seen.

Gary subtly pocketed the smooth plastic brick and, with an exasperated look at his watch, broke free of the scrum. He came to Clipper's side. "*Telegraph* reader," Gary said, "Might have let him off if I thought he only read the sport. Bastard was eyeing the International News."

Like a fair percentage of what Gary said, Clipper couldn't fully decipher the meaning, but he gave an appreciative chuckle. Gary always liked to explain why his marks deserved it.

"That was perfect," Clipper said, still amazed at how beautifully the whole thing had been executed.

"Not perfect," corrected Gary. "It's about time we talked about escape routes. When we're done, you'll see how this lift could be even better."

Then Gary had asked him to imagine what would happen if he stole a trog's wallet in plain view and then jumped on a train. "Just to make it more interesting," Gary said, "imagine you're wearing a t-shirt that says 'Thief' on it."

Clipper didn't really have to think about it. He said, "Well, they'd radio ahead to the next station, wouldn't they? Have someone collar me. Have them look out for the t-shirt."

"But what if you don't get off at the next station?" Gary asked. "Would they stop the train and search it?"

Clipper thought about the manpower involved and the disruption to the network and shook his head. "They'd probably only do that if it was a bomb or something."

Gary looked pleased with him. "So even if the trog asks everyone on the network to look out for you, you could still be anywhere. And even if they alert someone on every ticket barrier in London you could still get out using one of the fire exits or the old tunnels or through a substation. Mind you, there's a couple of stations where jumping on a train might not help." Plainly he wanted Clipper to work it out.

"Right before the end of the line," Clipper said, cheerily.

"Good," Gary said. "So look average and keep clear of platforms that lead you to the end of the line. Apart from that, if you've got the wind up, always choose a train over a platform."

They'd never got round to talking about how to improve the iPod lift Gary had demonstrated earlier and Clipper decided Gary wanted to 'leave it as an exercise for the reader', as he used to say – which meant Clipper was supposed to think it through on his own time.

***

Back in the present, the train had pulled in and Clipper was relieved to realise that Warren was no longer staring at him; he was scrutinising the train, scanning the passengers as they started to emerge. For a moment, Clipper took this as a sign: they were obviously not interested in him; they were after someone else, probably someone leaving the train. But then he glanced over his shoulder to see the other fake cop creeping up on him and he bolted. *Always choose a train over a platform,* Gary had taught him. Since Warren was hiding himself from the passengers behind one of the platform's massive pillars, Clipper headed for the other side of it and sprinted for the rear of the train.

Everyone else had finished getting on or off and Clipper had a clear path to the doors. He dashed for the rearmost double-set, and he'd almost made it when a thin man carrying a heavy briefcase came rushing out at the last minute and the two of them nearly collided.

Muttering an apology, Clipper skidded around him, scrambled inside the train, and looked nervously behind him for signs of pursuit. He couldn't see either of the fake coppers.

The thin man had slipped and was recovering himself. He leant on the edge of the door and peered out while adjusting his glasses, and tried to follow Clipper's gaze to see what he was running from.

"Is someone chasing you?" he asked, looking pretty unhappy about the possibility.

Clipper didn't respond immediately; he was much more interested in Warren and his sidekick than the man in front of him. The beeping sound that warned passengers that the doors were about to close was sounding as he absentmindedly answered, "Cops. Only they're not cops."

The slim man with the bag looked startled, and as the doors began to close, he pulled himself back inside the train, clutching the big, old-fashioned briefcase to his chest.

He was in his late twenties or early thirties, with wiry red-brown hair and he looked like a late-blooming grad student. His pale, checked shirt and scuffed corduroy jacket were from an earlier era – probably acquired from a previous generation of students by way of a charity shop. Fleetingly, Clipper wondered what his story was. Perhaps he was the fake-cops' real target and Clipper needn't have bolted. On the other hand, in Clipper's mind, Warren was high up on the list of people who might be behind Gary's disappearance (death? murder?) and therefore someone very much to be avoided. *Better safe than sorry*. If he'd bolted unnecessarily he could have a laugh about it once he was about twenty miles away sipping a cappuccino.

The doors closed with a bump, and Clipper and the weedy grad student both relaxed a little. Clipper realised their expressions were mirror images of each other and it almost made him laugh. But then a second later, Warren slammed heavily into the doors, stuck the fingertips of both hands into the rubber seal where the doors met, pulled them towards him and hauled them open again. Clipper hadn't thought you could do that. Some part of the door mechanism agreed and was groaning and squealing in protest.

Clipper backed away, but the grad student was even more rattled. He ran to the back of the carriage, as far to the rear of the train as it was possible to get. The seats in that section were all empty, but the few passengers over on the far side of the doors were looking up in surprise, unsure what was going on.

Clipper wondered what the driver would do, whether he'd stop the train, but then he remembered that the driver relied on the platform cameras to be working to see what was going on. And for whatever reason, they were suddenly all out of action.

Warren's gaze was now fixed very firmly on the grad student. Warren may or may not have recognised Clipper earlier, but his reason for being there was obviously the thin man with the glasses and the battered briefcase.

Then the second fake-cop pounded up, stopping just behind Warren. Clipper considered the possibility that it was only Warren who was the fake, but he couldn't imagine a real copper teaming up with an impostor and not figuring it out. Surely they were both crooks.

"Tian, hold the doors," Warren said, slipping in through the gap he'd opened and leaving it to the man behind him to prevent them from closing again.

An announcement came over the train's speakers: "This is the driver speaking. I can't see who's playing silly buggers, but would whoever is preventing the doors from closing kindly stop it so we can all get on our way. Thank you." The 'thank you' was delivered in what Clipper thought of as textbook tube drivers' sarcasm.

Meanwhile Warren was advancing on the terrified grad student who was pressed against the back wall of the carriage. The only thing behind him was the rear driver's cab of the train, which would be empty at the moment, and beyond that open track. He looked very much like he wanted to push himself through the locked doors behind him and sprint away down the tunnel into the darkness.

"You're Kieran, aren't you?" Warren said, addressing the terrified man. "We're not here to hurt you, Kieran. We want what you're carrying and we want you to come with us." Then he glanced over his shoulder at the concerned passengers watching him and added, "Down to the station."

Kieran said nothing. So Warren took a step forwards. "Realistically,

Kieran, you don't have anywhere else to go," he said pleasantly.

Kieran slipped a hand into the open top of his old-fashioned briefcase and began rummaging around, his search complicated by the fact that his eyes never left Warren's face.

Warren smiled, albeit without much warmth, and began to advance upon Kieran, who was thrashing his hand around inside the bag, desperate to locate something. A moment later he had it, and he withdrew his hand to reveal a fist clamped whitely around the grip of a gun. He snatched back the slide, chambering a bullet and raising the hammer. Several of the passengers on the far side of Clipper drew in their breath sharply enough that it sounded like a collective sigh. Someone whispered to herself, "Oh my god."

The driver was once again trying to close the doors and automated beeping filled the carriage as Warren adjusted to the presence of the gun. His smile finally gained some real warmth.

"What," he asked, "do you imagine you're going to do with that?"

Clipper, who was still in the little standing area by the doors, had lowered himself so that most of his body was screened by the row of seats nearest him. There was a piece of plate glass above him which gave standing passengers something to lean against and he peered cautiously through it now. He was aware that he was only a metre or so from the other fake-cop, but couldn't think of anything better to do than kind of cower where he was. It was what everyone else was doing.

Warren was apparently unconcerned, possibly even amused, at having a gun pointed at him. But at the same time he looked like he'd lost patience with the conversational approach; he took several brisk steps towards the armed man just as the annoyed train driver began making another announcement.

Kieran flinched at Warren's approach and simultaneously fired his gun, sending a bullet ricocheting off the roof above Warren's head; Clipper had no idea where it ended up. A moment later Kieran composed himself and fired point blank at Warren, who seemed to stagger slightly, but gave no sign that the bullet had penetrated his flak jacket. *You can't hurt them*, Clipper found himself thinking.

Surely the driver would hear the gunshot. Inside the carriage the sound of the shot had been tremendous. But the driver was several hundred feet away, in his own little cab, in the middle of making another announcement. Clipper realised that whatever sound made it through the gap in the partly-opened doors would probably be swallowed by the vast space of the station. From where the driver sat, the gunshot would have all the volume of a distant door slamming or a shutter coming down.

As Clipper watched, Warren had almost reached Kieran. Then Kieran fired a third time, his composure gone, this shot even wilder than the first. Glass exploded and Clipper gave an involuntary moan of fear, recoiling as splinters of shattered plate glass sprayed across his face and shoulder, pattering into his hair and rattling across the floor around him.

But it wasn't the partition on Clipper's side of the carriage that had been hit; it was the one by the partly open doors. And now Clipper was turning his head and looking up at the second fake copper who'd been twisted around by the impact of the bullet, which looked to have caught him somewhere around where his neck met his shoulder. As well as being shot, he'd also been raked by pellets of glass as the bullet punched through the plate glass screen beside him. Beneath one of his eyes blood welled like red tears. He made a slow deep sound of surprise and pain, like a groan.

Warren looked round and yelled, "Sebastian!" as the driver's announcement concluded – no one had heard a word of it – and then Sebastian toppled sideways and slammed to the floor beside Clipper, allowing the doors to clatter shut behind him.

Warren threw a murderous glance at Kieran, who visibly recoiled, and then he rushed to Sebastian's side while Clipper tried to shrink further into the corner, willing himself to be invisible.

Warren crouched by Sebastian's side. He was oblivious to Kieran, who'd taken a halting step forwards and kind of let himself half slump into the seat nearest him. Kieran looked like he was deciding whether to have a heart attack or not. His face was difficult to read, a blend of fear and uncertainty, and maybe some surprise at what he'd just done. He was still holding the gun in his outstretched arm and he looked twitchy enough to do just about anything. He was also… Clipper wasn't sure, but he watched, his gaze operating on autopilot, as Kieran's free hand moved across the upholstery of the seat beside him while his eyes stayed fixed on Warren. There was something in Kieran's hand, a tiny blade of some kind, that was slicing into the heavy fabric. Clipper's eyes seemed to track Kieran's clandestine movements of their own accord while his thoughts remained jumbled and panicky, thrown into a tangle by the shooting.

A metre or so from Clipper, Sebastian was trying to speak. Warren held his head up slightly which seemed to help. After a moment's effort Sebastian said, "I was just moving my shield to hold the doors." He tried to give a shrug. "Bad timing. I'm sorry."

The bullet had struck only a few seconds before but there was already a lot of blood on the floor. Sebastian had his hand pressed against the base of his neck, but vivid blood welled in pulses between his fingers. His eyes were flickering with pain and concentration.

Then, with a lurch, the train finally began to move and Warren glanced up as he registered the change. A groan from Sebastian brought his attention straight back to his wounded friend. "You have to stop the bleeding," he said, squeezing the man's arm to emphasise his words. "Concentrate."

Clipper, still pressed into his corner, was holding perfectly still. He was trying orient his thoughts, to figure out what was happening, what he should be doing – and for the moment he was having no success at all. He was aware that the train was moving, aware that an armed man had opened fire in this carriage, aware that someone had been hit, but he wasn't sure how to process any of it.

And for a moment he was back in that club, waiting for Gary, seeing Warren turn, and watching a broken bottle grind itself to pieces on the empty space in front of him, watching a punch that never landed slam his attacker to the floor.

Gary had said you couldn't hurt them, whoever *they* were. But surely this was one of them, lying at Clipper's feet, his blood leaking out onto the floor of the train, the spreading pool even now reaching the toe of Clipper's scuffed right shoe. The man was going to bleed to death while Clipper crouched, really only inches away, immobile, within the growing circle of his blood, and something about that seemed so wrong that it set him in motion.

Before he knew what he was doing, Clipper found himself speaking. "Pressure. We need to put pressure on the wound," he said.

Warren looked round at him and just stared.

Clipper was pulling off his tie, winding it round his hand and threading the end through to make a ball of material. He came slightly out of his crouch, eyes flicking nervously towards the man with the gun and then back to the piercing look on Warren's face, wondering all the while who he should be most afraid of.

"I could…" He held up the wad of material to show his intention. Warren's stare didn't slacken.

After a pause, the stare lengthening, Warren said coldly, "I know you, don't I?"

Just what I need, Clipper thought to himself, *more stress*. But he knew what to say. Another of Gary's tutorials had covered this. At Gary's suggestion, they had dreamed up half a dozen responses to this question, intended to be given to trogs, coppers and previous victims, should anyone recognise them. Clipper picked the first one that came to mind.

"My brother maybe. He does adverts. Posters and stuff. Like those crunchy cornflakes," he said and shrugged. It occurred to him that if he pretended not to be afraid of Warren it would make this easier, and might defuse Warren's suspicion. Because Clipper had a sneaking feeling that anyone who truly knew Warren would be permanently afraid.

Clipper was trying to reach Sebastian now, but Warren hadn't shifted aside, though his hostility had disappeared somewhat and for a moment he seemed lost in thought.

Then a voice by Clipper's ear said, "Let me help." And it was the girl from the plaza, the one with hair the colour of maple syrup, the one he'd spoken to. And he remembered their conversation, how much he'd enjoyed it, and how it seemed like it had happened at least a week ago.

***

Rachel hung up. That was the fun part over. She'd burned her bridges with some real gusto and now she wouldn't be able to back out or change her mind. But wasn't that why people used to burn bridges? Or was it ships? Whatever. They were burned.

Putting her relationship with Rudy to the torch had been particularly easy, once she knew she had nothing to lose. As a boss he'd been a disaster and now there was no reason to pretend otherwise; she'd laid it out for him. Ticked off his faults with chilly efficiency. It was a talent she'd inherited from her mother – what she thought of as the family curse. Whatever you called it, she had her mother's blistering forthrightness, even in German. Which was why she'd been putting off this second call for weeks. Putting it off until after she'd resigned. Putting it off until after she'd booked her plane tickets home. Putting it off until her last day at work, until her transatlantic flight was only hours away.

Time to call home.

No one had ever accused her or her mother of being two-faced, or of keeping quiet about other people's shortcomings. Her mother never got calls from old friends saying, "Why weren't you straight with me?" Naturally the main reason for that was her mother's total lack of old friends. But if any had stuck around long enough to give their opinion, they'd have told you: she was so straight with people it made your eyes water.

There was no puzzle to it; Rachel could see it quite clearly: her mother's way with people, the effect it had on them, and the woman's inability to follow the logic of her own bluntness all the way through to the damage it caused. And even though it seemed so obvious when she looked at her mother's life, she suspected that she had exactly the same faults and exactly the same blind-spot, the same obliviousness to consequences.

It never felt wrong, letting rip like that, hitting them right between the eyes. It felt pure and honest and simple. But it wasn't anywhere near as exhilarating sitting around waiting for them to come back, waiting for them to get over the initial sting of hearing the truth, and gradually realising that they never would.

Before she'd come to London, around the time that she realised living with her mother was no longer remotely bearable, Rachel had done her best to get through to her, to make her understand that she was driving everyone around her away. And she hadn't been a hundred percent surprised when her mother failed to acknowledge the truth of it – but had instead repaid the compliment by

rounding on her, proceeding to enumerate all the ways in which Rachel herself
was deficient, deluded or unlikable. It was quite a fight.

There hadn't been much left to say after that. Or rather neither of them were
interested in saying it. So that's how they'd left it. Their relationship a lifeless,
radioactive wasteland. Emotional Chernobyl.

It wasn't until Rachel had been in London a few weeks and had looked
back calmly on that last unrestrained, fully-nuclear exchange that she'd
understood what had happened, the forces that had been at work. Her own
certainty that she was right and her mother's monstrously stubborn refusal
to admit it were two sides of the same coin. Her mother would have been
feeling the same chill, thin wind of righteousness roaring through her and
marvelling at the pigheaded obstinacy of the woman in front of her. Really,
the whole thing was just her mother having a fight with her own reflection;
Rachel was simply the vessel by which this stupidity could annihilate itself
and simultaneously pass down to the next generation.

She had no idea what the solution was – it couldn't be dishonesty or
blandness – she couldn't very well start simpering, it would be more than
she could bear – but equally there had to be a way of wielding the truth that
didn't involve using it to mug anyone who wouldn't take the hint and drift
away of their own accord. The furthest she'd got in her search for an answer
was the beginnings of a suspicion that it had something to do with trust.
Maybe her caustic honesty was just about getting her retaliation in first.
Maybe if you could really be sure of someone, you didn't need to launch
pre-emptive strikes. Now if only she could persuade her mother of that.

Slowly she dialled her mother's number. In her heart it was still *her*
number too. Pushing the keys one by one felt like arming a bomb. A
thought occurred to her: what if her mother no longer got up this early?
Conversational bloodshed would be inevitable. *Oh well*. Rachel tried to
pull together a few words that might produce some effect besides silence
or a long-distance brawl. At the other end, the phone rang: long American
tones.

"Hello?" It was her mother's voice. The first time she'd heard it in
almost three years.

She let her breath out and spoke: "Hi Mom."

There was silence at the other end of the line and Rachel cupped her other hand around the phone to keep the wind away from the mouthpiece.

"Hi," her mom said eventually. Her tone gave nothing away.

"Mom, I…" How could she possibly phrase this? There was no easy way to express it. But then an unexpected swell of emotion pushed words out of her mouth: "Mom, the thing is… I miss you and I'd like to come home."

She hadn't said 'want' to come home, but 'like'. It wasn't a demand. She was throwing herself on her mother's mercy. A quality her mother had never given any sign of possessing.

More than anything Rachel had ever done, this felt like putting her neck on the block and waiting for the axe to fall. The first thing her mother would do was ask what this meant, what it signified. She'd want it spelled out that Rachel was capitulating, admitting that she'd been wrong. Then she'd lay down some rules about how it was going to be different this time – and by different she'd mean tighter, tougher, more under control, with less room for future rebellions.

Rachel could almost hear her speak the words: "So what are you saying? You've come to your senses at last? Well, let me tell you…" But those words never came.

Instead: "Are you…" Her mother's voice was strange. "Are you OK? Is everything OK?" Her mother seemed unsure. Rachel wasn't sure she'd ever heard her sound like that before.

This was unexpected, but it was too soon to relax; fighting could still break out at any moment. But the fact it hadn't yet was more than Rachel had expected.

"I'm fine," Rachel said carefully. "I'm quitting this job, though. I *have* quit it." She regretted saying it like that. 'Quitting' was a trigger phrase of her mother's. Not something she had ever permitted.

Her mother said nothing.

Rachel went on: "It's just that… I miss you and I miss the horses too." It was silly but true. "I don't know how things are, if they've changed, but if you… if it's OK with you, I want to come home. Help with the farm. See how it goes."

Her mother still said nothing. The pause lengthened.

Rachel spoke into the silence. "So might you, um… I mean, *is* it OK if I come home?" Her mother was really making her work for this, but Rachel wasn't going to chicken out now, no matter how agonising it was to say these things aloud. She'd been prepared for battle. She'd been determined not to provoke it, but she'd been expecting it. So she wasn't going to let the silent treatment throw her off track.

Then she realised her mother was crying. "Mom?" she asked, wondering if something had happened. Had someone died? Was something else wrong, besides their screwed-up relationship?

"Come home, honey," her mother said, between sobs. "I was scared you would never call. I couldn't bear it. Just come home and we'll make it work out."

"Really?" Rachel said, hope rising inside her. She felt stupid for making her mom repeat herself, and about five years old. But this was beyond her wildest expectations. "Are you OK? Is everything OK? I'm going to be home tomorrow sometime, if it's alright."

She could hear happiness in her mother's voice now, even though she was sniffling and her words were thick with emotion: "Everything's fine. Just come home. The horses miss you. Me too."

"I'll see you tomorrow," Rachel said. "We can… never mind. I'll see you tomorrow."

She hung up, feeling amazed and bewildered. And then a wave of relief washed over her so profound that she felt tears start to gather in her eyes, pooling along her lower lids and making the ground beneath her look blurred and indistinct. She blinked, and hot droplets ran down the cold skin of her cheeks. And then someone was talking to her, asking her if she was OK and she turned to tell him that she felt fantastic.

She smiled up at him. "I'm giving up a job I hate and I'm going back home. And my mom actually said she wanted to see me. So I'm fine thanks," she gushed, taking in the young man in front of her: scruffy, mid-twenties, OK looking, and with the most amazing look of concern on his face.

"You hate your job?" he said, as though he'd never come across the idea before. "What do you do?" he asked, sounding troubled.

"Well, there's the long version, but pretty much if you boil it down, I would say that I was a thief," she said. "Yes. That's it: a thief. Why, what do you do?" She didn't know quite why she was having this conversation, but he'd seemed so worried for her and he'd chosen a moment when her defences were absolutely down.

"I'm… well, I'm a thief too," he said. "Only I really am."

She smiled and sniffed away the last tear. "OK. Well, I'm pleased to meet you. I'm Rachel," she said.

"Matt," he said and stuck out his hand and they shook. With the formalities, it sort of felt like they were playing at being grown-ups. But somehow it was a good game.

"I love the name Rachel," he said.

"From *Friends*?" she asked him, narrowing her moist eyes.

"Nah," he said, "*Blade Runner*."

"You know that Rachel means 'ewe'?" she said.

"Ewww?" he asked, unsure.

"Exactly," she said, laughing. The conversation with her mother had released so much tension she felt almost high. She could talk to anyone about anything right now.

"You're really a thief?" she asked.

"Yup," Matt said. "Sorry."

"You like it?" she asked.

That seemed to stop him in his tracks. "I used to," he told her, and then he frowned. "It used to be exciting and I honestly didn't feel like I was really hurting anyone. But something's changed. I think I might have had enough."

"That," said Rachel triumphantly, "is precisely how I feel."

He lowered his head a little and said quietly, "But I don't know what else to do."

He looked like a little boy when he said it. Rachel wanted to wrap her arms around him. Her emotions were all mixed up, the wonderful warmth of relief still spreading through her, making this strange conversation seem lighter than air.

"Come home with me," she said enthusiastically. The words just popped out, like something in a dream. Surely she'd only thought them, not said them out loud? None of this felt quite real. She found herself asking, "You any good with horses?"

He looked surprised. "I don't know," he said. "I mean yes. I had a weekend job at a stables when I was living in California with my dad. And right now, when I think about it, that seems like the best thing I ever did. You've... have you got horses, then?"

She nodded. "My mom's farm in Oregon. It's beautiful there." She smiled at the thought and then looked down at the two huge bags by her feet. "It's where I'm going right now."

But when she looked up, he wasn't staring at her anymore. All through this dream-like conversation he hadn't looked away from her for an instant – she wasn't even sure he'd blinked. But now his gaze had flicked past her, over her shoulder.

"Listen, I..." he started. "I'm glad you're alright."

She wanted to say something, to stop him leaving – she had no idea what, but she didn't want this extraordinary conversation to come to an end. She opened her mouth, but no words came to mind.

"I've gotta go," he said and then he was gone, threading through the crowd, glancing back a couple of times, though not towards her.

Abruptly, she realised how cold it was outside. And she felt weird, but not good weird – sort of sick actually. Somehow the talk she'd had with Matt, wonderful though it had been, had left her with a sour feeling of loss that threatened to spoil the incredible elation she'd felt after things had gone so well with her mother. She tried to remember exactly how she'd felt when she'd hung up, the sense of enveloping calm, the way her anxiety had dissolved away leaving behind tears and a warmth that might have been love. It was still there, but somehow the moment was gone. Her encounter with Matt had spoiled it, which was ridiculous because she'd loved every second of their strange little talk. It was the sudden way it had ended. She felt cheated.

She was angry – and angry at her anger. She picked up her bags and moved towards the station entrance. This silly irritation would fade, wouldn't it? She would forget about the ridiculous conversation with the man who'd told her he was a thief. Then she'd have the whole long slow flight to Seattle to picture her mother's face and how it would look when Rachel walked into her kitchen. At last, after nearly three years, she could actually imagine her mother's face smiling back at her.

***

Now Rachel was crouching next to Clipper and talking to Warren. She was trying to avoid presenting a target to the gunman and she'd taken off her jacket. "I'm afraid that's arterial blood. It'll need surgery. But we can help a little if we sit him up and do like… um… Matt said." Clipper cringed slightly to hear Rachel telling Warren his real name.

She caught his eye and he wasn't sure if there was some message she was trying to send or whether she just wanted to acknowledge his presence.

She went on: "Yeah, like Matt said: pressure, and sit him up. Can you radio to the next station and get an ambulance on its way?" Her voice was calm, though Clipper could see a little sheen of moisture on her upper lip. She'd folded her jacket and was slipping it behind Sebastian's head. She'd had to lean across Clipper to do it and absentmindedly he realised that she did in fact smell fantastic, just as he'd imagined.

Warren didn't reply. He'd moved aside slightly to give her room, but he seemed totally distracted, circulating in his own thoughts. And then a moment later he was back. The hard look dropping into place like a visor. The momentary indecisiveness was gone.

He leaned over his fallen companion. "Sebastian," he said evenly, "I think this might not work out."

Clipper could see that something was missing that had been there earlier. The concern was gone. He looked down at his partner with eyes that were hooded and blank. He seemed to have reached some sort of verdict on the situation. The set of his features suggested that it wasn't a particularly charitable one.

Now his gaze left Sebastian and flicked for a moment towards Kieran. Then he turned to Rachel and Clipper. "Look after him," he said, flatly, like he was speaking to a servant. "I have work to do." That last remark was addressed to himself as much as to them.

Then he stood, leaving the wounded man to their care – but he ignored Kieran; instead he turned the other way, facing the few remaining passengers in the compartment.

Kieran still reacted to his movement with a start, rapidly pushing off the seat he'd been leaning against and jerking himself to his feet, gun extended. But he needn't have bothered; at that moment no one was paying him any attention.

Now Warren stood squarely, balancing easily against the motion of the carriage, and called out over the racket of the train to the three other people in the compartment. They were all crouching at the front end of the carriage, as far from both the injured cop and the gunman as possible. They'd pressed themselves into the corner, right by the door that led to the next compartment.

"I want you three to move towards the front of the train. Tell everyone you meet that there is a serious police situation back here and get them to move away. Everything is under control, more men are on the way, but when I look through those windows…" he pointed towards the next compartment, "I don't want to see any members of the public. Do you understand? Just leave everything to us, don't complicate the situation, and get everyone else to safety."

"Not you," he added firmly but quietly, addressing Clipper and Rachel.

The retreating passengers scrambled to get the connecting door open without exposing themselves to a direct shot. They didn't seem to notice that Kieran was oblivious to anyone but Warren. As they slammed the door behind them, Clipper thought he detected a change in the motion of the train. It was slowing. But from experience he knew they weren't at the next station yet. Either the driver knew that something was wrong… or maybe more likely, it was one of the thousand little delays the underground system experienced every day. Then the train's speed levelled out. They'd slowed down somewhat but it didn't seem like they were stopping. *Probably just congestion*, thought Clipper, *and not help on its way*. Then he turned his attention back to Warren.

Warren waited until the retreating passengers were a good distance into the next carriage before he finally turned back to face Kieran. Their eyes locked, and Kieran stepped back, involuntarily, before quickly correcting the aim of his gun. Then Warren began moving purposefully towards him with a heavy, steady walk that put Clipper in mind of a tank rolling into position. Warren looked like it would take more than a few bullets to stop him.

"If you put that gun down now I won't kill you," he said reasonably, as he advanced on the other man. His voice was low, just enough to carry over the noise of the train, but Clipper and Rachel could hear him.

Back behind the seats, Clipper saw Rachel's uncertain frown. It was easy for him to forget that she'd still got some catching up to do. Warren's words were obviously bothering her. They weren't exactly standard cop-speak. Warren's tone had been... well, the best word was probably 'sinister'. If you added in the fact he seemed to think he was bullet-proof, Clipper could see there was plenty to frown about.

He didn't exactly have all the answers, but Clipper felt he should share the little he did know. He looked down at Sebastian, whose eyes were flickering, half closed, his pupils twitching and unfocused. He gave no sign that he was paying attention to them, so Clipper leant across and whispered to Rachel, "Yeah, they're not really cops." He hadn't meant it to sound cocky.

He looked at her face to see if she'd understood him. Her eyes were wide and questioning – demanding that he say more. He put his mouth close to her ear and whispered, "I don't know much about them, but they're crooks. The uniforms... it's all fake." He was still keeping his voice low, though Sebastian had yet to give any sign he was aware of them.

A few metres away, Warren had halted. He was explaining the situation to Kieran: "Think about how much harm I could have done to you by now if I'd wanted to, but you haven't got a scratch on you. That's because I want you to talk to us, tell us who you've been working with. And for that, I want you in one piece. Isn't that what you want too?" His hands were spread in a gesture that was probably intended to be non-threatening and patient. But Warren's expression altogether spoiled the effect. If he'd had his face chromed it couldn't have displayed less warmth.

"You're really making this difficult," he said and it seemed like a little sarcasm might be creeping into his tone. He paused for a moment to let Kieran respond to his offer. Then he added, "Imagine all the ways this could end. There's only one version in which you're still breathing. And it's the one where you cooperate with me."

His words seemed to be getting to Kieran, who was really sweating now, and shifting awkwardly. He took a faltering step towards Warren, his gun lowering slightly, unsure, as though his determination was wavering. It almost looked like he was giving up.

On the other hand, Clipper could see the tension in Kieran's body. Even the arm that had dropped slightly was so taut it trembled. If his tendons had been any tighter Clipper reckoned you'd be able to play a tune on them. As it was, he could almost hear Kieran's body humming with tension. He couldn't decide whether the man was about to give up or hurl himself physically at Warren.

Whether Warren was fooled or not by the show of uncertainty, Clipper couldn't say, but a moment later the pretence was over. Having shuffled forwards a little, Kieran twisted around and fired two rapid shots into the door lock behind him. Then he snapped back towards Warren, keeping the gun trained on him, while using his other hand to snatch his bag from the seat beside him. Gun outstretched, he shoved himself backwards, bursting through the door behind and nearly toppling into the gloom of the deserted rear cab of the train.

Clipper was fairly sure you didn't need to shoot those cab doors open; there was a release-lever that passengers could use in an emergency; but he had to admit, the gun was quicker. Plus, if you already had a weapon in your hand in a situation like this, your survival instincts probably dictated that you didn't put it down while you fiddled with a door lock.

Kieran took two quick and stumbling steps backwards into the rear cab, but instead of going after him, Warren hesitated for a moment and Clipper found himself wondering about that. He was getting the distinct impression that whatever protected Warren and Sebastian from harm, it was at its least effective when they were moving. But then as soon as Kieran had disappeared into the dark of the cab, Warren dashed forwards to close with him.

Kieran must have expected this because simultaneously his arm came halfway up, lifting up out of the darkness of the rear cab, while the rest of him remained in shadow. The gun fired again, this time angled straight down at Warren's feet. The outstretched arm vanished into the darkness as Warren cried out and snatched his right foot away, slipping and falling back across the seats behind him. It was an ugly fall, with Warren's lower back coming down hard on the solid jutting edge of an armrest. His attempts to break his fall tipped him sideways almost head-first onto the vinyl-coated floor of the train. He lay there for a moment hardly moving.

Clipper craned his head and saw a splatter of blood on the floor and a chunk punched out of Warren's right boot. Clipper didn't know how serious getting shot in the foot was in the relative scheme of things, but even as he watched, Warren was scrambling to right himself, so it couldn't have been too bad. For his part, though, Clipper found the violence of it shocking. He was getting the definite impression that you needed to see a lot more than two people get shot in front of your eyes before it became something you could manage to be casual about.

'Shock' captured the feeling perfectly; for a moment you just couldn't believe it had happened. But while most of Clipper's brain was recoiling from the noise of gunfire and the terror of being trapped in a confined space watching people on either side of him get shot, another more analytical part of his mind was trying to learn something useful from what he'd seen.

For a second Clipper wondered if he was going to be able to think his way out of this situation: figure out what Warren's limitations were, what his agenda was, and use that knowledge to time a rapid exit. If he was really lucky Warren and Kieran would still be trying to kill each other when the train reached the next station and then he could just grab Rachel by the arm and run like hell.

He glanced at over at her, wondering if she was doing the same thing, trying to think this all through. It was hard to tell. She looked frightened – but then maybe he did too – but she wasn't looking panicked. He thought about how she'd moved to his side after Sebastian was hit. She'd been shaken, but she'd had it under control. He wouldn't be surprised if her mind was working just as hard as his. Which gave him a fair bit of comfort because she was very likely a lot smarter than he was. If he was really honest with himself, thinking his way out of a situation was not something he'd ever shown much talent for, and these weren't exactly the ideal circumstances for him to perfect the skill. His friend Gary had always been the brains of the operation. He'd done his best to turn Clipper into a thinker, but it had been an uphill struggle for both of them. Even so, if Gary were here, he'd be urging Clipper to think: to work out ahead of time what the important moments were so that when they happened he'd be ready.

That, and research; Gary had always been very big on research. Which was why Clipper found his gaze flicking down to the pool of blood by his feet. He was staring at its colour. It was that familiar shade of red. Though it was maybe a little brighter and more orangey as it welled from Sebastian's neck, but Rachel had said that blood was 'arterial' – Clipper had no idea what that meant, unless it was something to do with arteries – but she seemed to recognise the look of it. Besides, you couldn't really judge under these lights. The point was that so far as he could tell, Sebastian, and the blood he was losing such a lot of, were both human. He felt stupid for even questioning it, but what else was he to think?

But the twitching, delirious figure in front of him was bleeding what looked like real blood from what seemed like an honest-to-god bullet hole in his neck. He was pretty obviously human and he was pretty obviously dying, unless he got some proper medical attention. And now Warren had been hurt too. So whatever else Sebastian and Warren were, they were also men. It was one simple and solid fact in an otherwise insane situation and it made Clipper feel just a tiny bit better.

That feeling of reassurance grew a little stronger as he watched the superman who was probably responsible for his best and only friend Gary's death slipping in a patch of his own blood as he tried to scramble back to his feet.

A moment later, Warren had hauled himself upright, clutching a handrail with one muscular arm while he held his perforated foot above the floor and swore. Under other circumstances it might have been gruesomely funny, but not here and now. Meanwhile Kieran had completely disappeared into the gloom of the empty rear cab. Peering towards the open door, Clipper could see part of a dark window, and beyond, the occasional tunnel light receding slowly down the track. Kieran was moving about in there, but Clipper couldn't see what he was doing. Panicking, most likely.

Warren took a few deep breaths, steadied himself against the lurching of the train, and put his weight on his damaged foot. The bleeding seemed to have stopped straightaway, though when he took his first step he quickly took a second one to get his good foot back under him. From the location of the hole, the bullet must have gone right through the middle of his boot and out through the sole. No wonder it was a little tender.

Warren had reached the open door of the rear cab and grabbed hold of the frame for support. Then he paused for a moment and called out ahead of him, "You're really not making this easy, Kieran. You're not even trying to keep on my good side, are you?" Then he winced and bent to fiddle with his boot, yanking at the laces.

By Clipper's side, Rachel moved closer and whispered in his ear, "So do you have any idea what the hell is going on?"

"I don't really know," Clipper whispered back. "But I mean *obviously* that bloke, Kieran, has crossed these people somehow. And you've seen they… they seem to have some sort of… power." He wasn't sure he was contributing anything so he stopped talking for a moment while he collected his thoughts. Then he tried again. "I've seen *that* one," he dropped his voice even further and indicated Warren, "before. I reckon he killed a friend of mine. And he wasn't a copper then; he was bent as a nine-bob note."

"I've got no idea what that means," Rachel said coldly. Then a minute later she asked suspiciously, "So who *are* you?"

"No one," Clipper said, being defensive. His whisper was more of a hiss: "I just nick things. So did my mate, Gary. Then he did some work for that guy, who called himself Warren. And right after that, my mate disappeared. I don't know any more than that. Except I saw Warren do that trick once before, where it's like he's indestructible. Though it obviously doesn't work the whole time. I also saw him knock someone down without touching them."

Rachel was taking this in without commenting. He reckoned the fact she'd seen Warren shot point-blank and not get hurt must be lending a bit of credibility to his ridiculous-sounding story.

He went on, "Warren knows he knows me, but he can't remember where from. I really only saw him once, just before Gary went missing." He saw Rachel's look become calculating and said, "Honestly, I don't think I'm anything to do with this. It's just a coincidence I'm here. I swear."

Rachel considered his words, but said nothing. They were silent for a moment, watching Warren wrestle with his boot before going in to tackle Kieran. Clipper spoke to Rachel again, "Look, I reckon now's your chance. Get to the door back there while he's busy."

She hesitated a moment and then shook her head. "He'd see me. And… leaving you on your own doesn't seem the right thing to do."

He said, "Yeah, well, that's very nice, but I'm sure you'd get over it. Go on, at least try."

She shook her head again. "Look, I don't see that either of them," she flicked her eye towards the cab, "are actually trying to hurt me. You go if you want," she said and nodded towards Sebastian, "but someone should look after him." Then she took the wadded tie from him and pressed it more firmly against Sebastian's wound, adding, "It's not like you're very good at first aid."

He couldn't tell if she was joking. He thought maybe she was trying; it was just difficult with all the adrenaline. He whispered, "And you are? I thought you swindled people for a living."

She shrugged and said, "Well… before the swindling I had a year of vet's school. OK?"

He didn't bother to reply to that. He could see how anyone listening to them might think they were arguing. It certainly sounded like it. But it didn't *feel* like it. It felt like they were agreeing to stay together for a little longer. Clipper was surprised at how much better that made him feel.

At the back of the carriage Warren was triumphantly pulling off his damaged boot. He tipped it up, allowing a thin trickle of blood to run out. Tossing the boot behind him, he stepped into the doorway of the rear cab. With one boot on and one off, he was walking like a peg-legged pirate, but the look on his face was serious enough.

With Warren blocking the doorway Clipper couldn't see exactly what happened next, but a moment later there was another gunshot, the flash lighting up the dim cab, but not for long enough to let Clipper see anything, and then there was a rushing noise which didn't go away – in fact a moment later it jumped in volume again. The train was suddenly much noisier and cold air was moving quickly through the compartment.

Clipper tried to peer past Warren to see what was happening. It looked like the door at the back of the rear cab was now open. Clipper was seeing straight out into the tunnel beyond and he could catch the occasional glimpse of Kieran flailing around. With a shock, Clipper realised he must be hanging off the rear of the train. Clipper caught a glimpse of him holding on with one hand, while the other struggled to clasp his briefcase to his chest.

Even though the train was travelling more slowly than normal, the steel rails were still sliding past at maybe thirty miles an hour and there was nothing either side of them but concrete. Without meaning to, Clipper found himself picturing what a collision with metal and masonry at that sort of speed would be like – never mind the six hundred volts of electricity crackling through the live rail.

He could hardly bear to watch. There didn't seem to be any way back for Kieran; he had pretty much run out of options. His one hope would be to stop resisting and plead with Warren to help him back onto the train. Otherwise it would only be a matter of time. But it didn't look like Kieran was going to do that. Clipper's insides bunched at the thought of what came next.

And then, a moment later, his fears became real. Kieran pitched backwards and was snatched from sight, and Clipper could hardly stop himself from yelling out. He found he'd jammed the knuckles of his right hand into his mouth without realising it. From the glimpse he'd seen it was difficult to tell if Kieran had just lost his grip. It almost looked like he'd jumped. Clipper stared in disbelief for one very long second.

Then the moment passed and there was a bright spitting flash just beyond the rear of the train and fat, angry sparks filled the tunnel behind them. Clipper thought he heard a scream over the noise of the train, but he couldn't be sure. Then there was a loud wooden slap as all the brakes came on simultaneously and at the same moment all the lights in the train went out.

In total darkness, the train pitched beneath them as screeching wheels tried to bring several hundred of tons of metal to an instant halt. Broken glass and unidentified debris tumbled forwards. Blindly, Rachel gripped Clipper's arm in the dark and he reflexively grabbed onto her as they tried to avoid being flung across the carriage towards metal handrails and hard corners they could no longer see. She must have had hold of something solid because she was able to stop them both from being thrown around. Her unbreakable grip kept him from taking a dive headfirst into the dark.

Endless moments later the train had squealed and lurched to a final halt. And then, with the power off, it was abruptly silent – the sudden peace occasionally interrupted by pings, creaks and hisses as parts of the train cooled and contracted.

A few moments later emergency lights came on in the compartment and they could see again, though more dimly than before. It took Clipper a second or two to realise that his fingers were still digging deep into the flesh of Rachel's arm. It must have hurt like hell but she didn't show it. He released his grip and said, "God I'm sorry. I didn't realise. I was just trying to hold on."

"I know," she said, simple acceptance in her voice. Then she looked around, peering towards the rear cab. "Did you see what happened in there?" she asked. "Did he fall? I couldn't tell."

"I think he might even have jumped," Clipper said, "but I couldn't see properly." He realised how loud their voices sounded now.

Then he shrugged, without quite knowing why, and said a little more quietly, "I heard that you have a fifty-fifty chance of missing the live rail. We were going slowly; maybe he thought it was worth risking it." What he didn't add was that it really said something about Warren's reputation if the people he chased were willing to throw themselves off a moving train to get away from him.

As he finished speaking, it belatedly occurred to Clipper to wonder what had happened to Warren. Was he busy with something in the cab? Or maybe he'd fallen too? It hadn't looked like it, but perhaps Kieran had grabbed hold of him at the last moment and they'd tumbled onto the tracks together.

Clipper couldn't help hoping that's what had taken place. But if Warren didn't appear soon, Clipper really was going to begin edging the pair of them towards the door to the next compartment.

And where was the driver? Shouldn't there be an announcement? Wouldn't the intercom system work even on emergency power?

Or maybe there was a limit to the number of bullets you could fire into a tube carriage before you broke something important. Gary was always telling him things about the trains and the Underground, and encouraging him to find out more. Now Clipper wished he'd followed up on that.

Despite all those unanswered questions, he found his thoughts kept coming back to Rachel. He studied her face. "So, are you OK?" he asked her. She was busy checking Sebastian over. She looked up at him without saying anything and he found he couldn't read her at that moment. Nevertheless, something about the feel of her eyes on his affected him, just like it had done when he'd first seen her. He found himself volunteering: "I'm sorry I ran off before, when we were outside."

She was staring at him now and her hands had stopped moving, though her face still gave no sign of what she was thinking. He explained, "I got a bit scared," and then he laughed, adding, "Seems silly compared to all this."

And finally he said, "It was… really good talking to you. I meant to say that to you. Before."

Rachel said nothing for a while and then spoke quietly: "I… know what you mean. You caught me off guard. It seemed like… there might have been… more for us to talk about." She was obviously even more awkward about putting this it into words than him.

Clipper's instinct was to make a joke: "But, you know, here we are. We got a chance to have another chat after all." He did his best to give her a smile, so she'd know he was trying to cheer her up. She snorted in a way that he read as meaning a smile in return was expecting too much but she appreciated the effort. After a moment, she returned her attention to Sebastian.

The train had been stationary for a full minute by now and Clipper had begun to wish he'd being doing something useful instead of talking. If he'd got them out of that carriage straightaway they could have been half way down the train by now. Whether that would have done them any good, was another question.

Rachel had finished making Sebastian comfortable. He was barely conscious. He'd been shaken around as the train's brakes had locked but Rachel had propped him up again, hoping to slow the bleeding a little, and was once more pressing the wadded tie to his neck. The pool of blood around him was ominously wide now. And splotches of it were starting to get everywhere – on their shoes and clothes. Rachel's hands and dark blouse were streaked with it and a dark red smudge had somehow made its way to her forehead. Clipper tried to guess at the volume of blood. He found he had to imagine it was some more familiar liquid before he could even begin to work out how much you'd have to spill to make that much mess. It had to be more than a pint. Probably more like two.

"What do you think we should do?" Clipper asked. "I know he's in a pretty bad state," he nodded towards Sebastian, "but I *really* don't trust these people. I still think we should make a run for it."

Rachel was obviously working it through in her mind. After a minute she said, "Listen Matt, you don't know what that guy Kieran had done or who he was. I don't think I trust this Warren guy any more than you do, but he wasn't trying to hurt anyone else. He definitely wasn't the one firing in all directions: any of us could have been killed." She looked down at Sebastian. "And you don't even know who this is, do you?" He nodded, conceding the point. She said, "I need a pretty strong reason if I'm going to leave someone to bleed to death."

He could see she was making up her mind as she was speaking. Now she nodded to herself, the decision made. "I think we should go and see what happened to Warren. And we have to do what we can for this guy."

Clipper wasn't so sure. It seemed fairly likely to him that Warren was going to cause them both some real trouble soon enough. If Warren had killed Gary then he was absolutely ruthless, because Gary wouldn't have been a threat – he wouldn't have talked or caused trouble. What reason would anyone have for getting rid of him, except to shut him up permanently? If that was a reason to kill, then Warren obviously considered those around him disposable.

On the other hand, if Warren *was* now dead – if he'd fallen onto the rails along with Kieran – then Clipper wouldn't mind knowing that.

Slightly against his better judgement he said, "I suppose I should go and look. You can do more for this bloke than I can."

Rachel shook her head as if to say that what she could do for him wasn't that much – but she wasn't arguing with his suggestion. He stood, finding that he was still hunched over – it just seemed too weird not to duck down a little bit, what with all the shooting – but he forced himself to straighten up. He touched Rachel's shoulder, not exactly sure why, and give her the best smile he could manage, and then began moving towards the gaping door of the rear cab.

***

In that cramped driver's cab, Kieran hadn't had much time to think, but that was OK. He'd already done all the thinking he needed to do and made all the decisions he needed to make.

For Kieran, life had divided pretty neatly into two sections. There was his real life, the first one, where everything that happened was fairly normal – and occasionally exceptional – but it all tended to make about as much sense as anyone else's. And then there was the second part that followed, which was like something Kafka might have come up with if he'd been hungover and in a rush. This second life *seemed* real enough, but it was strangely twisted and the logic of it often eluded him. Some of the events just seemed to have squirmed their way out of an acid trip and into reality. Not that anyone seemed to do acid any more. But in Kieran's time it had been big.

He'd been pretty average as a child, though he was brighter than most, and he'd never had much time for rules. But he used his wits to get himself out of most trouble. He'd liked learning and he'd liked books. But he'd liked sex and drugs and rock'n'roll even more – though he'd always compartmentalised, and kept the two separate. And the former paid for the latter. His brains did the work, his body reaped the rewards – or at least felt the effects.

Even in his mid-teens he was insatiable when it came to new experiences, mixing with a much older crowd and often staying out all night. But no matter how much his leisure time was like something from the annals of the Hellfire Club he'd always made sure his studies didn't suffer.

Towards the end of the Seventies he was at university, attending lectures during the day, and by night living a life that would have blown the minds of his college friends. He was dealing to pay for it all, which is how he knew only too well when the Seventies really came to an end and the Eighties began. Even if you didn't know what year you were living in you could see the change in the way that the hash and the acid market dried up, and instead of selling tabs and bags of weed to hippies in Afghan coats he was selling a grand's worth of coke at a time to guys his own age who wore suits that cost more than his car – and drove cars that cost more than his flat. They looked like junior executives but they lived like the Borgias and for a while he found himself starting to get jealous. He was severely tempted to swap dealing for trading. But then he came to his senses.

He was halfway through a PhD in Economics and one day he was talking to a friend about the North Sea oil boom. His friend was explaining how the best place to be in a boom was in the second-tier. If the boom was a gold rush, you sold picks and shovels and mules. If the boom was offshore oil you sold underwater welding equipment or chartered out helicopters. There was less competition, you could charge what you liked and you could probably survive a downturn if you were smart.

That really resonated with Kieran, particularly as he was watching the financial boom of the Eighties get started. He'd been feeling like he had his nose pressed up against the window watching the party from outside in the cold. Right before his eyes, Wall Street and the City were waking up to all sorts of possibilities. They were getting a fetish for high-risk sex with the money markets: leveraged acquisitions, asset stripping, and kinky new ways to securitise or play fast-and-loose with bond issues. Simultaneously the government was flogging off public infrastructure like peddlers on Oxford Street unloading nicked jewellery. It had all the hallmarks of a boom with all the possibilities that entailed.

Kieran quickly forgot about changing jobs; he was better placed exactly where he was, he just had to make a few changes. If anyone managed to pull off the perfect Eighties hat-trick and asset-strip a recently-privatised utility while financing the deal with junk bonds, Kieran wanted to be right there to make sure the adrenaline-crazed twenty-eight-year-old in question was afforded all the appropriate luxuries, comforts and indulgences his ego-less id could desire.

Understanding the markets helped Kieran be in the right place at the right time, and when his customers got rich, so did he. Financially at least, the Eighties were very good to Kieran. By 1988 he owned two clubs and a boutique hotel on the edge of the City, both with members-only areas and private rooms and lots of security. He owned a very prestigious executive dining service that would deliver chilled champagne and fresh Cornish oysters right to your corner office – or whatever else you wanted: the menu was extensive, expensive and typically included little cloisonné boxes of powdered crystals as a side-dish. He also owned two dance studios and a PR firm. Both were legit, but any girls from the dance studios who wanted to earn extra cash could work nights for the PR firm wearing hot pants and draping themselves over new cars or handing out leaflets, whatever was required of them. And if any of the girls needed even more extra cash they could graduate to the third tier of that particular business enterprise – what Kieran euphemistically called 'executive hospitality'. It dovetailed beautifully with the other businesses, helped him make all the right contacts – and since Kieran's grasp of finance and accounting exceeded that of anyone in the City of London police force or Special Branch, the chances of him being caught were slimmer than a dance-studio drop-out on a cocaine-only diet.

Kieran was meticulously careful to maintain genuinely profitable and legitimate front companies for all of his lucrative *demi-monde* ventures – though sometimes reality could outstrip even his most optimistic expectations. For a while his ultra-high-end lunch service threatened to make more money than the drug dealing it was designed to conceal. It was what Kieran's lecturers would have called 'negative price elasticity': you put up your prices and that only increased the demand for your services because it made it clear to everyone on the sidelines that your clients were the real thing: vulgarly, profligately super-rich.

Logistically, financially and creatively the organisation he created was a roaring success. The one area he struggled in was security. In all other ways, every business was complementary to every other one: the girls, the clubs, the hotel, the drugs, the stratospherically priced dining service all overlapped; but security never seemed to fit. His clients wanted things easy, calm, hassle-free, low-key – but at the same time they wanted cast-iron, gold-plated security, so that no one – police, journalists or Kieran's rival entrepreneurs – could interfere. It was a difficult balancing act. So over the years he hired bouncers, martial artists, ex-policemen, working policemen, ex-army officers, disgraced CIA officers, avaricious KGB agents and out-and-out thugs, and still he never quite felt he'd got that side of things covered.

The fact was that every now and again he would brush up against another crime organisation – usually one much older, larger and nastier than his – and there'd be trouble. Often you didn't even know who you were dealing with; you just pulled back before you found out. He certainly didn't want to go head-to-head with anyone. The last thing he needed was shoot-outs and tit-for-tat killings with the Mafia or the Triads or the Yakuza or salt-of-the-earth East End villains. By spending a large slice of his turnover on security, and by constantly innovating his way into new markets, he managed to avoid coming to the attention of any of the big players. As a result, by 1990 he was a very rich man.

But as the Eighties waned, so did he. The change – what his lecturers would have called his personal 'inflection point' – was marked by two events, two signs that his fortunes had shifted. One was tiny, the other less so. The larger of the two was still rather on the slight side and took the form of a tall, slim woman with pale skin wearing a beautifully tailored suit who crippled two of Kieran's meatiest bouncers with an insouciance that was so total and so convincing that it actually made most of what she said to him afterwards seem plausible.

The second omen was far smaller. It was the virus Hepatitis B. Kieran had heard of it but he'd got the distinct impression it wasn't that bad, which for many people it wasn't. But in the years to follow he was to revise his initial view a number of times. To begin with, it took him a while to recognise that there was anything wrong with him, because all the symptoms – aches, persistent tiredness, nausea, headaches – were things he expected to feel anyway given the kinds of 'hobbies' he would pursue once he was done with the office for the day.

When he tried cutting back a little, taking a few nights off – even getting to bed before midnight on a couple of occasions – his health still didn't improve, so he went to see a doctor. That was the start of a whole era of visiting doctors, sitting in expensive waiting rooms with good art on the walls, being addressed by attractive receptionists with immaculate manners who still managed to be just as unwelcoming as the stressed-out old bats he remembered from when he was a kid waiting to see the family GP.

Initially he was told it was alcohol poisoning or 'substance abuse' or chronic fatigue. Reluctantly he began to cut back even more on his recreations. As his symptoms got worse he mounted ever more drastic incursions into the land of healthy living. After one very memorable six-week period in a 'celebrity retreat', during which he consumed nothing more exciting and harmful than camomile tea, his Harley Street specialist eventually concluded he had a chronic viral infection.

It was around this time he had his visit from the tall, pale, insanely-dangerous woman in the grey Donna Karan pinstripe. She didn't stay long, but she made him the most extraordinary proposal he had ever heard. She said she represented a group of people with pretty much unlimited reach and influence who, while they had no interest in working for a living, rather liked having money and power. She proposed that they take over the ownership of his business, though not its day-to-day running. He could remain in place, draw a handsome salary and give the lion's share of the profits to them.

While he was not an aggressive man, he hadn't grown wealthy living on the wrong side of the law by being soft. Whatever the truth of her claims, it didn't do for people to think you were a pushover. He squared up to her, ready to put on a show of righteous anger – all the while hoping that whoever was supposed to be watching the door downstairs still had enough unbroken fingers to dial a telephone and call in some reinforcements. But astonishingly he found he couldn't move, could hardly breathe. It was the first of many such surreal experiences, and while they never ceased to be troubling, he eventually began to accept them as emblematic of the less pleasant and more Kafkaesque second phase of his life.

With his breath stuck in his throat and the panic of suffocation beginning to flush blood to his cheeks he listened to her complete her proposal. She would be back to visit him in a week and he could do what he liked in the meantime. He could change his name and fly to South America, he could hire a mercenary army to protect him, he could call the police, or book himself on the next Space Shuttle flight. In one week's time she would return, she would kill or maim everyone who stood in her way, and she would expect him to shake her hand and accept that he now worked for her and the people she answered to.

It was actually the phrase 'the people she answered to' that bothered him the most: the idea that there was a hierarchy at work here and he wasn't even dealing with the top rung of it was heartily distressing.

In the intervening week he did his best, though sometimes it felt like he was just going through the motions. He found an old sea fort on the Norfolk coast that had been retrofitted with a fall-out shelter in the late Seventies and he locked himself in there. He hired half a dozen freelance Israeli snipers to patrol the ramparts and borrowed a security team from a supplier of his in the Shan States: men who were usually deployed guarding drug convoys and fighting off honest-to-god pirates in the South China Sea. It didn't do him much good, as some part of him knew it wouldn't.

His one consolation, looking back on it, was that the tall, pale woman – whose name was Karst – had needed some assistance in getting to him. It was slim consolation indeed because her 'team' had consisted of one other, a young woman who only looked to be about seventeen according to one of the snipers who'd survived. While Kieran never got to know Karst very well, he did have occasional insights into her thinking. She was nothing if not calculating. With hindsight he suspected the young woman she'd brought with her would have been selected largely for psychological effect. Karst had made sure to kick his ass with what his male chauvinism would have to assume was their 'B' team. She'd leave it to him to imagine what a team made up of half a dozen of their alpha males was capable of.

For a while, working for Karst was actually a pleasant surprise – not because it was a bundle of laughs, but because his expectations had been so very low. He really was allowed to carry on pretty much as before, with the obvious proviso that three-quarters of the profits now went to someone else. He also had to submit to random inspections by their accountant, who was a strange man: frightened for his life much of the time and yet living like a king on the salary they paid him.

After three months, Karst came to see him in person for a second time. She explained that the next day she was going to come back and break his left arm. He protested that he had done nothing wrong and that he'd obeyed every order he'd been given. She said she knew that, and that was why it was only an arm – that and the fact he had a low psychological tolerance for physical harm. She lingered long enough to give him a brief lecture on the psychology of intimidation.

You had to be careful with proud men, she said, because hurting them could be counter-productive. It was usually best to attack their sense of control over their environment, perhaps by hurting a family member. In Kieran's case, she said his pride was intellectual and hurting him physically would work perfectly well as a motivator, with the proviso that he must always be given a chance to protect himself first. This, she explained, would make it clear that he couldn't think his way out of the situation, no matter how cleverly he schemed. That, plus the fear of more pain, would ensure he didn't start looking for a way to regain his independence. She had selected the three-month mark because it was the time at which a sense of normality started to set in, and with it a possible resurgence of confidence, and thus it was a good moment to reinforce the lessons of their first encounter.

"Really," she stressed, "it's good that you fear pain and the prospect of being physically mutilated. If you didn't, I might have to do something far, far worse than break a single bone."

She turned to go and then remembered something: "Oh, and no painkillers. I'll take a blood sample tomorrow. If your blood contains anything I don't approve of we'll have to go through this again, and next time I'll be creative. That isn't something you'd enjoy."

He didn't sleep much that night, as no doubt she'd intended. The expectation was far worse than the event, which was still bad enough to give him nightmares afterwards. He just wasn't the sort of person who could take pain in his stride, not to mention the sensation of a bone snapping. And despite the fact that he would remember that experience as long as he lived, Karst had found a way to make it even more memorable. She had caught him in whatever invisible net she'd used to cut off his breath the first time they'd met and then she'd reached out towards him, not even making contact, and he'd felt his left humerus break.

As she left him with tears rolling down his face she gave him one last piece of wisdom, "Think about this too. I've never lied to you. When I tell you something will happen, it happens. That's important, because one day I will promise you something good and I want you to know that it's guaranteed, just like any of the painful things I predict for you. One day I'll tell you how you can retire in comfort. It will be something to look forward to. But it won't be for a while yet."

The 'good thing' she'd mentioned was a long time in coming, but eventually it did arrive. First Kieran had to go through most of a decade of despair and agony. The effects of the hepatitis grew worse. No treatment worked; he was one of the fraction of the population whose immune systems couldn't defeat the infection. Eventually it turned into cirrhosis. Which then progressed to a viral form of liver cancer.

Until it got really bad, Kieran carried on working. Even when he was spending most of his day lying helpless in an electrically-adjustable hospital bed he still got a kick out of directing the business – as Karst knew he would. It distracted him from the fact that he was dying. And of course since Karst's takeover, he never needed to worry about security any more. If someone caused him problems he had a number he could call and that was that.

As his condition grew worse it became clear that he needed a new liver. And even though they'd fudged his medical records to make him appear more eligible than he was, he'd still been on the waiting list for three years and no suitable donor had presented themselves. He couldn't wait much longer. And so in '94 he had his transplant; it took place in Costa Rica and Karst's people arranged everything. He didn't ask where the liver had come from or whether the donor had finished with it before it was extracted.

But rather than restore his health, the transplant brought with it a new set of problems. Tissue rejection set in, and the drugs he took to control his rebellious immune system allowed other infections to blossom. For eleven months he was more or less in a coma, getting weaker every day.

Time passed in a blur. And then one day he woke up. For a while he thought he'd died. He was dressed in white, in a beautiful room looking out over the mountains of Tuscany and he felt so healthy he thought he might burst. One look in the mirror convinced him that this must be some form of afterlife. His reflection showed a man in his late teens or perhaps the start of his twenties, whereas Kieran had just turned forty. The face he saw was his, though – except that his nose was different. Kieran's nose had been big and bent; now it was straight and rather average.

The sense that he was in heaven lasted for the rest of that day and into the evening. And then, as he watched the sun setting over the distant peaks, Karst came to see him to explain what had happened, and he realised he was still alive.

She said, "We consider this an honour. We have made you young and healthy, which is not something we would normally do for… an employee. I told you one day that I would make you a promise and that it would be something good. This is the beginning of it. Saving your life is a reward for what you have done for us up until now."

She gave him a moment to let that sink in and then went on, "We want you to go back to work. In fact, we want you to take on some extra responsibilities. You're an ideal choice to run several of our operations and I think you'll enjoy the challenges of your new job."

Kieran sensed there was a 'but' coming. This definitely wasn't heaven: no afterlife he'd ever imagined would have included working for Karst. This seemed a lot more like business as usual, but taken to a new level of weirdness.

Karst said, "We're good employers. The longer you work for us the better your retirement package will be, but we can offer you one thing no one else can. We'll give you back all the years that you give to us. When you leave us, you'll be young and rich and free. But first you have to earn it. Does that sound fair?"

Karst had him pegged. By now he knew that crossing her was certain death – and doubtless dramatically excruciating. This latest development proved that if they wanted to they could ensure that working for them cost him nothing and gained him everything. It really was an offer you couldn't refuse.

As she was leaving, Karst mentioned, "We threw in an old-fashioned nose job for free. It avoids various complications down the line."

Like having anyone believe his story if he chose to tell someone, he thought. His fingerprints weren't on record anywhere, he'd always maintained a low profile, he had no proper longstanding friendships or any living relatives he was in touch with – and he didn't even look like the old Kieran. He smiled in cold appreciation; Karst really knew her stuff.

It took a while for the reality of the change to sink in. His first job was to rebuild the top level of his old organisation, replacing anyone who'd known him before. The parts of the business that had been on the downturn in the early Nineties were on their last legs by now. It was time for a fresh start. Karst gave him control of a number of additional ventures she'd previously been handling directly. He was able to make himself useful by bringing his usual flair for synergy and clever logistics to each of them. As Karst had promised, he even enjoyed it for a little while. But then his curiosity began to stir and threatened to spoil it for him.

He would occasionally meet Karst's colleagues and found them to be as taciturn as she was. More so in fact, because Karst would sometimes give these little illustrative lectures aimed at realigning the sensibilities and motivations of her direct reports, whereas the others paid no attention to him at all.

Despite the danger, Kieran found himself trying to learn more about who these people were and how they were able to do the remarkable things they could do. From time to time he would see evidence of their strange abilities which, breathtaking though they were, certainly had limits.

Unfortunately for him, Karst eventually became aware of his interest and decided to give him another corrective lesson. But first, as always, she wanted to explain.

"You need to understand that my ability to manipulate you psychologically is what keeps you alive. If we ever reach the point where I can think of no way to make you do what I want, then your usefulness would be gone. That fact underlies any other deal we might have in operation."

She gave him a kind of moonlit smile and said, "Your intellectual curiosity is valuable to your work, but if I come to believe that work alone is not enough to occupy your thoughts we will have reached an impasse. And I only know one method for resolving those."

She continued, "You have the whole wide world to distract yourself with and a surfeit of professional challenges. Unless you can redirect the curiosity you feel in some new direction, I will be forced to replace you."

Kieran was doing his best to listen to her, but by now he was also aware that the talking part of the lesson would soon be over and the hurting him and breaking things part might be about to start.

But a thought occurred to Karst and she said in a voice that was almost kindly, "It might interest you to know that I was born a very long time ago, and believe it or not I once had a mother. There was a piece of advice she would sometimes give to people. It doesn't translate very poetically, but let me try: it was something along the lines of 'why study power when you can study happiness instead?'. I have never been able to do much with it, but perhaps you will. I think if you can take it to heart, it could save your life."

And then instead of hurting him or issuing some terrible prediction about what would happen a day or a week later, she drove him to one of their buildings in the City and locked him in its ancient cellar. She left him there in total darkness to 'give him some time to think about the nature of curiosity' and to 'make pacts with himself about how he would behave if she ever let him out'. Previously, she had fought his defiance by combining fear and pain; now she fought his curiosity by mixing fear with sensory deprivation.

Nearly two days had passed when she finally returned to release him. And he did indeed find that his curiosity was much lessened for a time, wonderfully so in fact. In that cellar, with absolutely nothing to focus on except his own thoughts, he'd done just as she'd expected and come to wholeheartedly regret his inquisitiveness. She had more or less cured him of his curiosity.

And perhaps things would have stayed that way if he hadn't met someone who offered him a way out from under Karst's control.

The fact was that Kieran was no longer happy. In fact, at his core, he was miserable. But the impossibility of escape and an appreciation for just how perceptive Karst could be kept him from acting on it. The problem was that he had changed. His old pleasures didn't satisfy him any more and he found himself gradually giving them up, only indulging himself sufficiently to stop Karst suspecting some fresh shift in his character which might lead her to look for new torments with which to manipulate him. He thought wryly to himself that perhaps he was just getting old. He was nearing his fiftieth birthday, feeling like he was ninety, while the face he saw in the mirror could certainly pass for late twenties.

The way out he was offered came from one of Karst's colleagues. Much as she would have done, he first made it clear how easy it would be to reciprocate if Kieran betrayed him. Then he explained that, much like Kieran, he wanted some independence. But before he could strike out on his own, he needed to get his hands on one or two of life's little comforts to make sure that his voluntary exile was as agreeable as possible. For this he needed information. Kieran wouldn't need to physically do anything. He'd simply need to compile a picture of the operations which he supervised and then hand that information over. In exchange, he would receive a lump sum of two hundred thousand U.S. dollars in cash and a chance to start over, with Karst and her friends thinking he was dead.

Once upon a time, two hundred grand U.S. would have meant very little, but these days his access to funds was severely restricted. Karst let him have almost anything he wanted, but someone else always paid; he had very little discretionary cash of his own. Unless he wanted to risk getting caught, then squirrelling away even fifty thousand pounds would be a struggle. Given his increasingly frugal tastes, two hundred grand would be enough. In fact, to his surprise, he realised he would have done it for no money at all; his freedom was what he really wanted.

Still it took him two months to work up the nerve to say yes – even though from the moment he heard the offer he knew he had to take it. It was just that crossing Karst was not something you did on the spur of the moment. In fact he'd come to think of it as playing Russian roulette with a fully loaded gun.

He never learned very much about the identity of the man who made him the offer, beyond the initial he used to identify himself: 'J'. Over the course of six months Kieran copied all sorts of data for him: e-mails, bank records, property transactions, travel information. Kieran was administering a large organisation, and while he often didn't know what purpose its activities served he was still in a position to record many of them.

He did his best to give no clue to Karst that anything had changed. But inside, he was the happiest he had been for a very long time. Though it hadn't had quite the effect she intended, he had found the advice Karst had passed on from her long-dead mother surprising memorable. It really resonated with him. So much so that he had had it engraved on a little silver card that he kept in his wallet. It had taken him a long time to get there, but he felt as though he might actually be ready to start enjoying the simple things in life.

As the time approached for him to hand over the information, and undergo his fake death, it even looked like he was going to get away with it. In the end, he never found out what had given the game away, but a full day ahead of schedule he got a call from J telling him to bring what he'd got right that second because someone was on to them.

"This will still work,' J told him, "They don't know that I'm involved. I can still cover your tracks when you disappear. In fact, this might make things easier."

They met in the big train station at Stratford in East London. J handed over a backpack full of bundles of hundred dollar bills; Kieran handed over two data CDs packed with files. He knew J would only need to pick up the phone and his life was over, but he also knew it would be difficult for him to do so without incriminating himself. Just to make things even more secure, Kieran had a second pair of discs in his old briefcase and they contained some extra files he hadn't given to J, including a couple of e-mails they'd exchanged. It wouldn't necessarily keep him safe – unless J anticipated something like this – but it *would* make it just that bit more difficult for J to get away with it, if he double-crossed Kieran.

When the exchange was complete, Kieran walked away from J with the beginnings of an irrepressible smile spreading across his face. He found a gents toilets, shut himself into a cubicle and transferred the cash into his old briefcase, wrapping two bundles of notes in cling-film and slipping them in alongside a 9mm semi-automatic and a fake passport, both of which he'd owned since before Karst had come onto the scene. Then he changed into clothes he'd bought in a charity shop, putting his Armani suit in the bag J had given him, and dropping that into a litter bin near the station. Then he boarded a Jubilee Line train for Canary Wharf, where he would pick up the rest of his things and get a taxi to City Airport. At that moment, he allowed himself to believe it was going to work.

And he very nearly made it. He was getting off the tube train, when the young man in the cheap suit came pelting towards him with someone chasing after him and Kieran realised that his one chance of freedom had slipped away. They'd sent a couple faces he wouldn't recognise and dressed them as police, but he instantly saw them for what they were. Very few ordinary people moved the way they did. You needed to be young for a lot of years to acquire that murderous grace. His spirits were in free-fall.

Dressing them as some sort of police SWAT team was a nice touch. Ideal if you wanted to haul someone away in broad daylight with no questions asked. No other criminal organisation would even dare to try something like that, but he knew that Karst's people could call on some astonishingly illustrious official connections if they needed to. Not that they'd probably have bothered; none of their kind would worry about being captured or questioned. They could break through any cordon, resist any attempts to contain them. Short of calling in the army, they were unstoppable.

So it seemed like Kieran was going to be captured and dragged back to Karst. Then she would want to know who he'd been working with. If he was lucky she would just kill him once he talked. But knowing Karst, she might decide to use him as an object lesson to her other direct reports. That was enough to turn your stomach, just thinking about it. Very soon now, he was going to die – one way or another – that was pretty much a certainty. And he found that finality lent him a certain determination, almost like courage, that he hadn't experienced before. The fact was that if he decided that he wouldn't allow himself to be hauled back to face Karst then that was all there was to it. He would find a way out whatever the cost. It was all he really wanted now anyway: to be free.

***

Clipper stood at the entrance to the rear cab and looked outwards towards the dark track. Light from behind him illuminated part of the dim interior and a little of the tunnel beyond. He could see that one of the train's rear windows was missing. Presumably that was the result of the gunshot he'd heard just after Warren cornered Kieran in here.

The outer door of the train lay open as well. It hinged, not along its side like a normal door, but along its bottom edge, which meant that it opened like a drawbridge – though this drawbridge had steps built into it and formed a descending ramp down to the level of the tracks. Plastic-wrapped steel cables ran out from the sides of the doorframe and down to the ramp, holding it at the proper angle. Sitting on the bottom step, legs dangling over the tracks, was Warren.

Clipper's eyes adjusted gradually to the gloom. A slight stirring of air in the tunnel brought to him the smell of dust and hot oil and… with a nauseating jolt he realised what that third smell might be and did his best not to think about it.

Once his eyes had got used to the low light, he could make out what Warren was doing. He had one arm raised and was gently flicking his right hand out in front of him and then slowly rolling his arm in a circle around his shoulder.

"Er… Are you OK?" Clipper asked, not sure what to make of it, but feeling as though he should say something to announce his presence. He'd been really hoping that Warren hadn't survived, that he'd fallen along with Kieran, so it felt strange to be asking him how he was doing. On the other hand, he'd seen no sign that these people could read minds, so he did his best to keep the guilt to himself.

Warren's tone was biting as he said, "Well, you see I pulled my shoulder out of its socket. It's still a little painful."

Presumably he'd tried to grab hold of Kieran as he jumped; Clipper could work that much out. But how had he *un*-dislocated his shoulder? He could vaguely remember tough guys in movies charging into walls to pop them back in. He wasn't sure he believed that would work. Still, if you could deflect bullets and stop yourself from bleeding through force of will, the shoulder thing was probably kid's stuff. Child's play. A doddle.

Was that a little hysteria creeping into his thoughts? Clipper took a breath and tried to settle himself. Warren still hadn't looked round as Clipper said, "I'm sorry but your, uh… your friend isn't doing very well. We don't know what else to do for him."

Warren sighed and began to haul himself to his feet. He still had on only one boot and Clipper could just about make out the black mark in the middle of his bare foot that must have been the clotted blood around the bullet hole. There was no sign of bleeding. Warren was even able to put a little weight on it as he stood.

Once he was upright he said, "Well, try not to concern yourself." More sarcasm? He grunted a little as he turned, his bad arm holding onto one of the ramp's steel cables. "I think Sebastian is going to have to chalk this one up to experience." His tone was conversational now – he was mainly talking to himself – and yet there was something troubling about his words.

Clipper edged back as Warren limped towards him. Wanting to get out of his way, Clipper turned and walked ahead, making his way back to Rachel's side. When Warren eventually reached them, he crouched down next to Sebastian, glaring at Rachel until she moved aside to give him some room. Then he gently touched his friend's face and called his name. Getting no response, he said it again and patted his cheek to rouse him. Still no response. A look of annoyance passed crossed Warren's features. He lifted his hand a little and gave Sebastian a hard slap across the face. Rachel gasped.

Irate, she demanded, "What the hell do you think you're…" but then she abruptly stopped speaking. Clipper couldn't figure out what was happening now, but Rachel's eyes bulged a little and there was a look of panic on her face. Her mouth was open but so far as he could tell she wasn't breathing.

When Rachel had challenged him, Warren's head had snapped round to stare at her and his eyes were still fixed upon her now as she squirmed and struggled to breathe. It was plain enough that Warren was doing this. Somehow.

Clipper needed to do something to help Rachel, but he had no idea what. Several options flicked through his mind, and all of them seemed likely to make matters worse – especially his first instinct, which was just to punch Warren in the face.

He realised he needed to say something to distract Warren and maybe get him to calm down a little, but all that Clipper's throat wanted to produce was a shout of anger. And that wasn't going to work.

He forced himself to sound calm as he said, "Hey, listen, she was only trying to help your friend, alright? That's fair enough isn't it?" He needed to sound reasonable, not like he was challenging Warren, but it wasn't easy.

A moment later Rachel dragged in a great lungful of air and Warren said to her, "Keep your mouth shut." Then he turned back to Sebastian, whose eyes had fluttered open. He was clearly having difficulty focusing on the man leaning over him. Clipper could almost see him trying to figure out whether someone had just hit him. It didn't look like his brain was firing on all cylinders.

"Here, look at me, Sebastian," Warren said, clicking his fingers and trying to get his attention. Then, very clearly and emphatically, he said, "You need to stop the bleeding right now. Right now, understand?" Sebastian said nothing, though he looked as though he was trying to speak. Then his eyes began to flick upwards again and the lids closed.

This time when Warren hit him, even harder than before, Rachel tensed and Clipper could see how tightly her nails pressed into the palms of her bunched fists, but she held her tongue.

Sebastian twitched and quivered from the blow, but his eyes opened once more. Warren said to him, "This is it, my friend. If you're going to save yourself you need to do it now."

Sebastian coughed a little, deep down in his chest, hardly making a sound and his lips moved, but all that came out was a wheeze. He tried again and managed to say, "It's no good. I can't maintain it…" He snatched another couple of painful sounding breaths and went on, "Hospital. Let them fix me up. I'll get out… when I'm stronger."

But Warren was shaking his head slowly. He sounded sad as he said, "Sebastian, that isn't how it works. You know the rules. You'd get us a lot of attention. And they'd take away these." He tapped Sebastian's wrist as he said it.

Sebastian looked confused and then just a little bit worried. "No. I can… Give me a moment…" he said, struggling to speak.

Warren shook his head again. Then he reached around and pulled a black tube free from the bottom of his backpack. Clipper tried to figure out what it was, but couldn't guess. Warren grasped it at either end and pulled his hands apart. A bright knife-edge came into view. It was a blade about eight inches long. Sebastian's eyes went very wide and he began struggling to move, but his arms had no strength in them, they did little more than flutter at his sides.

"No," Rachel said sharply. And when Warren shot her a warning look, she held her hands to her mouth and repeated quietly, "No," but she didn't try to stop him.

For Clipper it was like the moment when he'd seen Kieran hanging from the rear of the train. His mind raced – aware of what was going to happen next, but unable to think of a way to prevent it.

"Couldn't we…" he began, not caring if Warren turned on him. But Warren had already done it. He'd rested the tip of the knife on Sebastian's chest and pushed the blade in between his ribs. Sebastian twitched once, violently and made a sound that was halfway between a moan and a cough, and that was that. Clipper could hardly believe that was all it took to kill someone.

Warren waited a few seconds and then eased the blade out. He gave his wrist a violent twist which cast a line of blood droplets in a thin arc up onto the white of the door panel and then he shut the knife back into its sheath with a snap. He used his sleeve to wipe the handle free of his fingerprints and then tucked the sheathed knife into Sebastian's belt.

Since the moment she'd seen the mirrored steel exposed and realised what it meant, Rachel had been staring at Warren with fixed and silent hatred. Her gaze burrowed into him and Clipper thought he would surely be forced to look round in a minute, to react. Mentally Clipper pleaded with her to stop before she attracted Warren's attention and he was provoked into doing something awful to her. Given what he'd just seen Warren do, Clipper could picture it so easily: Rachel's body crumpling, her life extinguished, while Clipper looked on helplessly.

But Warren was busying himself with Sebastian's personal effects. He was removing the fastenings around Sebastian's wrists. One was a watch; Clipper wasn't sure what the strap on the other wrist was for. He also removed Sebastian's wool cap and a bright band of metal beneath it. It looked out of place next to the black uniform.

Was this what gave them their power, Clipper wondered. Was this like those stories where people had magic rings or wands and stuff? Or could it be some sort of technology, some kind of miniaturised gadgetry – perhaps secret military equipment beyond anything civilians had access to? He had no idea. For all Clipper could tell the things Warren was removing might simply be their equivalent of dog tags – or taking a man's wedding ring back for his widow.

Now Warren turned Sebastian's body onto its side – and despite the fact that moments before he'd ended the man's life, he was gentle about it. He opened Sebastian's backpack and removed a few objects, some of which Clipper could identify – like a wallet and a phone – and some he could only guess at, like the black tube that resembled Warren's knife but was much longer. Then he worked his way along Sebastian's corpse, expertly rifling the body and removing everything that could be removed. When he was done, he slipped his own backpack off and stowed Sebastian's things, and then shrugged it back into place.

When his task was completed he half stood, bending down to get his hands beneath Sebastian's body, and lifted it off the floor. Moving slowly and favouring his good foot, he carried the body past Clipper and Rachel, and took it into the rear cab, placing it on the floor behind the driver's chair. As Warren stepped back from the body, Clipper could see him pulling his sleeve down over his hand, before he bent down again. When he straightened he was holding the knife in the fabric of his tunic. He flicked his arm and the knife spun away into the dark of the tunnel. He must have loosened the scabbard too, for Clipper saw a flash as the blade caught the light. He could hear it clatter and ring as it bounced across the tracks. He wondered whether Kieran wasn't going to get the blame for the hole in Sebastian's chest as well as the one in his neck.

Now what? Clipper thought, ominously aware that there was nothing left to occupy Warren's attention apart from him and Rachel – and so far the recipients of Warren's attention hadn't lasted very long. But there wasn't any reason for him to hurt them, was there?

The problem was that Clipper just didn't know how to read someone like Warren – and that frustrated as well as frightened him. He'd been around some dangerous people, but you could usually tell when you were in trouble with them. They tended to shout a lot and threaten you, and they made it pretty clear when they were getting ready to do something physical. But who could work out what was going on in Warren's head? Should Clipper assume he was safe for the time being – at least until Warren got out another knife? Or should he be freaking out right now and sprinting for the other end of the train? Which just seemed guaranteed to force Warren's hand and make him do something unpleasant.

He looked over at Rachel to see how she was doing, and noticed tears in her eyes. She was looking towards the cab – to where Sebastian's body lay – and he realised she was crying for the man who had been killed, and the fact that she hadn't been able to save him – and that made Clipper feel worthless and low. He was busy worrying about his own safety while she was wishing she could have done more to help an injured man. He felt a wave of disgust with himself. This situation was just bringing home to him what he'd been feeling for a while now: he was a parasite who always put himself first.

He just hoped he could hide that from Rachel for a little bit longer. They were in a lot of trouble here, but it sort of felt like they were a team. And that was so much better than going through this on his own. Which meant he desperately didn't want her to notice what a self-centred loser he was.

Dammit, he was doing it again: turning it around so it was about him. He was going to think about somebody else's wellbeing for a change before his self-esteem just shrivelled up and blew away.

He reached out to touch Rachel's arm and said quietly, "It'll be OK."

He wasn't sure *what* would be OK – it didn't seem likely that anything very much would be – but that wasn't exactly the point.

Rachel looked up at him, and he tried to think of something else to say that would help her to feel better. "You really tried," he said, and he meant it. "You didn't know him, but you still did everything you could for him."

She didn't respond to that, but after a few moments she nodded a little and he reckoned that maybe he'd consoled her a little. Neither of them spoke for a few seconds, until Rachel lifted her head and said, "I think you were right about him." She meant Warren. "We should have just run."

Well, he wasn't going to get into that line of thought. And sadly, he couldn't change the subject by explaining his genius plan to get them out of there because he didn't have one. In fact there wasn't really anything useful he could do, unless it was just to distract her a little. He said, "You know, I really would like to see those horses you mentioned. I'm just a bit worried your mum won't take to me. She sounds like she can be awkward when she wants to be."

Rachel give a single laugh and said, "Well if *that's* all that's spoiling your day, I can tell you now, there's *no way* she'll approve. But you shouldn't let that put you off visiting. She hates it when people give up too easily." She didn't really smile, but she looked at him in a way that made him feel like they'd just shared a joke, which was what he'd wanted.

When Warren reappeared a moment later, Clipper felt like he'd been caught doing something he shouldn't have been, though he wasn't sure what. As Warren clumped towards them, passing between opposing rows of seats, he called out to them, "So what's the story with you two? Friends? Co-workers?"

Before he even thought about it, Clipper said, "She's my girlfriend." He sounded defiant and realised immediately it was kind of an idiotic thing to say. But he felt like he needed to put up some form of resistance, to obstruct Warren in some way, even if he didn't dare challenge him properly. Lying to him felt like a start; a small sign of independence. Plus, he couldn't help feeling a little protective towards Rachel. He wasn't exactly the expert, but out of the two of them, he had to imagine he'd spent more time around violent criminals than she had.

"Girlfriend? I doubt that," said Warren, "but you clearly know each other." Then he suddenly held his hands up, like he was making a big announcement, and said, "But listen, here's the good news. I only need one of you. Right? So you can go if you want. I just need her to stay." He sounded easygoing, but his eyes never left Clipper as he spoke.

When Clipper didn't react, Warren said, "I mean it. You can go. Get to the other end of the train with all the other passengers. If you get asked to describe me later, make sure you do a bad job of it and we'll be fine."

Clipper was looking from Warren's face to Rachel's. Warren was doing that trustworthy thing again, spreading his hands a little, trying to sound reasonable, even a little bit amiable. Rachel on the other hand now had a sharp look of fear in her eyes. It was evidently dawning on her that, bad as this situation was, there were ways in which it could get a lot worse.

"I…" Clipper said, not sure of what he was going to say. It was only a matter of time before Warren remembered why Clipper's face might be familiar, wasn't it? And if things turned ugly, what was the sense in both him *and* Rachel getting hurt?

Clipper half expected Rachel to say something, to demand that he stay, to make some sort of protest. Maybe even to beg him. But she didn't. She was making it easy for him; she was even avoiding his gaze. He studied her face trying to understand what she was thinking. She looked like she was working hard to keep the fear under control and… something else.

"Well?" said Warren.

But Clipper was still wanted to understand Rachel's expression. Somehow it mattered. It was clear that Warren's decision to split them up – and to let him go – had dropped the floor out from underneath her, but there was something else going on in her eyes besides fear. There was a struggle taking place. And then she spoke, quietly. "It'll be OK," she whispered. She was giving him permission to go, but her eyes were fixed upon her hands, which rested in her lap.

So that was it. He could read her expression now. She was struggling to persuade herself that she'd be fine on her own. She was clearly terrified, but she wasn't going to drag this out. That's why she wouldn't look at him or beg him. In her mind, he was already walking away, and she was doing her best to prepare for whatever happened next. She must know what Clipper would be thinking: that no one in their right mind would turn down Warren's offer of freedom just to keep a stranger company. He wondered, if things were the other way round, whether she would choose to stay. Well, she'd already decided against leaving him once. And now she was making it easy for him to walk away from her.

As always happened when he got stressed over some sort of decision, he found himself wishing he could ask Gary what to do. Of course Gary had never given him any advice for a situation like this. But he had once said something about nicking from people who might not be able to afford it. He'd told Clipper, "Don't do anything you'll hate yourself for. It's not worth it." And that was clear enough. Clipper wanted so badly *not* to be the kind of person who'd leave Rachel behind. He didn't want to despise himself; in fact he was desperate for a reason not to.

"I… don't want to leave without Rachel," Clipper said. He felt he should give a reason, but he wasn't about to launch into some crazy speech about his self-esteem. "You know how it is," was the best he could manage.

Warren studied him. "You're sure?" he asked. He was like one of those game-show hosts who tried to get you to change your mind the whole time, to make the game more fun for the audience. Clipper nodded.

And finally Rachel looked at him. He wasn't quite sure what the look signified – it certainly wasn't anything as straightforward as gratitude or relief. But at least she could look at him again. And he realised how much that meant to him.

"Excellent," said Warren. "I was hoping you'd say that because I've got a job for you. And we need to make a start before someone tries to get this train moving again and I'm forced to do something about that."

Clipper didn't know how to react. Warren had a job for him? So what was all that about letting him go? Clipper had felt nauseous but sort of noble about his decision to stay for all of maybe three seconds, but now the situation had shifted again.

"You see, someone has to go down that tunnel and get Kieran's things," Warren explained. "For the time being, I'm having one or two mobility issues. So, um, *Matt*? Why don't you go for me and I'll stay here with…

Rachel wasn't it? I'll look after her until you come back." Warren laid his hand on Rachel's shoulder, his fingers towards her neck – the fingertips were hidden inside the tumble of her hair. The gesture was both protective and unpleasantly intimate. Rachel looked like she wanted to pull away from him, but she didn't.

Clipper didn't need it spelled out: he knew how a protection racket worked. If Warren didn't get what he wanted, he'd stop 'looking after' Rachel. Earlier, he'd just been testing Clipper to see whether he was prepared to give up a chance to escape for Rachel's sake – and Clipper had passed. Or failed, depending on how you looked at it. Effectively he'd just volunteered Rachel to be his leverage.

It reminded Clipper of chess. In movies, whenever two people got into this cat-and-mouse stuff, someone would point out it was like game of chess. Well, Clipper hated chess. He'd tried it two or three times and couldn't make any sense of it. The rules seemed like they were plucked out of thin air, and any time you thought you'd worked out what you were supposed to do next it just meant you were about to fall into a trap. This entire thing was *exactly* like chess and he hated it.

And besides all the mind games, Warren wanted him to go out into the tunnel. Well, the more he thought about that, the more he wasn't too thrilled about the idea of being down there on the tracks. He also didn't like to think about what state Kieran's body might be in. It had been bad enough standing by the back door of the train and smelling something that shouldn't be familiar but somehow was: a combination of burnt hair and overcooked barbeque meat. He tried not to picture what was waiting for him in the dark of the tunnel.

"What if the current is still on?" Clipper asked. He knew the trogs called it 'traction current'; and if it was on it meant that the live rail could kill you.

Warren smiled unpleasantly. "Work something out," he said. "Maybe you could just be careful what you touch."

Clipper was trying to remember what else he knew about underground trains besides the words 'traction current'. He knew one of the reasons the door on the back of the train folded down to make a set of steps was to evacuate passengers if something went wrong. And obviously London Underground didn't want people to be electrocuted as soon as they stepped off the ramp. Yeah, that was it: there was a locker full of emergency bits and pieces in the cab somewhere. He was trying to think what the item he needed was called. His brain kept insisting it was a JCB, but he knew that wasn't it. Then he had it: an SCD. Short circuit device. It was like a long clamp that fitted across the rails. He'd never seen one, but he knew about them. If the electricity came on, the SCD sent it straight into the other rails and sort of blew the fuse.

Clipper was nodding reluctantly now. "OK. I know there's a gadget in the cab we can use to make sure the power stays off," Clipper said, "I just need a bit of rope maybe. To lower it onto the track."

Warren looked at him questioningly.

Clipper said, "Look I'll do what you say, but I'm not going to dab my finger against the live rail to see if it's on. There should be a short-circuit thing in the driver's cab and then we just need a way to lower it down so that I can tell whether the juice is on or not."

"Fair enough," Warren said, sounding impatient. "Get your short-circuit whatever-it-is. I've got some line here." He slipped his backpack off and unzipped one of the compartments. Reaching in, he pulled out a bunched coil of black rope. It was no thicker than clothesline, but it had an expensive satiny sheen to it that suggested it might be a lot stronger than clothesline, maybe some kind of superfibre.

Warren undid the coil of rope and produced a metal multi-tool gadget from one of his pockets. He thumbed open a wicked looking knife blade and held it up.

"How much line do you need," Warren asked. As he spoke, the tip of the knife drifted close to Rachel's face; it was almost absentminded, but Clipper was sure it was intentional. All part of helping Clipper picture what would happen if he legged it away down the tunnel instead of doing as he was told.

"I dunno, about ten feet," Clipper said. And then an idea like a snap of static electricity popped into his head. Bam. There it was.

It was more than a little bit crazy and right away he wondered whether he should forget about it. On the other hand, there was a chance it would work.

Warren was parcelling out the rope, getting ready to cut it, and waving the knife around near Rachel's skin. That clinched it in Clipper's mind. He didn't have to go through with his idea, he just had to set it up. He might need something up his sleeve if things with Warren really turned bad.

Half distracted, trying to think it through, Clipper said, "Nah, don't worry about cutting it." He reached out and Warren shrugged and handed him the rope.

Clipper was putting the steps together in his mind, ticking off the order of events.

"What's so funny?" Warren asked suspiciously. "Are you high or something?"

Clipper realised he'd been smiling. The idea that was even now unfolding itself in his brain had originally come from something Gary had said. It felt like one last gift from his old buddy, exactly when he needed it most. And that had made him smile.

"No," said Clipper, "It's just been a strange day, you know?" Warren gave him a look that suggested he thought Clipper was insane.

Setting the rope down on the seat nearest him, Clipper said, "Let me get the short circuit thing." He walked away from Warren and into the dim cab. As soon as he stepped into the gloom he started violently, having forgotten that Sebastian's corpse was waiting in there, leaning against the wall in the dark, legs out in front of him, staring into forever.

Doing his best to ignore the dead man's gaze he looked around for anything that might be an equipment locker. It was easy enough to find; he undid the lock and opened the hinged cover. Inside he could see a shovel and an ice scraper, a folded tarpaulin and a long complicated looking metal rod that had to be the SCD. He wrestled it free of its clips and closed the cover.

The idea that had popped into his head a moment before was still there, occupying part of his attention, and as it assembled itself he was able to see it from different sides. At that very moment, he spotted a problem and just as quickly realised the answer. Before he could change his mind, he set the

SCD aside and crouched over Sebastian's corpse. He'd just watched Warren fetch out a bundle of rope from his backpack. As swiftly as he could, he checked the same compartment in Sebastian's pack… and came up with an identical bundle of silky futuristic-looking line. Hastily he tossed it out onto the track, throwing it as far as he could and hoping that Warren wasn't watching. Then he tried to prop Sebastian's corpse back up, so that it was just as Warren had left it. Arranging the heavy limbs felt horribly wrong and Clipper had to avoid looking at the dead face or brushing against any bare skin. He did the best he could and left it. Then he grabbed the SCD and stepped back into the passenger compartment.

Warren was closer now that he had been; probably coming to investigate. Clipper held up the metal device and picked up the rope.

"You any good at knots?" Warren asked, sceptically.

Clipper knew a few. Like he'd told Rachel, he'd worked at a stables for a little while. You couldn't be around horses for long and not learn a bit about tying a knot. He shrugged noncommittally.

Warren interpreted that as a 'no' and took the SCD from him. He expertly wrapped a couple of turns of line around the centre of the device, did some clever looping and threading, and then pulled the whole thing tight. The SCD was now dangling from a little cradle of rope at its centre.

"Now get on with it," Warren said, handing the whole thing back to Clipper. "I want his bag and all his personal belongings. Make sure you get any paperwork or computer stuff: disks, memory cards. Don't miss anything."

Clipper nodded and then looked across to Rachel to see how she was doing. She looked like she wanted to say something. Clipper was half expecting her to say 'hurry back' or 'see you in a minute'. Then again, maybe she still wasn't sure he would return. So he said it for her: "I'll be back as quick as I can." She nodded, like she was doing her best to believe him.

"Yeah, yeah," said Warren impatiently and followed Clipper as he made his way to the rear exit steps.

Clipper got as far as: "I'm going to need…" half turning to say it, when Warren handed him a maglite, one of the little ones, about as long as his hand. "Right," Clipper said, taking it from him and turning it on. Then he stepped down to the last rung of the ramp and began lowering the SCD towards the live rail.

He wasn't quite sure what he expected to happen – a loud bang, a spark like a bolt of lightning, maybe the SCD would fly up in the air – but the reality was an anti-climax. He dangled the device, making sure it linked the live rail to the others and still nothing happened.

So he hopped down onto the level of the track and fiddled with the SCD until he had it fitted tightly into place. Then he dragged in a deep breath struggling against a chest that felt far too tight and started walking down the tunnel, away from the train and into the dark.

***

Rachel caught glimpses of Matt's flashlight beam as it bobbed and swung, gradually receding into the gloom of the tunnel. She was sitting on one of the rows of passenger seats just outside the driver's cab. Near her right toe was the bullet hole and splash of blood where Warren had been hit. To the other side of her, in the open space by the double doors, was a broad dark layer of drying blood within which Sebastian had died.

She sat now with her hands in her lap, the nail of one thumb fidgeting against the cuticles of her index finger, her mind fretting just like her hands. Turning her head, she could look over to where her bags lay among the seats, beyond all the blood, just as she'd left them. All ready to go. She tried to imagine for a moment how this nightmare could be sorted out, how she could still find herself on a plane in a few hour's time. The thing was, she could easily picture herself queuing to check in, shuffling those bags forwards a few feet at a time, frustrated that it was taking so long. She could see herself a little later, sitting on hard seats at the gate, among noisy families and sprawled teenagers in headphones, waiting for the announcement to board. Then she'd be on the plane. By midnight, she'd be drowsy and warm, her head propped on a tiny pillow, leaning against her business-class window, watching the faint thread of lights miles below and the occasional flash of moonlight from iced-over lakes. It was easy enough to imagine, and the idea comforted her, but it wasn't real. None of it was going to happen. Right now, it was difficult to believe she was even going to get off this train.

This disaster of a day was not just outside her experience, it was outside of what she had ever expected to experience. She knew bad things happened to people out there in the world, and like anyone who'd ever seen cable news, she'd thought about them happening to her – but not anything like this – not the impossible things she'd seen. They somehow made this ordeal seem... she wanted to say 'unfair'. It wasn't a word she ever used, but there were enough horrors in life you had to prepare for without the world free-associating new nightmares on the spur of the moment. What she'd seen shouldn't have happened.

Nevertheless, here was Warren. Only a few minutes ago he'd trapped the air in her lungs and held her arms pinned to her sides using only – so far as she could see – an angry look. And a few minutes before that she was pretty sure a bullet aimed right at his chest had lost its way and ended up in the ceiling of the train. Warren was a glaring error, a blatant mistake in her understanding of the world.

And yet she'd lived twenty-eight years without encountering anything like him. Her previous life had given no clue to the existence of anyone like Warren. And that left two possibilities. The first was that the world made no sense: it could spontaneously flip into some new mode that ran on different rules, and everything you thought you knew could just slide into chaos. The second possibility was that Warren, and anyone else out there who was like him, were a very tiny part of the world – so tiny that most of humanity went their whole lives without an encounter like this. That was the only explanation that made sense, the only way she could fit this situation into her life while keeping her sanity intact: she was right in the middle of some freak exception to the world's everyday rules. And there was a sparkle of hope in that thought. If Rachel could find her way off this train and onto a plane home there was a very good chance that she would never have to worry about Warren and what he represented ever again. There was no reason she couldn't go at least another twenty-eight years untroubled by the fact of his existence or what it might imply.

Of course, like any good idea, the problems tended to show up once you got down into the details. *If* she could get off this train, her life could go back to normal. But as 'if's went, this one was a bear. Though surely there had to be some chance that once Matt came back with whatever it was that Warren was after, that would be that. And she could almost allow herself to believe that he *would* come back. She was not a trusting soul, but Matt seemed... remarkable somehow, or at least different, though she couldn't put her finger on why she felt like that. Maybe it was just that she didn't know anyone remotely like him. He was an unknown quantity which made it easier to believe that maybe her usual low expectations didn't apply.

Or maybe he *was* a little bit remarkable. At the back of her mind, she was still turning over that strange conversation they'd had, outside, before all this happened. The weird chemistry of that encounter seemed to have left her with an unexpected residue of hope, an unexplained faith that he really was doing his best to help her. Common sense told her it was wishful thinking, but all the same, there it was.

So that would be the first miracle she needed: for Matt to return with Kieran's things. And then what? Warren would get the train moving, they'd finally reach the next station, and Warren would make his escape, leaving her to continue on to Heathrow with just enough time left to check in.

OK, that *obviously* wasn't going to happen. Not with a dead body on the train, another on the tracks and the floor of the train looking like something from an abattoir. But maybe after enough policemen had asked her enough questions, and the delays had stretched out longer than anyone expected, maybe then they'd let her go home. That sounded possible, didn't it? And for that to happen, Warren just needed to release them unharmed.

As it had twenty times already, Rachel's mind's eye dragged her back to the moment the knife went into Sebastian's chest, the gleaming blade slicing down into thick muscle and piercing his heart. There was something particular about the sureness with which Warren had done it. She had known without a doubt when she saw his hands move that he had performed exactly that motion before.

Perhaps the first time he had been nervous, his hands awkward. Perhaps the second time he had been a little steadier, more business-like, but maybe he had still hesitated. But he'd killed Sebastian with a simply, precise efficiency – and no more fuss than if he'd been twisting the top off a jar. So what number had Sebastian been? His third? His fifth?

And she thought back to the look on Warren's face when Sebastian had been shot. It had affected him. He'd been visibly upset. But it hadn't stopped him forcing a knife between his friend's ribs. Once he'd made his mind up, he hadn't wavered – no matter that Sebastian was someone he cared about. So what did that say about Warren? That he was ruthless? That he would do whatever he thought he needed to do? What worried Rachel most was that it suggested – in fact it did more than just suggest – that Warren didn't like leaving loose ends. Matt had said his friend disappeared after working for Warren. Getting rid of loose ends explained that too.

Was Warren going to make an exception this time? Would he leave witnesses behind – especially when he had such extraordinary secrets to protect – secrets that would be picked up by every single newspaper and TV station in the world if they got out?

Sebastian's only crime seemed to be that he might survive long enough to wake up in hospital, where he might say something, or do something, that Warren didn't approve of – or get so delirious with pain or medication that he'd demonstrate one of his impossible abilities to a room full of hospital staff.

Nope. Warren didn't seem like the kind of person who would run the risk of turning on the TV to see her and Matt telling their story on the evening news, followed by an identikit picture of his face filling the screen.

And if he didn't like leaving witnesses behind, was there anything at all she could to protect herself? Like, what if she promised not to talk? Crossed her heart. Really, honest-to-god *swore* that she'd say nothing. And then Warren would have to believe her and he'd be sure to let them both go without hurting them.

Of course he would.

She let her chin drop a little as she felt the hopelessness of the situation. And Warren chose that moment to poke his head round the corner of the doorframe and into the carriage. "Good," he said, seeing her sitting there, looking dejected and defeated. "You just sit tight," he said, and then disappeared back into the rear cab, to keep his vigil for Matt.

She returned to the thread of her thoughts. The endpoint of all that theorising was that she could either sit there waiting to die, or make use of what was probably only a handful of minutes to come up with a plan, a way out, before Warren decided to shut them both up for good. The problem was that her mind was blank. She needed to *think*.

But no ideas came... although... but that was really clutching at straws. A couple of times she'd seen people talking on cellphones on the Underground. She'd never understood how they got a signal, but sometimes people did. Or was that just on tube lines that ran near the surface, where the stations had those huge openings between the platforms where the rain would come in? She couldn't remember. At any rate, she could at least try it. Her cellphone was in her luggage.

Since Warren had just checked up on her, now was the best moment to make a move. She probably had at least a minute before he'd look in on her again. She slipped out of her shoes and padded away from the cab and towards her bag, looking back over her shoulder every few moments for signs that she was being watched. The fact that he'd poked his head around the door kind of implied he didn't have some sixth sense for spying on people. If he looked out and saw her away from her seat she'd say she was going for a Nurofen. I mean, who wouldn't need a Nurofen at this point in the proceedings? Maybe she'd write to them and suggest they used this situation in their commercials.

She edged around the broad pool of Sebastian's blood and reached her garment bag. The phone was in a velcroed pocket up near the handle. Gently, she started to ease the flap up, tearing the fastening apart. But the noise! Dear God, who invented this stuff? No matter how slowly she went, the velcro made a sound like a Geiger counter on full volume – a sound like a Geiger counter sizzling in hot fat. And it was taking too long. Working slowly didn't make the shredding sounds quieter, it just spaced them out. So she tried to arrange the ripping, crackling sound into regular rhythmic bursts so it would sound like the mechanical clicking of some part of the train.

It took more than a minute – probably more like two – before she had the pocket open. She slipped the phone out of its recess and then faced the next problem. She had turned it off before stowing it in her bag. As it powered up it would beep and chirp to let her know it was coming to life. Why did phones have to do that? Was it the same reason that computers in movies had to twitter every time text appeared on their screens? But maybe she could stuff the phone in with her suits and muffle the sound that way. Fortunately the suits were in a section that sealed with a zip – a good quality one that she was fairly certain could be opened silently. She bent down and took hold of the zipper's tab down at the bottom of the bag… and her hand bumped against something cold and solid. Kieran's gun.

Her last glimpse of Kieran had been him holding on to the back of the train with one hand and hugging his briefcase with the other. Before that, he must have either put the gun down or dropped it. Then, as the train's brakes had locked up, the gun must have tumbled forwards in the dark, sliding along the central aisle of the train until it finally encountered an obstacle: her bags.

Rachel was momentarily paralysed. She wanted to grab the gun, but where would she hide it – she was wearing a close-fitting skirt and a tailored blouse – but wouldn't you know it, no holster. And if she grabbed the gun now, would she have the guts to use it? Waving a thing like that at Warren wasn't going to work as a deterrent; he'd made it pretty clear he wasn't afraid of guns. She'd have to wait for a moment when he was distracted, and then she'd have walk up behind him and shoot him. And she wasn't sure she could do that: sneak up, stick a gun in someone's back and blow a hole in him – not even if it saved her life.

She made herself pick up the gun. Wrapping her fingers round the roughened metal grip felt symbolic, like she was agreeing to something before she was really ready. It was like those legal disclaimers that were plastered over every new product these days: by taking hold of this gun you agree to waive your consumer rights to a guilt-free existence; you hereby accept responsibility for the consequences of brandishing loaded firearms in volatile situations; you acknowledge that you may be required to forfeit the remainder of your life or to end the life of another, as specified in your purchase agreement.

She saw that the safety was off, the hammer pulled back. She was fairly sure the slide would be locked back if it was empty. So it probably had at least one round in it. But it must be nearly out of bullets because she could remember at least five shots being fired, maybe more. How many bullets did an automatic hold? She'd fired rifles a few times and watched about a million hours of cop shows. Six shots for a revolver, maybe more for an automatic – that's if the clip had started out full, which maybe it hadn't. At any rate, she wasn't going to be getting into a lengthy shoot-out. If she made her move, she'd probably only get one chance, only need one bullet.

A hissing sound made her jump and her hand tightened reflexively around the trigger, though not enough to fire the weapon, thank god. The sound was coming from all around her. And there was a weird voice, barely audible, horribly garbled coming from all sides. For an insane moment she thought it was... she put the superstitious thought out of her head. What she was hearing was the train's intercom, malfunctioning but still partly working. God, she must be freaked out if her first thought was that she was hearing the voices of the dead.

But there were more immediate priorities than her mental state. Warren would hear the noise and come straight out to investigate. She was standing there with a loaded pistol in her hands in plain view.

The indecipherable voice was trying to make an announcement – she could tell from the intonation – but the intercom was swallowing up the sense of it. Apart from the occasional loud crackle, the rest was just muffled murmurs.

Rachel's instinct was to bury the gun in her bag and retrieve it again later, but what if she never got the chance? She caught sight of her jacket, over by the pool of blood, discarded after Sebastian had died, no longer needed to cushion his head. She flipped the gun's safety catch on, stuffed it into the waistband at the back of her skirt and took four quick steps across to her crumpled jacket just as Warren looked out of the cab and frowned, registering the fact that she wasn't where he wanted her to be.

Making sure to face him, she dipped and came up with the jacket. Holding it up so he could see the reason she'd wandered. She brushed it with her hand, dislodging a few nuggets of broken glass and slipped it on, reaching around to make sure the back covered the grip of the gun. She gave a little shiver that she hoped didn't look too fake and pulled the jacket's sides around her.

Warren clicked his fingers and pointed to the seat where she'd been sitting earlier, like he was instructing a dog. He was watching her, alert for anything suspicious and this clearly wasn't the right moment to confront him. Obediently she returned to her place, angling her knees towards him as she sat down so as to conceal the bulge at the back of her jacket.

It looked like Warren was about to say something more to her, but a sound from behind him made him turn. Despite his injured foot, he twisted as quickly as a cat to investigate the source of the noise. Then, with a glance back to her, and a finger raised once to indicate that she should stay put, he withdrew into the cab.

Matt must have returned, though she couldn't see him. She could hear him though, and by concentrating she could make out what Warren was saying to him: "Pass it up here. No, you can wait down there. Stay put while I look at this."

Then Warren rejoined Rachel in the passenger compartment carrying Kieran's scuffed leather briefcase in his hands. It was one of the old kind that stood upright and hinged open at the top. It was fuzzy with age, the brown leather faded almost to orange, and now it was streaked with what looked like fluff mixed with axle grease. Warren popped the catch, pulled wide the jaws at its top, and then tipped it upside down, emptying out what was inside. For some reason it made Rachel think of gutting a fish the way the contents spilled out onto the floor of the train. The scene in Jaws, maybe.

Two irregularly-shaped bricks of money hit the floor: half-inch-thick bundles of green notes, piled into thicker blocks and stacked side-by-side, and then bound together with Saran wrap. There were also pens, a phone, a sheaf of papers, some keys and a CD-ROM. Warren flicked quickly through the papers – and Rachel could see the navy and gold of a U.S. passport – before he discarded them and pounced on the shiny silver disk. For a moment he looked triumphant. Then he turned it over and she saw anger tightening his jaw. She wasn't that far from him and surreptitiously tilted her head to read the scrawl across the disk's surface.

In red marker it said, 'J' and then separately, 'Disk 2'. If she'd had to guess, Rachel would have been inclined to think it was the numeral '2' that was bothering Warren, because there was only one disk. He was nodding his head impatiently and repeating 'J' to himself as though trying to remember where it came in the alphabet. Then he pivoted and stalked, stiff-legged, back into the cab. She could just make out the exchange that followed.

"What are you doing now? Get up," Warren barked.

"I thought I saw something. But it was just a bit of glass," Matt was saying.

"Where's the other disk," Warren demanded.

"What other disk?" Matt said. "And what do you mean 'other'?"

"Don't get clever. I can see you're lying," Warren said. "You know something."

Rachel craned her head. By rising up in her seat she could just see Matt's head over the ledge of the train floor. He was still down on the tracks. She looked at him sweat under Warren's gaze. He wasn't doing a very good job of appearing innocent and Warren didn't seem likely to let it pass. Rachel mentally pleaded with Matt to stop looking so guilty and to say something that would reassure Warren.

"Why would I hide something from you?" Matt said at last. "You can search me. And you can look in the tunnel. If there's something I haven't found yet, then maybe it's because he… maybe it's on the body."

"Fine. Search the body. Bring me everything. And I would be particularly delighted if you could find something that looks like this," Warren said, holding up the disk by its edge like a politician waving a manifesto. Then, as an afterthought he said, "And make sure you move the body off the tracks so they can turn the power back on when we're finished with this."

That one moment of confident defiance seemed to have used up Matt's entire supply. She saw him nod slowly and turn back towards the tunnel, his head low. He looked worn out, nervous and pretty much hopeless as well, and her heart went out to him. His job now was to find Kieran's ruined remains and to pick over the body like a grave robber. And when he was done with that awful task, he had to walk back again, probably wondering as he did so whether Warren would kill him when he arrived.

As he trudged off, looking dejected, Rachel found herself wishing he would just leave her behind and run. Whether he came back or not, she no longer really believed it would make much difference to her chances of surviving. He might as well save himself.

But if he was planning to run, wouldn't he have done it by now? The first time he'd got out of Warren's sight he should have made a break for it. But instead he had dragged himself back along that tunnel, carrying the briefcase, heading towards the man who killed his friend.

And there was only one way to explain that. He had come back because Warren had persuaded him that it was the price of her safety – and for some reason, that must have mattered to him. And now he was going to go through it again even though he was plainly scared stiff, even though she could see from his face he dreaded how this might end. If he returned a second time and then Warren cut him down, he would have died because he'd tried to help her. Warren was going to use Matt's desire to protect her to lead him to his death.

She couldn't quite identify the emotion that realisation stirred up inside her, but it burned painfully. It was sickening and strong and she suspected that it was some kind of fury because it made her want to stride into the cab right now and blow Warren's brains out, no matter how suicidal attempting that might be.

But if she tried it now and failed, she would be bringing both of their lives to an end. Better to wait, and choose her moment with a little care. Better to make sure there were no mistakes. She should wait until Warren had his mind on other things – and the best time for that would be when Matt returned again. That would be her chance.

She ran through it in her mind, trying to prepare herself. Warren would be looking down over the track, the light would be coming from behind him so she would need to be careful that her shadow didn't warn him of her approach. On the other hand, she couldn't sneak up slowly. She'd only have a second or two to close the distance between them. And she needed to get close because her best guess was that whatever it was that protected him from harm, it wouldn't work against a bullet fired from a gun pressed into his flesh.

If she'd had to do it right at that second, as she watched Matt drag himself back into the tunnel, she felt sure she could. And so it was agony knowing that she had to wait, that she had to risk letting the fire she was feeling go out. Because then the doubts would crowd back in, her nerve would begin to slip away and soon enough she'd feel cold with fear again.

She was so wrapped up in these thoughts that she twitched with alarm as Warren emerged unexpectedly from the cab. Though it was adrenaline, he would undoubtedly assume it was nervousness.

"I want to…" he said to her, clearly frustrated with whatever he needed to say to her. He tried again, speaking slowly as though telling off a child, "Do you know how I can talk to the driver? I can't make this thing work," he said, pointing back towards the cab.

"I…" she wasn't sure what to say, "I can look."

It was important that he not get behind her where he might see the gun. On the other hand, if they were manoeuvring around each other in a tight space, she might get her chance earlier than expected, which is why she'd offered to help. The difficult part would be to stop him noticing that she was concealing something. When he looked like he might be pausing to let her get by him, she pretended not to notice and rubbed her neck as though it was troubling her, like she'd paused to relieve the stiffness a little.

When she didn't move after a moment, he simply carried on walking and preceded her into the cab. She followed along behind and moved around to the side of him, trying to angle her back to the cab wall which left her tucked in behind the driver's seat. In the gloom, she had to stand uncomfortably close to Sebastian's corpse to do it, but it was the only way to keep the gun hidden.

When she thought about it, she realised that every one of the bullets that had been fired earlier had hit some part of the train. Even the two that had struck flesh had continued on until they encountered metal, glass or plastic. She could even see that one of the windows in the cab had been blown out. It was no wonder that the electronics were malfunctioning. There was a phone set half-way up the frame of the driver's side window and she guessed that would be the intercom. She lifted up the handset and looked at the array of buttons on it. But no matter which one she pressed, nothing happened.

"Great. Thanks for your help," Warren said, unpleasantly. He'd obviously been through this routine.

Then Rachel had an idea. "Listen, there are emergency intercoms all through the train," she pointed towards the compartment they'd just come from. "You can pull the alarm and it will connect you to the driver. We just have to find one that's well away from all the damage."

"OK then," he said, and waited for her to lead the way. Again, she pretended not to notice and held onto the handset as though she was taking one final look at it. He frowned and moved past her and out of the cab, but paused after a couple of steps to check that she was following. She fell in behind him wondering how much longer she could avoid turning her back on him before he noticed that something weird was going on. Then again, if she was frightened of him – which she was – maybe it would seem natural not to want him behind her.

As he turned his back on her and began walking through the train her hand slipped under her jacket and round to the back of her waistband as she wondered whether he was distracted enough to have dropped his guard.

No sooner had she thought it than he stopped suddenly and she nearly walked into the back of him. She snatched her hand away from the gun as he bent over and picked up his discarded boot, and then pulled it back onto his uncovered foot.

Rachel realised that for the last minute or so he hadn't been limping. Had he somehow healed already? She felt a rush of anxiety which brought with it a mental picture of her pumping bullet after bullet into him, unable to slow him down. But, she reminded herself, one stray bullet was all it had taken to put Sebastian permanently out of the picture. You just had to pick your moment carefully.

Warren left his boot laces untied as he walked away from the rear cab and forward through the compartment. He stepped over Rachel's bags and came to a halt next to a red metal handle set high up on one of the carriage's side panels. Rachel ducked into one of the seats opposite so Warren would be free to lead the way whichever direction he set off in.

Warren cleared his throat and pulled the handle down. There were two little red strips on the panel and one of them lit up now, illuminating the words written on it. They said 'Driver Aware'. A moment later, the other one lit up. It said 'Speak To Driver'. And a tinny voice said, "This is the driver. Who is that please?"

Warren gave Rachel a firm look and raised his eyebrows which she could tell meant she was to keep silent. Then he said, "This is Sergeant Chris Hawkins of the Metropolitan Police Counter Terrorism Unit. I have a badly injured colleague here and I need to know if you'll be able to move this train when I give the word."

The driver sounded flustered, "Sergeant, uh, Sergeant Hawkins. Listen, the power's off at the moment and the technical bods are looking into it. We can't go anywhere right now I'm afraid. Can you, er, can you tell me what's going on? You're at the rear of the train, yes?"

Warren said, "I can tell you that my colleague and I attempted to arrest a known terrorist. He turned out to be armed and he fired at my partner, who is now very seriously injured. Then our target jumped from the rear of the train, which I assume is what brought us to a halt. I used the, er, short-circuit device while I retrieved the body. I'm nearly finished now. Then I will remove the device, at which point I need this train ready to proceed to the next station *immediately*."

Rachel could almost hear the driver lick his lips nervously as he said, "A passenger has been killed? Listen, I can't move the train. We'll need to evacuate the remaining passengers and get a crew down onto the track. The investigators have to be informed. That's the rules I'm afraid. My hands are tied."

Warren raised his voice now and spoke with a cold and angry authority. "Now you listen to me. My partner is bleeding all over the floor of this train. He's been shot in the neck and he's dying. The only way to get him medical help in time to save his life is by moving this train. If you let him die you will have me to answer to." Warren paused to let that sink in. "You will be directly responsible for the death of a police officer and that's something which will follow you around for the rest of your days. Think carefully, because you are about to become the most hated man in London." He paused again, for effect. "Now, in a couple of minutes, I will give the word and then you will get the power restored, after which you will do everything humanly possible to get this train to the next station before my partner dies. Do you understand me?"

"I'll see if…" the driver began, tentatively.

Warren's voice was ice as he demanded, "I said, do you understand me?"

"Yes," was all the driver said. And then Warren slid the alarm handle back up cutting off the conversation.

"There," he said to Rachel, turning off the anger in his voice and sounding positively pleased with himself. "That should do it. Now let's hope your boyfriend finds that disk."

***

But Clipper knew he wasn't going to be finding any disk because he already knew where Kieran had hidden it. Nevertheless, he needed to go through the motions so that Warren would believe he'd run out of options.

Clipper's big idea, the one he had Gary to thank for, was nearly ready to go – all but the last part was taken care of. The problem was that he'd need a full-sized miracle for it to stand any chance of working. And, frankly, Clipper was beginning to have serious doubts that he'd even be alive by the time the opportunity to turn the tables on Warren presented itself. Not only wouldn't he have saved himself or Rachel, but in the meantime, by playing along, he'd have ended up actually helping Gary's killer. That easily made today the worst day of his life and he was still only halfway through listing his problems – because before he could screw up Rachel's rescue and get them both killed, he had to look for a burnt corpse in a railway tunnel and then go through its pockets.

At least he had a pair of latex gloves shoved into the back pocket of his trousers so he wouldn't have to touch the dead flesh with his bare hands. Gary used to buy the gloves from a hairdressing suppliers and they came in handy every now and again for going through swiped bags or luggage that they were planning to ditch. Clipper had always been disappointed that they were looser than medical gloves and never made that satisfying snap like on TV. He pulled on one of them now as his nose told him he must be approaching Kieran's remains.

The body was lying face down and was in one piece. He approached it slowly, trying to ready himself mentally for what he was about to do. The trick, he reckoned, was to narrow his attention down to just the width of a torch beam and not to think about anything else. He did his best to touch nothing, smell nothing and see as little as possible. At least, since he knew the disk wasn't on Kieran's body, he only needed to gather enough personal effects to persuade Warren he'd made a thorough search.

He got through it as fast as he could, and when he was done he had a wallet, a set of car keys, some coins, half a pack of indigestion tablets and a translucent red casino dice. He stuffed them into his own pockets as he found them.

There was only one moment when he thought he might puke, and he managed to get himself under control in time. But it persuaded him that he'd done enough corpse-robbing for one day. He had a plausible haul of personal effects – enough to stop Warren being suspicious – so he turned around and headed for the train. But he walked even more slowly than on the way there, as he tried to think through what came next. He needed to come up with some way out of this situation… and he just couldn't summon any answers. He felt like beating his fists against his skull in frustration.

He might just about have been able to cope with things ending up like this, if it weren't for the knowledge that Rachel was relying on him. He was used to screwing things up, and usually that was nobody's problem but his own. But now, for the first time, he had someone relying on him – and he was going to get her killed. He might even have to watch it happen.

Why couldn't she have picked someone else to rely on? There had to be all sorts of people who'd look at this situation and straightaway get some amazing idea that would sort everything out. But not him. He'd got one extremely long shot in mind that he'd never get a chance to even try. And about the only other thought that had even occurred to him was to sprint flat out to the next station and try to get back before Warren guessed what he was up to and took it out on Rachel. But he knew it was too far, he wasn't fast enough and he wouldn't be able to make anyone listen in time. Maybe someone else could do it, but not him.

So he traipsed slowly back, the light from the train growing brighter and brighter until it dazzled his tunnel-adjusted eyes, until he could make out Warren lurking in the shadows of the rear cab, looking out at him. He even caught a glimpse of Rachel, in the lit passenger compartment, gazing towards the tunnel, but without seeing him. He saw the anxiety on her face and it felt like she was accusing him, blaming him for letting her down. *Sorry Rachel*, he said to her, soundlessly. *You just picked the wrong person to depend on.*

As he came close to the base of the train's escape ramp, Warren stepped out of his corner and called out to him, "Did you find it?"

He didn't reply straight away. This being bad news, he didn't want to shout it. He wanted to be close enough to say it quietly. When he'd closed the gap he said, "There wasn't any disk." He was standing to one side of the ramp now, while Warren stood on its top step and looked down at him. He didn't look pleased.

"Did you check the track on the far side of the body? Did you make sure you didn't walk past it?" Warren demanded.

"I was very careful," Clipper lied. "There was no disk." Clipper unloaded what he had found, reaching up to place each item on the floor of the rear cab.

Warren leant down and snatched up the pile, glanced quickly through the wallet before swearing. And then swearing again. He tossed Kieran's effects into the light of the compartment behind him. Clipper waited patiently, knowing that they couldn't be very far from the end of things now. Warren would rant and curse and then he would think about his next step… and then his attention would come back to Clipper and what to do about him. And, unless Clipper was very lucky, that would be that – for him at least. Then, soon after, the same thing would happen to the girl in the next compartment who'd made him smile and who had no one else but him to help her.

"Can I come up?" he said at last, thinking it couldn't hurt to ask.

"Oh, I don't think so," Warren said, sounding far from pleasant.

That was pretty much what Clipper had expected. He stood there, waiting to see if there'd be any more instructions. He'd known he wouldn't make it back into the bright comfort of the passenger compartment again. He expected to die down there on the tracks, filthy and afraid.

"You know, I think I've finally figured out where I know you from," Warren said.

Clipper thought for a moment and then laughed. They were the words he'd been afraid of hearing since he'd first set eyes on Warren today. But now it was too late; Warren's little feat of memory could hardly make things any worse, could it?

"You were friends with Gary Wilson, weren't you?" Warren asked.

Hearing Gary's name on Warren's lips offended Clipper; Warren shouldn't be allowed to say that name. "And you killed him, didn't you?" Clipper said, angry, and figuring there was no point in concealing it.

Warren smiled and spread his hands. "He was too much of a thinker. I told him to stop, but he couldn't help himself. He was always putting two and two together. Sooner or later that causes problems." Warren looked down at Clipper and said, "What I really should have done was pick you instead."

Insults too? Great, thought Clipper. He didn't know how to reply. Perhaps there was nothing left to say. He stood waiting for whatever came next.

"Get that contraption disconnected," Warren said, nodding towards the short-circuit device, "and I think that will do it for you."

Clipper took a breath and turned around. He bent over and wrestled the metal clamp loose from the rail. Then he picked it up by its rope and carried it over to where Warren was pointing, before setting it down on the bottom step of ramp.

"Yup," Warren said. "I think you're probably finished now."

Here it comes, thought Clipper, and the feeling hit him a moment later. A tightness settled on him, pressing into his chest, his neck, his face – and with a jolt of panic he realised he couldn't move air in or out of his lungs. Warren might as well have taped a bag over his face: he couldn't breathe. And now his body was starting to react. He could feel the veins in his neck standing out and the thud of his heart growing heavier and more violent until each beat was like being thumped in the chest.

He was looking up at Warren who had a slight frown on his face – but it wasn't concern – he was simply concentrating. Clipper doubted that he was even the most pressing thing in Warren's mind at that moment. Clipper was a chore that needed finishing, that was all. Warren's thoughts would be on other things, like getting away, or what he was going to tell his bosses about all this.

Very quickly things were starting to get hazy for Clipper and his thoughts were scattering as fast as he could chase them. As he did his best to keep Warren's face in focus, he wondered whether his killer was even now thinking about how he was going to dispose of Rachel. Half delirious with oxygen starvation he found that thought still had the power to make him sad.

Clipper was starting to lose the edges of his vision now and his thoughts were scarcely more than a jumble, but it almost looked as though Rachel was there, pressing up against Warren in a way that Clipper's confused brain found unsettling. It was like she was hugging herself to him and Clipper hated that thought. He'd been hoping that she liked him instead. But now he was dying and she was getting cosy with his killer. He'd expected better from her.

But a moment later there was a sound like an explosion, muffled somewhat by the invisible barrier that was wrapped around Clipper's head, and then Warren was toppling forwards. Simultaneously, cold air burst into Clipper's lungs and it was like the lights came back on in his brain; everything around him became sharp and hard-edged, and he could think again.

Rachel was crouching over Warren, who had fallen to his knees. She had the gun pressed to the back of his head and angled up slightly so that the grip of the weapon was pressed into the fabric of Warren's backpack.

Down on the tracks, Clipper was on all fours, gasping for air, but he was looking up, trying to take in the scene. Warren was down too, and doubled over, but he wasn't dead. He groaned loudly and tried to rise. Rachel pushed the gun's barrel hard into the base of his skull and said, "I can fire this thing before you can stop me. So don't move until I tell you to."

Then she looked over at him and said, "Matt? Are you OK?"

He was still hyperventilating, but he could talk. "I'm OK," he said. "What do you want me to do?"

She said, "The driver's ready to move the train. So let's get the power turned on and get going. Can you take care of the short-circuit thing and get this door closed?"

"Yeah, no problem," Clipper said. "And, er… thanks very much." It sounded a bit stupid, saying 'thank you' for saving his life, but if that didn't warrant a 'thank you', then what did? Plus, Clipper wondered if he might not be just a tiny bit high from the combination of adrenaline and lack of oxygen.

Rachel was talking to her captive. "Stand up slowly. Turn *very* slowly. And then walk back to that intercom. Tiny steps all the way."

Warren managed to get to his feet with a bit of trouble. Clipper couldn't see exactly where he'd been hit, but he had his hands clamped over his chest high up on his right side. There was a strange wheezy noise as he breathed that Clipper could hear from down on the track. He looked pretty messed up, and yet he was able to stand.

Clipper reckoned that even with another hole in him, Warren would still be about as dangerous as a tiger on crystal meth, but watching Rachel, how sure she sounded, he was starting to believe that she and him had a chance of making it to the next station alive. As Warren turned and Rachel kept herself tucked in behind him, he was starting to feel a surge of hope. His stupid plan to take Warren out wouldn't be needed now, and thank god for that.

And then he saw something that made his breath stick in his throat all over again. Rachel pushed the gun into Warren's neck, urging him to start shuffling forwards and Clipper caught sight of it as it passed into the light that streamed through the open doorway. The slide was back, covering the hammer. The gun was empty.

If Warren suspected, if he decided to try his luck, they were finished.

As Clipper grabbed hold of one of the steel cables and pulled himself up onto the ramp, he thought of all the things that could go wrong in the few minutes it would take them to get to the next station and he wondered what he could do to help Rachel. Hopefully she'd just get Warren to lay down on his front as soon as they were clear of the rear cab, but he didn't want to risk suggesting it in case it gave Warren ideas.

At any rate, Clipper needed to get the track clear and the door closed as quickly as possible. So he grabbed the SCD off the bottom step of the ramp and poked it in through the busted window of the cab. Then he withdrew into the cab and tried to figure out how to get the steps folded up and the door hoisted back into position. A few seconds of trial and error and he had it slammed shut.

Picking up the SCD and holding it like a rather ungainly baseball bat he moved towards the doorway, praying that Rachel still had Warren under control and he didn't need to go hand to hand with him. That would be a short fight.

Rachel had got Warren most of the way down the carriage and now he stood, dripping blood and wheezing painfully, in front of the emergency alarm. Rachel was right behind him, the empty gun pressed into his back, the barrel tucked into the hollow at the top of his spine.

"Tell him," she said. And when Warren didn't respond, but just stood, slightly stooped, arms clamped across his injured chest, she repeated it, this time screaming it at the top of her voice, "Tell him to move this train or I'll kill you and do it myself."

Warren reached up, slowly and painfully, the motion putting a strain on his wounded flesh. Then he pulled the handle down and waited for something to happen.

A moment later there was a crackle. "Driver here," the voice over the intercom said.

"Everything's ready. Let's get moving," Warren said, his voice sounding hoarse and uneven. Then he folded the alarm handle back in place. A moment later he began to choke, doubling over, just as the normal compartment lights came on. They looked dazzlingly bright after the relative gloom. The noise of compressors filled the carriage, making the floor vibrate. It felt like the train was coming back to life.

"Stop moving," Rachel commanded, as Warren shuddered with each cough. "Just lay down on the floor."

Good, thought Clipper. *Get him to lie down and stay there.*

Clipper saw Warren get his choking under control and begin to straighten his back. He set one knee on the ground, ready to lie down. And then Clipper saw Warren's head turn a little and pause. Clipper followed his gaze and realised what had happened: he was looking at Rachel's reflection in the window, lit up by the full glare of the compartment's lights.

And Clipper knew what would happen next. There wasn't even time to shout a warning. Warren had seen the condition of the gun. He twisted around and caught Rachel across the jaw with his elbow, slamming her to the ground. Then he stood up carefully, swaying on his feet. He straightened up very cautiously as though wondering whether his wound was as bad as he'd been making out. Then he took his hand away from the wound and inspected the damage. Rachel was still at his feet, momentarily dazed by the blow and not yet able to find her feet. The empty gun lay on the floor nearby, discarded now.

Warren touched the oozing hole in his chest carefully and gasped. "You people," he said, sounding disgusted. Then he looked Rachel in the eyes and said, "This next part, you're not going to enjoy."

Clipper knew what to do. He couldn't wait any longer. The timing would just have to take care of itself. Before Warren could do anything, Clipper shouted out his name. Warren looked round to see what he wanted.

"I know where the other disk is," Clipper called out. He'd seen Kieran's hand fidgeting, seen the little knife cutting into the upholstery while Warren went to attend to his fallen comrade. And Clipper had seen the glint of the disk as Kieran slid it inside the hole he'd made. Now Clipper moved to that spot, halfway along the row of seats nearest the rear cab.

Warren was still directing his attention at Clipper; he hadn't turned back to Rachel yet. Clipper rested the unwieldy metal SCD on the floor, propping it up against the seat, and nearly tripping over the trailing rope in the process. Then he plunged his hand into the slit in the seat cover.

He pulled out the disk and held it up. "See?" he said. He looked at it himself and read aloud, "J. Disk one. E-mails, plans and accounts. That has to be what you were after. Whatever he stole, whoever he was working for, I bet it's all on here."

"Give me that," Warren said, that curious bloody gurgle evident in his voice. Then he started walking towards Clipper. "*Now!*" he yelled.

Clipper scuttled backwards to the door of the rear cab, wedged the disk in the doorframe and applied some pressure. "Stop right there or I'll break it," he commanded.

Warren stopped. For a moment. Then he began to edge slowly forwards. "Let's do a deal," he said. It was just like before, when Kieran had stood on more or less this spot and Warren had offered him a deal too. Clipper wondered if this reckless feeling inside him was what Kieran had felt too.

Warren was using that same old reasonable voice again: "Matt? You know I can track you down if I have to. Now that I know you were Gary's friend I can find out everything else about you. But that's good. Because it means right now I can let you go. If you cause trouble for me, you know I'll be able to hunt you down. But if you don't... then we're fine. You understand? So if you give me the disk now, I won't have to take it off you. You live, and I get the information I came for."

The curious wobble Clipper could hear in Warren's voice didn't seem to be emotional – the man was as sure of himself as ever; it was something to do with his injury. Clipper realised that Warren was trying to make a deal even as blood trickled into his lungs.

Then, with a lurch the train moved, and everyone grabbed for something to hold on to. A second later, the brakes slapped into place, the train shuddered to a halt and the compressors kicked in again.

"We'll be out of here in a minute," Warren said. "I bet you could probably be home in an hour. But if you break that disk, I'll kill you, and that will be that."

"And what about her?" Clipper asked, nodding towards Rachel.

"Of course. You can both go," Warren said. Clipper waited for him to argue, to explain his conditions and lay out the terms of the deal, but he just repeated, "You can both go if you let me have that disk."

Maybe if Warren had asked for Rachel's surname, demanded to see some proof of her identity, Clipper might have been tempted to believe him. But he didn't. And that meant Warren had no intention of letting her leave the train alive. Which pretty much settled it in Clipper's mind. Any doubts he'd had about what he was planning to do were gone.

Again the compressor cut out and again the train lurched, but this time the motion continued and the train began to move forwards at last.

As they pulled away, Warren was beginning to sound a little pressured.

"OK, we've run out of time, so let me turn this around and see if that helps," he said. "I'm going to come over there and kill you now. See if you can talk me out of it." Then he started towards Clipper, his eyes hard and fixed on his target. His hands were clamped so tightly over the hole in his chest that his fingers were white and the steps he took were slightly unsteady, but there was no mistaking his murderous determination.

"Right. OK," Clipper called out in a tone of surrender. He held up the disk. "OK." Then he leant over and set it on the floor, in the doorway to the rear cab, before clambering up onto the nearest seat, as though he was trying to get out of Clipper's way.

The train was accelerating now, the driver obviously having taken Warren's words to heart, and Warren was moving faster too. Clipper tried to get past him by hopping across the seats, stepping rapidly over the arm rests as Warren dragged himself down the aisle towards the disk. But as they passed, Warren threw out his hand, cracking Clipper across the side of the head with a solid punch and sending him sprawling headlong into the aisle.

Warren reached the doorway to the rear cab as, behind him, Clipper tried to get up. He'd smacked his head pretty hard and the fall had been awkward. His arm had been trapped under him as he fell. He thought it might be broken, which would explain why he couldn't seem to get it to work.

Rachel rushed forwards to help him and Clipper screamed at her to get back. He sounded so desperate for her to listen to him that she stopped dead.

Warren had the disk now and was tucking it into a pocket in the leg of his trousers. With the hole in his chest slowing him down, it took him a few seconds. By the time he was finished, Clipper had managed to crawl away as far as the double-doors – all of five metres forward from where Warren was standing. He was almost at the exact spot where Sebastian had died.

The train was really moving now, a fact Warren was obviously very aware of as he said, "I think we'd better make this quick." Then he threw out his hand with a stabbing movement, thrusting it towards Clipper. It was just like the punch that Warren had thrown in the club, the one that never landed. But this time it was Clipper who felt the awful impact of it.

It felt like a bomb had gone off inside him. His chest was lit up with pain as though he'd stepped out in front of a bus. Or maybe, as some part of Clipper's reeling brain insisted on suggesting, as though he'd been hit with the force of a train.

And at that moment it happened. There was a sound from the rear cab as the rope snapped taut. Clipper had wrapped a loop of it around the driver's seat, to hold it until the last second. With a crack like a whip, it snatched itself free. Then the metre-long metal bar of the SCD leapt backwards and flew through the door of the cab, encountering Warren as it did so. As the clamp struck him, the train was doing just under forty miles an hour and the rope, tethered as it was to a spot just under where the cab had previously stood, transmitted all of that velocity to the steel shaft of the SCD.

Clipper wasn't able to stay conscious long enough to see it hit. But he heard the incredible noise it made and knew it had happened. He knew Rachel was safe. He just wished he'd been able to see Gary one last time and explain that he'd solved the riddle of the perfect iPod lift. The trick was that you swapped it around. Always choose a train over a platform. You put *yourself* on the receding train with the prize and you left the cord behind, along with your unlucky victim. Gary probably wouldn't have approved of modifying it so he could kill someone, but he'd have been pleased that Clipper had solved the riddle, and even more pleased that he'd used it to save a life. It's just a shame it hadn't been Clipper's own.

His last thought was that maybe he was about to get a chance to see Gary in person and thank him for giving Clipper a way to keep Rachel alive.

***

Rachel sat in the kitchen looking out across the fields of home – perfectly familiar, but made new with a fresh fall of snow. She had coffee in her cupped hands. Her mother had made it at around six, before she went out to check on the horses. Rachel had slept in until after seven. The house had been warm and deserted, except for a sleeping dog toasting itself on the base of the cooking range. He looked up at her, whined politely, and then laid his head back down.

She tucked her feet in their thick socks beneath her and sat at the counter, half focusing on a distant pair of crows, arguing over something they'd found in the snow, while the other half of her mind was miles away.

She'd waited a fortnight before leaving the UK. There'd been questions to answer, even more than she'd expected. And it had been made a little trickier by her need to bend the truth in a couple of areas and to leave out anything that no one would believe anyway. Fortunately, it was fairly clear to the police that she was just a passenger who got caught up in something terrible. With the way things were, you didn't accuse US citizens of anything unless the State Department said you could. And you didn't inconvenience the employees of US banks, even once they'd resigned, unless you had no choice.

So Rachel turned Warren's death into an accident. Or rather, she said that she couldn't explain it and the police concluded for themselves that the trailing rope had snagged on something, all by itself. Any knots Matt had tied were gone. The fake cops, whoever they had been, must just have been careless. And the back of the train was sufficiently wrecked to make the exact sequence of events a matter fit only for theories and best guesses.

In Rachel's version, she and Matt had watched as the fake cops and an unidentified gunman fought. Both of the fake policemen had been shot. Had she seen a knife? She wasn't sure; she'd been hiding. And then the gunman had thrown himself from the train. So far so good. Then she and Matt had both been injured as the train slammed to a halt, which explained her bruises. With the train stationary, the least-injured fake cop had needed a hand retrieving the gunman's body and Matt had agreed to help, but he was unsteady on his feet and had slipped, falling from the back of the train onto the rails. The fake cop got Matt back on board, and decided to forget about the body on the tracks. He wanted to save his companion, who was in a bad way, by getting the train moving again. Shortly afterwards, the rope had snagged, a terrible accident had occurred, and that was that.

One or two problems arose when the forensics report suggested that her sequence of events didn't match the evidence, but no one knew what to make of that – and when Rachel could offer no explanation, there wasn't much anyone could do about it. Two crooks, posing as policemen, had cornered a third man and driven him to kill himself. No one could implicate her in any of it and Matt was in no position to contribute anything to the enquiry. The police had even retrieved a single fat brick of US dollars, which seemed sufficient motive for the violent squabble. The gun, when it was eventually located, shed no light on anything. It had been wiped clean of fingerprints.

So Rachel had returned home, later than expected, but more glad than ever to be leaving London behind. There'd been just one last piece of business for her to take care of before she departed. She'd gone to visit Matt in hospital and told him everything she'd done, what she'd said and what her plans were. And then she'd flown home to find that her mother – who'd been following the British news – was even more grateful to have her daughter home safe than Rachel had thought possible.

In fact these last three weeks had been a wonderful dream she didn't want to wake up from. Her mother and her hadn't quarrelled. There had been a few tears at first, but very little had been said, and now they had both settled into a comfortable peace. Rachel didn't know if it would last, but there was every reason to think it would be put to the test later that very day. Rachel was expecting a visitor.

***

Matt phased in and out of consciousness for a long while. The warm cotton-wool of painkillers kept him from understanding the few glimpses of reality he gulped down, before he sunk back into his concussed and medicated stupor.

It was a week before he had any control over the comings and goings of his mind, before he had any say in when his eyelids dropped closed. And it was ten days before they let him have a visitor. The first person they let in to see him was his girlfriend. Matt knew she'd only called herself that so that they would allow her in, but he liked the idea of it all the same.

Rachel looked gorgeous, although the puffy, yellowing bruise across her cheek hurt him worse than the ache in his ribs when he saw it. He wanted to get up, make a fuss of her, even just manage to sit upright, but he couldn't. After a moment he stopped trying.

Once the nurse had left, she looked him over, concern in her eyes. "Does it hurt?" she asked.

"Only when I'm awake," he said. He smiled at her. "Thanks for coming to see me. I was hoping you would."

She looked horrified. "Are you kidding? Of course I'd come and see you. You saved my life. And look at what it cost you." She took in the cast on his arm, the drips, and the contraption holding his splintered ribs together. "You don't do things the easy way, do you?"

Matt was worried that he was going to laugh for a second, which didn't bear thinking about. He'd probably fall to bits if he tried it. "Well, some of it is a bit vague," he said. "But I remember nearly dying and then I remember you being there and I could breathe again."

They said nothing for a moment, their eyes wandering, occasionally connecting, and then one of them would glance away.

"I've got something to tell you," Rachel said at last.

Matt said nothing. She went on, "I hid half of that money. It took them ages to come and get us. So I just grabbed it. The police didn't search my bag. A friend of mine is looking after it, though he doesn't know what's inside the case I left him. Here's the key." She pulled a little slip of metal out of the pocket of her jeans and laid it on top of his bedside cabinet.

"Why..." Matt said, looking confused. "Why are you giving it to me?"

"Well, you said…" Rachel sounded awkward. "You said you were unhappy. You said you were," she dropped her voice, "a thief and you didn't want to be. There's about a hundred thousand dollars there. It won't make you rich, but it might let you start over."

Matt didn't know what to say. Rachel added quietly, "It's enough for a plane ticket too. When you're feeling better."

"You want me to… You're inviting me to visit?" he said.

"You can visit," she said. In little more than a whisper she added, "Maybe, if you like it, you could stay?"

Matt's face was burning now. He wanted this more than anything, but he couldn't let himself believe it. This wasn't how real life worked. He needed to tell her the truth before she found out anyway.

"I want to," he said. "I think it's the best offer I've heard in my whole life. But, what about the fact… I mean we don't really know each other. You don't really know me, is the point. Someone like you…" he was struggling now, finding the words getting stuck in his throat. "I would just make a fool of myself and you'd be disappointed."

Rachel leaned over and kissed him carefully, once, on the lips.

"You've got a point," she said, "I don't know very much about you. And I don't think we've got much in common. It takes years before you really know someone. All I know about you is that you make me laugh – sometimes. And that I can absolutely trust you with my life." She smiled at him and gently took hold of his hand. "And I've noticed that you can't seem to take your eyes off me. I decided that was enough to be going on with."

"Well, if you put it like that," Matt said haltingly, but with a smile on his face. "We should probably at least *try*. Shouldn't we?"

Rachel was beaming at him. "Yeah, because if I set my standards any higher I don't think there'd be anyone in the world who qualifies."

They sat for a little while, not saying much, but both OK with that. And then Rachel explained to Matt the story she'd told the police. When she was done, he said, "You think they believed it?"

"I think they're used to things not making sense. They just don't have any better theories," she replied.

Rachel looked thoughtful for a moment and then pulled something flat and shiny from the back pocket of her jeans.

"Listen, Matt," she said. "The things we saw – the things that Warren could do – they were pretty weird, right?"

He nodded. And she went on, "As well as taking half the cash, I also had a quick look in that guy Kieran's wallet. I found this." She placed the metal rectangle, about the size of a business card, next to the key.

"I don't know why he carried it with him, but I've got a theory. I think it was to remind him that there were more important things in life then understanding people like Warren. I know it's not easy to walk away from a mystery, but I think this one time that you should. Tell me that you won't try to find out more about who Warren was. Just get better and then fly out to see me, OK?"

Then she leaned over and kissed him again, and said goodbye.

It was another three weeks before he could get out of bed and even then his doctors advised him against it, but his bones were knitting and he wasn't in any danger. He'd had thirty-one days to mend and it was enough that he could get around if he had to. The day after he got out of the hospital he picked up the money Rachel had left for him – and the day after that he booked a plane ticket to Seattle.

He slept through most of the flight and then they made him ride in a wheelchair from the gate. Rachel was waiting for him when a helpful Skycap wheeled him into the arrivals area.

He thought about the metal card she'd left for him as she drove them past white fields under a sky so pale and clean he could hardly believe he was on the same planet as London. He looked over at Rachel now. The bruise was gone from her cheek and she looked well and happy and beautiful. When she turned to smile at him, he thought his heart would burst with the feeling of it. He didn't think he could ever say it aloud, he wasn't brave enough, but all he wanted in the world was a chance to make her happy. If he never did anything else right in his life that was OK, if he could do that single thing.

After she'd left his hospital room he'd reached over and picked up the metal card. It had been a struggle to get his arm all the way over there and as he moved it, he found she'd left a picture too. It was an old photo of her, holding a horse's bridle and smiling. She had written 'see you soon' on it.

He read the words on the metal card: 'why study power when you can study happiness instead?' She needn't have worried. He didn't need to be told twice. He pushed the card so that it slipped off the edge of the table and into the bin. Then he propped the picture against a water glass, so that he could see it when he turned his head, and he settled back to think about the future.

The End

ADEPT

CHAPTER 1

L ondon after midnight – there are no stars; a lid of cloud like a damp old army blanket lies over the city. Sodium-vapour light from a hundred thousand street lamps leaks back from the sky, turning the corners of the world orange and making the night-time cloud glow faintly, like radioactive fog. The permanent false dawn nags birds from their sleep, punctuating the soundtrack of urban grind and rumble with sudden meadowland trills. On the edges of the old city a few foxes lope, a few late drinkers follow their homing instinct. In the warrens of the sooty Victorian warehouse district, things are still. One or two security guards drowse over magazines, killing time at their foyer reception desks.

Elsewhere the city never sleeps, but here the activity is commercial and, in a sense, solar-powered. At night the machines rest. All that moves through the folded streets are gusts of air with their freight of mist and pollution.

Then there's a squeak of bouncing springs as a scuffed white Transit van pulls up outside a silent stretch of offices. The driver peers up and down the street, scanning every nook and doorway. There's a full minute's pause before the engine is turned off and the doors open. Cautiously, three figures emerge, like the last three members of some endangered species.

The driver is bulky and energetic; he's in his late forties but of the type to whom age is largely a cosmetic consideration.

The second figure is younger – late twenties – with a lanky, wiry build. Where his companion looks energised, he merely looks frightened. He wears a baseball cap, which he tugs at, pulling it down on his head.

In contrast to the other two, who are wearing overalls, the third man looks dressed for a mild day on the ski slopes – black, high-cut jacket zipped tight, black trousers in some highly-evolved descendant of nylon. His head is covered in a dark wool cap. His compact build and easy movements do nothing to dissipate the illusion that he is there to perfect his racing turns. He needs only sunglasses to complete the image. His neat, shaped beard is dark like the close-cropped hair visible at his side-burns and it gives a slightly Eastern air to features that might have originated anywhere from Oslo to Kabul. His composed, unreadable face suggests a forty-five-year-old in perfect health.

Alongside the van, a narrow path leads a little way down one side of the offices, giving access to various hatches and maintenance doors set into the side wall. The driver lugs a heavy tool-bag out of the van, and sets up in front of one of the hatches. His nervous companion fiddles with his baseball cap and mutters, "Our cleaners are all black," to the larger man.

Without looking up from his work inside the open hatch the driver says, "Maybe you're the supervisor." The sing-song tone he uses makes it sound like he's talking to a child.

The younger man continues to tug at his baseball cap, his anxiety plain. Just above his pale forehead the badge on the cap reads 'T.J. Office Services'.

Meanwhile, the man in the ski clothes is at the main entrance of the building. Several steps up from the street, the unlit reception area is dimly visible behind the glass and metal double doors. The skier is working on the lock. He looks up, glances once to his left along the street, once to his right and then back towards the lock. Something in the door shatters with a sharp crack.

At the side of the building, the driver shoos his hovering companion back a couple of steps and, taking an involuntary deep breath, pulls on a handle inside the hatch. Nothing dramatic happens but an unnoticed background hiss is now silenced. Inside the building, the LEDs on the reception's switchboard wink out. The emergency exit lamp shines with lowered intensity. A red light begins to glow from a glass-fronted panel just inside the main doors.

"Count to one hundred and push this lever up," the driver says. "Give me your hand." He takes Baseball Cap's arm and guides his hand to the lever. "It won't bite you," he says, but the younger man doesn't look convinced.

"But it doesn't make sense," Baseball Cap says, a whine in his voice. He receives a sharp look but continues nonetheless, "Why don't we leave it off until we're done here?"

The older man is angry but keeps his voice down. "You leave that power off for five minutes and see what happens. We've turned off the lights and the fucking coffee machine; we've done nothing to the alarm system. It's got batteries to last a week."

"Then why bother…" The younger man doesn't get any further with his question. A hand clenches his overalls just below the throat and he stops talking. The larger man leans in, bringing them face to face.

"If you balls this up it'll be the last stupid thing you ever do. You understand me?" the larger man asks. He glances at his watch. "Count to seventy-five." Then he picks up his tool-bag and strides off towards the front doors.

Reaching the skier, the driver cocks his head towards the double doors, "They open?"

The skier nods. The driver pushes through the doors into the foyer and sets his tool-bag down in front of the glass-fronted alarm panel. The red 'Battery Power' light glows brightly. He sticks a steel rule in the gap between the edge of the glass door and the frame. Pushing upwards he presses in the catch and pops the door open. Dropping the rule into his bag he retrieves a pair of wire-cutters and hooks one handle into the pocket of his overalls. It hangs there like a cowboy's six-gun. Then he fishes out a cordless screwdriver and begins to undo the spring-loaded screws at the four corners of the panel. All the while, the flat of his left hand holds the panel in place.

Then he waits.

A minute goes by.

Beneath their feet, from somewhere in the basement comes a muffled thump, like the sound an anchor might make hitting the sea bottom. "There we go," mutters the driver. The red light winks out.

A green light marked 'Mains power' comes on. Beside it is another green light that begins to flash. It's marked 'Power On Self Test'.

"This is the clever bit," the driver whispers to the skier. Removing his hand from the panel he gets his fingernails under one edge and pulls the panel free. The back of the panel is festooned with criss-crossing loops of coloured wire. "Power cut? Might be trouble. Power back on? All's right with the world. Ideal moment for the system to run a quick diagnostic. Never occurred to the designer that someone would *restore* the power as part of a break-in." His fingers are teasing a bundle of wires apart. He selects two. Flipping the panel over he checks where they lead: a key-operated switch marked 'Offline'. He grabs the dangling cutters and snips the two wires, efficiently stripping the ends with his teeth and twisting the two sets of bared copper strands together. "And that's that," he says. He drops the cutters back into the bag and lets the panel rest against the wall, dangling from its connections. "Time for that little tosser to earn his keep," he says. He strides out the door leaving the skier on his own.

A minute later he's back, Baseball Cap preceding him. The skier speaks for the first time, "Treasury?" he asks in BBC English. Baseball Cap nods and sets off up the stairs. The other two follow him, the driver carrying his tool-bag.

On the first floor they move through a dark open-plan office, two rows of eight desks and computers, each decorated with stickers, pot plants and framed photographs. Stray light coming in through the windows partly illuminates their surroundings – sixteen little worlds – a pink crocheted cardigan stretched over a chair-back, a Weight Watchers diary, a lingering tendril of Opium.

At the end of this open space, they reach a locked door. The driver pulls a crow bar out of his bag and, with two fierce tugs, splinters the doorjamb around the lock sufficiently for the door to open. The noise sounds brutally loud in the silent office.

The private office within has a real wood desk by a large window. The chair is black leather, high-backed.

Baseball Cap opens a low cupboard underneath the window to reveal the front of a safe. The driver once again sets down his tool-bag and begins to size up the safe. Absent-mindedly he twists the dangling plastic pole of the Venetian blinds, gradually angling the slats to block out the view. The dark sky, the multi-storey car park opposite and the train tracks disappear.

Seeing the driver intent upon the safe, the skier turns to Baseball Cap and says, "The Chairman's office." They head back past the rows of desks, Baseball Cap leading the way.

They climb to the second floor. The décor is much more expensive, the carpet fitted, not tiled. "I only saw it the once," Baseball Cap is saying, "when I took him in the itinerary." He pronounces it *itinuary*. "I knew something was in there, but I thought it must be a drinks cabinet."

They arrive at the end of a corridor. There are no windows here; there's just enough light to sketch in the suggestion of a desk. The skier clicks on the desk's lamp, illuminating the triangle of deep red carpet on which the desk sits, angled across the corridor. Beyond are two doors of thick, polished beechwood. "It's that one," Baseball Cap says, taking his hand out of his trouser pocket long enough to gesture at the right-hand door.

The skier puts one of his gloved hands on the door handle and tests it. Locked. "I said they always lock it. I told you that," says Baseball Cap.

The skier runs his hand over the door lock, giving no sign that he's heard. "Look in the top drawer of the desk," he says in his newsreader's voice.

Baseball Cap moves round behind the desk, turning his back to the skier and tugs the drawer handle a couple of times. The drawer thunks against its lock. He pulls on the larger bottom drawer. "It's locked. They're both..." The rip of splitting wood interrupts him. His head snaps round, startled, frightened by the unexpected sound.

The right-hand door is now slightly ajar, the area around the lock and part of the frame are splintered. The skier has taken a step forwards. While Baseball Cap is still frozen, crouching behind the desk, the skier moves into the opened office. "Show me," he says without looking round.

The office within has no windows either. There's a set of three switches just inside the door and the skier turns on the bottom one. Halogen lights set in the tops of smoked-glass shelving illuminate a fitted wooden wall unit. It looks like something from the Presidential Suite in a modern American hotel. The six-metre glass and veneer unit contains everything: a small TV, glasses, a tiny black sink – all of it backed with mirrored glass.

A broad beechwood desk occupies another corner of the room. The remaining space contains a round table and two armchairs. There are several cupboards and free-standing sets of drawers.

Baseball Cap goes over to the far wall of the office and opens a full-height cupboard. A light comes on inside. Although the door suggests a place to hang coats, behind it is an alcove going back a couple of metres. It's less than a metre wide. There's a little vanity unit with a mirror at the end. On one side is a tiny bench, just wide enough to perch on. Shelves hold toiletries. Hanging from pegs opposite the bench are several suits and shirts on hangers. There's a faint smell of sandalwood.

"So that time, when I come in, the door's open and he's in here. It was just like this except you couldn't see the sink. This bit of wall was open," says Baseball Cap moving into the alcove. He pushes and prods among the hanging suits until he finds a catch. A section of the panelled wall opens in the middle, hinged like the doors of a cuckoo clock. From anywhere but between the doors it's difficult to see what's behind them. Because the hinged sections of wall include the two halves of the row of coat pegs, as the doors are opened the suits swing out with them.

"Now I didn't know what was in here. I thought maybe he kept the good stuff in here. But I got talking to one of the girls and she was in here once when the safe was open and she saw the door to it." And sure enough, behind the wooden panels is the grey steel door of a safe, complete with recessed dial and handle.

Baseball Cap has stepped back to allow the skier access to the alcove. He dips under the open panel, parting the suits, and regards the safe door. "Very good work, Peter. Find a window and make sure that all's well, then see if Alan needs you for anything. I'll join you when I'm done here," the skier says. Peter looks reluctant to leave. "Off you go," the skier says politely.

Peter heads back to the stairwell and finds a window that looks down onto the street. The road turns away sharply in both directions and the van is the only vehicle visible on their little stretch. It's all just as they left it: damp road, streetlights, night.

After twenty seconds, Peter's breath has fogged up too much of the window for him to see out properly so he makes his way downstairs. As he emerges from the stairwell on the first floor he can hear the distant sound of a drill. It gets louder as he moves through the open-plan area towards the private office.

Reaching the doorway, he can see the driver, Alan, over by the covered window. He's holding an industrial drill at waist height to the face of the safe. There's sweat visible through Alan's thinning hair. The drill has chewed its way through a couple of centimetres of door already. The noise, though considerable, is hardly deafening.

Peter raises his voice over the squeal of metal and calls, "All clear…" Alan starts violently, sending the drill bit skittering across the safe door. A wavy snake of bright metal is etched across the enamel finish. "…outside," Peter finishes weakly. The pitch of the drill drops as Alan's finger comes off the trigger.

"Christ Almighty. Did no one ever tell you, don't sneak up on people. Especially when they're busting into other people's safes," Alan says angrily, his voice rising towards the end of his rebuke. He puts the bit back in place and powers up the drill again, his gaze once again on the safe.

"Supposed to use goggles," mutters Peter under his breath. He watches for a minute, his face screwed up, unreadable. Then he wanders away towards the windows overlooking the street. He picks up a stapler from a desk by the window and looks around for something to staple. A movement catches his eye in the street outside. Four men in identical black clothing are moving quickly towards the front of the building. Two are carrying short rifles, the stocks tucked into their shoulders. Just at the bend in the road a high-end BMW, with the markings of a police car, is now visible.

As they near the front of the building, one of the armed policemen looks up at the window that Peter's watching from. Peter ducks down quickly.

Hunched over, under the window, he bites his lip. Panic is evident on his face. Then, still crouching to keep low, he sprints towards Alan, weaving between the desks. He collides with the last one, the corner catching him hard on the hip. The impact shunts the whole desk forward an inch, its feet eliciting a little yelp from the tortured nylon carpet. The collision scatters office supplies and knick-knacks from their nocturnal resting places.

"Shit," he gasps, clutching his hip. He rushes on, one leg held stiff, and bursts into the office, where Alan stands flexing his back, the hole finished, the drill silent.

"Police," yells Peter in the silence, one palm still rubbing his hip, "in the street outside, they're here."

At that moment, the skier comes racing up the stairs. He's moving very rapidly but his steps are almost silent. He stops in the open doorway that leads from their floor out into the stairwell. The door is made to open outwards towards the stairs; it was already open when they arrived, held in place by a fire extinguisher. The skier grabs the extinguisher. As he raises it, the door begins to swing closed and his foot comes down, trapping it. Lifting the bulky extinguisher to his shoulder he brings it down diagonally onto the outside handle of the door. Gold flashes at his wrist as he raises it high again. A second blow and the loop-shaped handle is bouncing across the stairwell carpet, the metal ringing like a bicycle bell.

Moving inside the office, the skier lets the door close behind him. Grabbing the middle of a nearby coat rack, he lifts the chrome centre-pole off its plastic base and inverts it, dumping the crown of hooks to the floor. Now he's left with a straight pole, which he spins once, expertly, and then feeds through the inside handle of the door at a forty-five degree angle. It won't pass all the way through; the end of the pole is gouging wood from the door when it's only a third of the way through.

With his hands spread wide, one on each end of the pole, he levers it round until it's level. With the pole wedged solidly, one end biting into the door, the other end hard against the wall, the door is now barred from the inside.

Although it only takes seconds to wedge the door closed, it's not a moment too soon. Already the police can be heard clattering up the stairs. They reach the sealed door at the same time the three intruders complete their retreat to the office at the other end of the floor.

The policeman in the lead paws at the door. With no handle to pull, only the frame of the little wired-glass window offers any purchase. It's not enough to allow a proper grip.

Alan is standing in the doorway of the small office watching the stairwell door. He turns his head to glance at the skier. "What were you doing downstairs?" he demands.

The skier makes no reply.

Peter, meanwhile, is panicking. "What do we do?" he says, repeating it several times under his breath. He yanks the cord on the blinds to reveal a ten metre drop down to glittering steel train tracks. His gaze flicks nervously from the tracks to the office door and back to the tracks again. He begins to scrabble at the frame of the window, trying to find a lock, but there isn't one. The window is a single sealed unit.

The skier steps past him, flexing his gloved hands. He bends over the tool-bag spread open in front of the safe, and grasps the handle of a screwdriver. He straightens up and runs the tip of the screwdriver firmly into Peter's chest.

Peter freezes. His stricken expression and seized limbs make him look as though he's just grabbed a live wire. For a moment, no one in the room moves.

Then Peter looks down, his twitchy frame still for the first time that evening. His chin drops and his gaze locks on the yellow plastic handle tacked to his ribcage. His eyes go wide like someone realising they have a scorpion pinned to their lapel. He raises one hand numbly and it's not clear if he intends to grasp the handle or swat at it. As his hand rises, his knees buckle and his terrified eyes roll back in their sockets. He crumples, to lay unmoving at the skier's feet.

Alan is paralysed for a second, then with a flinch the spell is broken and he's scrabbling frantically at the pocket of his overalls, a look of panic on his face.

The skier doesn't move.

A moment later Alan has located a revolver, tugged it free of his pocket and levelled it unsteadily at the skier who is standing framed against the window.

Their eyes lock and Alan takes an involuntary half-step back. Maintaining fierce eye contact the skier says, "I'm going to kill you next." Each word is clear, but the cut-glass accent is gone, the sounds no longer those of a native English speaker.

Alan's whole body is tensed, his muscles so tight that the gun trembles slightly in his sweaty hands. He is panting. His eyes, unblinking, are riveted on the skier who returns his gaze with feral intensity. Neither moves a hair.

Then the skier lunges violently towards Alan. Alan fires instinctively, but the skier's lunge is just a feint, he is moving sideways, not towards Alan. The bullet ricochets off something and shatters the sealed picture window. Glass tumbles onto the tracks below.

Coming out of his crouch, the skier asks, "Shall we try that again?" his crystal accent back in place.

* * *

Out in the stairwell, a police officer is working on the door with a crow bar. A black-clad figure with sergeant's stripes on his shoulder is resting on one knee, his MP5 semi-automatic braced against his shoulder and pointed towards the door. His trigger finger lays along the guard.

The policeman with the crow bar rips another chunk out of the door panel.

"What about a shotgun, Sarge?" asks one of the men.

The kneeling policeman shakes his head.

On the fourth attempt, the chisel end of the crow bar slips far enough under the edge of the door that the wood doesn't splinter. The policeman strains hard until suddenly the pole holding the door closed folds with a screech and drops noisily to the ground. Released, the door springs open a few inches. But with nothing to hold it in place it bangs closed again a moment later.

At that moment, from the other side of the door, there's the unmistakable sound of a gun being fired.

The policeman with the crow bar jumps to one side, out of the firing line. The man with the semi-automatic crouches lower, rapidly sweeping the barrel backwards and forwards, looking for a target. There's nothing to see through the little glass window of the closed door.

After a couple of seconds, the sergeant speaks.

"Who fancies holding that door open for me?" he asks, still sighting through the wired window. A couple of the others snort. Seeing that no one volunteers he says, "Slap, there was a mop downstairs, run and fetch it would you? Chris, I want you to pull the door open a crack then push it the rest of the way with the mop. Slide it along the floor and put your foot on it when the door's open so we can get past you. Dean, over there to give a bit more cover."

The mop is fetched and passed to the policeman with the crow bar who does as instructed. As the door slides open there's a crash from beyond. A few seconds later there's a second shot. Both armed policemen tense, their fingers resting on their weapon's triggers. They can see nothing of what might be happening in the office.

"Dean, through to the right and cover," says the crouching sergeant.

"OK Sarge," Dean says and darts through the door and to one side. He drops one knee to the floor and aims his weapon at the far end of the room.

"Slap, weapon at the ready, through to the left and cover." Slap brings his semi-automatic to his shoulder, draws back the slide, flicks off the safety catch and moves through the door.

"Chris, when I'm through, weapon ready and cover these stairs, up and down. No surprises please." Chris nods. The sergeant steps through the doorway and the door closes behind him as Chris wedges himself in the corner of the stairwell.

Advancing in several quick stages, using desks as cover, the three armed policemen approach the silent office. The sergeant holds up a hand. He calls out, "Armed police. Surrender immediately. I repeat, armed police. Put down your weapons now. Do. You. Understand?"

Nothing.

They wait for thirty seconds. A few papers rattle as a gust of wind spills them from a desk.

With a hand signal, the sergeant fans the other two men out and has them advance on the office door. He stays still, his rifle trained on the open door.

"I can see a body," says Slap.

"I see two bodies – they're not moving," says Dean.

The sergeant motions Dean to move in closer. Dean shuffles forwards like a hesitant fencer, sliding his feet along the carpet until he is at the doorway. He crouches, takes a rapid look inside and ducks back. "They're down," he says.

Standing, the sergeant signs for the other two to remain still. He walks slowly towards the office. He sees two bodies, one inside the door, one lying beneath the broken window. He moves through the open door. His foot slips slightly as he steps in a pool of blood. The body by the window has a plastic handle sticking out of its chest. An outstretched hand holds a revolver.

The sergeant places the sole of his boot carefully over the wrist, pinning it, his gun trained on the unmoving body.

"Slap, secure the other one," he calls.

The sergeant bends down, his foot still trapping the gun hand, and feels for a pulse. "This one's dead."

"Same here," says Slap bending over the other body.

The sergeant leans out of the shattered window, peering down at the tracks. He looks left and right. There's nothing to see except sheer walls and hard track. Pulling his head in he looks at the two dead bodies.

"What the hell happened here then?" the sergeant asks no one in particular.

CHAPTER 2

D avid Braun took a step back as his attacker flipped a fast right hand at his face. A second jab just missed the tip of his nose – a feature which, by the shape of it, hadn't always been so lucky.

His attacker, a beefy blond hulk with a fierce South African accent, was crowding him, throwing snap punches and keeping his guard high.

David took another step backwards. He was running out of room.

He dipped his left knee and twisted a little, pretending to stumble. He watched to see how his attacker would respond. The advancing South African pushed in quickly for the kill. Once his opponent had committed himself, David slapped away the next jab, pivoted on one heel and brought the other heel whirling round to crack the South African in the side of the head, knocking him down. His attacker sprawled on the mat.

David looked horrified.

"Jesus Tommy, I'm sorry," David said, instantly apologetic.

Tommy had risen to one knee, his head still down, one hand tentatively touching the site of the impact. He found a tender spot: "Eina! You kicked me in the head, man." Tommy sounded wounded – emotionally at any rate –

rather than angry. He was carefully tracing the outline of his reddening ear, assessing the damage by feel. "You've disfigured me, brah. Now I doubt I'll pull that Vanessa bokkie."

David laughed. "I'm really sorry," he said. Hunching forward he looked from Tommy's red ear to its pale pink partner. "I think it's evened them up a bit, actually."

Both of them were panting a little as they talked and sweat covered them. Tommy said, "Lekker bliksem, man. I'm done for the day. Help me up."

David hauled Tommy to his feet and gave him a slap on the back. "What about a couple more goes? Really and truly no contact," David asked. "Scout's honour."

Tommy gave him a sidelong scornful look, but there was no real harm in it. "We've been at it for two hours, china. I'm finished."

Retying their gi they walked towards the changing rooms. A minute later they were both in the communal showers.

Tommy stood, back bowed, one hand against the wall, letting the water hit him in the face. David was showing a little more industry, scrubbing himself with shower gel.

Tommy turned so that his face was out of the water. When he spoke now, his accent sounded a little more English. "You train pretty hard, man. I mean really hard. What's your rush?"

David was rinsing now, almost finished with his shower.

"You train just as hard, Tommy," David said. He shut off the shower and flicked some of the water out of his hair. His breathing was steady while Tommy's was still a little laboured.

"Not like you, I don't. I've never seen anyone so serious about training, but I don't see you going in for competitions," Tommy said. "Is it true you don't even have any belts?"

David walked past Tommy on his way back towards the benches in the changing room. "Where did you hear that?" he asked, "I got to blue belt in Judo when I was nine. I've still got it somewhere," he said over his shoulder.

A few minutes later, David had said goodbye to Tommy and made his way outside into the dark, rain-slicked car park. He was dressed now in indigo jeans and a black sweater.

He ran a hand through his damp hair and looked around for his car. It was in the far corner of the car park, parked on its own under a lamppost; the sodium light made the blue paint look black.

Swinging his holdall over one shoulder, he crossed to his car. Micro-droplets of rain touched his face and clung to his eyelashes until he brushed them away.

Once inside the car, David passed his holdall over onto the back seat. He started the engine and then retrieved his mobile from the glove compartment, pushed the power button. As he pulled out onto the main road, his mobile beeped to announce that he'd got voicemail. He steered one-handed while holding the phone to his ear.

"First message," the automated recording said, followed by a girl's voice sounding weary: "David, it's Judy. Give me a call if you get this before nine." He glanced at the dashboard clock: 9:45.

There was a little intake of breath and then, "Actually, you know what? Don't bother!" this last with a certain vehemence. "You might as well... Look, I've had enough. It's like spending time with a... a zombie. You're easily the nicest guy I've been out with, in fact I almost can't fault you. Except that you wouldn't care if I dropped dead tomorrow. Do you know how that feels? It's insulting. Well, you know what? You can drop dead." Most of this was delivered in the voice of someone obviously unused to shouting. Her voice warbled with emotion. There were a couple of seconds in which she could be heard breathing heavily and then the message ended.

"Next message," the machine said, then there was the sound of choking. "Jesus, I think I've swallowed a wasp." More coughing, then the message ended.

The machine again: "Next message," and then, "It's Banjo, mate. Bastard peanuts, they're a fucking menace, if you ask me. Thought I was going to need a tracheotomy. I'm getting it looked at now."

A woman's voice in the background said, "Same again, dear?" then Banjo continued, "They want to keep me in over night. Come and visit your old mate if you've got a minute. I'll be in the intensive care unit at the

Old Grey Goose getting mouth to mouth." The same woman's voice in the background commented, "Not likely," and then the call ended.

Smiling to himself, David drove towards Banjo's local. Ten minutes later he was parked and out of the car. As he walked into the brightly lit saloon bar, he saw Banjo at the bar, buttoning up his red lumberjack shirt. He'd clearly been showing the attractive, forty-something barmaid whatever lay beneath.

"I could come back," David said by way of greeting.

"Watcha, mate," Banjo said, looking up. "What are you having?"

David looked from Banjo to the barmaid, "I'm gasping. You couldn't get me a pint of water, could you?"

"And…" said Banjo.

"And a pint of Boddingtons, thanks."

"I'll have the same again, Helen love. And help yourself to anything that takes your fancy," Banjo said, pulling the neck of his shirt down to expose a freckly chest.

Helen pursed her lips in mild disgust. "Put it away. If that shark didn't want none of it, I'm hardly going to touch it, am I?" Helen said, pleasantly, and set about fetching the round. A moment later she returned and patted Banjo's hand. She whispered, "I'll have something after, pet." She pressed a button on the till which caused the display to register a sale of 50p.

Banjo indicated a quiet table by the window, David nodded, and they carried their drinks across.

Banjo looked David up and down. "Blimey, you look more like a bouncer every time I see you. You're probably saving up for one of them long leather coats, aren't you?" Banjo said. He poked curiously at one of David's biceps which bulged sufficiently to stretch the material of his sweater.

"If it was anyone but a ginger scarecrow saying that, I think I'd be hurt," David said. He took a long drink from his pint of water. When he set it back on the table the glass was nearly empty. He gave a little gasp of approval.

Banjo turned his attention to his pint. "So you been out scrapping this evening, then? Fighting sailors and wotnot? If you're going to exercise – and you know my views on the matter – why don't you go along to aerobics and spend an hour dancing around watching fit birds in Lycra waggle their arses at you?" Banjo said. "Common sense," he added.

"You've seen me dance. Imagine what I'd be like sober and wearing a leotard," David said. "Nobody wants that."

Banjo said, "Could have used you around earlier. My Uncle Jess dropped by. You remember Uncle Jess? From graduation?"

A look of pain crossed David's face, "The horror."

"Yeah, that's him. Anyway, you'll have to excuse the fact I'm a bit pissed. It's not easy persuading him to go while you've still got life left in you," Banjo said.

"I remember he likes to be the last man standing," David said.

Banjo took a swig of his pint. "So how's the world tour progressing? You're not letting all this stuff in the papers put you off, are you?"

"Nooo," David said. "Obviously I'm going to have to make some adjustments depending on, um, local developments."

"Like if they're actually bombing the place the week you want to stay, for instance?" Banjo asked.

"That would certainly be one factor, yes," David replied. "But I was thinking more about the air travel. Apparently flights are getting more and more unreliable and the airlines are cutting back their schedules."

"Well that might have something to do with them being war-torn, fucking combat zones," Banjo said, his voice rising. Helen glanced their way.

"It's really not as bad as all that," David replied. "Anyway, I might give the Middle East a miss. I haven't decided."

"Do you want to know what I think?" Banjo asked, leaning towards David and looking him in the eye. "I think you're so bored doing that pointless job of yours that you'd happily get yourself killed just to liven things up a little. Like all that martial arts business."

He went on, "When we were at college it was fair enough. Girls thought all that way of the warrior stuff sounded cool and there was a good crowd at the club. But you're still hard at it. I think you just do it now because kicking someone's head in, or getting yours kicked in, is the only way you can blow off steam and maybe feel a little bit alive at the same time."

David said nothing and Banjo continued, "All I know is there's tons of jobs you could be doing instead." He tapped a finger on his bottom lip,

"Look, why not take the trip, but do something fun with it. Learn to surf, trek round Thailand, drive across Australia. I'll even come with you. But don't get yourself killed in some place I can't even pronounce. The Nine O'Clock News isn't bloody Wish You Were Here. They show all that stuff so you'll know to stay away."

Nothing was said for a few moments.

David began, "Look, Banjo…"

But Banjo butted in, "OK, OK. Sorry. I might just possibly be exaggerating. But there's a few things I want to get off my chest," he said, his voice quiet now. He took another sip.

Softly he said, "I think people are always doing idiotic things in their private lives to make up for all the damage they do when they're at work. Human beings weren't meant to spend their days in cubicles…" He was picking up a bit of speed again now.

David muttered, "I don't work in a cubicle."

"…preparing next quarter's sales budget for some bloke called Prenderghast," Banjo went on.

"You know there actually *is* someone called…" David tapered off as Banjo showed no sign of halting.

"The human soul is more plastic than elastic," Banjo stated emphatically, taking another big swig from his pint. His eyes were off somewhere in the distance now. "If you squeeze it hard and let go, it tries to go back to its old shape, but mainly it's got someone's dirty big handprint on it now. Every time you try to change yourself to fit in somewhere, it leaves an impression. Jobs, school, getting on with the snooty in-laws, all of that. You get a job by pretending to be an 'enthusiastic self-starter with dynamic potential' or whatever. Basically, you claim you've got a hearty appetite for whichever kind of horseshit they produce there.

"If you fool them and get invited into their world it's because you squeezed yourself into the right shape to pass through their particular eye of the needle." Banjo had a manic look in his eye. "Now you're in. But you can't relax, you can't just flop back to whatever shape you were before or they'll catch you. You've got that unsightly belly of individuality pulled in and you can't let your breath out. If you do, you're marked. You're not one of them. You get the speech about 'thing's aren't working out as we'd hoped'. But keep up the pretence and you can pass among them and gorge yourself at the corporate trough."

"Steady," David said quietly, but Banjo was unstoppable.

"Now you'd *like* to think if you took off the suit and let yourself relax you'd spring back into shape. That the real you is inside, working the levers, the master illusionist, fooling everyone, but it's not like that." He shook his head sadly. "No-one plays a part for years. If you do it for years, it's not pretend, it's really you."

Despite the fact that Banjo was ranting and well along in his evening's drinking, he still had David's attention. The points Banjo was making hadn't completely missed their marks.

"The worst thing, David, is those places you have to stoop to get in to. You could really be something if you wanted to be. But you hunch yourself over and hobble along pretending to be just the same as all the grey little management pygmies around you. You could tower over them whenever you chose to let the secret out."

He drew a deep breath. "Maybe. Or maybe you couldn't anymore. Maybe you'll spend the next forty years bent double believing that you've got the last laugh because you're only pretending."

Banjo's gaze fell to his drink. He seemed to be winding down now and he looked melancholy. "We mutilate ourselves everyday just to fit in; we hardly wait to be asked. We like to show willing. And if there's a GTI with a CD-player at the end of it, we'll reach into ourselves and rip our own fucking hearts out. Most of us will carve ourselves up with a smile, because at the end of the ordeal, when we're done, we're hoping whoever handed us the knife will smile and say 'welcome aboard, son'."

Out of breath, Banjo finished off his pint.

"Jesus Christ, Banjo. Now I won't sleep tonight. Not a wink," David said sounding a bit horrified.

There was a long pause. Banjo's face softened as the intensity he'd put into his words began to ebb.

After a minute he began to smile again.

He said, "You know what? Best cure for not sleeping is plenty of hard work. Get yourself up to that bar and get some drinks in. Do you the power of good. I've got to make a quick detour."

Banjo levered himself to his feet and headed off, roughly in the direction of the gents. He was muttering something under his breath as he went, the only word audible being 'insurance'.

David ordered Banjo another pint of the keg cider the pub was famous for. He glanced at his own pint and found he'd only drunk about a third of it. Helen, following his glance, said, "I could just put a bit of a head on that. For the look of the thing, eh ducks?"

"Thanks," said David. He added, "Did you really just call me 'ducks'?"

Helen winked at him. "I'm big on tradition," she said.

As David carried the drinks back, Banjo returned.

"Helen's a star, isn't she?" asked David.

"A priceless jewel. She used to be a schoolteacher before her husband died." Banjo glanced at the bar. "Don't bring it up though."

Drinks were sipped. "About what you said," David began, holding his hand up to forestall Banjo's inevitable interruption. "I'm honestly not trying to get myself killed – but you're right, I am bored. And maybe I'm doing things I wouldn't do otherwise." He cleared his throat. "But if it helps, I'm not planning to stay in that job indefinitely. What you have to understand, though, is that I'm really pretty good at something that pays well. And a lot of the time I actually enjoy it. I know it's not 'me'. If I knew what was 'me' I can tell you I'd be off like a shot."

Banjo attempted to jump in again, but David again held up his hand, "No, let me get this out. I know what you're saying and I agree with a lot of it. And I appreciate the fact that you look out for me, even though god knows I'm ugly enough to look after myself." Banjo nodded seriously. "So how's this for an idea: I'll give you my word – right now – that I'll be doing something totally different a year from now. Even if it's not the right thing, I'll try something else." He sat back and looked at Banjo who was wearing a thoughtful expression. He added, "And while you're trying to talk me out of my current lucrative employment, I'd like to point out you don't seem bothered by the fact that I've paid for every curry we've eaten since 1995."

Banjo ignored the curry remark, just nodded slowly a couple of times and patted David's shoulder. "Yeah, OK. Good. And sorry if I went off on one."

After a minute, Banjo's expression lightened and he asked, "Anyway, how's the lovely Judy, then? God that girl's got legs that go on for weeks. Not to mention an arse that makes you want to take a bite out of it, if you'll pardon me talking about your future wife in those terms."

"Hmm. Things with Judy aren't too good," said David, rummaging in his pocket for his phone. "I think I've got the most recent update here." He pushed a couple of buttons and handed Banjo the phone.

Banjo listened to the message play.

"Hoo hoo," piped Banjo when he'd finished listening. "You haven't lost the old magic, have you? Still able to screw up while doing everything right," he said. "Now let me ask you something veeerrrry important and you must tell me the truth: are you going to try and get back with her?"

"No," said David shaking his head. "I'm honestly a bit relieved."

"Good," said Banjo, "then I can tell you that I never thought you two were right for each other. Mark my words, next time you see her she'll have married an accountant, who she'll bully something chronic. She'll be as happy as Larry and no hard feelings."

David agreed. "Yeah, to be honest I've been trying to think of a way out that didn't leave either of us too traumatised. This is better than I'd expected. You remember when I split up with Hope, after that talking to she gave me? I was so shaken up I thought I was getting a stutter."

"Yeah, you were a state," snorted Banjo.

"But, I think that was just because I couldn't believe she could hate me so much with so little warning. Judy and I never got that far." David sighed, "I like her and everything, but what worried me was how easy it was to forget she existed when she wasn't around. That's not a good sign, is it?"

Banjo said nothing and David went on, "Anyway, what about you? How are things with that nurse, Melissa, you were drooling over?"

"Actually, there've been a few developments on that front, mate," Banjo said, clapping his hands and rubbing them together. "And what a front it is."

They were still talking about Banjo's romantic prospects, and laughing, half an hour later when Helen called out, "Time gentlemen please. Hain't you got no 'omes to go to?" She winked at them both as she spoke.

David and Banjo brought their glasses back to the bar, Banjo draining the last of his, David handing over an almost full pint. "Night Helen," they both said and headed out into the night.

The smell of rain was still in the air, but a few gaps had opened in the clouds. Stars peeped through.

"I'll call you later in the week," David said.

"Right you are, matey," said Banjo, giving David a final clap on the shoulder and heading off on foot, leaving David to unlock his car.

* * *

David was home and fast asleep a few hours later when his pager began its piercing beep.

He clicked the bedside light on and swung his feet out of bed. He sat on the edge of the bed for a minute, rubbing his face and running both hands through his hair. Then he took a deep breath, shook his head a couple of times and reached over for his pager.

The pager display had a number to call. David stood, a little unsteadily, and pulled on a pair of shorts. Then he padded out into the living room and turned on the light. He picked up the cordless phone and the pad and pen that sat by it. He sat on his scuffed looking leather sofa, rested the pad on his knee and dialled the number from memory.

A voice answered after one ring, "David? Reg Cottrell." It was a very English voice and sounded like it belonged to an older man.

"Hi Reg. What's up?" David said.

"Apologies for the page. I think you'll need to get involved with this. I've just had a call from the alarm people. Interfinanzio's offices have been broken into. It sounds like a mess. Police are on site – armed police in fact. There's been some sort of incident, ambulances called. I don't know much more, except that the officer in charge is a DI Hammond of the Flying Squad; he's been told to expect you."

David had been jotting notes. "This is their offices in the East End? I think they've got another office somewhere."

"Errrm," Reg said, consulting his own notes, "Off Bow Road in Mile End. That's the one. Can you take it from here?"

"No problem, Reg. I'll get down there. Are you in tomorrow?" David said.

Reg muttered to himself, "Half three now," obviously thinking aloud. Then he said, "I might get a later train than usual, but I'll be in."

"OK, well I'll fill you in when I see you," David said.

"Good, good." Reg paused. "I mean I'm sure I don't have to say…"

"Absolutely. Have no fear. This is my top priority from this moment onwards," David said in reassuring tones.

"Splendid, splendid. Important clients. Well, tomorrow then," Reg said.

David was already on his feet as he replied, "Sure thing," and put the phone back in its cradle.

Ten minutes later he was shaved and dressed for work – dark blue suit, mid-blue shirt, dark-grey tie. He zipped the notepad into a leather portfolio, put his car keys and phone in his pocket and headed out the door.

CHAPTER 3

THAT SAME EVENING
MONDAY 7TH APRIL

S usan Milton was getting angry. She sat looking over a table spread with papers. Her assistant, Kevin, was standing behind her chair.

"I just thought you looked a little tense," Kevin said, in his Midwest accent.

"I'm tense, Kevin, because you're bugging me. Stop screwing around and sit down," Susan said. She was also American but her accent was trickier to pin down.

"Look…" Kevin said, in a soothing voice, letting the word hang. He parted her shoulder length blonde hair and laid his hands on her shoulders. His thumbs started to massage the muscles of her back.

Susan's voice was icy, "Stop that now or you'll look back and decide this was the moment when it all started to go wrong for you."

Kevin lifted his hands from her shoulders and laughed, albeit a little nervously. He held his hands out, palms up. "OK. Jesus. See what I mean, you're tense."

"Listen, genius, this is going to be difficult for you to grasp, but try. If I was Professor Shaw, would you be giving me a massage? You do that for everyone you work for? Seventy-year-old guys included?" Susan asked, sounding exasperated.

"No," Kevin said, peevishly, "But you're *not* my professor." Under his breath he muttered, "You're not even that much older than me," as though that clinched it.

"Right. And yet somehow the College thought you might learn something from assisting me – how to get your PhD finished, maybe." She twisted round to look at him, though he refused to meet her gaze. "Look, try to understand, I'm not your next big conquest, I'm someone you work for who thinks you're creepy. Is that reasonably clear?" Susan said.

Kevin snorted. He slumped down in his chair; his expression suggested he felt very harshly treated. He was sulking.

"We've got a lot to get through still," Susan said. Kevin gave no sign he'd heard. He was staring at one of his Cat desert boots, his leg stretched out in front of him.

Susan looked thoughtfully across at her pouting colleague. "Hey, I meant to say," she said brightly, "Jill said to tell you 'hi'."

Kevin's expression flickered for a second before he caught himself, erased the evidence of curiosity. "Yeah?" he said, sounding bored.

"Yeah, I bumped into her coming back from her dance class. Boy, that stuff really keeps you in good shape." Kevin was looking her way now. "God, I'd love to be that toned and flexible," she said to no one in particular. "Anyway, she says 'hi'." Kevin's expression was neutral, his mind elsewhere, as he considered Susan's words.

"Think I'll call it a day," she said in a whisper, standing up. She slipped her pale lavender denim jacket off the back of her chair and swung her courier bag over one shoulder. She headed out into the corridor and down towards the senior common room. She left Kevin sitting in her office.

It was early evening and the college was largely deserted. All the students had gone home and, this evening, so had most of the staff. As she crossed the hall and neared the common room door, she saw Professor Shaw himself approaching.

"Hey, Professor," she said, smiling. She held the door wedged open with her foot waiting for him to catch her up.

"Well here's a nice surprise. Are you coming in for a drink?" the Professor inquired.

"Just a cup of coffee. Want to join me?" she asked, warmth in her voice.

"What have I done to deserve this?" he asked, amused. "Never mind. If you've nothing better to do with your time, that's my good fortune."

The common room was a large, square, wood-panelled room filled with wooden tables and chairs, darkly varnished. High, latticed windows looked out onto a college courtyard and a Cambridge sky nearing sunset. On the opposite side of the room ran an oak bar.

Two coffee jugs sat on hot-plates beside the bar and Susan poured herself a mug from the fuller of the two. Professor Shaw exchanged quiet words with the waist-coated man behind the bar and received a schooner of sherry and a courteous nod.

They made their way over to a couple of elderly leather armchairs. Besides them, the room was almost deserted.

Susan's tan hipster cords and loose, white t-shirt – Polo written across the front in red letters – looked a little too style-conscious to be standard academic issue. The Professor, on the other hand, looked every inch the elderly academic: flannel shirt in some pale, buff tartan, sage green cardigan and trousers in a worn russet corduroy.

"The young men of today are obviously a less assiduous lot than I'd realised if you have nothing more tempting to do with your evenings," the Professor said, toasting her with his sherry. "My gain, however."

"Oh no, they're a pretty assiduous bunch if you ask me, and not just in the evenings. Kevin Hartman being a prime example," Susan said.

"Oh dear, is he making a nuisance of himself?" Professor Shaw asked.

"That was an off-the-record remark, Professor," she said softly, "it's not a problem. It's just a bit like working with an untrained puppy. He's got plenty of energy but not much focus," she said, examining the design on her mug.

He replied, "Well, I suspect notions of propriety have migrated so far since I was young that my opinions would only be of interest to a fellow historian. In my day, it was quite unthinkable to court a female member of staff, but perfectly proper to marry her. It makes you wonder how those things ever got started, doesn't it?" said the Professor.

"Well it's a minefield these days, I can tell you that." She stared at her mug, her fingers absently tracing the raised college emblem. She mused, almost to herself, "I wanted this top in a six, but then I'd never have got any peace."

Focussing again, she said, "You know if a guy did me the courtesy of focussing on work, I might actually be so impressed that I'd want to go out with him. That's a modern irony for you."

She went on, "It's probably best if we all get used to separating our social life from what goes on at work. Just a shame I only know people from work."

"Oh, I doubt that will be the case for very long. You're still settling in. I know you're a long way from home, but there are splendid people all around you; just allow some of the newness to rub off and you'll soon find yourself desperate for a little solitude. And what about that club of yours? Do they not have a social secretary? Or are they all terribly business-like and to the point?" He chuckled as though he'd said something funny, "Oh, I say, that's rather good."

Susan smiled wanly.

He said, "At any rate, let me know if Mr Hartman begins to make you uncomfortable. We have a veritable firebrand in Human Relations or Resources or whatever it's called this week, and I'm sure he'd enjoy nothing more than lecturing Mr Hartman in the latest fashionable thinking on appropriate workplace behaviour."

He smiled. "Or I could rough him up a little," he said. "That was very big in my day, too."

"Did the BBC show a Jimmy Cagney gangster movie recently?" Susan asked.

"It was Humphrey Bogart, actually. Rousing stuff," he said. "So tell me," he went on, "how's the paper progressing?"

Susan blew air through pursed lips. "Kevin's unwanted contributions aside, it's going slowly. To be honest, I'm not even sure I've got enough material. It looked a lot more solid before I got into it."

Professor Shaw suddenly raised his eyebrows and said, "Do you know what? I've just had a marvellous idea. In fact, I should have thought of it this morning."

He put his sherry down and pressed his palms to his thighs, leaning forwards slightly, "The most fascinating thing has turned up, down in London. I would have thought of you instantly except I knew you were up to your neck with that paper. But this way it works out perfectly."

She was smiling but with a little puzzlement in her expression.

He went on, "I should really tell you what I'm talking about, shouldn't I? The School of Antiquities in London have just come into possession of a totally unknown collection of documents after their last owner passed away. From what I've been told, most of them concern magical practices and beliefs and they originate from a number of different centuries. The school wondered if we wanted to send someone. They're more used to, well I suppose you might call it non-fiction: histories, letters and various sort of records. I was going to go down myself, although it's a bit of a bind. I'd much rather send you. Besides, it's all right up your street. You'd get first look at a collection of material that sounds absolutely fascinating. You might even find something useful for the paper and you'll give Mr Hartman a chance to cool off. Or better still to set his sights on whoever that woman is who wanders round in her underwear."

"Jill Jenkins," Susan enunciated slowly. "Great minds think alike. So tell me more. What do you know about this find?"

The Professor told her what he knew, which was really only enough to excite her curiosity. After a few minutes he enquired, "You have nowhere to stay in London, I suppose?"

"I thought I'd get the train down each day," she replied.

"I have a better idea," the Professor said, "although you can make up your own mind of course. But you're more than welcome to stay at my late sister's house. I've been meaning to let it out, but it's just so convenient whenever I have business in town – which I suppose is not that often these days. At any rate, if there's any justification for retaining it, this would be it: so that I can make the occasional *beau geste*."

"Well, that's very kind of you…" Susan said, unsure whether to accept.

"Terribly awkward these things, aren't they? Excess is just as off-putting as meanness. Well, I'll leave it up to you. Take the keys with you and if you do nothing more than pop round to make sure the place is still standing I'd be grateful. Doctor Williams has stayed there a couple of times, but he always leaves the place in such a muddle for the lady who comes in to dust that I'm afraid I've allowed him to believe it's no longer available," he said.

Susan's expression suggested her mind was now made up, "I'm quite sure I can be a better houseguest than The Walrus. Thank you Professor. First you find me a proper office and now this. You're a sweetie." Then she raised an eyebrow, "Hmm, I wonder if college policy allows me to say that?"

"I'll see that it does next time I'm forced to sit in on one of their incomprehensible meetings," he said. "And let's be clear, my dear. I'm sure we'd get along splendidly anyway, but it's the quality of your work that puts you at the top of the list. The last time I let charm or a well-turned ankle influence me on a matter of college business, George VI was still on the throne."

They carried on chatting and in the end Susan stayed for a glass of white wine. The Professor had a glass of college red and a ham sandwich while they discussed Susan's London expedition. While he had little more to offer regarding the collection, he knew a considerable amount about the School of Antiquities and its staff. Eventually, the conversation turned back to the house.

"You know Lizzy never could discuss her work and I never enquired. I do know that when she passed away, even though she'd been retired for several years, some gentlemen from the government came to take away all her papers. I suggested on several occasions that she settle somewhere like Hampstead, but her work kept her close to the City. By the time she was free to move I don't think she wanted to. I imagine you and she would have got on well. Both sharp as tacks."

A few minutes later, the barman came over to ask whether they wanted anything else before he closed the bar. It was just after nine, but they were the only two left in the common room. Both agreed it was time to be on their way.

Susan expressed her enthusiasm for the Professor's idea one last time and said she would head down to London the following afternoon, once she'd attended to a couple of loose ends in college. She left the common room wearing an expression that was far less troubled than when she'd entered it.

CHAPTER 4

Threading the pre-dawn London maze, driving southwards from Islington towards the old City, David followed the forgotten course of the River Fleet, sleeping these last hundred years sealed beneath the streets.

He neared his destination. Up ahead a silver, fluorescent-striped BMW blocked the road – executive police for executive victims.

David pulled his blue Saab into an empty, metered parking place a dozen metres short of the police car. His dashboard clock read 4.35am.

In the street beyond, partly concealed by a bend in the road, a three-storey office block had apparently made the switch to twenty-four-hour operation. While elsewhere in the street windows were dark and doors were closed, this building had all its lights on. Uniformed figures stood near the open doors and several official vehicles were parked at various angles in the street outside.

David walked towards the activity, his little leather portfolio case under his arm. The night air was still damp and the temperature had dropped while he'd slept. Tiny pieces of rain-misted gravel crunched under his leather soles. He was fifteen metres from a group of three uniformed policemen when they looked up from their conversation.

"Good morning, I'm here to see Detective Inspector Hammond. Can I go in?" David asked.

Radios squawked in the background. "Name please, sir?" asked the police officer closest to him. His expression was stern.

"I'm David Braun, I'm from the insurance company Marshall and Liberty." He held up a business card that identified him as an Account Manager.

"Is he expecting you, sir?" the policeman asked, without looking at the card.

"Yes," David said, simply offering the policeman a polite smile.

The constable nodded and eased up on the stern look. "Yeah, go on up," he said, sounding almost friendly. "And don't touch anything."

David nodded and moved past the little gathering, up the steps and through open doors into the glass-fronted lobby: lots of textured concrete, smart but not quite stylish. An alarm panel was open just inside the door; wires were spread out in all directions. A flight case sat beneath the panel, its open lid revealing several jars and plastic bottles. No one was around.

David climbed the steps to the first floor and met another uniformed policeman standing at the fire door leading off from the staircase.

The door itself was propped open with a fire extinguisher. The door and door-frame were dented, splintered and chipped. One of the door handles lay on the concrete floor nearby.

"I'm looking for DI Hammond," David said.

"Won't be a minute, guv," the constable said. "Would you wait here?"

"I'm not on the force. I'm from the insurance," David said.

"You just looked… Just wait here, sir," the constable said. No 'guv' this time. The officer headed into the open-plan office beyond.

David could hear voices from the other side of the brightly lit space. A breath of wind brushed his face and stirred papers on nearby desks.

A moment later the constable returned with a stocky man in his late forties. He was wearing dark suit trousers, a white shirt and a blue tie decorated with tiny penguins. He looked blankly at David and pushed his fingers through his few long strands of brown hair.

"I'm with the insurance company. Actually, we've met before, Inspector. I'm David Braun." David held out his hand.

And for a moment, Hammond just stared at it. Then he lifted his chin suddenly, as though something had occurred to him and pumped David's hand a couple of times.

"Yes, yes. Jewellers on Bond Street. That's right." Hammond didn't smile, but his body language suggested that David had ceased to be a stranger. "I remember that case. You helped us along with that one. All went a lot quicker once the owner was, er, forthcoming."

Hammond turned his back on David and walked into the office. He left one hand stuck out behind him, a single finger flicking, almost as though he expected David to take it and said, "Come. Come," without looking round. David followed.

"Want some fucking horrible coffee?" Hammond asked, pointing off to the right as they passed a little kitchen area.

"Maybe not," David said, following in Hammond's wake.

"Probably wise," Hammond said without turning round.

When they neared the door of the corner office, where most activity seemed to be concentrated, Hammond stopped and David came to stand beside him.

"You want me to tell you what we know?" he glanced sharply at David.

"Thank you," said David, unzipping his portfolio case to uncover the notepad inside. He took a pen from his suit pocket.

"Alarm was triggered just after one. Alarm company passed the call along. There've been several armed robberies in this area so an armed response vehicle was sent, a four-man team in this case.

"Main doors downstairs were open. They came in and found the door to this floor barred. They heard two shots fired while they were opening this door. Once through, they approached this office," he indicated the corner office they were standing outside. "Found two dead bodies. One was stabbed with a screwdriver, his partner was shot. The one with the screwdriver in his chest was holding a revolver – two chambers fired – but only one bullet hole in his victim. The window was busted, so maybe that's where the second shot went. The one who was shot also had half his rib-cage crushed, we're not sure how that happened.

"The safe over there's been drilled, but it doesn't seem to have been opened. It looks like they might have been disturbed by the ARV boys at the last minute.

"Also looks like they broke into the chairman's office upstairs. No obvious signs of theft.

"I'll let you know about the post mortems and forensic reports. Perhaps you could coordinate with your client to double-check nothing's missing. I'd be a bit surprised if you come back with anything though, because there was nothing on either of the dead men." Hammond concluded, "Questions?"

"I've got three, if you wouldn't mind," David said. Hammond nodded once. "Well, I'm wondering about the alarm system. Pardon me for asking this, but if the intruders set it off when they broke in, how did they have time to drill the safe before being interrupted?" David asked.

Hammond replied, "We're working on that. The alarm was disabled at the time of the break-in. Don't know exactly how yet, although the panel's obviously been tampered with. About a quarter of an hour later the alarm was somehow triggered. Sloppy job on the bypass maybe. I'll let you know what we turn up. Our response time, by the way, was just under five minutes, including the alarm company's handover. Next."

David said, "Have you ever heard of something like this? Two intruders dead, killed by each other?"

"No. Not as such. I've found bodies before where a gang has, er, made someone redundant right in the middle of a job. This is the first one I've heard of where no one's left alive. Did you want to make a point, Mr Braun?" Hammond asked.

"No. I only wondered how unusual something like this is," David said.

"Well they're all unusual. Usual is being at home in bed, not breaking into someone's office. But, I'll grant you, this is more like that telly programme America's Thickest Villains. I might have to write a monograph for the Detective's Gazette," Hammond said completely deadpan.

It took David a few moments to realise that Hammond had made a joke.

He snorted.

"What's your last question?" Hammond asked.

David said, "Can I look out that window?" indicating the office door from which the night-time breeze was blowing.

For the first time Hammond's face registered something emotional; his brows scrunched together. Perhaps it was irritation. He said nothing for a moment. Then he strode into the office. "Don't touch anything, either with your hands or your feet. There's a lot of clutter in here."

The floor was covered in markers, tape and various damp marks. A large stain was obviously blood. It was alarmingly large – the red appearing black on the dark grey, nylon carpet. They both stepped round the stain, keeping to the edge of the room.

David joined Hammond at the glassless window. Only a few jagged pieces of the double-glazing remained in the corners of the frame. David peered out and down into the damp night.

Beneath the window, maybe ten metres below, ran railway lines. There were two sets of tracks, the bright steel of their polished top surfaces reflected the faint ambient light. In between the tracks, broken glass twinkled. Some of the pieces were jagged shards as big as a fist; elsewhere a dusting of tiny fragments glittered like distant stars.

The train-tracks seemed to be lower than street level. Steep walls enclosed that section of railway for many metres in either direction. The tracks ran through an artificial canyon formed by the basement walls of the buildings on both sides.

On the opposite side of the tracks from where David looked out, a sheer wall rose ten metres. Above that, the featureless wall gave way to big rectangular windows in the plain concrete, but the holes were filled with chain-link not glass. The other side of the mesh, faint fluorescent burned. The building appeared to be a multi-storey car park.

Hammond said, "Nobody jumps – what? thirty-five feet? – onto broken glass and steel. At least not without putting themselves in the hospital. And it's a hell of a climb back out. We're shutting off the track for an hour to check it out, but only because there might be evidence down there. We're not expecting to find Spiderman's footprint."

David bent down and studied the bottom of the window frame.

Now Hammond's voice was clearly registering irritation at David's interest, "Braun, I want you to liaise with your clients, get me the information I want, keep them sweet. Don't start investigating this case. For a start, there's no theft."

David stood up, turned away from the window frame to face Hammond.

"Right. Thanks Inspector. I'm going to make some phone calls and some notes. Would you remind me of your phone number?" David said.

Hammond left his potent stare trained on David for a couple of moments before pulling a business card from his top pocket and handing it over. David offered one of his in exchange. "Call me if there's anything I can do to help," David said.

David made his way back through the office. Papers were beginning to blow around as the breeze stiffened a little.

Downstairs, there was now a technician dusting the alarm panel for fingerprints. David stopped and said, "Hi, DI Hammond was just telling me you haven't worked out yet why the alarm went off."

The technician glanced up quickly from his brushing, took in David's suit, his short hair and chunky frame. He said, "Well, yes sir, I suppose we haven't officially. But if you're in a rush, I can tell you what the report's going to say. These wires," he indicated a couple of bare-ended strands with one latex-clad finger, "were pulled apart. You can even see where they were gripped."

Two wires emerged from the panel in an arc, then they each went through a little zigzag. From the zigzags to the naked copper ends they ran straight.

The technician explained, "The kinks are where someone gripped each wire. As the wire comes off a drum in the factory, it's got a little curve to it. Outside of the kinks, the curve's still there. Inside the kinks – where the wires took the tension of being pulled apart – they got straightened out.

"Somebody disabled the alarm and then they either thought better of it or someone else came along to break this circuit."

"Thanks," said David and left the technician to his work. He went through the main doors and out into the damp darkness.

For a moment, David stood in the street outside the lit office block. He looked at the buildings on either side, then he began to walk back to his car, peering at the gaps between the buildings as he went.

When he reached the car he got in and started the engine. He didn't move off right away, but instead pulled a street atlas from the glove box. He found the street he was currently parked in and ran his finger down the adjacent railway line. His fingertip came to rest on a road which crossed the tracks.

Putting the car into reverse, he turned it round and then set off, following the route he'd scouted on the map.

A few hundred metres from the office block, the level of the tracks was nearly four metres below street level. A road bridge need only rise half a metre or so in order to cross the line. Sure enough, David found the little humpback bridge, crossed over, and then set about trying to find the multi-storey car park that had been facing him when he'd stood at the broken office window.

With a little trial and error he located it. Leaving his Saab in the street outside, he ducked under the entry barrier to the car park and peered into the little security hut. No sign of life. He walked up the ramp, through several levels without windows, until he reached a floor with openings and found himself looking out towards the Interfinanzio building.

No cars remained in the multi-storey and only two of the six fluorescent strip lights on his level were working.

David walked to the window and peered out through the chain-link, over the railway lines, and into the glassless window of the lit office opposite. The room was empty, but he could see activity in the large open-plan office beyond.

Taking a handkerchief from his pocket he grasped the bottom of the chain-link and pushed. It was solidly anchored to the concrete wall. He moved further down, passing the first of two pillars which divided up the aperture. Every metre or so he tested the barrier. None of the chain-link could be lifted, nor was it cut.

Putting his hands in his pockets he stood and stared at the chain-link, his lips pursed. After nearly a minute of deliberating and scrutinising, his eyes suddenly narrowed.

He walked to the particular section of chain-link that had caught his eye. Using his handkerchief to touch it, he stretched up high and pushed at the top of the barrier. It came away from the concrete. If a person were somehow suspended outside, they could pull the top of the mesh away from the wall and find enough of a gap to squeeze through into the fourth floor of the car park.

Now David turned his attention to the car park floor. He dropped down into a press-up position and peered sideways along the ground. He moved to a different spot and repeated his inspection. Five times he moved and dropped down low enough that the front of his suit was almost brushing the ground. He found nothing of interest.

He stood up, and gazed around the car park, slapping his hands together to dislodge the dust and grit. His face wore the same expression of thoughtfulness as when he'd studied the mesh covering.

His eyes roamed the concrete floor, then took in the walls – searching in every direction.

Then something occurred to him. Turning his back on that level, he strode down the nearest ramp onto a level with windows that overlooked the street where he'd just parked. The illumination was a little better; only one fluorescent fitting was dark.

This time he only needed to drop into his press-up position once before he sprang back to his feet, a smile on his face. He walked over to where a single splinter of glass twinkled in the dim fluorescent gloom.

There were four broad tyre marks in the parking bay, black rectangles half a metre long, the rear set wider than the front. One of them went right over the splinter.

Bending down, David took his pen out of his pocket and crouched down. He gently nudged the glass fragment a millimetre or two to one side. In the dim light, it was difficult to tell whether the concrete beneath the chip had rubber on it or not. He nudged the chip back to its original position.

He pulled his mobile phone out of its belt clip and retrieved Hammond's card. He dialled the first number on the card.

It rang once and was answered, "Hammond."

"It's David Braun. Listen, there's something I think you should know. My route home took me past that multi-storey car park the other side of the railway tracks from your crime scene. I thought I'd have a quick look round and I noticed a bit of broken glass in one of the parking bays. It isn't one of those little cubes you get if you break a car window; it looks like window glass. You might want to send someone to have a look over here," David said.

Hammond's response was angry, "Braun, did I not make myself plain? You don't investigate, you don't interfere, you keep the owner happy like it says in your job description. If you've screwed up a crime scene, lad, I'll have you charged with interference."

He might have continued but David butted in, "Hold on Hammond," David's voice had a hard edge to it. "You told me there were two people involved in this break-in and they're both in your morgue. If you're right, then this isn't a crime scene. And if I'm right, how does correcting your mistake constitute interference? This car park opens in an hour and a half, so decide whether you want to inspect the third man's tyre tracks before or after a couple of hundred early commuters have driven through here. I'll wait fifteen minutes then I'm going home." He pushed the red button on his phone ending the call.

Just under ten minutes later, a van pulled up beside David's car. He had gone out to stand by it and waved at the van as it approached.

A fifty-ish, barrel-shaped woman with bright, gingery hair got out of the driver's side door, immediately followed by the passenger, a thin, sad-looking man in his mid-twenties.

"You found something interesting?" she said, her voice energetic and horsy.

"I think so. Let me show you," said David, leading them into the multi-storey.

First he took them to the detached chain-link.

"Don't ask me how he got up there, but if he did, he could have slipped through here," he said, pointing to a section of the mesh. The younger technician pushed at the barrier with a latex-covered hand and peered up through the resulting gap.

Then David led them down one floor.

"On this side of the building you look out over the street and from here down there are no windows on the other side. So if he parked here he could drive down without being seen from the crime scene, even if he had his lights on," David said.

He approached the glass chip. "There," he said, "is a bit of glass I think came from the office window they broke."

"You could have tracked it in yourself," the woman said, brusquely.

"Well, firstly I didn't – I saw it before I reached this part of the car park. But look," he raised one foot and showed them the sole, "hard leather. There's almost no glass in that office, it all went out onto the tracks, and I had to walk about four hundred metres to get here. Very unlikely I could bring something this far. Compare that with a suspect who jumped down onto glass about forty metres from here, who – if he had any sense – was wearing rubber soles and who would have twisted his foot against the ground exactly here," he pointed at the chip, "if he were getting into the car that made these marks."

"Marvellous," the woman boomed, clapping her hands once. She turned to her assistant and said, "Now why can't you be more like that?" The assistant shrugged half-heartedly. She went on, brightly, "It'll probably turn out to be the wrong sort of glass, but it's a lovely story. We'll give this place a good going over."

She added, "You might want to be running along. Whatever you said to George Hammond, I think he's had enough of you for one day." She smiled at him.

Then she turned to her assistant and said, "Right then, mopey drawers, you can get the evidence case and the camera bag, while I measure up here."

David left them to it. He made his way back to his car and drove home. He just had time to freshen himself up before it was time to go to start his normal work day.

CHAPTER 5

LATER THAT DAY
TUESDAY 8TH APRIL – AFTERNOON

Mahogany map drawers, parquet floors, high windows and indestructible iron radiators: all the trappings of nineteenth century science. Susan stood in the Assyrian room at the London School of Antiquities gazing out of the first floor window.

She'd been wearing a knee-length white raincoat which was now draped over her arm. Over the other shoulder was her courier bag. Her simple outfit of dark jeans and a white lambswool sweater, plus her carmine boots, still somehow made her look dressier than the people she'd passed on the way in.

From the window she could see the oppressive tower of the Senate House Library rising to her left – Orwell's inspiration for the Ministry of Truth. More books than one person could count: a mountain of learning too high for any scholar to climb.

In the street outside a tourist couple paused to look at the building and started fussing with a camera.

"Ms Milton," a voice behind her said. She turned to see a soft-featured, plump man addressing her from the doorway, an uncertain smile on his face, his hands clasped behind his back. He wore a faded blood-orange shirt and washed-out black jeans. He looked to be in his late thirties.

"Yes, but Susan is fine," she said. Now that they had made eye contact, he seemed to be blushing a little.

"Oh well, I'm delighted to meet you. I'm Bernard, Bernie Lampwick." He gave a little laugh as he said it. "I'm mostly called Bernie. To my face at least." Another little laugh. He rocked a little on his heels, looking uneasy. "I'm supervising the Teracus collection."

Susan frowned a little, puzzled. Bernie explained, "Oh that's what we're calling the collection you're here to look at. Anyway, welcome." He began to put out his hand for her to shake. With her coat and bag, Susan wasn't going to be able to reciprocate. His arm dropped back to his side and he smiled nervously. "OK. Listen, put your stuff down, it'll be fine here. I'll give you the lightning tour and then perhaps we'll go to tea. Or coffee if you prefer. That's a bit more American, isn't it?" he said.

"Coffee would be good," Susan said. She laid her coat over the back of the nearest chair and placed her bag by it. "Here?" she asked.

"Oh yes, that will be fine there," Bernie said. "If anyone were going to pinch something from this room it would most likely be one of the priceless antiques." Susan laughed.

Bernie turned towards the door and indicated that she should precede him through it. They walked back to the reception area and through some double doors, chatting as they went.

Out of the corner of her eye Susan could see Bernie checking her out. She turned her head a little towards him and he rapidly transferred his gaze to the corridor ahead. His blush returned.

"So do you get many visitors like me?" she asked, catching his eye and holding it. "You know…" she left a pause, allowed it to lengthen. Bernie licked his lips nervously as he waited for her to continue. His face showed his discomfort. She finished, "…Americans?"

He laughed loudly, relief evident. "Indeed, no. No it's something of the monastic life here. Not a lot of contact with the outside world." He laughed again. "Apologies if the old social skills are a bit rusty."

This time when she looked away his gaze remained fixed forwards.

"So why Teracus?" Susan asked.

Bernie said, "It was the pen name of the owner of the collection. His real name was probably Terry Cousins – although there does seem to be some doubt about that. For whatever reason, he used more than one name when he was acquiring new documents. But most of the correspondence we've got is signed Teracus.

"He was quite a character, or a man of mystery I should say. He died in Greece in a car crash, but it took a while for the local police to work out who he was and track down some paperwork on him. They notified the British police, who sent someone to his house.

"He had no family, only a landlady who rented out her upstairs flat to him. He'd already been dead two months when they gave her the bad news, so the question arose of what to do with his collection. She knew he'd flown all over the world assembling it and she felt he'd have wanted it to be appreciated, so she donated the lot to the University. Apparently her husband had been a beadle here." He missed Susan's confused look at this last. "We sent someone over to have a quick look just in case there was anything to it." He explained conspiratorially, "We get back editions of Picture Post or Victorian copies of the Bible being left to us as priceless treasures the whole time. Anyway, the assistant we sent along phoned us almost beside himself at what he'd found.

"We're keeping it all downstairs in the Alexandrian room. There are over four hundred documents in all, ranging in ages from Teracus's recent notes to some leaves from a book written in the mid-seventeenth century, assuming they authenticate. Of course what's much more interesting is that a number of them are recent copies of much older documents. There's even one fragment where the ink is Biro but the words are in Hieratic. We've translated just enough to satisfy ourselves it's not gibberish or obviously part of a known work."

They arrived at a busy refectory. Bernie spoke a little more loudly to compete with the din of voices and the scrape and squeak of chairs being moved on vinyl flooring. He took a tray, and laid it on the guides that ran along the front of the food counter. He loaded the tray up with a mug of tea, a cup of coffee and a couple of doughnuts for himself. Susan chose a little pack of ginger biscuits.

When Bernie had paid, they found a quiet table away from most of the bustle and resumed their conversation.

"I'm most of the way through a first draft of a catalogue," Bernie said. "I've recorded what I think each document is, along with a few particulars of its style and appearance. It's obviously been important to draw a distinction between the age of the words compared with the age of the paper and the ink."

Bernie drank some of his tea. He said, "I'm thinking the catalogue would be a good place for you to start. Have a look through my classifications, maybe start checking them. If you think I've got something wrong, then sing out. I'm not precious about these things. The more mistakes you uncover, the better, I think."

Susan asked, "Have you scanned any of it?"

"No. Obviously we keep a digital archive of our documents, but we tend to get the classification sorted before we put them in the archive," Bernie said, slightly officiously.

"I'd *really* like to get some of them scanned," Susan said. "It will help me work if I can start annotating digital copies as soon as possible."

Bernie looked a little ruffled. "Well there is a process to follow," he said, not very reassuringly.

"Whose permission do we need? I can take care of that," Susan said, energetically.

Now Bernie looked alarmed, "Ah, now, hold on a minute. I didn't say we couldn't do it. Why don't you leave it with me?"

She looked him straight in the eye, "I was hoping we could get the scanning underway today, Bernie." She volunteered, "I'll work on documents you've already classified. That way I won't be holding you up. And vice versa." Her tone was very direct, but the effect was softened a little with a smile.

Bernie's slight huffiness had become resignation. "I'm sure we'll work something out if it's that important, I mean if it helps."

"Thanks, Bernie," she said, responding to his slightly beaten expression with a cheerful smile. "I'm fascinated by this man Teracus. Do you have any idea why he assembled this collection? Was he a dealer or a scholar?"

Bernie brightened, "Well, it's curious. Since the whole collection was locked away in his digs, it was obviously about as much of a private collection as you can get. And looking at his correspondence, he only seems to have acquired; I haven't seen a single record of a sale. So he wasn't a dealer. But on the other hand, he wasn't with any academic institution that I've been able to see. He seems to have spent the last thirty years building the collection purely for his own enjoyment. What he did for money, we have no idea. Like I say, a man of mystery."

"Really," Susan said, appreciatively. "That's so interesting. And does the whole collection relate to myths and magic?"

"There's a great deal about magic – legends of great sorcerers, manuals of instruction, spells, even some philosophy. Most of it is in Medieval Latin – I mean the language it's written in; the materials aren't medieval. Since it's mainly recent copies, it's not going to be easy to work out when the original sources were written unless we find references elsewhere. I'm reasonably sure they are copies, by the way, not fakes, but you should be aware of the possibility.

"It hasn't been easy figuring out what's what. I would have said some of his recent notes dated from the Middle Ages except he put last year's date on them. It looks like Teracus's Latin was pretty good," Bernie said.

He went on, "There are also some bits and bobs about mystical relics. The first document I looked at was absolutely fascinating. It looks to be the newest addition to the collection. It purports to be a Latin translation of a classical Tibetan text about something called the signs or sigils of the healer. Supposedly, the gods find certain patterns interesting. By marking the body of a sick person with one of these patterns, it will attract the interest of a god who may choose to heal them. Really very interesting.

"Then there's another text, supposedly 16th century Florentine, discussing ways around the rule banning sorcerers from attacking each other with spells. I find myself wondering who wrote that. Who was supposed to read it? Did they believe what they were saying? Whichever document you choose, they all seem to cry out for further investigation."

Susan nodded. "I can't wait to get started," she agreed.

Bernie replied, "Well, I'm done here." Somehow, as he'd been speaking he'd found time to eat a couple of doughnuts and drain his mug of tea. "Let's go below. You know, there's as much of this building below ground as there is above. We'll be in basement two, right at the bottom. Wonderful environment for storing documents, providing you keep the moisture level right down. You're not claustrophobic, are you? Anyway, you'll get used to it pretty quickly."

Bernie led Susan back to the main hall and around to an old, cage-style lift big enough to hold a grand piano. To enter the building Susan had come up a flight of steps, which meant that the ground floor she stood on was nearly two metres above street level. As the lift descended, it passed a lower-ground floor, set a little below the street outside. Beneath that were two more floors, where sunlight was replaced by fluorescent light. Above the lift controls, a row of indicators lit up in sequence, tracking their descent. As they reached the bottom of the building, the leftmost light was illuminated. The label above it read '-2'.

Bernie took Susan to a large room opposite the lift entrance. Overall it was dimly lit, but bright task lighting illuminated the tables or workstations that were in use. Bernie spent a couple of minutes showing Susan where everything was, how to open the document store and how to log on to a workstation. He left her looking through documents and went off to get her an ID card.

Susan inspected several documents in the store and removed one. She placed it on the stand which sat next to her chosen workstation and turned on its little halogen light. Then she pulled a yellow pad and a draughtsman's pen from her bag and began to make notes. She hardly looked up when Bernie returned.

Two hours passed before Susan paused. She put down her pen and turned to Bernie, reminding him about the document scanning.

Bernie showed her how to use their new planetary camera as well as the flatbed scanner. Susan got straight to work, spending an hour efficiently scanning papers before Bernie announced that he was going home.

"Thanks for all your help, Bernie," Susan said. "We'll catch up in the morning, OK? Make a plan for my time here."

Bernie agreed and said, "Don't work too late. They'll ask you to leave at nine, anyway."

"Hey, Bernie, is it possible to make a phone call? I want to call my Professor in Cambridge," Susan asked.

"Ah yes, the famous Professor Shaw. Our Dean here was one of his old students – possibly during the crusades. Oh, no offence intended," Bernie said.

There was a code for making long distance calls and Bernie wrote it on a Post-it note. Then with a little wave he was gone.

A couple of other researchers had wandered in and out during the course of the afternoon, but Susan now had the room to herself. Most of it was in darkness.

She moved to the next desk, which had a phone on it, punched in Bernie's code and then a number from memory. It was answered promptly.

"Professor, it's Susan Milton."

"Susan, my dear, how are you getting on?"

"Professor, it's fabulous. I have to thank you for sending me down here. They're going to have to throw me out or I'm never going to leave. This collection is amazing."

"There now, that's just as I hoped."

"Listen, Professor, are you OK to talk? I don't want to interrupt anything."

"I've just received a brochure offering holidays in Tuscany. Some of them look rather inviting, but I don't mind putting off a detailed review of their merits for a few minutes since you've been kind enough to call."

Susan said, "I'm sure you're right in the middle of something important, but it's really sweet of you to deny it. Can I tell you what I've been working on this afternoon?"

They chatted happily for a few minutes, with the Professor making occasional suggestions or asking for more information when a particular detail caught his interest.

After a little while, the Professor said, "And everyone is behaving themselves and treating you well, I hope."

"Oh god, what did you do?" Susan asked, suddenly aghast, "I heard the

Dean was an old student of yours. Did you threaten to call his parents, or something, if he didn't treat me like royalty?"

He chided her, "You really do have such an undisciplined imagination for an otherwise sensible young woman. I might perhaps, in passing, have expressed an interest in your well-being. I certainly don't recall any explicit threats."

"Well, my thanks to you and Humphrey Bogart. This guy, Bernie Lampwick, has been taking great care of me. He was a little jumpy at first, which at the time I put down to my arresting presence. Fear for his life might have played a part in it, I can see now. Although it doesn't help matters that these guys don't talk to a woman from one year to the next. Anyhow, we're getting on fine now."

"Splendid. So long as it's all plain sailing, I'll leave well alone. Now have you had a chance to visit the house yet?"

"No, I came straight to the School. If it's OK, I'd like to stay there tonight." She glanced at the clock on the wall, "I don't have time to make any other arrangements."

"And neither should you. Unless you really can't abide the place, it seems obvious to me that you should stay there." Then, as though he were thinking carefully, he added, "Though I suppose I could talk to the Dean about finding you somewhere else?"

Susan snorted, "Yeah, I'd probably end up with the keys to his place while he slept in his office. No, I can take a hint. If it's really OK with you, then I'd be honoured to stay there. I've got one more call to make and then I'm going to head over there, see it in the light."

"Maybe you'll let me know how you find it."

"Sure thing. I'll phone around this time tomorrow, if that's OK."

"I shall look forward to it. Now don't let me keep you."

"Yup, thanks again, Professor."

"Goodbye Susan."

Susan set the phone down slowly. She was looking off into an imaginary distance with a fond smile on her face. She didn't move for a few moments. Then, coming back to life, she rooted around in her bag and pulled out an address book. She flipped to 'D' and glanced at her watch. She paused and tapped one of her bottom teeth with a thumbnail. Then, resolved, she pulled out an international phone card, pinned the phone between her shoulder and her neck and once again punched in Bernie's code. Then she entered a long string of digits, three at a time, reading from the card and then her address book.

It rang a couple of times – the single, long hum of an American exchange, not the double trill of the U.K.

"Dee," a woman's voice said.

"Hey, Dee, it's Susan," she said, not sounding too sure.

"Wo, Sis," the tone effervescent and confident, "where you been? I've been leaving messages for a week."

"Sorry, Dee, I've been travelling with work," she said, sounding a little down-trodden. She volunteered, "I'm in London at the moment. Gonna be here a couple of weeks at least."

"That's perfect, Susie. I wanna come over. You've been there god knows how long, I never see you except at Christmas and I've never been to England. I've got a conference over there coming up and I thought I'd see my big sis and check out all those British guys you've got hanging round you. See if any of them look good enough to steal."

"Dee, that's not even funny. And what do you mean you're coming over? I thought you hated anywhere that wasn't New York."

"Listen, you can't say no, you're family, it's like a legal contract or something. *Sue casa, me casa*, remember? I've got it here in black and white. So have you got somewhere for me to stay in London or am I going to have to find some Fawlty Towers motel?"

"I don't know. I'm going to be staying in this place my Professor owns, but I haven't been along to see what it's like yet. Could you call me in a couple of days once I know more? You're really serious about coming?"

"Don't sound so horrified, Susie. I won't ruin your life or anything. Just tell your friends that I'm adopted or something, they need never know you've got a low-brow sibling."

"Dee, don't. It wouldn't make any difference to me if you'd never finished the eighth grade. I'm not embarrassed about you; I'm just busy. God, you make more money in a month than I make in a year. You're ridiculously successful."

"This is new. Flattery. Well, I could get to like it. So listen, I'll call you with the details in a day or two. Meantime, you want me to get you anything? I'm going shopping this weekend. Unless you've piled on the pounds you should still look pretty good in anything that fits me. How about that Betsey Johnson top I told you about?"

"That's really generous, Dee, but I don't wear anything with a neck line below my navel. The floral one was more my thing."

"God it's no wonder you ended up surrounded by books. I'll get you the little virginal embroidered one. So, um, you called Mom recently?"

"Have you?"

"I called her about a week ago. Well, maybe a couple of weeks. We should go and see them. Come over during your summer break."

"Nah, that's just a student thing. I don't get a summer break anymore, but I'll call her. I will."

"Good. OK, Susie, gotta hustle. We sure appreciate your call and y'all have a good day."

"Bye Dee."

Susan hung up. She flipped through her address book to 'M' and sat thinking for a while. Then she snapped the little book shut and began to gather up her things.

CHAPTER 6

TWO DAYS LATER
THURSDAY 10TH APRIL

D avid was back at the scene of the break-in. He'd parked a few streets away and walked, briefcase in hand, towards the office block. There was no sign that the building had been the centre of so much activity earlier in the week.

Climbing the front steps, he glanced at the lock on the front doors. The plate around the keyhole had a mirror finish – brand new. He pulled open the door and stepped into the reception area.

Glancing to his left, he could see, behind the smoked-glass cover, a new alarm panel. An LCD display featured prominently on the new model. Instead of black, the replacement panel was pale cream, matching the walls.

David approached the reception desk where an over-made-up girl in her late teens sat talking into a headset. "Gotta go, yeah?" she whispered into the mike and pressed a button on the console in front of her.

She activated a smile wide enough to display her back teeth. "Hell-oo!" she said, in the sing-song speech of switchboard operators, and tilted her head to one side.

"Hi, I'm David Braun from Marshall and Liberty. I'm here to see Alessandro Dass," David said. As he spoke the Chairman's name, the receptionist's smile lost a little power.

"Was he expecting you?" she asked. David nodded, "Nine thirty appointment." He checked his wristwatch: 09.25.

"I'll just…" she said and glanced up towards the ceiling. She tapped a number into her console.

"Mrs Billings, it's Stephanie. I've got a young man here," she glanced at David and pursed her lips, "to see Mr Dass."

David fished a business card out of his top pocket and handed it to her just as she asked, "What was your name again?"

Stephanie read the name, listened for a moment and said, "Right." She punched a button and looked back to David. "Someone is coming for you. If you'd like to take a seat." She indicated two orange banquettes set against the wall between a shrub and a low table. The table held newspapers.

David sat himself down and began to flick through the sports section of the Telegraph. He didn't get very far. A stern, stick-like woman dressed in a dark-brown sleeveless sack-dress appeared at his side with a tinkle of bracelets. She had the leathery skin of the perma-tanned and it suited her expression well.

"The Chairman was expecting you at eleven," she said flatly. David's jaw tightened a little. Then it relaxed.

Getting up he said pleasantly, "Whatever's most convenient for Mr Dass." He set down the newspaper. "Why don't I come back at eleven?"

There was an impatient sigh. "I'll see if Mr Dass is prepared to see you now anyway," she said, though her tone suggested it was asking a great deal.

"Please, Mrs Billings, don't put Mr Dass to any trouble. If he's expecting me at eleven, why disappoint him?" he asked amiably, spreading his hands, palms up.

Mrs Billings narrowed her eyes suspiciously at David. The slitted gaze made her leathery face resemble a baby Cayman's.

"There's no point now you're here," she said testily. "You might as well come up." She turned and walked to the stairs. David followed.

As David passed Stephanie at the reception desk she caught his eye, flicked her gaze to the departing back of the Chairman's secretary and, opening her mouth expressively wide, mouthed the word 'Bitch'.

David laughed despite himself, but not loud enough for Mrs Billings to hear. He followed her upstairs.

She took him to the second floor, down a long carpeted corridor. A desk set at an angle narrowed the corridor, creating a secretarial checkpoint which any visitors would need to pass. A sign on the desk read 'M. Billings'.

Beyond the desk were two doors.

Mrs Billings held up a hand, indicating 'stop' and tapped on the right-hand door. She opened the door a little and put her head round it. When she pulled back, the last traces of what must have been a sunny smile were giving way to hard frost. Winter had once more set in when she turned to David and said, "The Chairman will see you."

David squeezed past her into an expensively, if tastelessly, decorated office. Behind a broad and nearly empty beechwood desk sat an immaculately dressed man in a cream suit – the cut of which, and the way it blended perfectly with the pale silk tie and off-white shirt, made him look almost like a fashion plate. His skin, tanned and lined, but with the distinguished ruggedness cultivated by mature movie stars, glowed with health. His silver hair was thick and impeccably neat. He smiled – his teeth too were perfect – and the contrast with his dark, expressionless eyes was unsettling.

David approached the desk and held out his hand, saying, "Mr Dass."

Dass stood and gripped David's hand for a tiny fraction of a second. Mrs Billings was still hovering at the door. Dass said, "Thank you, Maureen." She closed the door behind her.

"What can I do to help, Mr Dass?" David asked. They were both standing now. Dass had tilted his head back and was staring at a point some distance beyond the ceiling. He pursed his lips, thoughtfully.

Dass's voice was rich, the accent Italian and cultured. "Marshall and Liberty – we have done business with them for a number of years. Just over one hundred if my history serves me."

He went on, "We have always found them to be attentive. They don't go in for this modern marketing." He said the word with great distaste. "Special offers or the like." His tone became firmer, "A company doing something well for their customers has no need of those things, all the clamouring and pleading for business. Do not beg for your customers' trust; earn it. Well, Marshall and Liberty have earned *our* trust."

Dass was still gazing at the ceiling, not at David, so David made no reply; he simply waited.

Dass said, "You – oh now what is that expression? – put the policeman's nose out of joint with your detective work the other night. The third man. That was you?" He glanced at David.

"Yes," David said.

Dass smiled and looked around him. He said softly, almost to himself, "My god, but this is a hideous office. Why does a country that could command an empire allow its greatness to slip away? Weak governments, lazy civil servants, corrupt policemen – the newspapers talk of little else," he pivoted his hand so that his pointing finger took in the room, "and designers who don't design." He swished his hand, waving the thought away.

"Yes, this third man intrigues us. One man on the inside who worked here, *yes*, a second who understands alarm systems and security, *certainly*, but a third man who has the brains," Dass tapped the middle of his forehead, "to conceive of the idea. Someone who thinks, someone who plans – perhaps someone who first observes."

Dass walked over to the far corner of his office and pulled open a door. Inside a light came on revealing an alcove. A moment later Dass pushed the door closed again. "Interfinanzio is an old company. In a sense it is a family company. Like any family it has its heirlooms, its little treasures."

Dass suddenly dropped down into one of the room's two armchairs. His movements were lithe, much younger than his grey hair and lined face would have suggested. "Forgive the unpleasant topic, but I once met a man, an American, who collected famous racehorses. Not, you understand while they were still with us, as it were. Dead creatures. What fascination does something like that hold? He had made for himself a private room, like a museum." Dass again made a dismissive gesture, a swipe of his hand. "No, it is unfathomable," he sneered.

He continued, "At any rate, I suspect he saw not the dead flesh but the former glory. The symbolism comes not from the thing itself; it originates in the mind of those regarding it. And how could it be any different? So it is with the matter that brings you here. You have come to discuss those things which to my people are powerful symbols, things which resonate with past glories."

Dass was still not looking directly at David; he was staring at a painting above his desk. It was a dark, abstract impressionist piece suggestive of too many paint colours mixed together. He looked slightly troubled by it, or by whatever he was thinking as his gaze rested there. David still stood in the centre of the room, his briefcase held in both hands in front of him.

Dass pointed to the door that he had opened a moment before. "There is a safe within. It has been opened."

David stirred.

Dass gestured towards the other armchair, "Sit. Make notes." David sat down, his briefcase on his lap. He opened the case, slipped out a pad and laid it on top of the case. He pulled a fountain pen from his inside jacket pocket and began writing.

Dass said, "I think somehow our third man learned that I was to be in England for a time. Perhaps he knew that there are one or two of our family treasures that we like to have with us. I am speaking of this because we have faith in Marshall and Liberty, in their seriousness, in their discretion.

"There are other institutions which inspire in us considerably less faith. Your detective work the other night revealed the error I would make if I placed myself entirely in the hands of the police. The police whom I read of everyday in my newspaper, the police who cannot count as high as three without assistance from a professional," he indicated David, "a competent and thorough mind dedicated to his company."

Dass looked directly at David now. He turned his dark eyes to David's with such sudden intensity that David flinched. For a moment David couldn't meet his stare. An expression which might have been fear rippled across David's face. But a second later, he had brought his gaze up to connect with Dass's. As eye contact was made, David blinked once, involuntarily, but did not look away.

Dass stood and looked down at David. His voice was light, almost airy, but the intensity of his expression was startling. "I may call you David? Listen to me David. I want you to investigate this theft. I wish you to undertake this task. I wish for the police to keep you informed of their progress so that you can add what they know to whatever you learn. I have not lived this long without making some friends, so this will not be a problem. But I must have someone in whom I can place my faith at the centre of this matter."

David began to speak, struggled to get the words out, but Dass held up a hand. His eyes still drilled into David's.

"Let us understand, I am not asking anything improper. I wish you to establish a liaison with the police, to acquaint yourself with this incident and to push forward independently whenever you discern that their efforts are falling short. I am aware that facts are checked whenever a client is suspected of misleading his insurer. Details are verified and investigators are hired in secrecy. Well, on this occasion it is to be done with the client's approval – and if it is successful – with their grateful appreciation.

"We would like to recover what we have lost, without publicity, without noise or untidiness." Dass paused and turned over one hand. "I could of course content myself with making an insurance claim." He waved his hands lightly to indicate that this was the easiest thing in the world. "I could satisfy myself with a sum of money in place of a treasure that has been held dear by our family since Alexander VI was Pope. Although I fear that Marshall and Liberty would find that a costly decision. One is hardly aware of the monetary value which something possesses until one comes to pay for its loss. No, I doubt Marshall and Liberty would survive such a decision and it is almost unthinkable to me that we would follow that course when it may still be that we can recover what we have lost." As he finished speaking, Dass disengaged his piercing gaze and once more let his eyes roam upwards towards the ceiling. His focus returned to whatever it was that he perceived beyond the walls of the office.

David found that he had been holding his breath and let it out quietly. He looked back down at his notes and readied his pen. A gleam of perspiration had appeared at his hairline.

Dass said, "I regret that I cannot give you photographs. We have always felt that invisibility to the world at large was the best protection for our treasures." He frowned and spread his hands a little, allowing that he may have been mistaken. "But we are speaking of something of great antiquity. A box of unusual construction, covered in leather, the structure made from bone."

He explained, "The building materials of the time." Then he went on, "Inside is an ornament, a filigree of intricate design. The metal is platinum, beloved of the Incas and the Ancient Egyptians, though we do not believe this piece originated in either of those two empires. It is from the East, from China and the only one of its kind."

Dass stood, crossed to his desk and opened a drawer. He took out a single sheet of paper and a pencil and began to sketch. "There was an attempt made to steal the piece some years ago. Very powerful criminals. Since then we have allowed no explicit reports of its existence to circulate. Your company's records, for instance, do list the item (though I trust they will not have volunteered that information to you until now) but they do so in a roundabout way. A precise weight, a length and width, the total distance the interlocking design would reach if it were stretched out. No pictures, no drawings.

"In effect, we have given them a riddle to which the lost item is the answer – enough to recognise it, but not enough to describe it." He was nearly finished drawing. "But you may require a little more information."

"The man who took this," Dass indicated the drawing, "must have reasoned that we would not wish the police – and moments later the world – to know of its existence and thus we could not report its loss. That in turn would mean the investigation would be closed – because there would be no reason for the police to suspect the involvement of a third man. Not only did you establish the third man's existence independently, but you also provided us with a way to report a theft without revealing our secret. The police have a misleading description of what has been taken; you will work alongside them, entrusted with the truth."

Dass stopped sketching and held up the results. A weaving, intertwining web of lines criss-crossed the page, forming an intricate Mandala. Overall, the pattern looked a little like a feather, but broad like a palm leaf and symmetrical about its centre line. "It was once revered for its mystical properties, in more primitive times, as I suppose is any item of exceptional antiquity. I'm told if one travels sufficiently widely in China and talks to enough people, one can still hear stories that link it with various fables and folk tales, despite the fact that it was removed from China centuries ago."

From the pocket of his immaculate suit, Dass retrieved a slim Dunhill lighter. With a tiny pop it produced a flame which Dass waved under the lower edge of the paper. "I have no wish for melodrama, but it will not be through me that a description of our lost treasure reaches the avid collectors of the world. I hope, likewise, it will not be through you," Dass said, giving David another dose of his direct, penetrating gaze. He maintained eye contact with David as the drawing burned brightly and little scraps of ash began to move around the room. When the paper had burned down to Dass's fingers he allowed the black, ash-ghost of the paper to drop into the bin by his desk. He appeared untroubled by the flames touching his fingers. "I love to cook," he volunteered, "It teaches one not to be afraid of a little heat."

He bent and stirred the perfect tissue of ash, breaking it up. With his other hand he produced a handkerchief in lemon silk and cleaned his fingers.

"Call my secretary if I can help with your quest. Perhaps you will be good enough to keep me informed of your progress," Dass said.

The interview was evidently over; David returned the notepad to his case with unsteady hands, stood and moved towards the door. Dass was still dabbing at his fingers. "Forgive me if I don't shake your hand," he said.

David nodded, numbly, and twisted the door handle with a damp palm. He stepped out into the corridor beyond and pushed the door closed, leaning back against it for a moment.

He made a fist with his hand, which was trembling. He was visibly shaken. He closed his eyes for a moment. Then, shakily echoing Dass's actions, he fumbled for a handkerchief, wiping at the perspiration on his forehead.

He opened his eyes to see Mrs Billings seated behind her desk, scrutinising him like a cat regards a mouse. She had an almost sensual grin on her face. "Is something wrong?" she asked, sounding delighted at his lack of composure.

He didn't reply. Gathering himself, David strode rapidly past her, with a curt 'goodbye' as he did so, and made his way briskly down to reception. He walked past Stephanie, without heeding her attempts to attract his attention, and out into the street. He headed towards his car.

On the corner before the car park stood a pub. Outside on the pavement a sign read, "Morning coffees, cappuccinos, open for breakfast." David went in. Two dusty looking builders were standing at one end of the bar drinking pints. Around them, several tables were occupied by people eating cooked breakfasts. David ordered a pint of Guinness, glancing at his watch as he did so. The time was 10.04.

Once he had been served, he made his way to the table furthest from the door and sat, sipping at his drink for some minutes. He placed one hand on the table in front of him. It was almost steady, though a slight tremor could still be detected.

He took out his mobile phone and retrieved a number from its memory. He held the phone to his ear.

"Kieran, it's David." He listened to the reply.

Then he said, "Fine, thank you. Listen, are you free for lunch? I want to pick your brains, so choose anywhere you like and the company will pay."

He listened and then said, "I'll tell you when I see you, but you're free then?"

Another pause and he said, "Yes, who'd have thought it? I'm sure I was never quite that critical about history, but I take your point. Let's hope all that expertise is what I need for this project."

Pause. "No, early is good. I'll meet you there then. Call me if you're held up."

Pause. "Great. See you at twelve."

David hung up and put the phone back in his pocket. He took out the notepad. He continued to sip from his pint and make occasional notes as they occurred to him, until his glass was empty.

He took the glass up to the bar and noticed that they sold mints. He bought a pack and put one in his mouth. Then he headed back to his car.

* * *

Two hours later he was seated opposite Kieran in a smart, West End brasserie. Many of the diners wore suits, most of the rest were dressed with an eye to fashion; Kieran was the only one wearing an open-collared polo shirt.

"I wish you'd given me more notice, I feel I'm letting the side down coming here in my civvies," Kieran said.

David smiled pleasantly, looking past him to the street outside the restaurant. He took a sip of his water.

Kieran asked, "Are you alright David? You seem a bit not-altogether-with-us. Tough morning in the salt mines?"

"Sorry Kieran. I met the most… Have you ever met anyone who just frightens the life out of you and you don't know why?" David said.

Kieran looked at him for a moment and said, "All the time. I'm a librarian. But the thought that there are people in the world who scare you is an unsettling one. Who is this Neanderthal?"

"A client. A businessman. He must be in his sixties, not big, not hostile – quite polite actually – but I almost couldn't look him in the eye." David was still gazing out at the street.

"God almighty. Well whoever he is, he must have something about him. Didn't he realise you could have killed him with your little finger?" Kieran asked.

David snorted and looked at Kieran, "Evidently not. Anyway, forget all that. How are you, how's things?"

"Things? You mean Hope? You know she's in Hollywood now? She's making some film about an escaped wolf that's the product of a CIA genetic engineering program. Sounds awful; will probably do well. We haven't really seen that much of her since you two split up. She calls home occasionally, talking nineteen to the dozen, all insider speak that's wasted on us and then has to dash. I think she's happy for once, though," Kieran said.

"I'm glad she's happy. It's always been important to Hope to feel appreciated. Ideally by several million people at once," David said, smiling.

"Really, I won't have you speak that way about my sister. That's *my* job," Kieran said.

They fell to studying their menus for a minute and then the waiter appeared. Once they had ordered, Kieran said, "Drinking at lunchtime? I thought you were very strict with yourself about that sort of thing. Not part of the warrior monk lifestyle."

David said, "I don't think your sister dates monks, Kieran. And I have a glass of wine every now and then," David sounded a little defensive.

Kieran held up his hands in surrender, "Sorry, didn't mean to get at you."

Just then the drinks arrived and David took a sip of his. "To tell you the truth, I'm still a bit jumpy from my meeting with the Demon Client this morning."

Kieran said, "Is it this client that brings you begging for my help?"

"Buying you an expensive lunch and asking politely for your help, yes. He's lost something and I need to find it. I need to find out who'd want this thing, where someone might try to sell it, who to talk to," David said.

"Sounds like you need an expert. Tell me about this missing bauble. What's he lost?" Kieran said.

"Well, The Count was reluctant to give me too much information, but I know it's old, valuable, some sort of intricate piece of Eastern jewellery. If you made a doily from platinum, it might look like that. He said it was from somewhere in China where they still have legends about its magical powers," David said.

Their hors d'oeuvres arrived and they each took a mouthful. Kieran, chewing, held up a fork and gestured towards David with it, "You know what? If it's got some superstitious significance the boys at the School of Antiquities might be able to help you. They've just set up a team to look at all things mythic and venerable. I know the fellow who runs the team, Bernie Lampwick – he was in my house at school."

David nodded, unsurprised. "If he wasn't in your house at school he would have been a friend of the family's or his dad would have been one of your father's indentured servants or something."

"Don't let my father hear you talking like that. He hasn't been allowed to put the rent up in any of the estate's cottages since 1981. He says they live better than he does," Kieran said.

David let that pass and said, "Anyway, can you talk to this Bernie guy? See if he might be prepared to do a couple of day's consultancy for us. The company are fairly generous with this sort of thing; he should get a new set of tweeds out of it."

"I think Bernie's more grunge than county, but I'll call him. Do I get a cut?" Kieran asked.

"You get smoked salmon, followed by *boeuf en croute*, followed by *tarte tatin*, two glasses of wine and a coffee. Not bad for ten seconds work," David said.

"Ten seconds to tell you and a lifetime to build up the contacts and the encyclopaedic knowledge that goes with them. You're getting all that, you know," Kieran said.

"Fair enough. I'll throw in a brandy," David said. "Is Bernie any use at legwork? Would he be prepared to talk to a few dealers, assuming they exist for this sort of item?"

Kieran considered. "Mmm. Bernie's not what you'd call a people person. He gets ulcers if they make him give a lecture. Anyway, leave it with me, I'll find someone capable, with a bit of nous – who's desperate for the cash."

The conversation turned back to Hope, and Kieran's attempt to explain the plot of her current film. He suggested that David come to dinner when Hope returned in the autumn. David wondered aloud whether that was such a good idea. The matter was left unsettled, but they agreed to meet again in a few weeks to catch up properly. No more was said about David's encounter with Dass.

CHAPTER 7

THE NEXT DAY
THURSDAY 10TH APRIL

S usan showed her new badge to the security guard, who nodded and
pushed a foot pedal allowing her through the hip-height turnstile.
She crossed the foyer, glancing up once to catch a glimpse of the
ornamental ceiling. To the right of the main staircase stood the wide cage-
door of the lift. The lift car was waiting for her. She rode down to the lower
basement.

A minute later she was entering the subterranean Alexandrian room.
Bernie was already in and he waved from his corner as he saw her.

Susan put down her bag and her coffee, hung her white rain-coat on the
coat-stand by the door. Bernie sidled over.

"Good morning, Susan. How are you today?" Bernie asked.

"Peachy. You OK?" Susan said cheerfully.

"Oh, yes. Marvellous. Um. I wanted to talk to you about something,"
Bernie said, his tendency towards nervousness evident once again.

Susan, who was now sitting down, thrust out one of her legs and pulled
a nearby chair out from under its desk with her foot. "Sure. Sit down,"
she said, rotating her chair towards Bernie's and reaching back over her

shoulder to retrieve her Starbucks cup.

Bernie sat down, leaning back. He looked uncomfortable like that and leaned forwards instead. "I had a call from an old friend of mine last night. It seems he knows someone who works in insurance. They've got a client who's lost a rare antique and they want some expert guidance on where it might turn up. The piece they're looking for seemed like the sort of thing you might know about."

Susan said nothing and Bernie hastily added, "I didn't say you'd definitely do it. Certainly not." Bernie was smiling nervously as though there was more to his tale than what he'd said.

"But…" Susan said, inquiringly.

"Mmm. But I said you'd talk to the man from the insurance company," Bernie said, raising his eyes to Susan, gauging her reaction.

Susan showed no sign that she was displeased. "They pay for that sort of help, don't they?" she asked, intrigued.

Bernie nodded. "Good money, I believe. My friend suggested they were looking for a few days assistance, probably not all at once, but spread out over a couple of weeks. Research the lost item, write a little memo pointing their investigator in the right direction, maybe accompany him to a couple of dealers or auctions. He wasn't sure of the specifics, but you get the idea."

Susan said, "Well, you know, that actually sounds kind of fun. I'm not up for taking much time out, though. How did you leave it with him?"

"Well, I said I'd ask if you'd meet the insurance chappie this afternoon. I've got his number here," Bernie said, attempting to hand Susan a Post-it note, which remained attached to his fingers. He tried again, but it was still stuck to his hand.

"Bernie!" she said firmly, to attract his attention. As he looked up, she darted out a hand to pluck the note from his grasp so swiftly he didn't have time to move. She turned it around so that it was readable and looked at the number.

"Thanks for setting this up, Bernie. I might get kind of a kick out of it. And god knows I could do with a few extra bucks," she said.

"Oh well then," Bernie said, looking happier, "that's good." He got up to return to his workstation.

"Oh, hey, Bernie," Susan said. "I'm going out in a little while. I'm going to drop in on the woman who donated this collection, Teracus's landlady. If I meet this guy this afternoon, that might be it for the day. I thought someone should know where I am. You might think I'm playing hooky or something."

Bernie didn't look sure what to do with this information. "Don't think me... I hope you don't mind me asking, but why do you want to see her?"

"Lots of reasons. I want to know more about where all this stuff came from. I want to know if there could be any more. I'm also pretty curious to know who this Teracus guy really was." She concluded, "I'll tell you what I discover tomorrow."

Bernie smiled appreciatively and nodded a couple of times, returning to his side of the room.

Susan took another sip of her latte and stuck Bernie's Post-it to her phone. She hooked the handset under her shoulder and started pushing numbers.

"David Braun," a voice said after the second ring.

"David, hi, I'm Susan Milton. Bernie Lampwick gave me your number," Susan said.

"Ms Milton, hi. So do you think you might be interested?" David asked.

"Could be. Bernie said you wanted to meet with me this afternoon. Have you got a plan?" she said.

"For this afternoon? Not really. Let's make one. When are you free?" David asked.

"If it's Central London, I can be anywhere by four. We could do earlier, but I'm taking a little trip and I don't know how long it will take," Susan said.

"Then let's say four. How about the Natural History Museum by the big dinosaur in the entrance hall?" David said.

Susan laughed. "You're for real, right? This is about insurance."

"I swear on my actuarial tables. You can come to the office if you'd be more comfortable there. I just thought..."

"No, no. The dinosaur's fine. I've been meaning to visit that place since

I came to England," Susan said.

"That's easy then. Save any travel receipts and I'll reimburse you," David said.

"Not a problem. So, er, what do you look like?" Susan asked.

"According to most of my friends, a security guard. Anyway, I'll be the one visiting a museum in a suit. Call my mobile if you can't see me," David said.

"Great. Listen, I gotta run. I'll be there at four," Susan said.

"Bye."

Susan hung up. She fished her address book out of her bag and wrote David's name and number into it.

Then she flipped to 'H' and dialled again.

The phone was answered with, "Hello?" It was the brittle voice of an older woman.

"Mrs Harris, it's Susan from the University," Susan said.

"Oh, call me Hilda, pet," Mrs Harris said.

"Thank you. Is it still OK if I drop in to talk to you a little later?" Susan asked.

"Of course, dear. You come when you like. I've made some scones. There's too many for me anyway."

"I hope you haven't gone to a lot of trouble… Hilda. If I come over at midday, is that OK?" Susan said.

"It's no bother. I'll be here all day. 'Cept I might pop to the shops for a bit of fish later. I love a bit of fish for my tea and so does Herbert. You'll meet my little boy later. You're not allergic are you?" Hilda said.

"To cats," Susan guessed.

"To the fur."

"No. I like cats. I'll look forward to meeting you, and Herbert, at twelve," Susan said.

"Won't that be nice for us," Hilda said, though apparently not to Susan.

"See you later Hilda," Susan said.

"Righto, dear."

Susan hung up.

She had nearly completed the scanning of the collection. After making her calls, she finished running the last few documents through the planetary camera. Then she burned a CD-ROM with the entire collection on it. She slotted it into the optical drive of her iBook, before slipping the laptop into her courier bag.

Then it was time for her to leave. She caught the lift up to the surface, emerged into the bright April sunshine, and strode towards Russell Square tube station.

An hour later she was in the far west of London, walking through Brentford, an A-to-Z in her hand.

The residential street she was walking along had a kink near its halfway point, almost as though building work had started from both ends but hadn't quite met in the middle. Susan's destination was set in the crook of the first twist.

When she found herself outside the right address, she took a moment to look up at the house. It was a large, but shabby, detached house, circa 1920s. Set in the centre of the crazy-paved front garden was a tiny oval of flowerbed. It contained healthy-looking roses with huge, floppy, pale-pink blossoms already in bloom.

Susan opened the wrought iron gate and stepped up to the front door. She pushed the buzzer and heard a distant, electronic rendition of *Green Sleeves*. A moment later a woman in her late sixties, her lacquered hair a vibrant blonde, opened the door. She wore beige slacks and a white, long-sleeved top with a tiger embroidered in sparkly gold thread on the front. Underneath the tiger was the word 'Nepal'.

"Hi, I'm Susan," Susan said.

"Oh hello dear. Did you find us alright? Come on in," Hilda said. Inside the main door, a tiny vestibule contained two more front doors. The one to the left was open, revealing walls decorated with red textured wallpaper and a room dominated by a three-piece suite in light pink.

Hilda led Susan through. "I'll pop the kettle on. Tea or instant?" Hilda asked.

"Tea please," Susan said.

Hilda had Susan sit on the large sofa by the window. Behind her, ruched, fuchsia curtains framed the view of the street. Once Susan was seated, Hilda went off to fuss in the kitchen, occasionally calling back partly audible snippets concerning the weather and the amount of litter in the street.

In a little while, the tea was made and brought through, a plate of bourbon biscuits had been placed on the teak-veneer and glass occasional-table by Susan's knee and Hilda had taken her seat by the door. A red square of cloth lay over the right arm of Hilda's chair and the reason for this soon became apparent when a chubby black cat wandered in, from the direction of the kitchen, whined once towards Susan and jumped onto the cloth. He folded himself up neatly so that his legs were tucked beneath him and then he looked towards Susan.

Hilda seemed to take this as a signal to begin and said, "Terry was a lovely man. Very quiet. Always very wrapped up in his collections but never a bit of bother to me. I shed a little tear when I heard he'd passed on. He had my upstairs room ever since Herbert, that's my husband as was and not his little namesake here, kitted it out, which must have been 1977, because the tea-towels were all silver jubilee ones," she whispered, "from the market." Then continued, "Don't you think all her pictures since then are a fright? If I was the one took that picture of her that's on the money now, I'd be waiting for my trip to The Tower. I can't see why she puts up with it," Hilda said.

Susan was about to speak when Hilda picked up the teapot, swirled it a couple of times and poured out two steaming cups of tea. Even with milk added, there was a red tinge to the brew that suggested considerable strength.

"Thanks," Susan said when she was handed her cup and saucer. The crockery was bone china with pastoral scenes in pastel colours adorning its white surfaces – mainly maids with streamers.

"Do you know what else Terry did, besides work on his collection?" Susan asked.

"I never saw him take much of an interest in anything else. I think he did other work, but not for long. He was away a great deal. A lot of his little scraps he collected were foreign, and I don't mean nearby foreign. Proper foreign, like Africa or Nepal." She glanced down at her top. "He brought this back for me. I was always teasing him that he never got himself any sort of colour while he was away. How can you spend a month in Africa and come home pale as a bed sheet? But I don't suppose he stirred from his hotel. Somehow I can't picture him outdoors," Hilda said, looking thoughtful for a moment.

"Do you know why he kept the collection? He doesn't seem to have sold anything, so it wasn't really a business. Was it just for him?" Susan asked.

"I've never really thought about it, but he never had anyone round. So it wasn't exactly a lending library, if you know what I mean. No, it was his hobby, was what it was. There's lots worse things to collect than old paper and I reckon there's probably some valuable bits of history in there." She caught Susan's eye. "Have your lot gone over it yet?" she asked.

"Well, there's a great deal more to do, but, yes, we've spent a lot of time looking through it. It's extraordinary and we're all very grateful that you passed it on to us," Susan said.

"Well, even though Terry wouldn't be happy with a lot of strangers going through his things, I had a long think about it, and I reckon he'd have liked it even less if the whole lot went in the bin. No, it came to me that I needed to find a home for it. If it had to be strangers who got their hands on it, I like to think Terry would have preferred it to be someone who'd take good care of it and get pleasure from it like he did," Hilda said.

"So where did he keep the collection?" Susan asked. At that moment there was a thump from the room above.

Hilda heard it too and looked up towards the ceiling. She answered Susan's question absent-mindedly, while cocking her ear towards the door. "He had a big tin footlocker bolted into the wall up there. The key was with his things when the police returned his effects. All his collection was in there except…" There was another sound from upstairs, like a rusty hinge and the sound of weight being shifted. Hilda looked up at the ceiling.

"Is everything alright?" Susan asked.

"I wonder if Herbert's got himself shut in… Bless me, what am I saying, you're right here aren't you darling? I must have left a window ajar or something. I better have a look-see in case the wind's whistling through the place."

Hilda set her tea down and went in to the kitchen. She came back a moment later with a brass key on a loop of postman's string.

"I won't be a minute, dear. Help yourself to more tea," she said and opened the front door. She slipped the key into the lock of the other door in the vestibule and then Susan could hear the hollow thump, thump of footsteps as Hilda climbed stairs that must have lay just the other side of her front room wall.

Susan sipped her tea, barely wetting her tongue. She made a face and set the cup down. She could hear Hilda moving around upstairs.

Then there was a heavy thump and a sound like a gasp or a cry. Susan stood up. She called in the general direction of the door, "Is everything alright, Mrs Harris?" while her eyes roved the room.

In the brick fireplace stood an electric, flame-effect fire and by it a set of ornamental irons. Susan took the short poker, gripping it firmly in her right fist and went out the open front door.

She stepped in through the door of the other flat and began climbing the stairs, the poker held out in front of her. "Mrs Harris, do you want one of us to come up?" she called, loudly.

She heard a yelp and climbed the rest of the uncarpeted stairs quickly.

At the top of the staircase was a large room. One side held a bed, the other a writing desk and a filing cabinet. The far wall was mainly windows. On the floor in the middle of the room lay Mrs Harris struggling to get up. A figure, a man all in black, was standing just outside the window.

The figure looked towards Susan once and then ran along whatever he was standing on and dropped from sight. Before he did so, his right side was visible. He was wearing a long-sleeved black top from which most of the right sleeve was ripped. Susan could see his muscular upper arm. A large, dark blotch was spread across the olive skin of his bicep. Two smaller patches marked his forearm.

Holding the poker high, Susan rushed to the window. The house had been extended on the ground floor, but not upstairs, which left a flat roof, like a terrace, stretching five metres beyond the upstairs window.

Susan looked out, but the man had gone.

She quickly latched the window closed and ran back to where Hilda lay.

Hilda was struggling to rise and to speak, her mouth working soundlessly and a look of wild-eyed panic on her face. She didn't seem to register

Susan's presence.

"Mrs Harris," Susan repeated several times, but Hilda didn't focus on her. For a moment, Susan tried to help her up, but the older woman's legs weren't solid and she tumbled back to the floor, nearly dragging Susan with her.

"Don't worry Hilda, I'll be right back," Susan said. She ran back downstairs and into the front room. A white, cordless phone sat on the table by the armchair (which Herbert had vacated). Susan grabbed it and pushed the green button to get a dialling tone. She dialled 999 and asked for an ambulance. She gave as many details as she could, guessing Hilda's age at a little short of seventy. She had no idea what her injuries might be. As she talked, she made her way upstairs again, extending the aerial of the cordless phone to maintain reception.

When she was finished with the call she hung up and laid the phone down at the top of the stairs. Taking a pillow from the bed in the corner, she put it under Hilda's head and tried to persuade her to lie back and to stop her struggling. Susan held her hand, patting it gently.

A few moments later, she released Hilda's hand and picked up the phone again. She dialled 999 once more, pushing the numbers with her thumb, and asked for the police.

It was the police who arrived first, about three minutes after her call. When she heard the doorbell, Susan released Hilda's hand and took up the poker again. She went downstairs to the outer door where she could clearly see, through the frosted glass window, two figures in uniform. She opened the door, letting the policemen in.

She led them straight upstairs.

"What happened, Miss?" asked the policeman who was crouching next to Hilda.

"We were downstairs. She came up here to investigate a noise and someone was here. I thought I heard – well I don't know what exactly – but she sounded like she was in trouble. I called out and came up. There was a man on the roof, but he disappeared a moment later," she said.

The other policeman had been examining the metal footlocker by the bed; its lid was torn nearly off its hinges. He moved over to the window, opened it and stepped out onto the roof. He began talking into his lapel mike as he peered over the edge of the gravelled, asphalt surface.

The first policeman talked soothingly to Hilda, "Don't you worry, love. You're alright now. Don't you worry." Then to Susan he said softly, "You can probably put that poker down now." Susan was still holding it in her left hand and she let out a little sigh, almost a laugh.

"I think I hear the ambulance," she said a moment later. She went downstairs, detoured quickly to return the poker and the phone, and went out to greet the two ambulance men who were moving quickly towards the front door. She led them to Hilda and told them what little she knew.

With the upstairs room getting a little crowded, Susan returned again to Hilda's front room and retrieved the cordless phone. It had four speed-dial buttons, each with a name next to it. The first button was labelled 'Daisy'.

Susan pushed the button.

When a woman answered, Susan asked, "Excuse me, you're a friend of Hilda Harris's?"

"I'm her sister," the woman replied.

Susan told her what had happened.

Daisy's reaction was shock. She began asking Susan questions, not waiting for the answers, beginning to panic. Susan interrupted in a firm, calm voice, explaining to her what needed doing, reassuring her, and then she began to help Daisy get organised.

Susan gave Daisy her mobile number and had her write it down. Susan would travel with Hilda to the hospital, Daisy could find out what was happening by calling Susan's mobile.

Then Susan asked whether Daisy had a key to Hilda's house. She did. That meant Susan could leave the police to close up and Daisy could let herself in later, if the need arose.

Susan suggested that Daisy take a couple of minutes to calm herself and then travel to the hospital in her own time. Susan would meet her there.

Asking Daisy to hold for a second, Susan checked with the ambulance men which hospital Hilda would be taken to.

When that call was completed, Susan went through the kitchen into the bedroom, found a little valise and packed a few essentials for Hilda. She had just finished when the ambulance men started carrying Hilda down on a stretcher.

Susan took a piece of notepaper from her bag and wrote her contact details on it. Then she gathered up her coat and bag. Once the stretcher had passed the door, the policemen came down. Susan explained to them that she was going with Hilda, gave them the piece of paper listing her details and asked them to pull the door closed once they were done.

Then she flatly refused when the ambulance men told her she should get a taxi. Reluctantly, they let her ride in the front of the ambulance with the driver, while Hilda and the other ambulance man rode in the back.

"Herbert," Susan said, suddenly, remembering. She pulled out a pen and wrote the name on her hand.

CHAPTER 8

S usan Milton was late. David looked at his wristwatch again – 16.49. He paced very slowly round the Diplodocus.

"David Braun?" a soft, female American voice said. There was a little Southern in it and a little East Coast.

David turned to see a pretty girl in dark jeans and a white cotton blouse, clutching a bag and a raincoat and wearing a worried expression.

"Ms Milton?" David said. "Actually, it's Doctor Milton, isn't it?"

Susan didn't answer him directly. She dragged the strap of her bag further up her shoulder and stuck out her hand. They shook and Susan said, "OK. In no special order: I'm really sorry I kept you waiting. Two: call me Susan. And three: I've had an unbelievable bitch of a day, excuse me for saying it, so you might have to go easy on me."

David ticked the points off on his fingers, "No problem. Hi, Susan. And I'm sorry to hear that." He smiled. "Let's get to the café before it closes so at least you can sit down," David said. He led the way and Susan followed.

They entered the cafeteria, which was mostly deserted. David put his folio case down on a chair and gestured for Susan to sit.

"Normally people get dinner for agreeing to talk to me about work. Let me at least fetch you some coffee while you catch your breath," David said. Susan nodded with a weak smile on her face.

As he turned to go she called, "Can you get me a sandwich? I'm famished."

"Absolutely," he said and walked over to pick up a tray and join the queue.

David was the last person in the line. He paid for coffee and several packs of sandwiches and brought them back to the table.

While he'd been queuing, David had glanced over at Susan a couple of times and seen her hunched over, running her fingers through her hair, her head low. As he finished paying, he saw her take a deep breath, and compose herself. She pulled her shoulders back and her chin came up.

He returned to the table and set the tray down. "I don't know what you like so I got tuna, cheese and pickle or ham salad. Help yourself and I'll eat whatever you don't fancy." He passed her over a cup of coffee and spread the sandwiches out in front of her. She immediately went for the coffee.

He said, "Listen, I must apologise; I'm a bit slow on the uptake sometimes. You told me you've had a disastrous day; would you like to do this another time?" Susan was just peeling back the plastic on the tuna sandwich and she looked up. David laughed, "You can have the sandwich either way."

"Just try taking it back," she said, biting a big chunk out of it. She chewed for a minute. "No, I'm OK. I'm a bit wrung out, but that's all. Let's just say today could have been a lot worse for me."

David held her gaze for a moment, gauging her sincerity about continuing, and then nodded. "Well let me tell you what I need help with and perhaps you can tell me whether it's in your area of expertise and if you might be interested."

Susan was busy munching but she nodded enthusiastically, twirling one finger, signalling for David to keep going.

"OK," he said. "I work for what you might call an up-market insurance company. Most of our clients tend to be wealthy individuals or families.

It's my job to make sure everything goes smoothly whenever they want something or they need to make a claim. I do all the running around and the form-filling and even things like talking to the police, a lot of the time.

"Earlier this week, one of our clients had a break-in at their offices. It was quite elaborately planned. Whoever was in charge made it look like they were after money in the main safe, but what they really wanted was something rare and valuable in the Chairman's personal safe.

"That's where you come in. If someone stole some eighteenth century silver I'd have a fair idea which dealers to talk to because I've had a little experience with that sort of thing. I know something about the way these things get passed on and sold. With this piece, I don't know where to start, so I need some help."

Susan swallowed her last mouthful of tuna sandwich and reached for the cheese and pickle while saying, "I thought that was police work, not insurance work."

"Well, if we're lucky, it's both. The police investigate, we poke about a bit, everything gets shared and hopefully something good happens. Obviously an investigation like that goes a lot faster if the policemen involved are experts on, say, eighteenth century silver – but there aren't many of those. But, yes, a lot of times we'll just leave it to them. In this case, there are several reasons why we want to do all we can, not least of which is that the client has asked us to. His firm have been paying for our services for over a century; it would be good if it wasn't me who let the side down." David smiled.

"So what's been *pinched*?" she asked, playfully.

He gave her a sarcastic smile and said, "Oh yes, the Dick Van Dyke school of Cockney English. Very good." She nodded as though taking a bow and got stuck into another sandwich.

"Well I don't have very much. It's a leather and bone box containing a piece of ancient platinum jewellery. Like a piece of filigree. I can draw you a rough sketch based on a fairly rough sketch I was shown," he said, pulling his notepad out of his folio case and starting to draw.

"I thought platinum was a modern thing, like aloom…" she paused. "Alum*in*ium," she said carefully.

"Well, not so, apparently. According to my client, the Egyptians and the Aztecs both made platinum jewellery. Or it may have been Mayans," he said, unsure.

"I'm guessing Incas, actually," Susan suggested. "Point is, people who lived a long time ago. So is this Egyptian or South American?" she asked.

David had finished sketching. "Apparently Chinese, although I don't know from where exactly." He turned the pad round and slid it towards Susan. "Not exactly Michelangelo, but…" He broke off when he saw Susan's expression. "What is it?" he asked.

Susan was trying to open her bag and in her haste failing to unclip the catch. "Hold on," she said, getting the bag open, pulling out her iBook and flipping up the screen. She turned on the power. "When you say Chinese, might you maybe mean Tibetan?" she asked. The iBook was coming to life.

"Well, all I have is China and the fact that there are supposedly legends told about it there. You being an expert in legends and mythology…" he trailed off.

She was clicking on things. "Sorry, won't be a minute," she said. And then said triumphantly, "Yeah, there *are* legends about it and here's one of them." She rotated the laptop around so that David could see the screen. The image displayed was a piece of paper containing a lot of hand-written text, in the roman alphabet, and a sketch that looked not unlike the one on David's notepad.

"Damn, you're good," said David. "So what is it?"

"You don't understand," Susan said, "I was reading *this*," she tapped the screen, "this morning. And then this afternoon you ask me to identify it. How spooky is that?"

David didn't say anything for a moment, just raised his eyebrows. Susan on the other hand had a very curious expression on her face. She suddenly leaned forwards and looked David in the eye.

"Let me tell you what was so awful about my day," she said earnestly.

"OK," David said, stretching the word out in his uncertainty.

"I'm based in Cambridge, normally, but I've come down to London because of a big find. The School of Antiquities inherited a private collection of documents when its owner died a few months ago. It's full of the most remarkable documents, so I went to have a chat with the woman who donated it: the landlady of the collection's owner."

She continued, "The owner was always going off on trips to acquire new documents, only one time he didn't come back. I visited his landlady this morning to see what she knew about the collection or its owner. While I was there," her voice gained emphasis, "someone broke in and attacked her. I've just come from the hospital where they took her. She's in pretty bad shape, internal bruising like she was beaten with something. The guy who attacked her had broken open the box where the collection used to be kept." She tapped the screen again, "Where this document used to be. The one that describes your stolen antique. How's that for a coincidence? Whoever was after the antique might also be after the paperwork about it."

They both thought for a moment. "How did the owner of the collection die?" David asked meaningfully.

"I think the word the police used was 'unexplained'." She too had a question. "Was there any violence in your break-in?" she asked.

"Plenty," David said. "What's the opposite of pacifist? Two people dead apparently just to help misdirect the police."

They paused again, both thinking.

"So where's the collection now?" David asked.

"Safely locked up at the School of Antiquities," Susan said, though the sentence tapered off in its confidence level towards the end.

David lifted an eyebrow, "Well, I think you should have a talk to DI Hammond of the Serious Crime Squad and tell him what you've told me." David began looking for Hammond's details. "I think it would make a lot of sense if that collection had some extra security." He took a moment to copy the details out and then tore the page from his pad.

He said, "I'll call him too, to let him know what's going on." Then his features fell and he said, "My god, I'm sorry. I've just realised, you mean you were right there when it happened?"

Susan said, "Yeah, pretty much. The old lady went upstairs to see what the noise was and I heard something and got worried. I called up and said something about there being a bunch of us. When I got to the top of the stairs someone was climbing out the window."

"Are *you* OK, though?" David asked.

"Listen, I did volunteer work in New York City for a year. I've seen a lot worse than the back end of a mugger. It's just sitting with that poor old lady... It took about twenty seconds for her to go from someone who was on top of the world, to a frail old woman who they were saying... who the doctors think might not recover." She sounded quite choked up as she said this last. But then it slid away and Susan was collected once again.

David asked, "Why didn't you just call me and cancel? In fact, just not turn up. I could hardly have blamed you."

"That's not really how I work," she said. "God, if I fold up when I don't have a scratch on me, how would I cope with a real emergency?" she asked. David looked impressed.

"Pardon the cliché, but let's hope you don't have to find out the answer to that question," David said. His eyes wandered, in search of something to gaze at besides the distress on Susan's face. He found himself looking at the screen of her laptop. He stared more carefully at the image it showed.

He said, "Listen, let's swap roles. I'll be in charge of close shaves and you can handle the research. Like this for instance," he indicated the text on the screen, "can you read it?"

"Sure," Susan said, "it's in Latin and supposedly a translation from Tibetan. That's what it says at the bottom, anyway."

Susan's voice was back to normal now.

She said, "It's a story about a Magic Marker." She gave a little laugh, as though realising what she was saying as she said it. David looked blank. "Sorry, American humour. A Magic Marker is a big, thick kind of pen in the States. It's like you guys say Biro or Sellotape. Anyway, this Marker, in the story, is magic in that it attracts the attention of the gods. They get fascinated by the pattern. The idea is that you place it on a sick person and if a god happens to notice the Marker he might heal them."

"It's like a divine medic alert bracelet?" David said, a little flippantly.

"Well, it's not a bracelet, but yes, basically," Susan said. She got a far-off look in her eyes which David noticed.

"What?" he asked, gently.

"You just made me think of something. It's really crazy, but it's just such a weird coincidence. No, forget it," she said.

"What?" David asked again, encouragingly.

"When I told you about doing volunteer work it got me thinking about some of the homeless people we'd see. Listen, I'm not saying this is true, it's just a thought, but this guy who attacked the little old lady, I got a look at him. She tore his sleeve and I saw these funny marks on his arm," she said.

"Like tattoos?" David asked.

Susan shook her head. "Not tattoos. They reminded me of something a couple of the addicts at our shelter had. Do you know what Kaposi's Sarcoma is?" she said.

David said, "That's something to do with AIDS, isn't it?"

"Yeah, it's a kind of skin cancer that used to be pretty rare before AIDS came along. You generally only get it if your immune system is shot."

After a pause she went on, "I mean it just occurred to me reading this." She nodded towards the laptop. "You said this guy is really violent. Well I watched him jump off a roof. One of the quickest ways to get AIDS is to be a serious drug-user. It fits with violent, it fits with reckless behaviour like jumping off a roof. He might even be on something that makes him aggressive and stops him feeling pain, like PCP."

David added, "It looks like he jumped out of a thirty-foot high window to escape after the break-in."

"Right. So that fits," she said.

"So he's a drug-user," David concluded.

"Maybe. But I was getting at something else. What if he's a violent junkie and he's pretty sick? If he's on something powerful enough to make him imagine he's Batman he might be thinking some pretty strange things," she said. She seemed reluctant to go on.

"And…" David said, gently coaxing.

"What if he doesn't want this thing in order to sell it? What if he actually believes it will cure him?" she asked.

They both considered that question for a few moments. David didn't look convinced, but neither of them said anything.

The conversation then turned to more practical matters. It was obvious that Susan should be involved in David's investigation; they didn't even bother to debate it. David explained the sorts of things he needed and what his company would pay.

Susan agreed to put her work on the Medic Marker (as they called it) at the top of her list – which it pretty much had been anyway, even before the day's events.

"When can we get together again?" David asked.

"Well, I need a couple of days. How about Tuesday?" she said.

"Fine by me. What's a good time?" David said.

"Well I tend to finish work around six…" Susan said thoughtfully.

David looked slightly surprised, "Oh. OK, we can meet in the evening if that's easier."

"No, I just meant… I was just thinking out loud. I mean unless… It would probably be easier, actually. But maybe you don't usually work in the evenings?" she said.

"If only. Listen, my pal Kieran got a three-course meal out of me and all he did was spend two minutes calling your friend Bernie. On that scale you certainly deserve more than a sandwich." He glanced down at the empty wrappers. "A measly three sandwiches."

"I hadn't eaten all day," she said, coyly.

"OK. How about," he thought for a minute, "Villandry on Great Portland Street, seven thirty on Tuesday. Paid for by the company, of course. Including taxis." He jotted himself a note about reservations.

"Sure," Susan said, perhaps a little uncertain.

"And do call Hammond. Lots of people must know where that collection is by now. If someone's looking for it…" David said, seriously.

Susan nodded. "Don't worry, I'm not likely to forget."

They packed up their things and began wandering towards the exit. It was just a few minutes before closing time.

"Next time I'm going to have a look round," Susan said as they left.

They walked out of the main entrance towards the tube station, David asking about Susan's research work and how she was finding London.

Still chatting, they made their way down into the tube station and through the barriers. It turned out they were getting on different lines.

"Tuesday evening," Susan called stepping onto her escalator.

David waved, "See you then," he said. He stood for a moment watching her back before turning and heading towards the other set of escalators.

CHAPTER 9

Four days later
Monday 14th April

D avid sat in Reg Cottrell's office discussing the Interfinanzio account.

Reg said, "So you've met their Chairman." It had the tenor of a leading question.

David looked at Reg's face, gauging his meaning, and said, "He's got quite a presence, hasn't he?"

"Presence, quite so. Presence is a good way of putting it. Perhaps I should have said something beforehand," Reg considered this for a moment. "How did the interview go?"

David said, "Well I won't pretend I wasn't rattled by him, but we seemed to get on well enough. He was very keen for us to get involved. He wants us to investigate, to supplement what the police are doing. Actually, to be honest, he seemed to be saying he wanted us to retrieve the missing item and bugger the police."

Reg looked a little taken aback.

David said, "Perhaps I could have phrased it better, but that's the gist of it. That and implying that Marshall & Liberty would be bankrupted if it came to making a claim."

Reg nodded seriously, "There's a very real chance of that, unless we could work something out on the valuation. Times are a little tougher for our sector than when that policy was drafted." Reg went on, "At any rate, the ball's in your court. How do you think you'll play it?"

"Well, I was hoping for some guidance from the partners," David said cautiously. "If I do too little, I'm jeopardising not only one of our best accounts, it seems like I'm risking financial ruin for the company. If I push as hard as Mr Dass wants me to, I'd say I run a good chance of getting on the wrong side of the police, which won't do us any good. We rely on a good relationship with the police and we don't want the bad PR – both of which could be a problem depending on how much trouble I get myself into."

Reg looked rather uncomfortable as he considered his words. "As I say, it's your decision, and it's a tricky one. But bear in mind that Alessandro Dass is quite a heavyweight – he's been known to pull quite a few strings in his time. He's certainly not a fellow you would want to let down. And by the same token, whatever meets with his approval will go over pretty well in other quarters too – he'll see to that. I doubt the police would get their knickers in a twist over something that suited Dass and his associates, not unless some gross impropriety were involved."

David considered this, "Reg, perhaps I'm being a little slow to get the message, so I hope you'll forgive me for being dogged, but why isn't one of the partners handling this?"

Reg looked even more awkward. "I don't know, er, how much more there is to discuss here. Let's just say that the partners believe you show a great deal of promise. This is really your chance to show us what you're capable of, without someone looking over your shoulder. You're being given a free hand and I'm sure you can imagine how grateful the firm will be if you're able to bring matters to a satisfactory conclusion."

David nodded slowly, an expression of weary comprehension on his face, "That's what I thought: a chance to shine and no one looking over my shoulder. So I'll get all the credit if it goes well. And if it all goes pear-shaped…"

Reg said briskly, "Well let's not dwell on that. I think you've got a good grasp of what we're dealing with here."

"I think so," David said, and added significantly, "Thanks for putting me in the picture."

Reg didn't meet his eye, but busied himself flicking through some papers on his desk, making a show of looking for something.

"Well that's marvellous then," Reg said. "Let me know if I can help with anything else."

David stood and made his way to the door. Reg was still avoiding his gaze, scrutinising a page in his desk diary. "See you later," David said.

"Cheerio," Reg replied. "All the best."

* * *

"Hi, I've got an appointment with DI Hammond," David told the constable on the desk.

"Won't be a minute, sir," the constable said, picking up a phone. He consulted a tatty, photocopied phone directory and dialled a number. There was a brief conversation that David couldn't hear.

"Come through please," the constable said, pointing to a door in the corner of the reception area. He pushed a button beneath the counter and held it down. The door lock buzzed loudly, indicating that the lock was disengaged. Once David had passed through, the constable released the button and the buzzing stopped.

The policeman peered around a nearby doorway, "I'd take you up, but I'm on my own here. Just go to the second floor and turn left. The DI's office is the first one you reach."

"Thanks," David said and started up the stairs. He found Hammond's office easily enough and knocked on the cheap, veneered-plywood door.

"Come," a voice called.

David opened the door and stepped into a small office. Directly ahead was a single desk, behind which George Hammond sat. The room also contained a filing cabinet and a small table. Opposite the door was a dusty window through which David could see a lime-scaled drainpipe and a section of brick wall. Scattered about the office were lots of papers, some loose, others in folders.

"Mr Braun," Hammond said, by way of greeting.

"Detective Inspector," David replied.

Hammond wore his default half-scowl. He nodded towards the room's one empty chair. David sat.

Hammond spoke first, "So, your client has connections."

David said, "He told me he was going to make some calls. Is that what you mean?"

"Yes, that's what I mean," Hammond said, rather nastily. David was unfazed.

"So do you want to go first or shall I?" David asked.

Hammond merely frowned.

Seeing that he wasn't going to get a proper reply, David said pleasantly, "OK I'll go first, but before I do, can you tell me if it's me you're pissed off with or my client?"

Hammond continued to scowl.

David said nothing.

"Alright, get on with it then," Hammond said in a tone that might have been his gruff version of conciliatory.

"Fair enough. You got my message about Susan Milton, I hope. Has she called you?" David asked.

Hammond nodded.

"She's an academic historian. She's tracked down some copies of old documents describing the piece that was stolen from the Chairman's safe by the third member of the gang. If you've spoken to her then you know that someone has come looking for those documents."

Hammond still volunteered nothing.

David continued, "Dr Milton is going to be finding out what she can about the piece and, if we're lucky, a little about dealers we should talk to. I'm happy to let you have whatever we find out before taking any action." He added, "I'd also be happy to talk to a few people myself."

"You'll do no such thing," snapped Hammond.

David's temper flared, "Oh grow up, Hammond. I just said it was your choice."

Hammond looked furious and leaned angrily forwards, planting his fists on the desk, ready to lever himself to his feet.

David didn't blink. He said, a little more calmly but with equal force, "I'm sorry if someone's put pressure on you to involve me in your investigation. It wasn't my idea and I didn't want it. But don't go in the opposite direction just to be stubborn. When I speak to Mr Dass, I won't pretend you're being helpful if you're not. He could get me fired with one phone call. If he asks me how it's going, I'll tell him the truth. If you choose to make an enemy out of Dass, you're on your own."

Hammond glared at David for a few more seconds, his weight still on his hands as though he were about to jump to his feet. David didn't waver.

After a pause, Hammond asked, all irritation having vanished from his voice, "You ever think of joining the force?"

David surreptitiously let his breath out. He shook his head in answer to Hammond's question, "There's exams and so forth. Plus I'm not that good with people."

Hammond laughed loudly, tipping his head back. "Cocky little shit," he said agreeably.

Hammond was clearly amused, though there was no smile, just a little scrunching of the skin around his eyes. It faded and he said, "Don't do anything else like you did the other night or we really will fall out. Clear?"

"Yes," David said levelly. "I won't get in your way."

"Then we'll get along fine."

Hammond turned his attention to the piles of paperwork on his desk. He rummaged around until he found a particular file. He took a moment to gather and stack several dozen others that littered his desk. Then he moved them to one side and laid the first one open in the space he'd cleared.

"We had a result with forensics," Hammond said, scanning the top page in the folder.

While Hammond's eyes were focused on the report, David stole a quick glance too, reading upside-down. He looked back up again before Hammond noticed.

"The glass in the car park *does* match the office window. Which means the tyre tracks were very likely our suspect's – given that they were fresh and they went over the splinter of window glass. You want to guess what the getaway car was?" he asked David.

"A big old Jag?" David offered.

Hammond snorted. "A…" he looked down again at the report and read aloud, "new Porsche 911 Turbo. That's a ninety grand car, so even in London there aren't that many of them. We're still working through the list of owners, but we've already found one registered to someone who died in 1996. Our guess is that a car like that gets stopped all the time, so unless the real owner wants our lot following him everywhere he most likely keeps it properly insured. Which means even if the name's a dud, the address is probably something to do with him – he needs to be able to get his post. Anyway, there's no one at home, so we've got it staked out in case he comes back. That do you?"

"That's all good news. What about the two men who died in the break-in?" David asked.

"Right. One worked in that office. He's the one who would have known where the safe was and what was in it. The other was an old lag. Been inside twice for taking what didn't belong to him. He's the safe-cracker – though it looks like they didn't need him for the Chairman's safe. The insider must have had the combination," Hammond said.

"But they didn't really kill each other, surely?" David said.

Hammond shook his head. "It was nicely staged. There's a couple of little hiccups, though. First I'll tell you what we were *supposed* to think, OK?" Hammond pulled his sleeves up a bit. "There's a falling out – maybe because the Bizzies have turned up – and the safe-cracker stabs the inside-man with his screwdriver. The insider pulls a gun and fires two shots – one goes out the window and the safe-cracker bangs himself up getting out of the way of it. But the second shot gets him through the heart. Then the inside-man expires a few moments afterwards.

"Now, what we think *really* happened is that the third man stabbed the insider with the safe-cracker's screwdriver – he's got gloves, so only the safe-cracker's fingerprints are on it. The cracker pulls a gun, realising he's next, but misses the third man and hits the window. The third man clobbers the cracker with something, doing enough damage that he's incapacitated.

Then he puts the gun in the dead man's hand and pulls the trigger for him, killing the cracker. Then he's off out the window," Hammond concluded.

"Any idea why he didn't break his neck jumping that far?" David asked.

"We're still working on it. In fact we've got a little sweepstake going within the department. We've had all sorts of suggestions." He glanced at a list, "That car park opposite is five floors high with a hand-rail at the top; hook a rope over that rail and you could swing across. Someone else thought maybe he was a pole-vaulter. Don't know about that one. Someone else thought he chucked an inflatable mattress down there, jumped onto it, then slit it open and took it with him. They're all a bit barmy, but most of them might actually work. We reckon he got lucky with that first bullet missing him, but chances are he was wearing some Kevlar."

Hammond closed the folder and stood up. "That's going to have to do you. I've got to be somewhere else."

David said, "I appreciate it. I'll get out of your way."

Hammond asked, "So are we square? You're happy? Not going to tell your boss on me?"

"There's nothing to tell him, except what a good job you're doing. Speak to you soon," David said, politely.

Hammond just waved a hand in a gesture that could be interpreted either as dismissal or a wave. David left.

He hurried downstairs, out through the security door and back out into the street. As soon as he was clear of the police station he pulled out a pad and wrote down an address. It was the address that had been visible, albeit upside-down, on the top-most piece of paper in Hammond's file.

* * *

That evening, David was heading home after training. He'd hung around afterwards for a quick drink in the nearby pub. It looked like everyone else was going to be there until closing time, but David excused himself just after ten and began the drive homeward.

Behind the passenger seat of his car, tucked out of sight, sat his folio case. As he drove, he reached over, steering one-handed, and retrieved it. He laid it on the passenger seat.

His gaze kept returning to it.

At the next red light he reached over, unzipped the case, and pulled out his notepad. Nearby streetlamps gave just enough light to read by. Several pages in he found the address he'd copied from Hammond's report. It was an address in Notting Hill.

He tapped the steering wheel, waiting for the light to change, glancing occasionally at the pad.

As the lights turned green, he glanced both ways – the street was clear – and made a u-turn. He headed west.

Traffic was light. He dropped down to the Euston Road, was swept along with the flow westward. Dropping a little further south, he reached the Westway.

Once he was roughly in the right area he turned off the main road, pulled in and fetched a map from the glove box. One finger wedged into the map book, marking his destination, he wound his way towards it, driving slowly.

The house he was looking for sat on the corner where a quiet side road joined a slightly larger residential street.

He approached the property, driving along the larger road, his eyes scanning ahead, looking for the corner.

He caught sight of it and began to indicate left. Just before he reached the turn he noticed a dark blue Mondeo with two men sitting in the front seats. Two pairs of eyes in synchrony tracked his approach. "Subtle," he muttered to himself.

He avoided looking directly at his observers and turned smoothly into the side street. Cars lined both sides of the road and there were few opportunities to pull in. Twenty metres from the corner, one or two parking places remained unoccupied. He ignored the first couple, only pulling in when he was a hundred metres from the corner.

He turned off the engine and the lights and sat there unmoving. He adjusted his mirror so that he could see the street behind him. All was quiet. It was getting on for eleven in a very smart residential area and there seemed to be little activity – certainly nothing untoward.

For a couple of minutes David sat waiting. Occasionally he glanced in the mirror, though there was nothing to see.

After a little over five minutes he shook his head, as though disappointed with his own foolishness, and started the engine. He tapped the wheel thoughtfully for another few seconds as the engine silently idled and then he reached to turn the headlights on.

He paused before completing the motion; a car was coming towards him down the little side street, heading towards the corner and its lights were off.

Instinctively he ducked down, laying flat on the passenger seat. A powerful engine burbled slowly past his door, moving almost at a walking pace.

He could hear the deep chuckle of the engine grow quieter, more distant. Moving just his fingers, he pushed the button to lower his window a few centimetres and strained to hear. The engine sound was still there. It sounded like it was idling.

He slowly raised himself to an upright position. The headrests on his front seats helped to hide him from view. He looked in the mirror.

A low, black Porsche was pulling into a double parking space twenty metres behind him. He turned off his car's engine.

Very slowly he lowered his head again, leaning over the passenger seat. The left-hand wing mirror was adjustable and he moved it until he could see back along the pavement from his ducked-down position.

A man, dressed all in black, appeared a moment later from behind the Porsche. He crossed the pavement swiftly and flattened himself against the wall. Overhanging branches created little pockets of gloom into which his dark shape blended. He was only visible if one knew where to look.

The figure raised a hand, pointed towards the car, and a set of keys momentarily caught the light. But the indicators on the Porsche didn't flash; there was no chirp from the alarm system.

The figure lowered the hand again and the keys went into a jacket pocket and were zipped up.

"Changed your mind," David whispered to himself.

Moving stealthily, the figure crept towards the corner, getting further away from David. His dark outline became even more indistinct as he moved deeper into the shadows.

The front door of the corner property lay in the next road, where the policemen waited. From David's vantage point, all that could be seen was the side of the house and a high garden wall.

The figure drew level with the far end of the garden wall. The corner property was sufficiently large that he was still thirty metres from the corner and comfortably out of sight of the policemen.

The man took two quick steps and jumped the wall, placing one hand on the top of it as he vaulted over. He made it look simple and fluid enough but it was a strange motion nonetheless because the wall stood a metre taller than he did.

David continued to watch. A full minute went by. Then he reached up and changed the setting on the interior light of his car so that it wouldn't come on when he opened the door. He also pulled a cleaning cloth out of the driver's side door compartment.

He opened his car door and got out slowly. He pushed the door closed gently with the palm of his hand. It didn't shut completely, but he left it that way.

Keeping to a crouch, he made his way to the side of the Porsche and peered in. The passenger seat contained a briefcase. With the cloth covering his hand, David gripped the door handle. He looked up and down the street and then, seeing no one around, tried the door.

It was unlocked.

David leaned in and, still using the cloth, flicked the catches on the briefcase. He raised the lid and looked inside. It was full of loose papers.

Grabbing a handful, David began to rapidly flick through them. It was difficult to make out what they were in the dim light. As with David's car, the interior light in the Porsche had been turned off.

Several papers were bills. Another was written in some language other than English. He found a piece of paper printed on headed notepaper and held it up, angling the paper to catch the light from the streetlamp.

It was from a letting agency. It appeared to be a rental agreement for an

Adept 199

apartment. David read the address.

A dog barked and elsewhere a door slammed, almost simultaneously. It sounded like it came from the direction of the corner property. Quickly David pulled his head out of the car and scanned the street. Nothing.

He dropped the documents back in the case, closed the lid and snapped the catches down. Then he pushed the door closed, quietly, but firmly, using the flat of his hand still wrapped in the cloth.

He walked, half-crouched, back to his car. Moving around to the driver's side, he opened the door, but didn't get in. He gave the ignition key a single twist and the warm engine caught immediately, making hardly a sound.

He left the driver's door wide open, sticking out into the street and walked to the car behind him. He placed his cloth-covered hand on the wing of the Mercedes and pushed down hard. The car bounced on its springs. He did it again even harder and this time the alarm shrieked into life, destroying the silence. Lights flashed.

David ran back to his car, jumped in and, as quickly as he could, pulled out of his parking space. He sounded his horn and kept it blaring as he drove rapidly up the street.

A light came on in a nearby house.

He drove rapidly, horn still sounding, until he reached a bend in the road fifty metres on. Releasing the horn, he turned on his headlights and dropped down to the speed limit.

From there he headed home. He found he was driving like someone over the limit – too cautious, geriatrically legal.

CHAPTER 10

THE NEXT EVENING
TUESDAY 15TH APRIL

This time Susan was early.

The restaurant was also a delicatessen and Susan wandered among the bottles, tins and boxes, peering at anything which caught her interest.

Her navy suit gave her a business-like appearance, without seeming severe. The faded-pink silk blouse she wore underneath was sleeveless with a deep v-neck, giving her the option of a much softer look if she chose at some later point to shed the jacket.

Her straight blonde hair was down and it had picked up a slight wave since the previous week. Her skin had the healthy bloom of someone with no use for cosmetics – an effect that had taken her quite a while to create.

She happened to glance up as David entered the restaurant. He was wearing a charcoal suit with a midnight-blue shirt and tie. His short, dark hair was spiked a little and he looked freshly scrubbed and shaved.

"Hi," said Susan smiling.

"Hi," said David. "You look…" he paused as though remembering something, "very well. How are you?"

"I'm great." She looked around. "This is a lovely place."

"Well, the food's usually good, although I'm not exactly a restaurant expert. I don't really eat out that much," David said.

"Me neither, unless you count a muffin in Starbucks," Susan said.

David glanced towards the restaurant area.

"Let's see if they've lost my reservation," he said conspiratorially, leading the way.

The restaurant area was invitingly dim. Glowing lamps set on pillars throughout the room gave the impression of candlelight. The outside wall was floor-to-ceiling glass, looking out onto the smart town houses opposite and the night beyond.

A waitress seated them right in the centre of the room.

After a quick discussion, they agreed to share a bottle of Chablis. They both contemplated their menus for a moment.

Susan was the first to mention work. "I spoke to Mr Hammond. I don't get the impression he's going to do much, though. He apparently called security at the School and made some suggestions to them. There's now some sixty-year-old guy in what looked to me like a UPS uniform sitting by the elevator. What that's supposed to do if our evil junkie mastermind turns up I don't know. Fortunately, we're all the way down in the lowest basement. He'd have to get past the front desk and then find his way down a couple of floors before he'd reach the Senior Citizen on Patrol, so we should be OK." She gave an ironic smile.

A waiter brought the wine, which David nodded at rather than tasted. Their glasses were being filled as David said, "I'm sorry Hammond wasn't much help. I think he might be my old maths teacher reincarnated. He seems to be either miserable or angry depending on what sort of day he's having."

He added, "Hammond and I nearly had a falling out when I went to see him yesterday. My client had pulled some strings and done the worst possible thing in Hammond's eyes: put him in a position where he has to be helpful. I can see it's causing him real pain. I should say though, that he's probably a pretty good copper, aside from his personality."

They sipped their wine.

"Listen I was thinking about my junkie theory," Susan said, but just then the waiter returned to take their order.

They chose, Susan having soup then fish and David opting for bruschetta followed by a steak.

"Junkies," David said, prompting Susan, when the waiter had gone.

"Yeah. I don't like the idea any more," Susan said.

"Because?" David asked.

She narrowed her eyes at him. "I think you already know," she said suspiciously.

David offered, "Because he's organised, disciplined and a meticulous planner. It doesn't sound like an intravenous drug user losing touch with reality. Plus, physically he's the most amazing gymnast I've ever seen."

"You've seen him?" Susan said, surprised.

"Well, I…" For a moment David seemed about to backtrack, but he didn't. He looked awkward, sucked air through his teeth and admitted, "Yeah, I saw him last night."

Susan's mood, which had been warming as they talked, now chilled by several degrees. "What did you do?" she asked, scrutinising him.

"It was just coincidence," he said. "I drove past the address Hammond thinks he lives at. The Old Bill have a couple of men outside waiting for him. I just thought I'd drive by; I don't know why."

"And you saw him? He was there?" she said. She didn't sound impressed.

"Well, someone was there. The car matches the one Hammond's looking for. I saw him sneak into the garden of the house. The coppers at the front wouldn't have been any the wiser so I made a bit of a racket and set off a car alarm. If they came to investigate they would have seen his Porsche. If they didn't… well what else could I do? I couldn't go and tap on their window. At least this way they would have stood a chance of catching him," he said, somewhat on the defensive.

"Why on earth would you…" Susan began, incredulous.

Then an angry look of comprehension crossed her face. She pointed at David. "Your client didn't ask you to investigate this theft at all, did he? This is some sort of macho fantasy you're acting out," she said, accusingly.

Her voice was getting louder.

"Hey, calm down," he said, in hushed tones. "I am acting on the express wishes of my client and with the approval of my company. If it hadn't been for the most incredible coincidence, our villain would have had a chance to pick up his things, the police would have been none the wiser and my evening would have involved a quick look at the outside of his house, nothing more. What did I do that was so wrong?" he asked.

"Nothing that Rambo would have considered over the top," she said a little more calmly, but she was only half-joking.

"I might be wrong," David said, "but I don't have the impression you always do what you're told. When the old lady was attacked you went upstairs unarmed, didn't you?"

"I had a poker," Susan said quietly. David laughed, humourlessly, and nodded.

Susan spoke softly, but her intensity hadn't lessened when she said, "I was trying to help someone I thought was in trouble. I wasn't barging into the middle of a police investigation just because there was nothing to watch on TV."

They were both getting a little heated. David looked like he was going to make some piqued response when a beaming waiter asked in generic Mediterranean, "Oo is 'aving ze bruschetta?" This last was pronounced with an indulgent flourish.

"Thanks," David said.

Susan was served with her soup a minute later.

Neither touched their food for a moment, then they both reached for their wine simultaneously.

David took a breath and let it out. "You're right – it wasn't my job to get involved, but for some reason I did."

He went on, before she could say anything, "Did I tell you that the police thought there were two men involved in the break-in? That's how it would have stayed except I poked around and proved there were three. It was wrong of me; I'm a bad person. But everyone is better off because of the evidence I found. We wouldn't have even known about the Porsche and the house in Notting Hill otherwise. We'd have nothing.

"And last night, he would have come and gone – picked up his things and vanished without a trace. Again, because I broke the rules and poked my nose in, I have a pretty good idea where he's going next." His voice was level but with a hint of urgency that suggested he really wanted Susan to understand. "And I'm not saying this to be antagonistic, but it's not your job to tell me off about this, is it? But you're getting involved too, you're taking it personally."

Susan said nothing but looked somewhat mollified. They began to eat their food.

After several seconds, the beginnings of a twinkle returned to Susan's eyes. "So you know where he's going, Sherlock?" she asked.

"I thought I was Rambo," he reminded her.

"The jury's still out." She paused and then said, "I'm sorry if I got high and mighty with you. You're right, it's not my job to tell you off."

David gave a smile of relief, his shoulders relaxing, "If you hate apologising as much as I hate asking for someone else's approval then I think we're even."

"So you wanted to tell me to butt out just now?" she asked, teasingly.

"You didn't deserve it, but that's what I'd normally do. I'm not good at teams," he said. "So do you want to know what I know?"

"I'm not going to beg," she said, pretending to be angry.

"OK. While he was inside I had a look in his car," David said.

Susan's eyes went wide.

David held up a hand, "Don't crucify me until you've learned all my secrets; your curiosity will never forgive you." He took a sip of wine to wet his lips. "He left his car unlocked and I found a briefcase full of papers. One of them was about renting an apartment near the City."

Susan looked troubled, "Our mastermind can't remember to lock his car?"

"I think he thought about it. I reckon he's got one of those irritating alarm systems that gives a little *bip bip* to let you know it's armed. When you've paid ninety grand for a car, it's important everyone looks round when you get out of it. One of the many reasons rare sports cars make bad getaway vehicles," David said.

"So you found an address?" Susan asked.

"Yes, it's just off the Great Eastern Road, down from Old Street," David said.

"What are you going to do with it? The address?" Susan asked. It was clearly a leading question. She wasn't giving him a hard time, but neither had she let him off the hook yet.

"Well, I think it will depend on whether they caught him last night. If we're lucky, it might all be done and dusted by now. He might be behind bars," David said.

"You don't sound convinced," Susan said.

"You should have seen this guy. He hopped over a wall that must have been nine foot high. I've never seen anything like it and I've seen a lot of amazing things," David said.

"Maybe he's some sort of martial arts guru," Susan suggested.

"Believe me, I know a few people who fit that description and none of them can do what he did," David said.

"Really? You've got an interesting circle of friends," Susan said, raising an eyebrow.

David shrugged.

Susan reached over and took David's arm, holding his wrist through his jacket. He didn't resist. She turned his hand over and inspected his knuckles. The first two had a glossy callous, almost like wax, covering them.

"You must train pretty hard to get knuckles like that," she said, releasing his arm.

He shrugged again, "Some people do crosswords." He looked down at her hands.

"What do you do to keep in shape?" he asked.

"Guess," she said, turning over her hands which had no calluses on their backs, but looked a little more resilient on the palm side.

"You row?" David said.

"Nope," she said, but didn't elaborate.

The waiter returned, clearing away their empty plates, re-filling their wine glasses. The bottle ran out as he was topping up David's glass.

"So who can jump a wall like that?" Susan asked.

"That's a good question," David said, "and there's also the riddle of how he escaped from the office break-in. It's a thirty foot drop onto railway lines. Then somehow he climbed a sheer wall the other side. One of Hammond's lot suggested he was a pole-vaulter. This might sound stupid, but instead of a pole, imagine you had a ladder. You could step onto it and then push off behind you."

"Like Buster Keaton? So this guy's a field and track athlete using his pole-vaulting and high-jumping skills to pull off daring raids. Please." Susan said.

"What? Professional athletes never go bad? What about O.J.?" David asked.

Susan laughed.

David said, "I don't know. But he managed this stuff somehow. For someone we think is terminally ill, he's in extraordinary shape."

Their main courses arrived.

"This is good," Susan said, after her first mouthful.

David asked, "Have you learned any more about the Medic Marker?"

"A lot," she said, "but nothing that will help us get it back. I have no idea yet where someone would go to sell a thing like that, and I'm less convinced than ever that the thief intends to sell it."

She continued, "If you just wanted to raise some money, there are lots of better things to steal – cash, for one. You said there was a safe full of money they could have had instead."

David said, "Well, he might have been planning to take that too, but ran out of time. Except Hammond did say the main safe was actually open when they arrived. So there's a good chance he passed up the cash in favour of the Medic Marker."

"Of course it could be worth a lot more than the cash was," said Susan. "I've found what might be a reference to the Marker from the reign of Emperor Shi Huangdi. He offered a prize to anyone who would bring it to him. It could be irrelevant, or on the other hand this could be a Chinese cultural treasure from the third century B.C."

"Huangdi?" David said.

"First Emperor of all China. Qin dynasty. Built the wall," Susan said.

"So this thing would be like the crown jewels. It would be priceless," David said.

"If it's the same thing. But how would anyone ever prove it? You can't date metal and there are no pictures of it that I could find. The Huangdi reference is about a piece of jewellery made from a metal more precious than gold that conferred immortality. I found it because I was looking for references to jewellery with amazing healing powers. But the idea that it's got healing powers comes from a document found in someone's attic in Brentford. There's nothing to tie the stolen jewellery to the Huangdi story except that passage I showed you," Susan said.

"So you couldn't really sell it?" David said.

"Well, it's still a fabulous platinum filigree, so it's certainly worth thousands, and you could probably prove that the platinum came from China. But, all in all, I don't think you could ever demonstrate it was the Huangdi piece. So, I think you'd still be better off with a bag full of money," Susan said.

"Unless your AIDS theory is right," David said.

"You don't believe it," she said.

"I wouldn't say that. I just think there might be several possible explanations for what you saw. I'm beginning to think this guy is some sort of Special Forces character – maybe someone left over from the Cold War – trained to do some government's dirty work, who's now out of a job. We know he's a patient planner as well as being hands-on. Maybe he used to be a spy? And it's bound to be a pretty rough lifestyle; could be what you saw were burns or injuries. Or perhaps he really does have AIDS and the legends about the Marker are just a coincidence."

He went on, "If he thinks the legends are nonsense he'd be better off with the cash, so maybe he believes in them. But then I just can't quite square the black-ops stuff we know he's capable of with the idea that he believes in fairy tales," David winced at his own words and said, "myths and legends, I mean. Sorry."

Susan flicked her hand in a 'don't worry about it' gesture. "Me neither. We're not just talking superstitious – like, no thirteens or something – he'd have to really be into the occult." She added, "The only other thing I can think is that it's stealing-to-order. If someone knew your client had this thing and arranged for it to be stolen, then authentication wouldn't be a problem."

David looked interested, "That makes a lot of sense, you know. If you wanted something stolen, our mystery man is just the sort of person you'd try to hire."

He noticed her look of unease and said, "It fits the facts better than anything else we've come up with. What am I missing?"

"Just one thing," she said. "Say he's a mercenary and he's stealing the Marker for a collector somewhere; why did he come after the collection too? Those documents aren't valuable except to an academic. They're nearly all recent copies of older works. The one you saw the other day is written in ballpoint pen. It's worthless except for the information it contains."

"Well maybe he's after that information. What exactly does it say?" David asked.

"There's a little bit of background about a mad monk who made it, but mainly it's just the same as you'd get with a food processor or a stereo," she said.

David looked puzzled and said, "Which is?"

"Directions for use," she said. "He came back for the instructions. Whichever way you slice it, someone – either mercenary guy or his boss – believes in the legend."

They were both quietly considering this when a waiter asked them, "Is everything OK?"

David said, "Great thanks. Do you think you could get me a glass of the house red?" He glanced at Susan.

"Yeah, the white for me. Thanks," Susan said.

Then, turning to David, she said, "You didn't really answer my question about the address you found. What if mercenary guy isn't in custody? You have information the police need and the clock is ticking."

David looked uncomfortable again, "Well, there's no way I can tell Hammond directly. He was pretty pissed off about the third man thing. You'd think I'd got in the way of the investigation instead of helped it along."

Susan said, patiently, "He does kind of have a point. You see that, don't you?"

David said, "It's the old vigilante dilemma, isn't it. When the authorities let you down, are you supposed to shrug and say, 'oh well', or are you allowed to lend a hand?"

Susan asked, "Are you sure you're giving them a chance to fail before you jump in?"

"Well I definitely did with the third man's getaway car. They had no plans to search the car park that night. Their crime scene would literally have had a thousand vehicles driven through it by the following evening."

Susan shrugged, "OK. Well we might disagree on whether you've got your testosterone set a little high, but I think we're both clear that it's not my job to smack your wrists. But I really think you could get yourself into a lot of trouble, even danger, if you do much more of this lone ranger stuff. I'm just saying that as a friend."

David, who had been examining his plate, looked up at her. She looked away and added, "or a paid employee, at any rate."

"Oh well, in that case…" he said, laughing.

Susan said, "Listen, can't you just phone this address in as, you know, an anonymous tip-off?"

David didn't look convinced, "I don't know. I don't want the police spending too much time thinking about who the informant might be. Before you know where we are, they'll have a theory that it's two guys behind it all. On the other hand, I wouldn't be surprised if Hammond ignored a tip-off completely."

Susan touched a finger to her lips, thoughtfully, "Well, you've done this sort of thing before. Why don't you say it's your tip-off? Call Hammond and say you can't explain but you think he should check it out."

David was considering it. "I like that idea better. Hammond won't be happy, but equally he'd be risking his job if he ignored it."

"Cool," Susan said. "Just do it soon, OK? The police need that address."

"That reminds me, I must phone my mum." David said, sarcastically.

Susan made a face, "Don't start getting me confused with your mother," she said, slipping off her jacket.

As she twisted to put the jacket on the back of her chair the tailored waist of her blouse rose to reveal her trim midriff. David's eyes wandered a little. "I don't think that's going to be a problem," he said.

The waiter arrived with their glasses of wine.

Impulsively, David picked up his wine glass and held it forwards, making a toast, "Here's to our little team!"

"Here's to Rambo and his mother," Susan said, clinking glasses with him.

Work matters were left behind for a while and the conversation moved on to their personal histories. Susan talked a little about her work and David followed on by explaining more about what he did. Both of them were jokey and self-deprecating in their accounts.

Instead of desserts, they opted for Irish coffees.

David took a couple of sips of his, getting cream on his nose. They both laughed and he dabbed at his nose with a napkin.

"You know that's not actually funny," he said. "We're drunk."

"I might be," Susan said, "but you're twice my size. It must take more than three glasses of wine to get you drunk."

He held up four fingers, frowned and then folded one of them over, "Three and a half and they were large." He asked, "Have you ever done one of those magazine questionnaires where you work out how many units of alcohol you drink a week?"

"Might have," she said playfully.

"Mine was easy – two units a week – a pint with my mate Banjo. Never could hold my drink. And I train a lot; believe me, you never want to turn up for a training session with a hangover – it's torture."

"I know," said Susan, holding up her toughened palms to remind him that she trained too.

"Bell ringing," he said, decisively.

"Uh uh," she said, wagging a finger to indicate an incorrect answer. Then she said, "No, my parents were pretty strict Methodists. The churching seems to have worn off, but not the attitude to the devil's tipple."

"Except this evening," David pointed out.

She looked confused, "Yeah, I don't know what happened there. This won't go on my personnel record will it?" she said, gravely.

"Don't be silly. I might have to call your parents though," he said.

They talked a little about London as they drank their coffees. It felt as though the evening was winding down and when the glasses were empty David called for the bill.

"Let's talk in a couple of days. I should be sober again by then," David said.

"OK. Let me know what happens with Hammond, won't you. And call me if it turns out our guy's in jail." She wrote out her mobile number on David's copy of the bill.

"Remind me to scribble that out before I pass it on to accounts," he said. She laughed.

"You know," she said, "this is the most fun I've had in a business meeting."

"Yup, you'd hardly know we were working, would you?" David agreed.

They stood, Susan put her jacket back on, and then they made their way out of the restaurant. It was a mild night and they walked along the street for a hundred yards or so, hardly speaking, until David spotted a taxi. He hailed it, saying to Susan, "Get a receipt."

The taxi pulled in. Susan told the driver her address and then she opened the back door. Before getting in, she turned to David and said, "I've had a really nice evening."

"Me too," David said and for a moment things were awkward. It didn't seem right to shake hands, but it wasn't clear what they should do instead.

"Get home safely," David said, his arms hanging stiffly at his sides.

Susan nodded, smiling, and hopped into the cab. He closed the door behind her and watched it drive away.

CHAPTER 11

THE NEXT DAY
WEDNESDAY 16TH APRIL

D avid was in DI Hammond's office again. Hammond was being reasonably civil today, but then he'd been on the phone for most of the ten minutes David had been sitting there, so his opportunities for hostility had been limited.

Much of Hammond's phone dialogue consisted of little grunts. At last he said, "I'll hold you to that. Must get on." He hung up.

He turned to look at David who sat the other side of his desk. "So you heard what happened with our stake-out?" Hammond said, adding a stream of swear words under his breath.

"No I didn't," David said.

Hammond's face twitched into a humourless smile and relaxed again. "Your third man beat the tar out of two officers and disappeared. It seems he'd returned to the house to pick up some of his things. The officers came upon him as he was returning to his car. They drew their weapons and cautioned him. When they attempted to handcuff him, he went for them. Somehow – and believe me I *will* get to the bottom of this – he managed to disarm them and then gave them a good battering as well. I've got a list somewhere – broken this, punctured that. They're not going to die and neither will they win any beauty competitions for a bit. He made quite a mess of them."

Hammond, who had been glancing through papers on his desk as he spoke, looked up and caught David's eye. "Satisfied?" he said. David's jaw muscles tightened a little.

"I'm very sorry to hear that – I mean that your men were hurt." David paused a moment and said, "There's something I've learned that I think you should know. On the other hand, you might consider it interference."

"What have you done, Braun?" growled Hammond.

"Me? Nothing. But as you know, my company has recovered hundreds of stolen items over the years; they've got quite a lot of contacts. One of them passed some information on to us," David said.

Hammond's hands started to twitch in agitation. "Come on, spit it out," he said aggressively.

David leaned forwards and spoke softly, "Calm down, Hammond, you're starting to give me a headache."

"If you're winding me up…" Hammond said, his voice rising. He didn't finish the sentence.

David said nothing for a few seconds either, just breathed evenly. Hammond sat glaring at him. David pulled a piece of paper out of his pocket and laid it on the table. He said, "A Porsche Turbo, black, with this registration," he tapped the paper, "has been spending a lot of time parked outside this address," he tapped a bit further down the same sheet, "and our informant thought it looked suspicious."

"You leaked details of the car we were looking for?" Hammond asked, still belligerent.

"I don't like the word *leaked*. Your people made several hundred phone calls identifying themselves as police officers on each occasion; I asked a few very discreet contacts to keep an eye out. It's hardly the same thing," David said, his voice level.

"And what do you want me to do with this?" Hammond asked.

"Well, if it's the right registration, I'd like you to arrest the owner and put him in prison. If not, then accept my apologies for wasting your time,"

David said.

Hammond drew the paper towards him and pivoted it round so that he could read it. His head began bobbing as he read. He stuck out his lower lip.

He continued making little nodding motions and said in a monotone, "Leave this with me."

When David didn't respond, Hammond asked, in the same monotone, "Anything else?"

David shook his head and got up to go. "Goodbye," he said. Hammond gave no sign that he had heard.

* * *

Through some unknown process, the smell of stale beer and cigarette smoke had mixed and matured in the walls of the pub to become the scent of home from home, a comforting yeasty tang as instinctively familiar as the house you grew up in.

Breathing pub air, at a table within reaching distance of the bar, Banjo was giving David what he called his 'media briefing'. David watched almost no TV and Banjo took it upon himself to give David the executive summary of what he was missing.

"So what's special about these people?" asked David, confused.

"Nothing. They're whiney, mindless drones," said Banjo.

"I thought they were celebrities," David said, not getting it.

"Well there was one done with celebrities and then there was another thing in the jungle called 'Get me back on telly, I used to be a celebrity'. And of course, they're all celebrities afterwards because the entire nation has watched them pick their nose and loaf around looking bored for weeks," Banjo said.

"So that's what they're talking about constantly in the office – half a dozen ordinary people doing more or less nothing and never going anywhere?" David said.

"That's it," Banjo said, brightly. "It's like watching monkeys at the zoo."

"Why do they volunteer for it?" David asked.

"Well there's a prize, but I think most of them do it because it's a way to stop being a talentless, vacuous nobody for a little while…"

"And become a talentless, vacuous somebody," David interjected.

"And it's a lot easier than doing something with your life," Banjo finished.

"So you're not a fan. Certainly sounds like they've got your back up," David said.

"I've nothing against any of them, if I met them in the street. They're like my postman, in a way – he's a nice enough fella, always seems very cheerful. Brings my post, which is nice. But he wouldn't half start to get on my nerves if he got his own chat show. Or imagine if I went to the Tate and all they'd got was my niece Siobhan's crayon pictures of her dog, Pokey," Banjo said. "Pointing a camera at someone doesn't make them more interesting or more special. To believe the nation will want to watch you eat breakfast and sit on the sofa you'd need an ego the size of a water buffalo. You can't help but dislike someone who believes the fact of their existence constitutes prime-time entertainment."

David said, "Watch the eloquence, Banjo. Someone from the snooker club might wander in and hear you talking like that. Better tell me an offensive joke to make up for it."

"Blimey mate, you're such a snob," said Banjo, with listless scorn.

David said, "I don't mean to be. But that's not what I'm getting at when I'm, you know, getting at you. I just find it funny that you're overeducated. I thought that sort of thing died out with Queen Victoria. But the truth is, you'd probably be happier if you didn't know so much."

He went on, "If you'd never moved away from Bromley, you'd have the same outlook as everyone else in that mob you grew up with. And you wouldn't know that there was anything wrong with that. I just think it's ironic that something that's such a power for good, like education, can be such a thorn in someone's side."

Banjo seemed lost for words. It was difficult to tell from his expression whether he was hurt, but he was certainly off balance.

David looked concerned and said, "I meant funny peculiar, by the way, not funny ha ha. I'm not taking the piss, I'm just saying that I think sometimes you feel a bit of a traitor to your gang back home. Even though you didn't mean to, you've outgrown them."

He continued, "Everybody does it, though. You have to decide which world you fancy living in. And it's not easy. The biggest crime in a group like that is to think you're better than everyone else, but it's difficult not to feel like that when you can see that they're being a bit simpleminded about a lot of things."

Banjo blew out his breath noisily, his eyebrows raised, his eyes staring into the imaginary depths of his pint glass. "This is private stuff. It's not really pub chat," Banjo said, avoiding David's gaze.

David looked worried. "I'm sorry if I just dumped this on you, but I'm allowed to be wise and insightful occasionally." He said very gently, "It's not your job exclusively."

Banjo gave David a glum smile and showed some signs of rallying, "You're right, you know. I can dish it out, but I can't take it. It's what you're talking about, really. I like to pretend I take the world at face value but I also like to show off by telling someone their fortune. Maybe I can't have it both ways."

David nodded, encouragingly, "That's sort of what I'm saying. You're deep, but you try not to look it because you're actually a bit embarrassed about it. You'd rather keep it as a party trick."

David continued, "Remember your speech about fitting in? The more I think about it, the more I think you're right – but I think it applies to you too. Not that I think any less of you for not being perfect."

Banjo gave a sort of comic sneer, "You smug bastard. So is that it or have you got any more turn-the-tables-on-Banjo penetrating insights?"

David replied, "I don't know what the answer is, if that's what you're asking. If you succeed in bettering yourself – whatever that means – it can drive a wedge between you and the people around you and if you don't… Well I don't suppose wasting your potential feels that wonderful either. Look at me and my parents – I have nothing in common with them now. We live in different worlds. I thought they'd be proud of me if I got a good degree and all that, but all it did was make me a mystery to them and make them seem a bit small to me."

Banjo said, "And you think I'm suffering from a bit of the same?"

David nodded.

Banjo acquiesced, "I think you're right mate. So should I button my lip when I'm with the gang or should I show them what a clever old stick I am? It's a pretty crappy choice, isn't it? Lie to your friends about who you are or risk losing them instead?"

David shrugged, "Well, I went with the second one. You tell me how it's working out."

"Well, since we're being all truthful and soul-searching," Banjo said, lowering his voice, "I sometimes think you're a bit lonely and maybe a bit frustrated with your lot."

"You might not be a million miles from the truth there," said David, awkwardly. Now it was his turn to avoid the other's gaze. "You know I hate to talk about this stuff, but it almost feels like I made a deal – don't ask me with who – and they haven't come through. That choice we're talking about: whether to try and lift yourself up and reach your potential, or sort of hang back with the rest of the pack – well I knew there'd be a price to pay if I pushed myself. I knew I'd risk cutting myself off from people, but... I dunno, I just thought there'd be a few more compensations, a bit more of a payoff."

"Like what?" Banjo asked, fascinated.

"It sounds a bit simple, now I'm saying it out loud, but I just thought if I pushed myself, you know, trained and worked hard and studied, I just thought something would come along that was bigger and better than if I hadn't bothered."

"Build it and they will come?" Banjo asked. "Like a sort of karmic communism. To each according to their needs, from each according to their abilities."

"I suppose. In a way, I'm still waiting for my life to start – the real one in which all the really big stuff happens. I suppose somewhere deep down I thought the more capable I made myself as a person, the more impressive my destiny would be when it finally arrived." David threw up his hands, "It sounds demented."

Banjo's face said the opposite, "Everyone believes in destiny, David, everyone. Listen to birds talking about their blokes and going on about 'is he the one?' If life was random there'd be no right person for you, there'd be no correct choices. No one could say, 'is this what I'm meant to do, is this the right thing?' because it wouldn't mean anything. There'd just be one random day after another. Even people who don't believe in god, or superstition or heaven or anything, believe that there's a link between today and tomorrow and the future. No matter how faint it is, everyone believes they have some sort of destiny."

David said, "Right. And to tell you the truth, I'm feeling a bit gypped by mine. I feel like I put my name down for something, I kept my end of the bargain and then nothing happened. God, I sound so ungrateful."

"I don't think it's about being grateful," Banjo said, frowning. "You've probably got it a lot easier this way than if your big, bad destiny turned up. After all, it's about being challenged, isn't it? Finding out what you're really made of? Like going off to war. Lots of blokes wonder how they'd cope. It's not supposed to be a picnic."

David said, "You're not making it sound any less stupid, but at least put that way I can see I'm not the only idiot who thinks like this."

"Human beings are storytellers; we can't help it if we want our lives to make a good story." Banjo said. "Maybe even a legend," he added, melodramatically.

"I should talk to Susan about that. She's the expert on legends," David said.

"Ahh, yes. The woman ever-so-briefly known as Ms Milton. How is Susan?" Banjo asked.

"Don't get carried away. She's an interesting girl, but we're just working together," David said.

"Oh, make it a bit more difficult for me, mate. This is too easy. I like a challenge too, you know." Banjo closed his eyes, put his fingers to his temples and said haltingly, "I'm sensing something. I'm getting a message from beyond. It says… It says…" His voice became tremulous and moaning, "'David likes this girl.'"

David laughed.

Banjo continued hamming, "Wait there's more." The moaning voice again, "'David wants to ask this girl out but he's too much of a pink girl's skipping rope to risk it.' And what's that the voices are saying? 'David...'"

David interrupted, "Maybe now's a good moment to show you this move I learned at training. If I do it right, I should be able to crush your larynx without anyone noticing."

"At your own peril, mate" Banjo said haughtily. "As a master of Dimac, I have access to the legendary Count Dante's full array of crippling, maiming and mutilating techniques."

David did his cockney pensioner voice, "Alright Banjo, I was only joshing with you. You wouldn't hurt a man whose round it is, would you?"

"Now that's more like it. I've got to turn me bike round; I'll expect a pint of Old Nasty to be waiting for me when I get back, unless you want a taste of the quivering palm," Banjo said, warily holding up a trembling hand as though even he was afraid of its power. He sauntered off towards the toilet as David turned to the bar.

When Banjo returned there was a fresh pint of cider waiting for him. David too had a full pint.

Banjo commented, "Not switched to the elderflower cordial? You've become a drinking machine, man. Three pints? Whatever next."

David said, "Susan and I ended up hoovering back quite a lot of wine last night. There's nothing like drinking too much to give you a thirst." He looked down at his drink and puffed, "Actually, you're right. I don't even want this and I've got to speak to this hard man from the Flying Squad again tomorrow. Best done without a hangover."

"That's more like it," Banjo said as David put aside his untouched pint. "Wuss," he whispered, not that quietly.

David ordered a coke. "This is going spare then?" Banjo asked, indicating David's beer. David nodded.

Banjo hopped up, taking the full pint with him, and wandered over to the other side of the pub. There was an elderly man sitting at a table on his own, hands folded over the top of a walking stick, the tip of which rested between his boots. A broadsheet newspaper lay folded on the table, exposing a partially completed crossword. The man wore a species of old black suit which somehow looked as comfy and informal as Banjo's tatty jeans, and about as expensive.

David couldn't hear the conversation but Banjo came back without the pint. The old man lifted his chin and tipped his stick at David in neighbourly acknowledgement.

When Banjo sat back down, David said, "Listen, I want to ask you something."

Banjo said, "I'm all ears."

"This bit of stolen jewellery I was telling you about..." David said. Banjo nodded. "Well, it's from China and apparently in the old days they used to believe it had healing powers. What's weird is that the thug who's stolen it seems to believe the stories. Susan thinks he's dying and that he wants this thing – the Marker we've been calling it – he wants it to cure him."

"Sounds pretty weird. What did you want to ask me about?" Banjo said.

"I'm wondering if it's completely out of the question," David said, closing one eye and glancing up at Banjo.

"What's out of the question?" Banjo asked, not following.

"I reckon I've said enough stupid things this evening that one more won't hurt. I'm wondering if there might be something to the idea of being healed by a two-thousand-year-old piece of metal," David said.

"You mean, as opposed to being healed by a twentieth century piece of metal like a radiotherapy machine," Banjo said.

David didn't respond, but instead went on with his account, "You remember I said I had this client who frightened the life out of me? Well, the guy who stole the Marker from him isn't much better. In fact, considering he's killed several people he should be a lot scarier. There's just something about both of them. It's like they're aliens or something. They look like people but there's something about them that just makes your hair stand up," David said. He glanced thoughtfully at Banjo's heavily spiked red hair.

Banjo puckered his lips thoughtfully. "I don't think I've ever seen you scared. You remember when we went to Rebecca Stevenson's twenty-first and her brother's townie mates wanted to kick the crap out of us. You remember? You should have been scared then, they were huge."

David smiled, "That's the best thing about training – once you've been beaten up a few times by experts, you don't get so worked up about the amateurs having a bash."

Banjo shook his head. "Well maybe you ought to think about that, then. You said this guy frightened the life out of you. If you're not afraid of getting hurt, what are you afraid of?"

They sat quietly for a moment and then Banjo returned to the question, "Just thinking about bizarre cures. I reckon I believe in faith-healing – some of it anyway – and maybe hypnotherapy. And I think most people are prepared to believe that some of the Chinese remedies for things, like cures they've been using for thousands of years, might have something to them. Maybe this Marker is like, I don't know, like acupuncture. Have you seen those pictures of people having operations while they're awake and the only thing stopping them feeling it are a couple of needles?"

"That's true," said David. "I'm sure if people could debunk acupuncture, it would have been done by now. And that's just sticking little bits of metal in someone."

"In the right place," Banjo pointed out helpfully.

Banjo thought of something. "Didn't you say one of your senseis used to be paralysed?"

"Yeah, they had the x-rays pinned up in his dojo – a fracture of the spine. I forget which vertebra, but he couldn't move his legs for a year. It's supposedly an incurable condition, but he got better. He claimed he did it with meditation and breathing techniques," David said.

"And you believe that?" Banjo asked.

"I suppose I do," said David, considering. "It's a lot of trouble to fake. If he was going to falsify a story he should have claimed he knocked out Bruce Lee's front teeth or at least whomped a bar full of bikers. If you were going to bribe half a dozen people to back your story, you'd pick something a bit more macho and hands-on, I reckon."

Banjo said, "So it's not that difficult to see how your man could talk himself into believing in miracles."

Then he looked at David's expression and asked, "Are you saying you believe it too?"

David paused for a moment, made a face, "Naah. He might be as fit as Captain America's stunt double, but that doesn't mean he knows what he's talking about."

"What, is he a bit tasty then?" Banjo asked.

"Like you wouldn't believe. He's either popping something or he's got a training routine that makes me look like your old Uncle Jess," David said.

"Well you'd best keep out his way then, hadn't you?" Banjo said.

CHAPTER 12

THE NEXT DAY
THURSDAY 17TH APRIL

S even in the evening and outside it was still light. Two floors below
ground, in the School of Antiquities' vaults, Susan was finishing up
her notes.

Her fingers rested on the keys of her pearl iBook, the pad of her right
index finger tapping gently on the 'H' key without pressing it – a metronome
to her thoughts.

Then her fingers sprang to life. "Reference to hydrargum," she wrote,
"exception to the Aristotelian elements?"

She had set the laptop a little to her left; a document from the collection
was clipped to a stand on her right. By twisting her head a little she could
type at the same time as she scrutinised the yellowed paper with its precise,
tiny script. She had been sitting like this for a number of hours.

She lifted her hands from the keyboard and hunched up her right
shoulder, rotating it in its socket. With her left hand, she squeezed and
released the side of her neck several times.

She made a decision. "M'out of here," she said, saving and closing the
on-screen document she was working on. She began shutting the laptop

down, then carefully removed the piece of paper from its stand and slid it back into its transparent plastic envelope. While her computer still whirred away, preparing for sleep, she took the sticker-covered envelope with her out into the hallway.

There was now a second document store in a separate room to the researchers' workstations. Fishing a key-ring from the pocket of her sea-green jeans, she opened the heavy fire door and snapped on the light.

Cabinets and racking lined the walls and were stacked in the centre of the room. Though apparently spotless, the room smelled of dust – dust that began to singe if the bare light bulbs were left on for any length of time.

In the corner opposite the door, the document store had been set on a wooden pallet. In appearance, it was halfway between a safe and a filing cabinet. It had no combination dial, just a covered key-hole and a large chromed handle.

Undoing the lock, Susan levered the handle upright (it made a metallic swallowing noise) and pulled open the door. On three shelves, plastic envelopes and yellow-tagged folders were arranged, their code numbers and hand-lettered labels facing outwards.

Sliding the envelope she carried back into its assigned slot, she closed the door. On top of the store lay a clipboard. Half a splintered Biro was attached to its metal clip by a length of frayed, white-plastic twine. Glancing first at her watch, Susan filled in a couple of boxes on the form – its ghostly outlines and titles faded by endless serial photocopying.

She walked out of the room, turning out the light and locking the door behind her. To make room for the document store, a pallet of ancient odds and ends had been removed from the storage room and now lay stranded in the hallway near the door. Susan noticed an ancient green filing cabinet, swathed in polythene. It lay on its side – a sure sign that its end was near. Enamelled card index drawers and an aging roller blind, backed in perished black rubber, shared the cabinet's bier.

Stopping at the drinks dispenser by the silent lift she selected tomato soup and started slightly as the machine snapped a plastic cup into its dispenser with a gunshot rapidity that made its front panel rattle. The machine's explosive 'chunk', followed by a rising gurgle, was the only sound on the quiet floor.

Susan was the last person working on her level. The occasional daytime noises had ceased. A sound like a ball-bearing being repeatedly dropped onto marble flooring would sometimes filter down to her, but in the evening everything was peaceful. Even the new guard was nowhere to be seen.

Taking her soup back into the Alexandrian room, Susan dropped down into her chair. The dim overhead strips, and her single bright, halogen task-light, were the only illumination.

She slurped a few atoms of piping hot soup into her mouth and then began rooting in her bag for her address book. Wedged into its spine was her phone card, which she placed on the table.

Flicking through the addresses, she found the page she was looking for and pinned the address book flat with the palm of her hand. Tucking the phone under her ear she punched the long sequence of numbers and waited for it to start ringing.

"Shoot," Dee's voice said.

"Dee, it's Susan."

"Hold on Susie." Then Dee's voice, slightly muffled, could be heard yelling, "Get it out of my office before I kill it, Jack. Scram. And get the door behind you."

The muffled quality vanished and Dee's voice, quiet and calm, said, "Sorry about that. And sorry for calling you Susie. How are you Sis?"

Dee's sudden warmth caught Susan by surprise. She said, "Err, great. I'm great; how are you Dee?"

"Like gangbusters." Then Dee hesitated momentarily, "Have you thought any more about my visit?" Hardly giving Susan time to respond she continued, "I could maybe cancel if you don't think…"

Susan butted in softly, "Dee, I just meant I was pretty busy. I'd love to see you. I feel bad because I've got a lot to do at the moment. I won't be able to spend anywhere near as much time with you as I'd like. That's what was giving me reservations."

Dee considered for a second. "Well, what if I'm self-sufficient? I'll get a guidebook, show myself around. Maybe I can get a hotel downtown."

Susan brightened, "Oh that place I'm staying in, the one that belongs to my Professor, it's priceless," she said enthusiastically. "You have to stay with me – even if I'm not around that much. Imagine Miss Marple bought a townhouse. Décor's all Edwardian. Everything's an antique – so no TV. You'll love it."

"Sounds great. So you're OK with this?" Dee asked.

"Yeah, Dee," Susan said with sincerity in her voice, "I'm looking forward to it."

"Well, I'm getting in on Tuesday. Is that too soon?" Dee said.

"This Tuesday? Like five days from now Tuesday?" Susan said, sounding a little taken aback.

"Yup," Dee said, in a small voice.

"I just thought… Never mind. That's fine. Great I mean," Susan said.

Dee cleared her throat and then said brightly, "So what's keeping you so busy? Would I understand it if you told me?"

"You know what paper is, right?" Susan said, teasing. "Well, I'm going through a ton of it. Lots of old paper that needs reading and analysing and alphabetizing. Only a nerd could love it. Fortunately…"

Dee asked, "So you're not party-towning it every night then?"

"Cocoa, and in bed by eleven," Susan assured her sister. "Although, one cool thing I'm doing is help investigate a robbery. This insurance company is paying me to do some background research on a stolen antique. Real cops and robbers."

"Nancy Drew. So not just librarians, you're hanging around with insurance types too. Good job," Dee said, amused.

"He's not your stereotypical insurance guy," Susan said, snipping off the last word as though regretting she'd said anything.

"Who guy? Which guy?" Dee demanded.

"From the insurance company," Susan said breezily. She added, "His name's David."

"If he were a celebrity impersonator he'd be…" she asked.

"God, I don't know. A young Clancy Brown, darker though," Susan said.

"The Kurgan? Selling insurance? My mind refuses to form an image," Dee said, slightly incredulous.

"Bad choice. He's not scary looking, just solid. Anyway, the point of the story was the interesting work I'm doing, not the guy I'm doing it for," Susan said.

"Sure, sure," Dee said dismissively. "He single?"

"I guess," Susan said nonchalantly. "Stop quizzing me about him. He's just something on the side." She corrected herself, "It's some work on the side, and it's one of the reasons I thought I might not have enough time to see you." She added emphatically, "He's not my type anyway."

Dee said, "OK. I get the message. He's kind of a hunk, he's available and you're not interested in him. I get it. Say no more." Dee sounded conspiratorial, like she'd just figured out what was going on. "So can I give you my flight details? See if you can meet me. No sweat either way; I can get into the city by myself."

Susan blinked. She seemed surprised that Dee was dropping the inquisition about David so readily. "Ah yeah. Let me get a pen. OK, shoot."

Dee was getting into London Heathrow on Tuesday evening. Susan would have enough time to get to the airport without cutting into her working day.

"So do you look any different? Taller? Tattoos?" Dee asked.

"Don't worry. I'll hold up a sign," Susan said. "I'll see you Tuesday, Dee."

"Yeah, see you then, Sis," Dee said, hanging up.

Susan held the phone in her hand for a moment, her elbow resting on the desk. As she returned the receiver to its cradle, the small click of plastic on plastic happened to coincide with a distant thump, as though she were hanging up a phone weighing tons.

Idly flicking through her address book, she found herself looking at the page that contained David's number. She stuck out her lower lip for a moment, considering the entry. Then she spent a minute entering the number into the memory of her mobile. She accidentally erased it all and had to input the details a second time before she had it successfully stored. Still holding the phone in her hand, her thoughts wandered.

A sound cut suddenly through her daydream, a sound like two fist-sized flints being slammed together. It came from the other side of the wall – the storage room.

Susan cocked her head, straining to hear more, holding herself completely still. A faint, drawn-out squeak reached her ears, like the sound of something being slid over lino, or perhaps the shriek of distant metal being twisted and deformed.

She looked around the room, alarmed, her eyes searching. Whatever she was looking for, she didn't find it.

She picked up the phone and hit zero. It rang several times, but no one answered. She hung up.

On silent feet she moved to the door, pushed down the handle with infinite slowness, one hand covering the other. When the handle was fully depressed, she pulled it open a fraction. She could make out the storage room door ajar, the light on.

Just as slowly as she'd pushed it down, she cautiously released the handle. She pulled the door open far enough for her to squeeze through.

Before moving through the gap, she studied the pallet of oddments that lay between her vantage point and the opened door. Her eyes alighted on an old, oak window pole – a metre-long oak shaft capped with a tilde of black iron, designed to hook the looped catches of high Victorian windows. She crept towards it, weight on her back leg, sliding her front foot forwards in stealthy increments.

Her hands closed around the window pole and slid it carefully from its tangled nest. The pallet was in the corner of the hallway between the two rooms. She was out of sight of anyone who might be in the storage room, but neither could she see in.

A snap, like a steel cable parting under tension, echoed from the unseen room.

Placing her hands shoulder-width apart on the pole, she gripped it like a shortened quarterstaff, and advanced – in her silent, sliding gait – closing the distance to the open doorway.

Reaching it, she looked in and saw a man, dressed in black and grey, sitting on one heel in front of the opened door of the document store. A scatter of folders lay fanned around his feet. In his hands he held a piece of paper on which an intricate design was evident – it was the same document she had shown David on her laptop.

The intruder was holding the paper up, inclined to catch the light, and was apparently captivated by what he saw.

He wore a tight-fitting, black wool cap which, seen from behind at an angle, was shielding his face from Susan. But in partly obscuring his features, it also blocked some of his peripheral vision, helping to hide Susan's presence from him.

Susan took a step towards him. She froze as he turned suddenly (but in the direction of the document store) and snatched another folder from the rack.

He hadn't spotted her yet, but she could see that it was the same man she had glimpsed as she rushed to help Mrs Harris. He was clean-shaven now, but there was no mistaking his face.

She stepped forwards again. And again. She was almost there.

One more step and she twisted the pole up over her right shoulder before bringing it down hard, the wood and metal whacking him across the side of his head, sending his cap flying, knocking him sprawling.

The impact made a curious sound, sharp and inorganic. A flash of glittering metal caught Susan's eye. The displaced woollen cap lay at her feet and visible within it was a gilt band. The intruder had been wearing a circle of metal around his temples.

A blow of such force on an unprotected head might have been fatal; as it was, although blood streamed from a raw groove in his short, dark hair, and his eyes seemed momentarily unable to focus on anything, he was very much alive. The metal band had deflected part of the blow's momentum.

He was now lying on his side, one elbow beneath him, his other hand held with its palm in front of his face as though he were struggling to see it clearly.

Advancing on him, Susan raised the pole for another blow.

The intruder sprang back, with a scrabbling of feet. He collided with the sharp edge of a tall, grey cabinet, but was standing upright a moment later.

He was unsteady on his feet, and his eyes seemed to track a point that wandered, like a heat-dazed fly, in an orbit around Susan's head. Nonetheless he took a step towards Susan, his hands held up in a boxer's guard, but with the hands unclenched and twisted edge-on to her.

Without diverting an ounce of her attention from her adversary Susan screamed at the top of her lungs. In the confined space it stopped the intruder dead.

A moment later he sprang at her.

As soon as he moved, Susan brought the butt end of the pole whipping across in front of her. It connected with his jaw. Susan's grunt of exertion covered the noise of heavy wood on bone.

He dropped, felled, to one knee and then immediately came bounding back up, like something springing from a trapdoor, to slam the pole from Susan's hands and twist her off balance. She put a foot back to steady herself and stepped forward straight into a punch, a fast left jab that caught her high cheekbone, instantly buckling her knees and sending her toppling backwards. Her head caught the corner of the document store's open, twisted door on the way down. She fell onto her back, the intruder's metal band painful beneath her.

A clattering sound came from the hallway.

The left side of the intruder's face, where Susan had first struck, was painted with blood, droplets of which fell, one a second, from his chin. His right jaw-line was marked with a purple channel of wounded skin, the imprint of the makeshift staff. His mouth was hanging open.

He took a step towards Susan who was struggling to get a hand beneath her, momentarily unable to rise.

Two figures in uniform pelted into the room and stopped short. The intruder twisted his head to see them, his neck turning stiffly and with an unnatural motion of his shoulders. The two newcomers wore the patches of security guards.

"The police will be here in seconds," the young, black guard yelled at the intruder who stood, wounded and panting, glaring at them. "Come away from her," the guard ordered advancing towards them. The guard's hand came to rest on a collapsed metal tripod which lay atop a packing case, its telescoped limbs bunched and stubby enough to make it a possible weapon.

"Come on," the guard said, firmly but with a coaxing tone, his hand neither raising nor releasing the metal stand. The other guard, pale and nervous-looking, remained by the door.

The intruder took two hesitant steps towards the guards, his back bowed, his head lowered, blood running down his cheekbone and dripping from his down-turned nose. He walked like a man crippled.

It was a feint and suddenly the intruder scooped a handful of documents from the ground and ran, shoulder first towards the door. The first guard was knocked sideways as he attempted to tackle the intruder. His colleague, who merely grabbed at the intruder's sleeve, found the cloth torn from his grip as the man forced past him. Something on the intruder's wrist glittered in the light before the sleeve was released.

"Ernie, see to the girl," the black man barked, scrambling to his feet and running after the fleeing intruder who had already banged through the echoing fire door adjacent to the lift and was taking the stairs three at a time.

The remaining guard looked anxiously at Susan and then at his receding partner.

Susan held out her hand to him and quickly he came over and helped her to her feet.

She was quite unsteady and was forced to throw an arm over the guard's dandruff-sprinkled shoulders to keep herself upright.

"Help me into the other room, quickly," she said to the guard. He steadied her as she made her precarious way back towards her desk. Several drips of bright blood fell from a strand of her blonde hair and stitched a scarlet ellipsis across her white cotton t-shirt.

She tripped and almost fell into her chair. The address book still lay open, her mobile phone sitting in its centre, an outsized bookmark.

She snatched up the phone and dialled as quickly as she could. She winced as it touched her cheek.

It rang – once, twice and was answered.

"David," she said.

CHAPTER 13

MOMENTS LATER
THURSDAY 17TH APRIL

"I'll call them, but I'm only minutes from there myself," David said, phone to his ear, other hand on the steering wheel.

He listened to Susan's voice on the line. "My god, are you OK? Jesus."

He listened some more. "Jesus. Listen, you're right near University College Hospital. I'll call you there on your mobile. Are you OK?"

He listened. "Yeah, yeah. I'm calling them now." He paused a moment to concentrate on swerving around a bus which was slowing him down. "Get to the hospital, I'll call you really soon." He hung up and dialled 999.

It took a little explaining, but he managed to make it clear to the woman on the police switchboard that a man who had just committed a violent crime in one part of London might be heading to a second location. He mentioned DI Hammond's name and gave his own details. After a few minutes he received assurance that a car was on its way and hung up.

He was momentarily stuck in traffic, waiting for the lights to change, on the road from Islington down to Old Street. He searched the memory of his mobile phone, found Hammond's mobile number and dialled it.

"Hammond," a voice barked on the first ring.

"It's David Braun," and without giving Hammond a chance to speak went on, "our third man just attacked Susan Milton at the University and stole those papers she told you about. Have you got anyone at that address I gave you?"

"Not right now," Hammond said.

"Well I've called 999, but I thought you should know. Maybe you've got an ARV in the area," David said. Holding the wheel steady with his knee, he pulled at his tie, sawing the knot down until it slipped free. His jacket was already off, laying on the passenger seat at his side.

Hammond said, "I need to take care of this. Goodbye Braun." He added curtly, almost under his breath, "Thanks."

The address David was racing towards lay on a side road off the Great Eastern Road, the thoroughfare which ran from Old Street down towards the City and the Tower. The area was a warren of red-brick, three-storey studios and workshops – many still with hayloft doors on their upper storeys and old iron pulleys anchored beneath their roofs – remnants of their hard-working, pre-gentrified past.

Somewhere, the sun was dipping down beneath the unseen horizon. The gathering gloom made the switchback streets seem narrower. Hidden in the warren of lanes, David was now driving over cobbles.

He turned a final corner into the beam of headlights. A black Porsche sat idling, tucked into the kerb, just short of a recessed entranceway. Tall, blue-painted, wooden double doors barred access to the ground floor of a workshop. A dark-dressed figure had one of the doors open and was tugging at the lower bolt of the second door.

Once David had rounded the corner and the halide-purple sparkle of the Porsche's headlamps no longer dazzled him, he could recognise the man from their encounter earlier in the week. The man he had seen vault a three-metre wall stood in front of him, tugging at the doors' left-hand bolt, unable to pull it out of the ground. The figure's dipped right shoulder and the way his left hand held on to the heavy iron door handle suggested that his legs were doing less than the door was to hold him upright.

The high wooden doors, when opened, would be wide enough to admit the Porsche. A bare concrete floor just visible within had the look of a garage space.

David didn't begin to slow until he was level with the open door, giving no advance warning that he might have reached his destination. As he passed the struggling figure, he braked hard and put the nose of his Saab across the street, stopping inches from the Porsche's front end and blocking the street.

David burst out of the car, but the other man didn't run, he merely raised himself from his stooped position and squared his shoulders.

One side of his face was now black, a skin of drying blood covered it from forehead to chin. On the other side, his jaw line bulged horribly, the swarthy skin tight across his distorted cheek. The record of an impact was imprinted in the flesh.

He spoke through tight-clenched teeth, his lips drawn back from his blood-soaked gums; the effect was of a talking skull. "Only one hound and him without tribute. I'm insulted," he sucked blood through his teeth. "Perhaps mortally," he said with a little hiss, possibly intended as a laugh.

David had stopped a few paces short of his quarry, who stood unmoving in the doorway.

The battered figure studied him. "How clever of your master to send a loyal child. A hundred years from now you'll wish you'd kept it for yourself."

David said nothing.

"Well, let's see how well you've learned your lessons," the figure said, the final liquid sibilant forcing a pink bubble of blood to catch in the corner of his mouth. He took a step forwards and bringing his left hand out from behind his back revealed a knife clutched in his sticky fist.

David took an involuntary half step backwards, instinctively reacting to the sight of a weapon by creating more space. He shifted more weight to his back foot, the added danger of a knife making a kick preferable to a punch. He lifted his guard higher, making it more defensive, his hands now in front of his face, the bony points of his elbows presented to his enemy.

The wounded man transferred his knife to his right hand, holding it out as though he were about to hand it to David. Its tip made little circular patterns as its owner stirred the air in front of him. He took a small step towards David and another, forcing David to retreat. He began to back David towards the parked cars.

The knife suddenly flashed out towards David's guard, aimed high, at the level of eyes and fingers, but the attacking arm was not fully extended which left David room to dip back from its glittering point.

Twice more the knife arced out, forcing David back. He was almost against the flank of his slewed car, wedged in the vee between side panel and open door. He was trapped.

He glanced quickly to one side as though gauging his retreat, his eyes left his opponent's. The instant eye contact was broken the knife was swinging towards his face. Just as he dipped his gaze, David took his weight off his right foot. As his attacker swung, he brought his right heel straight up into the kneecap of his adversary's front leg. He allowed his upper body to fall back, out of the path of the knife, dropping him against the side of the car.

David's opponent stumbled backwards, his damaged knee buckling, his hands going up and out to steady him.

David pushed off from the car, thrusting forwards and driving his left foot flat into the centre of his opponent's chest. His adversary was thrown backwards, knocked off his feet, his head glancing off the glassy granite of the kerbstone, his hands thrown high. He lay sprawled on his back.

David stepped forwards and grabbed the man's out-flung wrist with one hand, covered it with a second, and pulled, meanwhile placing his right foot on his fallen attacker's shoulder. The arm was wrenched straight, the elbow holding, but the captured hand could barely retain its grip on the knife. The injured man gasped.

David wrapped one palm around the other's fist, grasped the base of the thumb and rotated his attacker's hand until the fingers opened like a flower and spilled the knife out onto the cobbles. Twisting further he stopped pulling and allowed the other's straight arm to bend at the elbow. The arm folded until the knifeless hand was up by its owner's ear. The downed man's shoulder came off the ground in an attempt to lessen the painful tension in his twisted arm.

Still holding the thumb and twisted wrist, David continued to rotate the arm until he had forced his opponent to turn completely over. As the injured man lay face down in the street, David dropped a knee into the centre of his back. Pinned, wrist-locked and battered, the fallen man had ceased to struggle.

Neither spoke nor moved for several minutes until sirens, high revving engines and finally the sound of running feet announced the arrival of the police.

Two officers approached while a third and fourth fanned out to either side. David said, "There's a knife to my left. I won't move if one of you wants to retrieve it. My name is David Braun. DI Hammond of the Flying Squad can vouch for me. This is the man Hammond's looking for." An officer was approaching David from behind, just visible in David's peripheral vision. A kick and a clatter and the knife was skittering away across the cobbles.

"Tell me when you're ready for me to let him up," David said.

"Just stay there, sir," an officer said. Then he spoke into his lapel mike. "Let's ascertain who's who before anyone starts moving around."

A couple more minutes passed with David and his captive locked together and immobile while the policeman conducted a radio conversation. Eventually the officer addressed him again, "I think it's pretty clear that you're Mr Braun, sir. If you'd let me put a handcuff on that wrist you've got there, you can let him go."

David held up one and then the other of his captive's wrists so that the officer could fasten them together. Then he stood up and moved aside, brushing dirt from his trousers and inspecting himself for injuries. He was still breathing fast despite the fact he had hardly moved for five minutes.

David produced a business card and said, "DI Hammond has all my details, but here they are again anyway. I assume there'll be some paperwork…"

The officer nodded and muttered, "Ohhh yes."

"…just get in touch when you want me."

The captive, who was now in a sitting position in the middle of the road, spoke to David. "Were your orders not to kill me?"

"I don't know what you mean," David said, as much to the policemen as to their prisoner.

"You might want to get yourself checked out," the officer said. "It's very easy to hurt yourself and not notice when the adrenaline's flowing." Turning to his colleagues he said, "You two take a quick look inside, check there's no one in there. Watch yourselves. We'll take the prisoner in. And get that towed," he said, nodding towards the Porsche.

Once the prisoner was folded into the back of one of the police cars, it set off, reversing up the street.

"I'd better move this," David said, indicating his car and received a nod from one of the two remaining officers.

David walked over to his car and got in. The keys were still in the ignition. He held up his hands which shook a little. He turned the key, started the engine and reversed until the car was straight again. Then he drove forwards, past the Porsche and pulled in.

He got out and wandered back to the open garage door, but the policemen had gone inside. David took a couple of steps through the open door, seeing only a bare patch of oil-stained concrete and a wooden staircase leading to an unseen upper floor. Businesslike voices drifted down the stairs.

He turned around to go and something caught his eye. His attacker had never managed to open the second of the double doors. In the deep shadows between the bolted door and the wall rested a bag.

David took a closer look. A smart black holdall, almost brand new and still spotless, sat on the filthy concrete floor. It plainly hadn't been there long. It sat just where someone who momentarily needed both hands might place it.

David looked up the stairs. No sign of the policemen. He looked back at the bag. It was almost invisible in the gloom.

He grabbed it and walked rapidly and stiffly back to his car. As quickly as possible he got the vehicle moving. There was still no sign of the policemen as the street vanished from his rear-view mirror.

CHAPTER 14

AN HOUR LATER
THURSDAY 17TH APRIL

S usan sat with her head in her hands. A few of the hard orange chairs around her were occupied, but the majority remained empty. Most would not be required until the pubs began emptying out. She had, a droll British-Asian doctor told her, picked a good time to drop in.

She had only waited half an hour to be seen. The presence of a police constable taking her details and asking the nurses how long she would have to wait helped ensure that she was given prompt attention. The constable left when she went behind a curtain to have her wounds cleaned and stitched.

The cut to her scalp, where she'd banged her head, had received five stitches. The blood had dried, matting her hair and plastering it to her head. The blow to her cheek had split the skin and would bruise spectacularly, she was assured. The doctor had closed the wound with a steristrip. They concluded her treatment with a tetanus jab.

Not yet ready to make the trip home, she returned to the waiting area. In the warm, bright room, surrounded by alert and watchful staff, she had found her eyelids beginning to droop, though it was only just after nine in the evening.

The doctor who had treated her emerged from behind a curtain and wandered over to her.

"You look pretty tired," he said and gave her a professional smile.

"It's been quite a day," she said, looking up.

"You remember what you were doing just before all this happened?" he asked.

"Sure. I called my sister," she said.

"And you didn't black-out," he asked.

"Like I said, I don't remember it if I did. I don't think there was time," she said.

He looked troubled and placed his fingertips on her head, tilted her head down, peered at her skull again.

"Is there anyone at home to keep an eye on you tonight?" he asked.

At that moment, a voice said, "Susan," and she looked round to see David standing there in a creased and dirty, grey business shirt.

"Have you come to collect the patient?" the doctor asked David.

"Yes. Is she OK?" he asked, a frown of deep concern on his face.

"There's no reason to think otherwise, but a bang on the head is always unpredictable. Can you do me a favour? Can you keep an eye on your girlfriend tonight?" He looked towards Susan. "You're probably just worn out, but if you find yourself getting groggy, confused," he looked back to David, "or if you can't wake her up, call an ambulance. There's only the very smallest risk, but we might as well be safe," he said.

Susan began to say, "He's not…" but David interrupted, saying to Susan, "You're welcome to stay. I feel responsible."

The doctor looked from one of them to the other. "So you're not quite at the 'staying over' stage yet. Well, guess what? You are now. Think of it as fate."

He turned to go and paused, "Those stitches can probably come out in a week. Drop in here, or get your GP to do it." He strode away, calling out, "Good luck."

David sat down beside Susan. He put his hand on her shoulder and said, "I'm so sorry. What's… What kind of shape are you in?"

Susan gave him a weak smile. "I'm alright. Did they get him?"

"Yup," David said, grimly triumphant. "He's in custody. Somebody really knocked him around before I got to him."

"You tackled him?" she asked, glancing up sharply.

"And you did too?" asked David, looking at her eye.

Susan gave a tired little laugh, "I hit him with a window pole," she said. "Twice."

David returned the smile, raising his eyebrows. "He looked like he'd been hit by a bus." His smile receded. "What did he do to you?"

"Just what you can see," she said indicating her swollen and patched cheek, "plus I hit my head on something."

"I'm so sorry for getting you involved in this," he said.

She shrugged, "I think I got myself involved. I want to be mad at you for going off on a one-man crusade again, but I don't suppose anyone forced me to take a swing at him instead of running like hell. Anyway, I'm too tired to think about it. He's behind bars and we're both in one piece."

She stood up, stiffly, and he helped her. "I meant what I said," he assured her, "you're welcome to stay with me or we can go to your place if you'd prefer."

"Are you trying to pick me up?" she said narrowing her eyes at him.

"No, I just meant…" he began, stumbling over the words.

She leant on him and said, "I'm kidding. Relax. If it's all the same to you, let's head to your place. A big, old Victorian house is not what I feel like at the moment. I want somewhere cosy. Is your place cosy?" She was talking more and more slowly, holding his arm to steady herself.

"I'm straight, male and under fifty, so no, it's not cosy. But it's comfortable enough and, thank god, pretty tidy at the moment," he said.

David found himself steering Susan towards the doors; she could walk, but she didn't seem too good at navigation. She was almost asleep on her feet. "Boy, that adrenaline really takes it out of you. Or maybe it's the local," she said.

David had parked on a meter a few minutes walk from the hospital. The cool evening air seemed to wake Susan up a little, though she still held on to David.

"You know what I think?" she said. "I think it's a miracle we're both still alive."

David said nothing.

She went on, "I was going over this while I was waiting back there. He's killed two people – maybe took a gun off one of them to do it. He's put two police officers and a security guard in the hospital, as well as one little old lady. And he can force open a locked door and then wrench the front off something that's basically a safe, apparently with his bare hands – god knows how. And you saw him jump a nine-foot wall. We were unbelievably lucky not to get ourselves killed. Everyone else who's encountered him has met some sort of monster; for some reason we only had to deal with a man."

David nodded gravely.

He said, "I got to his place before the police did. I should have left him alone. I was just… I didn't know what he'd done to you and I didn't want him to get away."

"You weren't afraid?" she asked.

"At one point. Not beforehand though. I just didn't think about it. I didn't get scared until I saw he'd got a knife."

Susan squeezed his arm, "Oh my god."

"He could have had a gun. He could have had half a dozen friends. In fact, if you hadn't given him such a hiding, I don't think he'd have needed anything, maybe not even the knife. And I knew that; I'd seen him move. Somehow it didn't matter. I was such an idiot, but I didn't care. I wanted to stop him."

"So what were you thinking about when you tackled him?" she asked.

"I was thinking, 'I can beat him'," David answered. "I think maybe all the training's warped my mind. Somehow it just seemed like a test, something I had to get through." He threw up his hands. He looked at her, "So, what's your excuse?"

They had arrived at David's car. He unlocked it, separated himself from Susan's arm and opened the passenger door for her. Once she was in, he closed the door and went round to his side, got in.

She was thoughtful as he started the car, waited for a break in the traffic.

"I caught him by surprise," she said. "He'd found the document describing the Marker and he just *had* to have a peek. I knew for a couple of seconds he was off guard. After that, maybe he'd go back to being pretty much unstoppable. Obviously, I wish someone else had caught him with his guard down, but there was just me. So I took my shot."

David reached over and squeezed her hand. "Like you say: we were pretty lucky."

They drove in silence for a few minutes. Susan turned to look out of the passenger window, let her forehead rest against the glass.

Suddenly she asked, "Did the police recover the documents? The ones he stole?"

"Not exactly," David said, mysteriously.

She waited for him to speak.

"I picked up his bag," he said. He didn't explain for a moment. Then he said, "He had a bag with him. It's got the papers in it. And something else in a box. I think it's the Marker." He glanced over at Susan, taking his eyes off the road for a second, trying to gauge her reaction.

For a moment she said nothing. Then she began to laugh. "Oh well, why not?" she said, almost recklessly, in between laughs, a wild tone in her voice.

David found himself smiling, her good humour contagious, despite the fact she sounded a little manic. After a minute or so she got herself under control and said, "Why aren't I surprised?"

David couldn't think of a reply.

"Have you got a plan?" she said.

"I'll hand it over tomorrow, make up some story," he said. "But I wanted to see this thing." He sounded emphatic.

He glanced at her. She was watching him, waiting for him to go on. He said, "You've seen him now. You know there's something weird, bizarre, whatever you want to call it, about him. Well the owner of the Marker is the same. There's something strange about him too. And both of them are obsessed with the Marker," he said.

She was still listening, patiently.

He went on, "He thought I'd come to kill him." He shook his head in disbelief. "He called me a child and said that in a hundred years I'd wish I'd kept it for myself. I didn't know what to make of it. And he said something about tribute," he paused. "Whatever's going on here, I want to figure it out. I want to know who the hell these people are and what he was talking about," David said, his voice loud with exasperation.

"He said 'tribute'?" Susan asked, curiously.

"Yeah, he said I had no tribute. Does that mean something to you?" he asked.

"It's in one of the documents in the collection. It talks about tribute. It's… It's like a badge of office, something you wear. I think the derivation is sort of a pun. Tribute means, literally, an offering from the tribe, but it also means three of something. Whatever tribute is, I think it's in three parts. The scroll mentions tribute on someone's brow; one part is obviously a headpiece."

She was quiet for a moment.

"We're not totally different, you and me," she said. She gave a crooked smile, "You're worse, no question about it. But I'm guilty too."

"What do you mean?" David asked. "What are you talking about?"

"I kept something from the police," she said, quietly.

"What?" David asked, his voice quiet and level.

"He was wearing something on his head, a metal band. I think it might be gold. When I hit him with the pole, what I really hit was the band. I think maybe I might have killed him otherwise." She stopped talking for a minute. She was very quiet, her hand over her mouth. She made a tiny sound, a single sob. Then she lifted her head again and her voice was stronger, "I kept the band. It's in my desk."

David asked, "Are you saying that's what he meant by 'tribute', the gold band he was wearing?"

Susan shrugged.

"What does it mean?" David said passionately. "Is this some sort of secret society? Like, I dunno, the Templars or the Illuminati or something?" he said, sounding incredulous.

"You know about that stuff?" Susan asked.

"I don't know anything about them except that they're popular with conspiracy theorists," David said.

"Or you could have said the Masons or maybe the Priory of Sion. There's a ton of them," she said.

"You don't believe any of it?" he asked.

"Not at face value, no. I don't think every last detail is made up, I just think most conspiracies are bits of disconnected things linked together when they shouldn't be," she said.

"So how do we link this together properly so that it makes sense instead of looking like a paranoid delusion?"

Susan sighed. "Maybe we can't. We'll look at the Marker. You'll give it back to its owners. The bad guy will go to jail, or maybe a lunatic asylum. Maybe we never get to work it out. Maybe we don't have enough of the pieces. Maybe that's how conspiracy theories get started, by taking half the picture and pretending it tells the whole story."

David drove in silence, brooding.

Susan put a hand on his shoulder and said softly, "It might not be such a bad thing. We had our brush with danger and we found out that neither of us are cowards – or maybe that both of us need our heads looking at. This is a good point to get off the ride. I don't think I'd care to go round a second time."

"You might be right," David said. "I'll have a happy client, you'll get to look at your collection in peace. We're both still alive. That's not a bad outcome, is it?"

"Definitely not," she said, reassuringly. "We might even end up as friends," she said, smiling.

While they had been talking, they had reached David's flat. He found a parking space right outside.

David's flat was the upper floor of a converted, turn of the century terrace. It had a large main bedroom and a second much smaller one, with a single bed in it, currently piled up with boxes.

David offered Susan his room, but she insisted that she'd be a lot happier in a small bed than he would.

Susan, whose white top was gruesomely bloodstained and whose matted hair hung stiffly, asked if she could take a shower.

While she was doing that, David searched around for clean clothes, finding a comfortable old rugby shirt, tracksuit trousers, a pair of towelling socks and some white cotton boxer shorts – all laundry-fresh. He laid them out on the single bed once he'd moved the boxes and put fresh bedclothes on. Susan was still in the shower.

She emerged, after nearly twenty minutes, wrapped in various towels and scuttled into her new room.

David tapped at the closed door. "Hot chocolate?" he called. "Everyone needs hot chocolate when they're feeling a bit banged up."

She opened the door a little and peeked round the edge, displaying wet hair and a bare shoulder covered in droplets of water. "Got any of that almond stuff? The liqueur?"

"Amaretto?" asked David.

"Yeah, that," she said.

"I might have, if my pal Banjo hasn't hoovered it. He tends to assume if I don't drink something within a month I need help with it. You want it in the hot chocolate or on its own?" he asked.

"In the chocolate. To start with," she said.

"You don't look like you're dressed yet. Have I got time for a shower?" he asked.

"Hey, it's your place. Help yourself. I don't suppose there's any hot water left in the whole street though. Sorry about that," she said.

David put some milk on to heat, on a low setting, and headed for the bathroom. When he returned, he was wearing similar clothes to Susan's, who sat on his black leather couch, legs tucked under her.

"The underwear was a nice touch," she said.

David looked a little awkward, "I didn't know if you wanted… If you'd wear…"

"Easy. I'll have to stop teasing you; it's no challenge. Actually, I used to wear men's boxers when I was in high school. Sort of undercover rebellion," she said.

"Don't tell me that," he said, shaking his head, "there's no way I should know what you used to wear under your school uniform. In fact I'm probably guilty of some sort of crime now."

"Oh, now you're worried about committing crimes," she said. And then pointed to the pan of milk. "Be a good boy and find that Amaretto," she said, and then in a throaty Southern drawl, "Momma needs her medicine."

David laughed. "Hold on," he said, wandering into the kitchen area, which was just an extension of the living room. He began looking in cupboards. "Are you even allowed alcohol?" he asked. "I don't remember the doctor mentioning that."

"Gimme," she said. "I get cranky otherwise."

He chuckled again. "OK." Pulling a dusty bottle from the back of a cupboard he said, "Here we are. Banjo is obviously slipping."

He made two mugs of hot chocolate, topped hers up with liqueur. He put a splash of Irish Whiskey in his and then grimaced as he tasted it. He brought the drinks over to the sofa. Susan took her mug and pulled her feet in enough so that he could sit next to her. She sighed and let her head loll back against the sofa for a minute. "I need a holiday," she said.

"Where would you go?" he asked softly, sipping from his mug.

"An island somewhere," she said dreamily. "Maybe a Greek island. One bar, one hotel, a restaurant and a post office. Maybe a goat."

"Sounds nice. What would you do there?" he said, his voice even lower.

Susan, when she spoke, sounded almost asleep, "Sit under a tree with my books. Look for olives. Talk to the goat."

The mug in her hand started to tip and David leaned across to catch it, cupping his hands round hers. She opened her eyes and lifted her head in surprise. She sat up a bit, which brought them very close. Their fingers were tangled up and it took David a moment to disengage.

"You got it?" he asked.

"I've got it," she replied.

He let go of her hand and they moved apart. Neither of them spoke for a moment.

After a few seconds they realised they were staring at each other and Susan looked away. "I'd better get to bed," she said. "What's your plan for the morning?"

"The doctor said I should keep an eye on you. I know it's a pain, but I want to check in on you every couple of hours," he said.

She made a face but conceded, "Oh yeah, he said that, didn't he?"

"I'll tap on your door, that's all, just let me know you're still functioning. I'll probably get up around six, so when I check on you then, we can make a plan," he said.

She took a few more sips of her chocolate and set down the half-finished mug. "Can I borrow a toothbrush?" she said standing up and shuffling towards the bathroom, dragging her feet in their oversized socks and baggy trousers.

"I left one out," he said.

When she had pulled the bathroom door closed behind her, he went into her room and scooped up her clothes. Her jeans and underwear went into the washing machine on a cool wash, the bloody top he left to soak in a bowl of cold water. While he was doing that, he heard the toilet flush and sock-muffled feet padding about.

"Night," she called and then he heard her door close.

When he tapped on her closed door at one, he called, "How many fingers am I holding up?"

"Better be more than one," a drowsy voice said.

At three he called, "Who's President?"

"Al Gore," she said.

He put her clothes in the dryer while he was up and set his alarm for six.

CHAPTER 15

THAT SAME EVENING
THURSDAY 17TH APRIL

The car contained three people: driver, passenger and prisoner.

"Name?" repeated the officer from the front passenger seat, this time more harshly.

The prisoner was on his own in the back, head down, his breathing audible even over the engine noise of the rapidly moving police car. There was a harsh catch and rasp to each breath which, when considered alongside David's shoe print plainly visible on his chest, didn't paint a picture of perfect health. The bleeding from his head wound had stopped, but it was unclear from his appearance whether the police station or the hospital should be his first stop.

His hands lay in his lap, his wrists linked by handcuffs. Instead of fastening his hands with the palms together, his arresting officer had folded his arms – each hand reaching for the opposite elbow – before the cuffs had been attached.

His head was down, his gaze lost in infinity. His posture was hunched, his focus turned inward. There was no sign that he was aware of his surroundings or registering the questions occasionally directed at him.

Having received no reply or reaction, the officer in the passenger seat turned away from the prisoner. As he did so, the battered figure croaked, "Jan."

"Jan or Chan," the officer asked, but there was no response.

A few seconds later, Jan began a quiet bout of coughing, his fastened arms pressed against his chest as though to hold his ribs together. His face was taut with discomfort.

After a minute or so, the silent fit subsided and he was still. He sank down to lie on the back seat, his eyes closed.

The officer in the passenger seat said to his colleague, "Get the duty doctor to check him out as soon as he's locked up. And get some pictures of those injuries. I don't want anyone thinking they happened in the cells."

The driver glanced quickly over his shoulder, took in the inert form. "He doesn't look too good," he said quietly. "Should we wake him up?"

"No, leave him," said the first. "Be good if they were all this easy."

With both officers facing forwards, the figure on the back seat began to stir. Using his teeth, he began to inch one sleeve up his arm. He'd pinch the cloth just below his shoulder and pull, angling his head back. The dark grey cloth gradually receded from his right wrist exposing a wide metal bracelet.

"What are we booking him with?" the driver asked, eyes intent on the road.

"The Sweeney are handling that. You might want to make sure someone's been down to start the paperwork before you go off tonight," the passenger replied.

The underside of the prisoner's bracelet had two raised pellets of metal set in grooves. Jan began to tug at one of them, manipulating it with his front teeth, trying to unhook it from the slot in which it sat.

Once he had succeeded in releasing one of the pellets, it became clear that a cord ran through the hollow interior of the bracelet, winding round and round. The pellets capping each end of the cord were secured by hooking them into the channels cut into the bracelet's shell.

The back part of the bracelet was open, allowing the cord, made of braided metal, to be withdrawn from the hollow interior. Jan slowly extracted the glittering strand, concealing it in his fist until he had it all.

Moving stealthily and greatly hampered by his handcuffed wrists, he began to wrap the cord – which extended perhaps a metre when unravelled – around his head, wincing each time the metal encountered the edges of his clotted wound.

He fastened the cord by knotting the ends in front. Then, methodically, he began to repeat the process with the other bracelet.

"I might as well get the doc on his way," the passenger said, unhooking the microphone on the side of the police radio. The driver's attention was fully occupied dealing with traffic as the police car moved briskly through the twilight London streets.

Less than a minute later, Jan had fastened the gold cord from his other bracelet around his temples, knotting it tightly in place. Now he held his handcuffed wrists in front of his face.

The passenger carried on a radio conversation with a remote voice, the squawked replies unintelligible to the untrained ear. When he'd finished, he said to his colleague, "So have you met Saunders yet, the transfer?"

"Bumped into him in court. Didn't get much out of him. What's his story?" the driver said.

"I don't know how reliable this is but I heard…" he paused. "Is something burning?" he asked, leaning forwards and sniffing in the direction of the radio.

The driver tilted his head and sniffed too. "It's outside," he said, dismissively.

At that moment, they were driving past massive Edwardian town houses set back from a wide boulevard. There was nothing visible along the magnificent sweep of expensive homes to suggest a fire.

The passenger continued sniffing the air and after a moment turned his head and caught sight of the prisoner, still laying flat, his linked wrists held in front of him.

The handcuffs he wore were of the one-piece kind, with no chain; the two loops and the wide, metal centrepiece that joined them were a single solid unit. But now there was something strange about the middle section of the prisoner's handcuffs. It was damaged. As the officer looked round, a curl of smoke rose from the black, disintegrating metal.

"What are you doing?" the passenger commanded, noticing the yellow metal which wrapped the prisoner's forehead. "Stop that," he said sharply, sounding alarmed.

With a grunt, the prisoner strained to pull his hands apart. The cuffs' centre bar separated like unmoistened clay, opening a vee-shaped gap along its middle, until only a narrow twist of metal secured the two halves.

Straining hard, the prisoner rotated his forearms in opposite directions, putting pressure on the join. With a sound like a pebble dropped onto stone the final strand broke. The prisoner's wrists were no longer fastened.

"Stop the car," the passenger called out, turning in his seat to grab one of the prisoner's arms and attempting to immobilise it.

The driver was at that second overtaking a slow-moving vehicle – a driver under instruction. He accelerated hard, the quicker to complete the manoeuvre. He attempted a rapid glance over his shoulder, but could see little before snatching his eyes back to the road. The engine roared as he floored the right-hand pedal.

The officer in the passenger seat, having gripped the prisoner's right arm just below the elbow, was attempting to capture the man's other hand. It was pulled back out of reach, but the prisoner himself was not fighting back. He was immobile. Instead of struggling, he was holding himself completely rigid. For a moment the prisoner's eyes flickered up into his head and his eyelids dipped.

With a bang and screech of torn steel, the rear left-hand door of the car exploded from its frame and blew out into the street.

The police car had barely pulled ahead of the vehicle it was overtaking. The jettisoned door whipped across in front of the startled learner-driver to collide with one of the huge iron lamp-posts spaced along the pavement. The door rebounded, disappearing under the wheels of the driving-school car, which swerved violently, mounting the curb.

The police car too slammed on its brakes. The wheels locked, throwing the car into a slide, the back end threatening to slew round. The driver twisted the steering wheel in the opposite direction, attempting to maintain control.

The animal squeal of shredding rubber was deafening for the two seconds it took the police car to slither to a halt. In those moments the officer in the passenger seat, twisted half round as he was, lost his grip on Jan's arm. He was thrown sideways, his shoulder and the back of his head striking the side window. The smack of skull against glass was drowned in the mechanical din, but the officer's eyes went wide and he doubled instinctively over, pulling his face down into his chest, arms wrapping his head, lips pursed for an uncompleted curse, as the pain incapacitated him.

Almost before the police car stopped sliding, the prisoner was boosting himself upright, scrambling out of the hole where the door had been.

The driver, a second slower off the mark, wrenched at his door handle and flung the door wide. He pushed up from the steering wheel, attempting to propel himself from the car only to be gripped fast by his seatbelt. Another fraction of a second was lost before his brain registered the problem. His hand clawed at the belt release, finding it on the second try, popping the metal tongue free from its slot.

The prisoner was sprinting along the pavement in the direction the police car had been heading (and was now almost at right angles to). Fifteen metres away he halted.

He turned to regard the vehicle from which he had just escaped, taking in the two occupants, one stunned, the other fighting to free himself.

His neck muscles tightened and his eyelids drooped, as though a heavy current was being drawn elsewhere in his body, leaving his eyes momentarily without the strength to open. His hands rose in front of him, turning, the fingers folding, until he looked as though he were pleading for something. He touched his clenched fists to each other and drew his face down almost to meet them.

The driver, finally freed, planted one foot on the tarmac of the roadway and rose rapidly from the vehicle. At once, he saw that his prisoner had not disappeared, but instead was standing facing him some metres down the street. He checked his impulse to rush towards him and raised one hand, saying in a firm and level tone, "Stop there. Don't move." One hand crept down to his holster and unbuttoned his side-arm.

And the prisoner didn't move – for a moment. He simply drew a breath in deeply and lowered his head to his touching fists, his eyes unseeing, his shoulders high and hunched.

The explosion threw the driver sideways and onto the other side of the road as the police car's petrol tank ignited. The occupants of the crashed driving-school car – which had struck a garden wall – were the only other witnesses.

The majority of the burning fuel which erupted from the burst tank flew out and up, issuing from the shattered filler cap like steam from a ruptured boiler. Flame instantly transformed the cloud to blinding orange-white, erasing all detail.

The sound of exploding gas punching out of its container sounded like a shotgun blast and was instantly followed by the monstrous 'whump' of ignition which boomed and rattled for several seconds, just like thunder, as it shook window-frames and rolled in echoes around the neighbourhood. Burning droplets showered from the cloud, spraying the ground with incendiary rain.

The massive surge of heat was such that hair on the sprawled policeman's head shrivelled. The blast had knocked him down, face first, leaving only the back of his head and his hands exposed to the wash of scorching air.

Stunned for several seconds, he turned over, pressing several burning spots on his uniform into the tarmac. With one hand over his eyes, he struggled to move back from the flames, the fire billowing above him, preventing him from rising.

Scrambling backwards to the opposite curb, he hauled himself to his feet, clutching a litter bin for support. His grilled hand shielding his eyes, he took in the scene: his whole vehicle was wrapped in flames, its interior so crammed with fire nothing else could be discerned. There was no sign of its other occupant, but the front passenger door was still closed.

Only after ten seconds had passed, having taken one sudden, lurching, abortive step towards the burning wreck, did he look round. There was no sign of his prisoner.

CHAPTER 16

THE NEXT MORNING
FRIDAY 18TH APRIL

"Coffee," David called softly, tapping on the bedroom door.

"Hnnggh," Susan said faintly from within.

"Suuusan?" he enquired gently, holding his ear close to the door.

"Adyawant?" a husky voice responded, torpor running the words together.

"Do you want some coffee?" he said.

"Got to sleep," the dreamy voice replied.

David sighed and knocked again. "Can I come in?" he said.

There was no answer. He opened the door and peered into the dimly lit room. Outside, the sun was rising and light was just creeping in around the edges of the curtains. There was just enough illumination to reveal the bed and something of its occupant. A mop of blonde hair and one arm poked out of the top of the duvet. No other features were visible, beyond a covered, person-sized hump in the centre, the lair of some hibernating creature.

"I'll put this over here," David said, tiptoeing over to place the mug of coffee he held on top of the bedside cabinet.

A moan coincided with some motion beneath the covers. The outstretched arm withdrew.

"Susan," David said again, laying one hand on the quilt-covered form and gently shaking. He stopped suddenly halfway through the motion.

"Take your hand off that," a clear voice said from beneath the covers, the muzziness of sleep completely dispelled.

His hand quickly withdrew.

From within the cocoon, fingers emerged and folded down a flap of duvet. Blue eyes were revealed. They regarded David, blinking once.

Susan drew the duvet back a little more, uncovering her cotton-covered shoulders. She had been lying contorted, back arched, one shoulder buried in the pillow, the other one raised, pulled up towards her ear – which would have placed David's hand somewhere around her left breast.

"It's like being back in my undergrad dorm," she said.

"I thought it was your shoulder," David said, humbly.

"Uhhuh," she agreed, without conviction.

David stepped away from the bed, backing towards the door. "I'll leave you to wake up," he said and nodded towards the coffee. He was already dressed; he had on a cream-coloured shirt with dark trousers and no tie.

"What time is it?" Susan asked, reaching for the mug.

"Just after six," he replied. "I'm not going to go into the office until later. I've got some thinking to do and I'd appreciate your input," he looked momentarily irritated at his phrasing, "I mean I'd like your help, if you're up to it. How are you feeling, by the way?"

Susan propped herself up on one elbow and took a sip of the coffee. Setting it down, she touched her bruised cheek gently.

"I feel fine," she said. "Just give me a few minutes and I'll be with you. The bathroom free?" she asked.

"It's all yours. Your clothes should be dry by now," he said. He made to go.

She raised her voice a little to halt him, "I'm starved. Got any food?" she asked.

"Get dressed and we'll go to the café on the corner," he glanced at his watch, "they open early."

While Susan was in the shower, David took her clothes out of the dryer. The top was still bloodstained. Although the blood had faded, it was still conspicuous.

He sneaked into the vacated spare room and began to rummage through the cheap pine wardrobe at the foot of the bed. Clothes of varying vintage and ancestry had been relegated there. He found a silk blouse in dark blue and held it up, attempting to judge the size. It was still draped in clear plastic from the dry-cleaners. He made the bed and left Susan's other clothes – along with the blouse – spread out on top of it.

Susan's head wound had left several spots of blood on the pillow. He caught sight of them and turned the pillow over.

He was sitting in the living room a few minutes later when Susan, her hair still damp, appeared. She was dressed and wearing the blouse. It was a good fit.

"So whose is this?" Susan asked. "Mom? Sister? *Girl*friend?"

He said, "Ex-girlfriend. She never came back to collect it, and since she already owns 4% of the world's supply of clothes…"

Susan shrugged. "Anyway it fits. I'll get it back to you. Thanks for the thought. I guess my top…"

David shook his head with melodramatic sadness. "It didn't make it," he said with a sniff, indicating where it lay on the arm of the chair. Susan examined it, inspecting the spots and putting it down again.

David watched her move around the room. "You look tired," David said.

"You just haven't seen me without make-up before," Susan said with a thin smile. "It's not easy looking glamorous twenty-four seven. But I guess you're out of eyeliner."

David said softly, "I didn't mean that. I wasn't complaining."

She shrugged, gave him a smile that was weak, but more sincere. "And another twelve hours sleep would be good too," she added.

"Yeah, I'm in the same boat," David said, emphatically. He continued, "The sleep I mean; I don't really care about the eyeliner." Her smile was genuine this time.

Susan picked up the empty coffee cup she had brought through from the bedroom. She raised it with a little jiggling motion. "Got any more before we head out?" she asked.

"Yeah," David said. "Same as before?" he asked, getting up from the sofa.

"No milk, thanks," she said, distractedly, her eyes alighting on a black, leather holdall which lay on the sofa.

"Is that," she nodded in the direction of the bag, "what I think it is?" Her voice had acquired a little tension.

David moved past her, poured coffee. "It is," he said over his shoulder.

Susan looked nervous, as though she were drawn to the bag but at the same time didn't want to approach it. "I want to see it," she said.

David returned to the sofa and handed her the replenished mug. He sat down next to the bag and twisted round so that he could reach it properly. Unzipping the top, he lifted out a heavy wooden box.

Susan stood and moved round to sit behind him, on one arm of the sofa. The box had her full attention. She placed a hand on David's shoulder, leaning over him to get a better look.

The box looked like a very beautiful, old-fashioned cigar humidor, though it was a little on the large side for that role – about the same dimensions as a stack of a dozen or so magazines. It was constructed from rosewood so dark, smooth and close-grained it seemed more like black chrome until the light caught it.

David moved the bag to the floor and placed the box on the sofa. It stood about 10cm high – featureless polished wood, except for a little button on the front for releasing the catch.

He pushed in the button and lifted the lid.

There was a box within the box.

The rosewood case was even more beautiful when seen this way. An interior space had been smoothly excised from what must have been a single piece of lustrous, glassy heartwood. The centre had been scooped out until the outer box was no more than a thumb's width thick at any point. Into the cavity had been placed something greatly at odds with the perfect sheen of its ruby-grained enclosure.

The inner box was a strange, ragged-looking thing. The top was made of sagging grey leather, its texture like unfinished paper. At the edges, the skeleton of the box was visible. Scrolled ivory-coloured rods, yellow with age, formed a frame over which the mottled skin was stretched to form the sides of the box. Some species of translucent thread secured membrane to bone. The needlework was fine and accurate, but the stitching had long since begun to disintegrate. The wrinkled top covering, with its blotchy colouration, seemed to have been water-damaged.

"It looks like the wing of some dead thing," David said, sounding uneasy as he looked at the inner box.

"Like a bat maybe. A big, mangy, mildew-eaten bat," Susan agreed.

A smell of rich, creeping damp rose from the box. It was an unhealthy smell that tickled the back of the throat with each breath taken, making it easy to imagine bright yellow spores taking root in soft pink lung tissue.

"Are you going to open it?" Susan asked, almost whispering.

"I don't even want to touch it," David said. "It looks like it died from the plague."

Susan hopped off the arm of the sofa, stepped to the table and picked up a pencil. She handed it to David, offering him the end with the eraser.

"I'd call you a wimp, but then you might make me open it," she said, looking at the box with disgust.

David took the pencil, holding it by the sharpened end, placing the little rubber pad in contact with the front strut of the box.

Susan said, "You really haven't opened it yet?"

David shook his head, pausing a moment and withdrawing the pencil. "I just opened the outer box to see what I'd got," he said.

Without detaching her eyes from the box, she said, "Thanks for waiting."

David put the rubber end of the pencil back in contact with the lid of the inner box.

"What kind of bone is that?" he asked unhappily, as he began to raise the lid.

"I don't know much about bones. It looks like a radius. Some part of a front leg. Don't know what critter it came off." She held up her hand, gauging the length of her own forearm. "The ones at the sides would need to have come from something much smaller than a man."

"Like a child, maybe," David said blackly, lifting the lid the rest of the way.

Both of them drew in their breath as they saw the Marker. It lay on a folded pad of black velvet, pinned in place with numerous, tiny, ivory hoops. The intricate lace of interlocking platinum had all the minute, ordered complexity of something organic – the veins of a leaf or the delicate, branching barbules of a down feather.

The Marker was about the same width and height as one of David's large hands when fully outstretched.

"It's beautiful," David said.

They both stared at the Marker – Susan moving round to lean against David's leg, so that she could peer into the box. She took the pencil from him, folded the lid of the wretched inner box back and put her hands on the rosewood outer case. She tilted the whole thing to catch the light. The platinum had a buttery lustre like silver as it begins to oxidise. Holding her breath, one hand over her mouth, Susan leaned right in to scrutinise the tracery.

It was made from slender platinum wire which tapered as the pattern wound further from the centre. It was unclear what held it together. The metal branched and met, crossed and joined, as though it had been cast as a single piece. And yet if it were moulded, molten metal would have needed to somehow fill the metres and metres of whisker-fine capillary – with no breaks or bubbles – in order to create the filigreed pattern. No tool marks were evident either.

David went to his bookshelf and took down an encyclopaedia. After a minute he said, "One thousand, seven hundred and sixty-eight degrees Celsius. That's over three thousand Fahrenheit."

Susan looked up at him questioningly.

He said, "The temperature platinum melts at. I just wondered how someone makes a thing like that." He carried on reading. "Hey, listen to this, 'Platinum is unique in that it corrupts metal tools used to work it. By combining with the edge of the tool, platinum weakens even tungsten carbide cutters.' I didn't know that."

"Me neither. No wonder McDonalds use plastic for their cutlery," she said.

He didn't hear her; he was pondering. He said, "I don't see how this could be anything but recent. The only way to make those joints is to weld them, but that makes no sense."

Susan said, "Huh? What's the problem?"

David said, "I studied engineering at university – so I know a certain amount about metalworking. Good steel is a new thing, relatively speaking, because you need exceptionally hot fires to make it and to work it. Welding is even newer, because it involves getting your very high temperatures confined to one precise spot. If you could make this filigree, then working steel would be child's play. That's modern technology. There's no way this could be more than a couple of hundred years old. I think we're having our legs pulled."

Susan said, "It could be a one-off. Look at the Phaistos disk – writing made with metal type three thousand years before Gutenberg was born."

David said, "Yeah, I'd forgotten about the Phaistos disk," a look of total incomprehension on his face.

She gave him a pretend pitying look, "Next you're going to tell me you haven't been to the Herakleion museum."

Susan tried a different tack. "Well, take the library at Alexandria then. A city-state with free speech, a passion for learning built around a vast, ever-expanding reference library. But it didn't last. The industrial revolution might have been underway before the end of the first millennium, but it takes more than just a single concentration of knowledge." She passed a hand over her forehead. "Listen, can we talk about this over breakfast? I'm about to pass out with hunger."

He said, "Oh god, of course." He closed the lid of the inner then the outer box and returned it to the holdall. He looked around for somewhere to put it. "Stand back a minute," he said to Susan who was still kneeling by the sofa. She got to her feet and moved to the doorway.

With one hand he lifted up the back of the sofa, pivoting it forwards onto its front legs. The webbing on the underside was ripped, revealing the hollow interior. David placed the holdall on the floor and carefully lowered the sofa on top of it, aligning the bag with the tear in the webbing. The bag disappeared up inside the couch.

Susan said, "Not the first time you've used that trick."

David smiled. "It is actually. But I remembered we ripped the webbing open carrying it up here when I moved in." He stood back and examined his handiwork. "Somehow I couldn't just leave that thing sitting on display."

Susan nodded. "I know what you mean," she said.

As they left the house, David found himself looking around, checking the activity in the street. A postman was delivering letters. A middle-aged woman was walking her dog. Nothing seemed out of place.

They cut through an alleyway that divided the terrace opposite, emerging onto a small parade of shops. Between a post office and a cab company, a greasy spoon café was open for business. Three of its tables were occupied by young, fit-looking men. By their clothing and paraphernalia – a toolbox near one table, a spirit-level resting on a chair – they probably all worked in the building trade.

David suggested Susan take a seat by the door while he went up to the counter. They had discussed food on the way over so David was able to order for both of them. He returned to the table with two mugs of tea.

Waiting for their breakfasts to be cooked, they sipped from their mugs. Susan spoke first. "Do you have any idea what's going on here?" she asked.

David looked uncertain of her meaning. He smiled, about to make a quip. She jumped in with, "I mean the robbery, the third man, the impossibility of most of it."

David shook his head. "No, I don't really have any idea what's going on."

Susan said, "Because I don't see how the thief pulled off that break-in." She was starting to look distinctly irritated. "I don't see how he got in and out of the old lady's house. I don't see how he opened that footlocker or the document store at the college." Her voice was rising, "I don't understand how he could jump that wall. I don't see how he could overpower two armed policemen. And I don't know what that thing is," she lowered her voice, "you've got in a bag back home."

She went on, "Not only do I not understand any of it, I'm starting to add up how many people have been hurt or even killed so far. And what I see is us, blundering about in the middle of something dangerous – suicidally dangerous, if you ask me. And I want to get the hell out of it before I get myself killed."

David looked at her, taking in the whispered anger with which she spoke. "You blame me for this, don't you?" he said, the beginnings of an edge in his voice.

"Of course I don't blame you for it. You're not the madman behind all this." She paused and it was clear there was a 'but' coming. "But you don't have a clue what's going on and still you're determined to get into the middle of it."

David said, "It's my job to be…" but she didn't let him finish.

"It's not your job," she said dismissively, almost contemptuously. "All you had to do last night was leave that bag for the police. Hammond could finish tidying this up. But you found a way to keep yourself involved, to keep me involved. Don't you get it; it's not your job? That's what the police are there for, that's what they do."

Susan had been keeping her voice down, despite the emotion in her voice. David sounded worked up when he spoke, but he too managed not to raise his voice. He said, "Do you honestly think Hammond knows more than you do, that he's brighter than you are? If I had left this to the police, I'd be out of a job and my firm would be bankrupt."

He counted off points on his fingers, "First off, they wouldn't have had a lead on the third man, in fact they wouldn't have even known there *was* a third man. Second, they wouldn't have known where to look for him – they even let him clear his things out of a house they were supposed to be watching. Thirdly, if they did know where to look, they wouldn't have caught him. They didn't catch him the last time they had the chance – a chance I created for them."

He leaned forwards and lowered his voice a little more, "It was made very clear to me that if the client put in a claim for that piece," he gestured over his shoulder, meaning the Marker, "I'd be out of work even if the business survived – which was doubtful."

He went on, "Dass wants his property back and he's got contacts at high levels. If I told Dass that Hammond was a nuisance, I'd bet you it wouldn't take twenty-four hours for Hammond to be reassigned. The police aren't some ultimate authority in this, they're just civil servants.

"I've managed to get Dass his prize back, I've seen to it that the thief is behind bars, I've stopped my employers from going out of business and I've kept my job. Not one of those things would have happened if I'd left it to the police. So how exactly do you work out that I'm not doing my job?"

He sat back, silent. Susan too was quiet. A woman in a bright apron bustled up with their food and still neither of them spoke.

They ate for a while.

After several minutes had passed, both of them had calmed their breathing. They were once again taking in their surroundings, instead of staring at one another or into space.

Holding up her knife, pointing it towards the ceiling, Susan said in a level voice, "I don't want to fall out with you. I know you're trying to do what you've been told to do and you're right: you've achieved it against all the odds. But don't forget that there's a lot more to this than a job. We've got every reason to think we're standing between a professional killer and the thing he wants most in the world. He knows who you are, he knows who I am and – for reasons I *think* I understand – we've put ourselves in his way again." She took a breath. "Have you considered what happens if it's not just him? All he'd need was one accomplice still on the loose and we'd be in huge trouble. Somehow, last night both of us got away with just a few knocks. Do you think we'd be so lucky a second time? No one else has been."

David didn't reply and Susan went on, speaking slowly, calmly, "I've been known to struggle with the idea of trusting people." She said it with a little, self-mocking smile – like it was a private joke. "I want to trust that you're thinking about more than keeping your job when you pull these stunts of yours. I want to believe that you're aware that people might die – have already died. I want to believe you'll think twice before you do something that could get one of us killed. I *want* to trust you, but you're not making it easy for me."

She put out one hand and laid it for a moment on top of David's. She squeezed it once and let go. They looked into each other's eyes. Neither of their expressions were easy to read, the mixture of emotions and the residue of their recent tense words clouded their features.

Someone's phone started ringing.

After a moment, David realised it was his. "Who the hell's this?" he wondered aloud as he reached into his back pocket.

Having retrieved the phone, he looked at the display. "It's Hammond," he said.

"Take it," Susan said.

David answered the call, "David Braun."

Susan watched intently as David listened to a monologue she couldn't hear. It went on for twenty seconds before David said, "What happened?"

David's face had become taut. He was listening to something that was making him very uncomfortable, but he didn't interrupt. The voice on the other end continued talking. A minute went by and David was still listening.

He asked, "What do you suggest? I'm talking to Susan Milton right now. What should we do?"

He listened again for another minute.

"Oh, believe me I'll call," David reassured Hammond. "Please let me know if anything changes," he said. "OK. Goodbye." He slipped the phone back in his pocket.

Turning his eyes to Susan, a mixture of discomfort and disbelief on his face, he said, "Their prisoner escaped. They couldn't stop him. They don't know where he is now."

Susan took a moment to absorb that information. Her only response was a single sarcastic comment, "Great."

A moment later she said firmly, "Let's get out of here."

CHAPTER 17

CONTINUING...
FRIDAY 18TH APRIL

D avid was stuffing clothes into a bag. "Let's just start driving and figure out what we're going to do next, OK?" he said.

"I agree," Susan said. "But tell me what Hammond said while you're getting ready." She stood in David's living room watching him rush around.

"Give me two minutes and I'll tell you everything I know." David hurried into the other room, taking his bag with him. When he came back he was zipping it up.

He said, "Right. Anything else we might need we stop and buy." He lifted the side of the sofa with one hand, slid the holdall out. "Can you take this?" he said, handing it to Susan.

Holding a bag each, they left David's flat and made their way downstairs towards the front door. Susan held up her hand suddenly and David, who was following her, halted.

Through the frosted glass of the front door a figure could be seen. The outline was stationary. Then there was a rattle as the figure did something to the door.

A moment later a beige envelope dropped to the mat and the figure began to recede. They both relaxed. "Now I remember why I'm not a spy," Susan said, laughing nervously.

When they got outside, the postman was two doors along. He waved to David.

Quickly they got the two bags into the boot of the Saab and got themselves buckled in. Moments later they were pulling away. David put a little bit of distance between them and his flat before he started speaking.

He said, "OK. Sorry to keep you in suspense. Right, what did Hammond tell me?" he said, as though trying to think how to phrase it. "I'll tell you his exact words as best as I can remember them and you can interpret them yourself.

"OK, something like, *You should know that fucking madman is on the loose. Your third man* – Hammond always likes to call him my third man. Like, if I hadn't pointed him out, he wouldn't have ever bothered anyone. Anyway, he said, *Your third man never made it to a cell. He incinerated a police car with an officer still inside it and made a run for it.*"

Susan said, "My god!"

"So I asked him what happened," David said. "He said, *The driver's still not sure which way's up, but in his story he claims the prisoner told them his name was Jan and then promptly passed out from his wounds. Sure you never thought of being a copper?*"

Susan said, "What does that mean?"

"It's police humour. I beat the prisoner up – you're supposed to leave that to the authorities. So then he said, *The next thing the driver saw was this Jan with the handcuffs off. He'd somehow burnt through them, like with a cutting torch, the driver said. Then the door came off its hinges and the prisoner jumped out. He ran a few feet down the street, turned and looked at them. Then the car blew up. Driver's in the hospital, his sergeant's in the mortuary.*"

Susan was staring straight ahead as she quietly took this in. David went on, "Let me think, what comes next? Yeah, he said, *I'm always telling them to search their prisoners. This bloke must have been loaded up with more gadgets than James Bond's Christmas stocking. How can you miss a grenade? The driver also claims the prisoner had wrapped a load of gold wire round his head. That'll be to stop us reading his thoughts, no doubt."*

"Tribute," Susan said. "I knocked the gold band off his head and he replaced it. It's got to be more than just a fashion statement," she said forcefully. She looked over at David. "What else? You asked him what we should do?"

David said, "Yeah, that was next. He told me he thought Jan would be going back to retrieve the jewellery he stole – which is what he thinks the Marker is – or maybe to get some of the papers he missed at the School of Antiquities. Hammond said they'd got four men waiting for him there. Of course, what he didn't know – and I didn't tell him – was that Jan doesn't have the Marker; we do. He said we probably weren't in any danger, but we should take a few precautions nonetheless. Oh and to call him if we should happen to run into his escaped prisoner."

Susan said, "Well we can have a good game of I-told-you-so some other time. What do you think we should do?"

David said, "Well, Jan doesn't know where the Marker is. He'd have to assume the police would find it, so if he's going after it, he'd be going after them not us. In the meantime, we get the Marker back to Dass. Dass can make up some story about how his people got it back. If Jan doesn't know what's going on, then he'll think the police have what he wants and if by some chance he's got a contact in the police he'll learn the Marker's back with Dass. Either way we're off the hook."

Susan said, "Unless his contacts are *really* good, in which case he knows that right this moment, the Marker's unaccounted for."

David said, "Yeah, so we have to be cautious for a few hours until we meet with Dass."

Susan asked, "What does Jan know about you?"

"Not that much," David said, then winced. "Unless he was paying attention when I told the police my name and who I work for."

There was silence for a little while and then Susan asked, "Where are we?"

It was 7.15 a.m. and they were heading west on the Marylebone Road. Traffic was heavy but it was still early enough that they were making progress.

David said, "I'm vaguely heading for the motorway. I want to get out of London. Pick somewhere you've never been and we'll drive there."

Susan said, "OK. But listen, let's not phone Dass until we've thought this through. A few hours won't make any difference provided we make sure we're good and lost before we stop anywhere."

David said, "Alright. Where do you want to go?"

"Brighton," Susan said, decisively. "Can we do that?"

"It's perfect," David said.

* * *

It took another hour and a half before they were flying down the M23 towards the coast. The sun was out and they'd been listening to the radio for much of the trip. By unspoken agreement, either of them could turn the music down if they wanted to say something.

They were just passing Gatwick airport when David cut the Sugababes off in mid-refrain. "He didn't have a grenade," David said.

"What do you mean?" Susan asked, intrigued.

"You saw what he was wearing. Where would you keep a grenade, just supposing you thought it was a good idea to carry one with you," David said.

"Well, I guess I'd try to find a little clutch bag that went with these shoes. If I were Jan, though… I don't know. Pocket? Clipped to my belt?"

David said, "That's about all I could come up with. I sat with my knee in the small of his back for about five minutes and I can tell you he didn't have anything bulky on him. Do they make miniature grenades? Likewise that cutting torch he was supposed to have. I've seen them small, but small like this," he spread his fingers, "not small like a lighter or something. Plus there's whatever he used to rip the car door off."

Susan said, "What about your black ops theory, that he used to be some sort of spy? If those miniature James Bond gadgets exist, it's spies who'd use them. When a secret agent wants a cutting torch they probably don't go to B&Q."

They were out in the country now. Fields and trees flanked the motorway.

David glanced over at Susan. He said, "That's another thing. Did you ever think it was funny that at the start of each film, James Bond would be given two or three gadgets that turned out to be just the ones he needed later on? He never got issued with a super-powered magnet and it later turned out that he needed the watch with the laser in it."

Susan smiled. "Right. Or found himself tackling a shark armed only with a miniature camera. I think I saw a comedy sketch along those lines."

David nodded and went on, "So even if Jan did somehow have two lots of explosives and a cutting torch on him, how did he know that's what he'd need? He didn't expect to be caught or he wouldn't have returned to that address."

Susan said, "What, you mean in real life, you'd have to carry two dozen little gadgets just to guarantee you'd got the three you actually needed?"

David said, "That's sort of what I'm saying, yes."

Susan considered. She said thoughtfully, "They *are* the things I'd take along if I was going to break in somewhere and open a safe. In fact, that's exactly what I'd take."

David made a face. He said, "You're right. Forget the James Bond stuff." He looked a bit sheepish. "I was just thinking out loud."

Susan said, "Hold on there. Don't give up yet. I said that's exactly what *I'd* take – that and maybe a gun. But I'm not Jan."

David looked puzzled, "Clearly. Are you saying he'd take something different?"

Susan said, "Who knows? He might have had pockets stuffed with explosives and tiny cutting torches and he might not. But if he did, they weren't there to help with the break-in, because he didn't use them. He cracked a door-lock and then peeled the steel front off a document store without blowing anything up or burning a hole in it. Did you happen to notice whether he was concealing a sledgehammer and a hydraulic jack while you were sitting on him? That's what it looked like he'd used."

David looked astounded, "You don't think he can… How can he do that stuff?"

Susan said, "What do you want me to say? Do normal rules even apply here? One thing's for sure, I'm going to read up on this deal with wrapping gold round your head. I wish I had my laptop – the whole collection's on there."

David said, "The papers he stole are in the holdall with the Marker. There's only a handful of them – literally – but you can start with them today if you want."

They drove in silence for another five minutes. Susan only spoke once. She pressed her index finger suddenly against the passenger window and said, "Baby sheep." She sounded excited. David glanced out at the field and then smiled at Susan. She noticed his amused attention and shrugged.

David said, "You know Brighton, traditionally, is where bosses take their secretaries for a dirty weekend."

Susan said, "I think I can guess what that quaint little phrase means. This would be in the days when 'boss' automatically meant a guy, right?"

David said, "Yeah, it's funny. Plenty of bosses are women these days, but none of the secretaries are men. Where's the equality in that?"

Susan gave him a mildly scornful look, "Gee, what a mystery. Just doesn't seem to be as much competition to get to the bottom of a company."

Susan looked at fields for a few seconds more and then said, "So is that why you were keen on Brighton? Take your little employee there?" Her words were full of sarcasm.

David looked outraged. "What? You picked Brighton!" he spluttered.

Susan replied haughtily, "And you said 'Perfect'. I just wondered why you thought it was so perfect. The only comment you've made about it is bosses screwing their female workers."

David was obviously insulted. He said forcefully, "OK. One, it's about the right distance from London. Two, it's an easy drive. Three, it's awash with tourists and visitors who we can blend in with. And four, it's a place where people go to have fun, so it's the last place you'd expect people in danger to think of."

Susan didn't say anything. David was still pretty worked up. "Why do you do that?" he demanded. "We'll be having a nice conversation and you'll say something to get me totally on the defensive."

Susan spread her hands and lifted her eyebrows. She said acidly, "Hey, how was I to know you didn't have a sense of humour?"

David shook his head, not accepting that. He said, "No, when you want to be funny, you're funny. This is something else. It's almost like it bothers you if we go too long without a few tense words."

Susan was the one on the defensive now. She said, "What, our argument over breakfast about you recklessly endangering the lives around you doesn't count as a few tense words? Wouldn't that keep me going for the rest of the day?"

David said, "That was for real. Despite the fact you feel strongly about it, you were fair with me. Just now though, you didn't believe for a moment I'd set this up to seduce you but you accused me of it anyway, knowing you'd get a reaction."

Susan was facing away from him now, staring fixedly out of her window. "I don't know what you mean," she said coldly. Her gaze was directed sideways, out of the car, towards the woodland they were passing, but her eyes weren't focussing on it.

David kept his eyes fixed on the road. He looked like he was fuming. They drove on in silence.

Motorway turned to fast A-road. Five minutes passed.

Eventually Susan said, "So are you saying you find me unattractive?" her voice hard and accusing.

David's nostrils flared and he glanced sharply at Susan. She was smiling sweetly back at him. He burst out laughing, relieved. She laughed too.

When they'd stopped laughing they were still smiling. After a minute David asked, "Is there a boyfriend somewhere who gets tortured like this?"

She pretended to be offended, saying, "You think I'm torturing you now?"

"Not really," he conceded.

After a little pause she growled, "No, I've driven them all away." Then she asked, "So where's the owner of this blouse?"

David said, "Hollywood. Seeking her fortune."

Susan chuckled, "Oh nice work. I've never driven anyone *that* far away before. Is five thousand miles your record?"

David looked pleased with himself, "It was nothing really. A little emotional neglect, a few hints about cheap airfares."

Susan asked, with a little less levity, "What happened?"

David considered for a moment and said, "Can you ever really summarise a relationship? She's just a very hungry person – hungry for more attention, more excitement. We couldn't find a compromise between what I wanted and what she wanted."

Susan asked, "So are you friends now?"

David replied, "Probably we are. Now. I would think Hope would have forgiven me and I was never that annoyed with her."

Susan said, "Maybe that was the problem?"

David gave her a questioning look.

She explained, "She's an actress, right? Maybe she wanted the full range of passion, not just the good stuff. A leading man in the movies is a lot more than just someone who's nice to you."

David said with resignation, "That's as good an explanation as I've heard. Anyway, she'll be in her element where she is and I'm happy to let her get on with it."

"*Lasciate speranza*," Susan said, without explanation and David didn't ask.

David said, "So anyway, you're American, you must be on about your fourth husband by now."

Susan smiled. "I see you know your stereotypes. Just between you and me, that's why I had to leave. I wasn't getting married enough and it was dragging the average down. Elizabeth Taylor was on double shifts trying to balance things out."

David asked, "So not even one husband?"

Susan shrugged, "Nope. A few lucky escapes. One false alarm. My sister is the expert at telling that story. She's flying over next week, maybe she can fill you in." A look of concern crossed Susan's face. "Jesus, I nearly forgot all about her visit. It's amazing how a brush with death will distract you. I hope all this is sorted out by then."

David said authoritatively, "Once Dass has the Marker the excitement's over. Whatever happens after that, it's not my problem. And you'll be left in peace to do whatever it is you do when I'm not trying to get you killed."

Susan nodded.

They carried on talking about relationships for a while. Whatever had surfaced to make them angry at one another had disappeared. They talked naturally and with light-hearted ease.

Soon they were driving past manicured municipal lawns on the outskirts of Brighton. It was only half past ten in the morning and yet both of them found themselves yawning uncontrollably.

David said, "Can I trust you not to go berserk if I suggest a change of plan?"

Susan said, "I don't know that I like 'berserk'. But I'll do my best. What's your suggestion?"

David seemed hesitant. "Listen, this is nothing more than what I'm saying, whatever it might sound like…"

Susan interrupted. "Spit it out, for god's sake, or I will get pissed," she said, but without conviction.

David got to the point, "You know we're both tired and we've got some important thinking to do and some calls to make. I was thinking we need a base here. So why don't we get a hotel room?"

Susan gave David an appraising look and as she did so she yawned widely. David said, "See? Let's get two hours sleep and some lunch and then work out how we're going to play things with Dass."

Susan said, "And I suppose it should be one room instead of two because…"

David said, "Because the last thing we should do is split up if we're going to get some sleep."

Susan said, after a moment's pause, "That's actually an excellent idea."

David added, "It doesn't have to be the Bridal Suite or anything, just so long as the Jacuzzi's big enough for two."

She gave him a sarcastic smile.

David said, "I've only stayed here once – on business. We can use the same hotel; it's right on the sea-front."

Susan yawned again while trying to say, "Fine."

* * *

They got a twin room at The Grand, looking out over a sea that had turned grey. The early morning sun had retreated behind midday cloud and a stiffening breeze was raking spray onto the promenade.

They had both made phone calls to say they wouldn't be at work that day. Susan had set the alarm on her watch for half three. Now David pulled the curtains. They were thick and lined, but they still let in a certain amount of light. The room was dim, but not dark.

Neither of them were happy with the idea of laying, fully clothed, on top of the covers. On the other hand, neither of them was about to undress in front of the other.

"Wow, I feel self-conscious," David said. "I think people usually do this for the first time drunk."

Susan volunteered to change into a robe in the bathroom. When she had closed the door behind her, David undressed rapidly so as to be in bed when she returned.

"This is very weird," she said when she emerged.

"It can't be any weirder than hiding from a thief with super powers," David said.

"Different weird," Susan replied. "This feels like the time I played Doctors and Nurses with Arty Hickson." She slipped into her bed and wriggled out of her robe.

David asked innocently, "He's someone you work with?"

Susan looked for something to throw. "He lived next door when I was six. I still believed in hell in those days, was sure I was going there," she said. "You know what's funny? He actually *is* a doctor now."

A few moments later, she asked "Are you actually sleepy? I'm suddenly wide awake."

There was no reply – just steady breathing.

Somewhere in the hotel the distant sound of a Hoover waxed and waned. It blended with the faint sound of the sea. Through the thick walls, the occasional far-off bump as the Hoover struck a chair leg was muffled into quiet timpani and the distant screams of gulls were robbed of their melodrama.

They both slept.

CHAPTER 18

Later that afternoon
Friday 18th April

It was the end of the afternoon and the temperature was dropping. David and Susan had wandered aimlessly through the town, talking and occasionally stopping to look in shop windows, until the sharp breeze began to make their eyes water.

They ducked into the first restaurant that looked warm and inviting. Now they were eating a very late lunch gazing out at the grey world.

Susan was eating spicy tomato soup, breaking off chunks of crusty bread to go with it. She said, "I feel worse than if I'd never slept."

David said, "I know it seems like that, but you were looking pretty pale before. I think the sleep's done you some good."

A waitress arrived with David's dish of baked ravioli. Despite its volcanic heat he made rapid inroads into it.

While they'd been walking they'd talked about Dass and the handover of the Marker. David now picked up the thread again. "So why did you think we should be cautious about calling him?"

Susan replied, "I started thinking over the things you said about him – how you felt when you first met him. You said you got a bad vibe from him

– and from Jan – but it was worse with Dass. Well, Jan's the ruthless killer; what does that make Dass?"

David said, "Yeah, but that wasn't really based on anything. It was just a feeling. With Jan I was all revved up on adrenaline and able to take some action. It's different when you're in a social setting, in someone's office, when you're constrained. Like I bet you'd find there were soldiers who were much more intimidated by the thought of getting a medal from the Queen than by whatever they did to earn it."

Susan said, "I think you're rationalising it. The first time you told me about Dass, you said he'd really got to you. I think you're talking it down now. A couple more renditions and you'll remember it as mild unease. Remember, I keep telling you to show a little caution, to keep in mind the danger, so I'm the last person to accuse you of being a coward. You had what sounded like a really visceral reaction to this guy. I just think we should bear that in mind before we trust him."

Susan suggested a few precautions they might take in dealing with Dass. David was still not convinced there was any need. He said, "I'm doing what he told me and he's getting what he wants; I don't see that I've got anything to worry about. If I crossed him, then I think all bets would be off, but I reckon I can trust him as long as I'm being a loyal foot-soldier."

Susan shook her head. "Woodward and Bernstein, man – trust no one."

"Except you, right?" he said.

"Oh, absolutely. Trust no one – except Susan," she said.

"Does that mean you've decided to trust *me*?" he asked.

She nodded with genuine seriousness a couple of times. "I'm really working on it," she said sincerely.

They carried on talking through another course and through coffee, Susan suggesting possibilities, David for the most part sceptical about the need for them – but nonetheless he allowed himself to be swayed. Susan managed to persuade him not to rush back to London for an evening handover.

After thirty minutes they had a plan which didn't strike Susan as reckless or David as unbearably paranoid.

David glanced at his watch. It was a little before five. "I want to call before anyone goes home for the weekend," David said.

They hurried back to the hotel so that David could make the call from the quiet of their room. He used his mobile and called the switchboard of Interfinanzio, asking for Alessandro Dass. He was put through to Mrs Billings, Dass's secretary, who told him it was impossible for him to talk to the Chairman.

David said politely, but with evident concern, "Mrs Billings, it will probably cost us both our jobs if this message isn't delivered at once. I assure you, this is information Mr Dass is extremely eager to hear. Please do your very best to get me in touch with him."

"Let me have the message and I'll see that it's passed on," she conceded snippily.

"I would need Mr Dass's express permission before I could do that. He made himself very clear on this point," David said.

Mrs Billings was silent, obviously considering her next move. When she spoke again it was with a much more agreeable quality to her voice. "Let me have your number and I'll see what I can do," she said.

David gave it to her and hung up. "Dass is going to call me back," he said to Susan.

David sat at the room's reproduction desk, his back to the window. Susan was sitting on her bed, facing him, her feet tucked under her. She was gently chewing her bottom lip. Neither of them spoke.

Less than two minutes after the end of his conversation with Mrs Billings, David's phone started ringing.

"Mr Dass?" David said, answering it.

The elegant voice said, "Mr Braun, do you have good news for me?"

David said, "I do. I've recovered the box that was taken from your safe, with its contents intact."

Dass breathed a sigh and said, "*Mirabile!* It is gratifying to have one's confidence rewarded. Tell me where you are and one of my people will be with you shortly."

David said, "I'm afraid we'll have to make a slightly different plan Mr Dass. You might have heard: the thief is no longer in custody and nobody knows where he is. My first priority was to get the box somewhere safe, so I took it out of London. I can get it to you tomorrow morning, but any sooner will be difficult." He paused a moment. "Would you like me to come to the office?"

Dass replied, "Initiative, such a rare quality. The office would not be ideal, no. By the time any interested parties learn of the item's return I would like it already to be on its way elsewhere. This would be considerably more difficult if you must make your way through a workplace full of eager eyes in order to meet with me. It will be too busy, even on a Saturday. Perhaps you would be so kind as to come to my house?"

"No problem," David said and wrote 'at his house' on the pad in front of him. He held it up so that Susan could see. She nodded when she saw it and gave a grim little smile.

"Let me give you the details," Dass said and dictated an address.

"I don't want to spend too much time in stationary traffic," David said. "It's too vulnerable a situation. So I'd like to travel after the rush hour. How would eleven o'clock suit you, Mr Dass?"

Dass said, "That's quite acceptable. There is a reserved parking space immediately outside; I'll see that it's free. I'd rather you didn't linger on the street."

David said, "Don't have any worries on that score. I'll see you tomorrow at eleven."

David hung up and set the phone down on the table. He let his breath out. "It's arranged," he said.

Susan asked, "What do you think the chances are that someone could trace that call back to a physical location?"

David replied, "Well, the mobile phone company could do it, no question." He let his gaze travel around the room as he thought about it. "But I think you'd need either a warrant or exactly the right man on the inside in order to arrange for the trace to be done. Same with tracking my credit card usage. Be tough to do quickly, no matter how much clout you had – if you didn't want questions asked later. I think you'd only do it as a rush job if you didn't mind jeopardising your connections. Maybe if Dass thought we were planning to keep the Marker – but then why would we have just volunteered to bring it to him? And I can't see how any other interested party would know we've got it."

Susan looked impressed. "You've been using that brain of yours, haven't you? I'm glad it's not just me who's decided that paranoia is the better part of valour."

David nodded. "I don't think there's anything more we can do to make ourselves safe for now. Maybe the police could track us down if they wanted to, but the thief doesn't have access to police info. He didn't know the cops had the address of his own hideout, so I don't see him using police resources to learn about ours."

Susan nodded in agreement and flopped back onto her bed. Her hands stretched up to touch the headboard. "What do you want to do now?" she asked.

He shrugged, "Can't eat any more, can't sleep any more. I don't know. I want to take my mind off all this for a little while." He moved to the window and looked out over the sea, leaning down to rest his elbows on the windowsill, one hand holding the net curtain aside.

"There's a cinema nearby, we could see what's on," he said. He didn't look round to see her reaction, but continued to stare out of the window. "It seems trivial with all that's going on, but I can't think of anything we need to be doing except giving ourselves a rest."

While he'd been speaking, Susan had hauled herself wearily off the bed and came to stand behind him. She looked over his shoulder, out through the window at a pencilled world of greys, devoid of colour.

"It looks how I feel out there," she said, resting a hand on David's shoulder and leaning closer to the glass. After a moment, David stood and turned to look at her – which brought them very close.

They were standing almost facing each other. Susan's gaze was still directed outside. She was watching the distant grey-green rollers filing through the dense sea.

David looked at Susan. He held up one hand to her cheek, not quite touching it. "Are your cuts bothering you?" he asked. She didn't retreat from his hand. He laid it gently along her jaw, tilted her head very carefully to one side and leaned forwards to look at her bruised cheek.

Rather than pull her head back to allow her to speak normally, she left David's hand cupping her jaw and spoke, hardly moving her mouth. Her voice was quiet and muffled-sounding as she said, "It just aches a little."

With a tired sigh a little energy seemed to go out of her and she allowed her head to drop forwards and rest against the upper slope of David's chest.

She said, "I'm exhausted, but I know I wouldn't be able to sleep."

He wrapped his arms around her, completely enfolding her. "I know. I know," he said, with no apparent meaning beyond the soothing sound of the words.

Susan relaxed in the circle of his arms, allowing her body to slump a little, letting him hold her up.

David brought one hand up to her head and eased his parted fingers slowly through her soft blonde hair, allowing it to divide around his fingertips. She stood without moving, leaning against him, breathing into his chest.

He laid his palm against the bare skin of her neck and began to delicately knead the muscles. She gave a quiet murmur of approval.

He turned his head a little and placed a soft kiss on her forehead. His fingers continued to gently explore the stiffness in her neck. He tilted his head a little further and placed a second kiss on her unblemished cheekbone.

She stiffened and a moment later pushed slowly away from him, his arms coming unwrapped and falling to his sides. "No," she said quietly and shook her head sadly. "This isn't right. I don't want this." Her voice was hardly audible.

David stepped slowly back so as not to crowd her. "I'm sorry," he said, the words quiet, the tone sincere.

Susan's eyes were downcast; she wasn't moving, just looking at her feet. She was wrapped now in her own arms, hugging herself, seemingly unaware of how the gesture mirrored David's attentions a moment before.

"There's nothing to be sorry for," she said. Her voice was laden with sadness as she said, "But this isn't what I want from you."

They separated further, Susan gradually retreating to sit on the edge of her bed, David moving to the other side of the room and occupying himself listlessly flipping the pages of the hotel directory, which lay on top of the room's tiny TV. Their faces showed that they had both withdrawn into their own inner worlds. They were immersed in their own thoughts.

David turned another page in the hotel directory, not really taking it in. His gaze wandered.

Next to the TV was a chest of drawers on top of which sat a tray. There was a kettle, with a neatly knotted cord, along with cups and saucers and various sachets and packets.

His eyes settled on the kettle. He picked it up and took it into the bathroom, where he half-filled it with cold water. Bringing it back to the tray, he plugged it in and flicked its switch.

After what seemed like many minutes, the kettle began to make the distant-traffic sound of heating water.

Five minutes had passed since their abandoned embrace and David said, "I don't want to be a cliché or anything, but do you fancy a cup of tea?"

Susan smiled. "Sure," she said, with an effort at brightness. "What do you suppose is on at the movies?"

David had returned to flicking through the transparent pockets of the hotel directory. "There's a flyer somewhere here," he said. Eventually he found it, just as the kettle finished boiling and turned itself off.

"So have you got *any* interest in watching Spiderman?" he asked, sounding unsure.

She said enthusiastically, "Modern mythology. It's practically my duty to see it. It'll be fun."

David looked at his watch and said, "OK. I'm game. We've got about an hour before the next showing." He looked at his watch again, calculating, "Then we can eat fish and chips – can't come to the seaside without doing that."

Susan said, "Fish and chips. Of course," as though she'd been foolish not to mention it earlier. "I've been meaning to get my order in before the North Sea is completely empty. Maybe we can grab the last two cod."

David said, "That's the spirit," slightly sarcastically. "We'll ask for whatever's most endangered." As he spoke he was pouring hot water, making tea. "I was thinking we could also get you a change of clothes. We've just got time to pick something up if you're not too fussy about being fashionable."

Susan nodded. "Now that's a good idea. Can we hit The Gap or something? I'm starting to feel a bit scuzzy wearing the same outfit. Even though you did a great job on the laundry."

They drank their tea quickly and then headed out. From the hotel, they walked up the hill towards the shopping centre. Susan, who had been shivering as she walked, made her first stop at an outdoors shop and headed straight for the sale rack. David offered her the services of his company credit card. She found a shiny black puffer jacket reduced to half price and asked David if she could have it. Two minutes later she was wearing it as they left the store to continue their shopping.

* * *

After the film and the fish and chips, David and Susan sat in the hotel bar. It was ten thirty. David had a glass of Jameson's Whiskey in front of him, Susan a glass of Canadian Club.

Susan said, "The movie was fun, huh? In a mindless sort of way."

David said, "I liked everything except the action sequences. As soon as he put his mask on it was like a cartoon. Like watching a rubber ball bounce round the scenery. How worked up can you get watching a piece of elastic in danger?"

Susan took a sip of her whisky and gave a little shudder. "Just at the moment, I don't see that as a weakness. I don't know if I could have stomached anything too realistic. Tom and Jerry action sequences suited me fine."

When their drinks were gone they ordered replacements. It wasn't many minutes before the conversation dwindled and the silences grew longer. They were both feeling drained. By eleven it was clear they should turn in. Little was said as they returned to the room and got ready for bed.

Susan was in the bathroom for nearly fifteen minutes. When she finally emerged, her bedside lamp was the only illumination. David was in bed, facing away from her, his breathing quiet and even.

She didn't enquire whether he was asleep but got quietly into her own bed and turned out the light. In moments she was asleep.

CHAPTER 19

THE NEXT DAY
SATURDAY 19TH APRIL

D avid was in the heart of Belgravia, driving slowly along Dass's
street. He passed a house with a flag fixed to its ornate portico and
a policeman stationed outside. A few metres later, the road turned
to the left and the embassy disappeared from view.

David was alone in the car, driving slowly – his eyes roving constantly,
peering in through the windows of the elegant townhouses, scrutinising
parked cars, exploring doorways.

It was almost eleven and he was nearing his destination.

His speed had now slowed almost to a walking pace. Beside him, on the
passenger seat, sat the holdall he had taken from Jan.

He continued to search the quiet street for anything out of the ordinary.

Up ahead he could now see the empty parking place waiting for him,
the word 'Reserved' in white paint across its centre. The parking bay was
directly outside a gleaming black front door set into an otherwise featureless
brick wall. The residence within appeared to have no windows on the ground
floor, at least none which overlooked the street.

It was a curious building. It seemed to have been built facing onto a road that no longer existed. Instead, the street ran along what appeared to be the blank right side of the house. From the pavement, all that one could see was unadorned brick rising three storeys until it met the edge of the roof. Just below the roofline was set a single broad window; it was an ideal vantage point from which to monitor the neighbourhood. And anyone gazing up from the street, hoping to look inside, would find themselves defeated by the steep angle – all they'd see would be reflections of the sky.

Almost at the reserved bay, David took a final look around before it was too late for him to change his mind about pulling in.

Fifty metres further down the street a half-seen figure flitted between two parked cars. At that distance it was difficult to make out details; the figure was now stationary, partly concealed by a plane tree. From David's point of view, all that could be seen was a glimpse of black clothing and a few hesitant movements that suggested someone hanging back from view, trying to avoid detection. His hands tensed on the steering wheel.

Then the figure moved and he could see a female outline, an orange shopping bag in her hand. It wasn't Jan. He relaxed.

He was now at his destination. Seeing no one else around he pulled quickly into the designated parking space and turned off the engine. He got swiftly out of the car, taking the holdall with him. With three rapid steps he was at the glossy black door.

No one rushed out at him from concealment, the street remained deserted.

To the right of the door was an intercom. He pressed the button set below its speaker. Despite the mildness of the bright spring morning he was wearing a heavy leather jacket. He shrugged his shoulders within it now as though he was cold.

Only a second or two passed before the door was opened by a pale young man wearing a dark-blue tracksuit with the hood pulled up. "Inside," the man said.

David stepped into the hallway and the door was closed swiftly behind him. The man in the tracksuit dropped a metal bar across the door once it was closed.

A second man appeared. His features were East Asian. He was wearing jeans, a grey t-shirt and a baseball cap. The t-shirt was tight over the flat blocks of muscle visible in his arms.

The man in the tracksuit began to pat David down for weapons. "Is that really necessary?" David asked. The Tracksuit didn't answer him; he simply continued his inspection. As his hands slapped and prodded he encountered something in the pocket of David's jacket. His gaze met David's meaningfully. The other man noticed and took a step towards them, close enough that David was within easy reach.

David lifted his hands slowly until they were level with his head, palms forward, allowing access to his jacket. Tracksuit leaned in, sliding a hand into David's pocket.

He withdrew a cell phone.

David shrugged. Tracksuit replaced the phone and continued frisking. When he was finished checking David's person he examined the bag, finding only a polished wooden box within it, which he avoided touching. Tracksuit nodded to the Oriental man who said, "Come with me."

The Oriental in front, Tracksuit behind, they led David up two flights of panelled staircase and out onto a landing heavy with antiques. A sea of carpet in toned-down burgundy lay between walls twining with William Morris flowers on pale paper.

A dozen tiny, hand-carved picture frames were scattered about the walls, but none of them contained pictures. Instead, each held a scrap of paper or parchment. On some a dark brushstroke or penned inscription was visible. Others appeared to be blank, simply corners torn from some antique document.

They stepped through double doors into a windowless sitting room artfully lit to seem filled with sunlight. Everything within was deep red, gold or ivory. It was a heavy colour scheme somewhat relieved by the magnificent proportions of the room, which occupied nearly the entire storey. Various cabinets and tables in red cedar and dark-stained cherrywood were spaced around the walls. Ox-blood Chesterfield sofas and armchairs formed a cluster in the centre of the room.

Fresh tulips in buttery yellows and natural scarlets were arranged in half a dozen vases scattered about, their scent a bright note amidst the background of beeswax and old leather.

There was no one else in the room. The Oriental pointed to an armchair facing the door and commanded, "Sit," then he turned around and left. Tracksuit took up a position to the side of the door, like a bouncer, hands crossed in front of him, his eyes on David.

Instead of sitting in the armchair, David found a high-backed chair tucked under a writing desk and moved it to the centre of the room. He sat down on it, setting the holdall beside the chair, and slipped his hands into his pockets.

A minute passed and the Oriental returned, followed by Alessandro Dass a few steps behind. Dass was wearing a suit of similar cut to the one David had seen him in previously – this one, though, was a pale misty grey. His tie was a vibrant, robin's-breast of red, engorged with colour, against a shirt the colour of ash.

As Dass crossed the room it became clear that a mark he bore across his forehead, which from a distance looked like a deep wrinkle or an old scar, was in fact a slim metal band. Its finish blended with Dass's skin tone, so that from any distance it was invisible.

Dass said, "You made it here without incident. Good." His cultured voice was full of charm. He took the armchair facing David and sank down into the leather. "Where did you disappear to when you left London? Don't feel you have to tell me, of course. I wonder, was there anyone you trusted with the secret of your hiding place?"

David replied, "I thought it was best if I just disappeared. I couldn't see why anyone needed to know where I was going. It would just have multiplied the risks unnecessarily." His voice was inflexionless, like a wary suspect giving a statement.

Dass parted his clasped hands in a little 'just so' gesture. "But I suppose your employers will have been curious. You will undoubtedly have told them of your plans to leave London..." he said with a solicitous interest in his eyes. His gaze met David's as he continued, "your plans to come here?"

As he had been speaking, the Oriental had moved stealthily round until he was standing almost behind David. Now David became aware of the

Oriental's presence close by his right shoulder. He made to rise from the chair. The Oriental reached forward to press him back into his seat.

David broke the Oriental's hold on his shoulder before it was properly established and sprang to his feet. His high-backed chair pitched to one side, colliding with a glass-topped table. At the same time the Oriental closed on David who skipped back, hands held high, ready to defend himself, his shoulders side-on to his potential opponent.

The toppled chair bounced off the edge of the table, making a great deal of noise and spoiling the smooth finish of the wood, but leaving the glass intact.

Again, the Oriental took an aggressive step towards David who shifted his weight a little in preparation for rapid movement.

Dass barked something exceedingly curt in a language other than English. The Oriental stepped back so quickly it looked almost as though the words had stung him.

"Please," said Dass more calmly. "Do let us retain our composure." He addressed the Oriental, saying, "Kim, I don't think you're helping to put our guest at his ease. Why don't you take a seat?" He gestured with a couple of flicking fingers to the furthest armchair.

Kim kept his eyes on David but sat down as he was commanded. He looked awkward now that he had been forced to sit.

Dass said, "Now where were we? I believe I was going to invite you to stay for lunch if you have time." He leaned forwards and enquired earnestly, "Tell me, when exactly is your office expecting you?"

David was able to meet Dass's gaze without apparent effort now. He looked appraisingly at the older man and it was several seconds before he spoke. "People know I am here," he said deliberately.

Dass raised an eyebrow. "I'm sure they do," he said reassuringly, leaning back again. "I must commend you on your precautions this morning. You've evidently been at pains not to draw unwanted attention to your visit here. In fact, I'm sure no one at all saw you arrive. Very impressive." Dass paused as though giving David time to absorb the implications of what he was saying. Then he went on, "And I must also say how relieved I am that you were able to join us. If you had failed to appear today, if you had not returned from wherever it was you disappeared to overnight, how would anyone learn what had become of you? How would we have come to your aid? It would be as though you had vanished." Dass's voice was conversational, carrying no menace except what was implied in the subtext of his words.

David sat listening. His face looked grim. He said pointedly, "Let's imagine you denied ever having seen me today; what would you gain from my disappearance?"

Dass made a display of somewhat astonished innocence. He looked for support from his two henchmen, both of whom remained alert but impassive, staring at David but giving no sign that they were listening to the conversation.

Then it seemed a thought occurred to Dass. "Oh, I see; you are being hypothetical. We are exercising our imaginations." He looked around to see if his colleagues had also come to this conclusion. They remained stony-faced.

Dass said, "Well if we were playing a game, I might say that the return of our lost treasure brings with it the return of unwelcome scrutiny from those who covet it. For the world to think it lost and for us alone to know it was safe might be the ideal outcome," he nodded at David and waved a hand airily, "assuming it could be accomplished without anything underhand taking place, of course." He shifted a little in his seat and then continued, "Who knows, there are also those in the world who might want to eat their cake and have it still. Perhaps you are familiar with those breathlessly venal American game shows where the victorious contestant must choose between a sum of money and the contents of a mysterious box. Even the Americans would consider it unacceptably greedy to reach for both. But hypothetically it would be possible. A truly avaricious person might allow an insurance claim to go ahead even now," he indicated the holdall by David's side, "as a means of throwing others off the scent." He stretched out his left hand, "It would protect our assets," then he stretched out his right, "even while it paid our bills."

Dass leaned forwards in his seat. "But before we spend any more time exploring the hypothetical, shall we just make sure of the facts of our situation. Would you be so kind as to return to me what is rightfully mine," he said, extending an arm towards the bag.

David considered for a moment and then reached for the holdall. He lifted it onto his lap and unzipped it. He took out the rosewood box, laid the holdall back on the floor and rested the box across his knees.

He made as if to open the box and then paused and leaned back. He blew out his breath and pushed his hands into his coat pockets; he seemed to be wrestling with a dilemma. "What worries me Mr Dass," he said, "is that you have no intention of letting me leave here."

Dass said nothing and David continued, "Which is why I decided to call the police before I came to your house." For the first time since David had met him Dass smiled with a look of genuine amusement.

David went on, "I told them that one of your people had recovered the box and that you had invited me over to be present as it was returned to you."

Dass smiled benevolently as though delighted by the story. David said, "I told them that I was worried that the thief might try again. In fact I mentioned that I *might* have spotted him lurking nearby."

Dass was nodding thoughtfully as though he were getting ready to speak. David pressed on, "And I asked them to call for me here," he said. He shrugged inside his coat, as though there was little point in saying more.

Dass stretched out a hand in the direction of the box. He said, "A very entertaining tale, if a little lacking in originality. Kim, fetch me the box."

As he said these words, David slipped his right hand quickly inside the box and withdrew something. As soon as he had done so, he jumped out of his seat, the box clutched in his left hand, and sprang to the far corner of the room. With a sharp downward flick of his right wrist the device in his hand extended into a metal baton. He held it out in front of him ready to meet any attack.

Kim and Tracksuit both advanced instinctively on David's position. "Wait," Dass snapped at them. They paused, like dogs straining at their leads, waiting to be released.

Dass stood and took a casual step towards David. "When I heard you had bested our little stray I did wonder how you could possibly have achieved such a victory. Jan, while no match for me, should have trampled you underfoot."

Dass reached out a hand towards the box and David brought the metal baton crashing down on his wrist. But Dass didn't react, except to pause momentarily as the blow fell. The heavy shaft of the baton encountered an invisible obstacle before it reached Dass's arm. The impact made a sound like a hammer hitting a cement floor.

They remained frozen in position, Dass reaching for the box, David's baton resting a few centimetres above the outstretched arm. David seemed to be pinned to the corner of the room, as Dass said, "I began to suspect that you possessed some special quality which allowed you to overcome one of us – even an exile."

David was struggling to move. There was no sign of any impediment, no apparent reason why he shouldn't burst past Dass, shoving the older man aside – but David was twisting and tensing as though he was encased in something solid or perhaps pressed against the wall by something massive.

The expression on Dass's face wavered for a moment as though a bad memory had flitted through his mind. Simultaneously, the baton was wrenched from David's hand and flew across the room – pulled by an unseen force.

Dass leaned close to David until their faces were a hand's width apart. Dass said, "I think I've realised what that quality was."

A line of perspiration ran down David's forehead as he continued to strain – totally without success.

"You were lucky," Dass said, turning his back and allowing David to topple forwards, the invisible barrier suddenly gone. Dass strode back to his chair as David pitched forwards, almost falling. "Simply lucky."

Dass dropped into his armchair, bringing David once more into his field of view. He looked at David who had regained his feet and was now glancing nervously around the room. Dass wore an expression which combined interest with disgust as he regarded his prisoner.

"I think I've learned all I'm going to," Dass said. Then his voice hardened, "Kim, take it from him," he said. Kim smiled.

As he took his first step towards David, a buzzer sounded elsewhere in the house.

Now it was David's turn to smile, albeit a little weakly. "Speaking of luck – that will be the police," he said.

Dass looked sharply at David, but his words were evidently aimed at Tracksuit, as he said, "See who that is, without answering it." Tracksuit darted out of the room.

Dass seemed to be sizing David up. He was clearly calculating his next move. David helped him along in his analysis. "My car's sitting right outside," he said pleasantly.

A moment later Tracksuit put his head back round the door and said, "There are police cars in the street outside." He added, "Karst is nearby. I could..." but a look from Dass silenced him.

David said, "I was particularly concerned that the thief might overpower you and lock the police out. I hope they remembered to bring their battering ram. But I don't suppose you'll wait for them to break down the door, will you." It wasn't a question.

Dass looked angry now. His eyes bored into David, who chose that moment to get to his feet.

Everyone tensed.

But David simply leaned towards Dass and offered him the box. "On behalf of Marshall & Liberty, I'm pleased to be able to return this to you, Mr Dass. I would say that we look forward to serving your insurance needs for years to come, but regrettably I'm going to have to recommend a full review of your account. We will of course continue to respect your privacy."

The buzzer sounded again and this time the button was held in for a number of seconds.

A look of sullen resignation came over Dass's face as he took the box. He said, "Let's all go down to meet our visitors shall we?" He lifted the lid of the box and peered inside the inner compartment. Then he snapped it shut again and, handing it to Tracksuit, said, "William, perhaps you would take care of this."

Dass led the way downstairs. After a few moments he seemed to recover some of his characteristic composure. "Where are my manners? Thank you for your help Mr Braun. I shall have nothing but good words to say about you to your superiors. Under other circumstances I might be tempted to recruit you…" Dass said. He looked back at the Oriental and said, "You can't greet the police wearing a baseball cap, Kim; what would they think?" He darted his eyes to one of the doors they were passing and Kim, taking it as an instruction, ducked in there. A second later he emerged without the hat, smoothing his short hair into place.

David peered at Dass, craning his head slightly as they descended the stairs, surreptitiously trying to get a good look at him. As they passed a tiny window which let a little daylight into the dim stairway, he could see that Dass had already removed the metal band from his forehead. Wherever he had stashed it, it wasn't in evidence now.

When they reached the door, Kim unbarred it and opened it wide. David and Dass stood back to let him do so. On the step outside stood two police officers; behind them was DI Hammond and beyond him were several men in body armour.

A second group of policemen stood over by one of the three official vehicles parked in the street. With them was a woman wearing a black jacket and carrying a bright orange shopping bag – it was Susan.

She caught David's eye for a split second and then turned away, her back to the door. Dass was already focussed on Hammond, thanking him profusely for his interest. Hammond and the first two uniforms stepped inside at Dass's invitation. Once they were in the hallway, David slipped past them into the street; no one was paying him very much attention.

Dass and Hammond were talking and the police officers were peering around, looking for something to fasten their interest upon. They eyed the muscular Oriental suspiciously and he returned the favour.

Once outside, David called back through the open door, "Inspector Hammond, you don't need me for anything do you?" He held up his car keys, indicating that he was about to depart. Hammond grunted. David said, "Congratulations again Mr Dass. I'll get the paperwork started," he said, offering a cheery wave.

He got into his car without anything more being said.

Susan was standing some distance from the open front door, out of line of sight of Dass and his people. She was talking to a policeman who was glancing periodically at his notebook. She looked up as David's car pulled away and they locked eyes for the briefest moment. Then he was gone and she continued smoothly with what she had been saying to the officer at her side.

CHAPTER 20

LATER THAT DAY
SATURDAY 19TH APRIL

A few hours later, David's mobile rang.

He was at his desk, in the Marshall & Liberty offices, trying to organise an emergency partners' meeting. Despite the fact that it was Saturday, several of the partners were currently in the office. The rest he was phoning at home.

He glanced down at his mobile's display; it was Susan calling.

His desk was largely screened from the open plan area where the assistants sat, but still he turned in his seat and brought his shoulder up to block the sound of his words. He said gently, "Hey," as he answered the phone.

Susan's voice was anxious as she said, "David? Are you OK?"

He replied, "I'm fine – absolutely fine." He paused a moment and said quietly, "You were right. He was going to kill me."

She said, "God, I'm so glad you're alright. I mean you looked fine, but I didn't know… I would have called earlier but they kept me talking for ages."

David's forehead wrinkled. He said, "Have they been grilling you all this time?" He looked at his watch. It was after three.

"No," she replied, "but I didn't want to call you from the street; I'm home now. The police ran me back to the station with them and I signed my statement about the break-in last week. Have they called you yet? Because they will."

"No, they haven't been in touch yet," he said. "What did you tell them in the end?"

She said, "Just what we agreed. We were getting together for lunch after your meeting with Dass. I was early and I thought I saw Jan. I ducked behind a bush and called them – didn't move 'til I saw a police car coming down the street. Dass obviously didn't mention *your* version of the story to the police because they seemed quite happy with what I'd told them."

David asked, "So are you in trouble for phoning in a false report?"

Susan replied, "They don't think it was false. Now they know that Dass was getting his treasure back, they think I really did see Jan, but he bolted when the cops showed up. They think they saved the day." A moment later she said, "You know you could have just told Dass you had an accomplice. If he'd compared notes with Hammond we could have been in trouble."

David said, "I think it was worth the risk. I'm even more glad now that we didn't let Dass know you were involved. Why have him carrying a grudge against both of us? He's angry with me for refusing to be bumped off; he might as well blame me for calling the cops too."

Susan said, "They took so long to arrive. That was me pushing the buzzer the first time; I couldn't wait any longer. God knows what I'd have done if someone had actually answered the door. But then the first police car arrived a few seconds later. While I was waiting I was going crazy imagining what Dass might be doing to you."

Shaking his head in recollection and disbelief, David said, "Well, whatever scenario you imagined, I somehow doubt it was 100% accurate." Then he said with seriousness, "You know, you talked me into having a plan, then you did exactly what you said you'd do and you got the police there just in the nick of time. It's down to you that I'm still breathing." He considered his own words for a moment and asked, "How many times did I call you in the end? I was just hitting redial and cancel over and over. I kept thinking Dass would ask me to take my hands out of my pockets."

Susan said, "While I was talking to the police there were nine missed calls from your mobile – plus there was the one that made me phone them in the first place. It was almost a relief in a funny way. I kept thinking, what if they take your phone off you and I'm sitting outside while they... you know, while something terrible happens. As long as you were calling I knew there was still a little bit more time. But you'd only been in there about two minutes before the first call."

David said, "Yeah, well it was pretty obvious from the first question that Dass was up to something. He was sounding me out, asking who knew my whereabouts. By the time the Old Bill turned up, Dass had worked out that he could get rid of me and I wouldn't be missed."

"Well, I'd have missed you," Susan said. "You're quite sure killing you was what he'd got in mind?"

David said with black humour, "Ohhh yes. He was even good enough to explain why my permanent disappearance would be such a good thing for him. Things were getting a bit physical by the time the doorbell went. He'd brought in a couple of blokes who can't have had any other use besides hurting people – not that he needed any help in that department."

Susan sounded puzzled, "What do you mean? Dass wouldn't stand a chance against you by himself, would he?"

David struggled to explain, "I don't... Listen, there's no easy way to explain this. Well, there is I suppose, but you're not..."

"David?" Susan said, cutting into his preamble.

David said, "Sorry. I can't tell you this over the phone. I need to say it face to face."

Susan said, "Come on, that's for the movies. Tell me now."

David was firm. "You're going to want to look me in the eye when I tell you the story. Believe me." He looked down at the list of partners, counted the un-ticked names. "I'll be done in another hour; can you meet me?"

Susan was obviously not happy, but she said patiently, "Sure. Tell me where you're going to be."

David glanced at his watch and pursed his lips for a moment. "I'm starved," he said, "can you come to Islington? There's a place called S & M on Essex Road just off Upper Street."

"S & M?" Susan said, unsure.

David laughed, "Don't worry; it stands for sausage and mash. Can you be there for 4.30?"

"I'll be there," she said.

"OK. See you then," David said, hanging up.

* * *

Susan was already sitting at one of the little blue Formica tables when David arrived. The restaurant was a tiny, low-key fifties diner – black and white colour scheme, lots of chrome. David gave Susan a quick kiss on the cheek before sitting down. She squeezed his arm and gave him a concerned smile.

David said, "Before we get into this, let's get the food on its way, OK?"

Susan pursed her lips and narrowed her eyes as if to say he was pushing his luck, but she agreed and turned her attention to her menu. "Sausage and mash," she said thoughtfully, "or sausage and mash."

A minute later they ordered from a friendly American waitress. As soon as she had gone, Susan pounced. "What?" she asked dramatically, "You can tell me that someone tried to kill you," she lowered her voice to say the word, "but you can't tell me the rest of it over the phone. What's bigger news than attempted murder?" she demanded.

David made as if to speak but nothing came out. His shoulders dropped as though he were giving up on whatever he'd been planning to say. He tried again while Susan watched him, a look of borderline exasperation on her face.

Finally, he began to speak firmly, and the words just tumbled out, "I know how Jan can open a safe and jump thirty feet out of a window and let himself get shot at and burn his way out of a set of handcuffs – I know how he does it. Well, I don't know how he does it, but I know what he does... I mean..."

"David!" Susan said in an angry whisper, determined that he should stay on track. Her expression said that she might scream if he didn't get to the point soon. "What happened?" she pleaded.

David took a deep breath. "OK," he said. He let the breath out and then he began, "Dass pinned me to a wall and tore that asp, that baton thing, out of my hand and he did it without moving. I hit him with it before he took it off me and it just bounced off him – or rather it bounced off something before it reached him. It was like I'd tried to hit him and hadn't noticed there was a wall in the way – except there wasn't a wall. Do you know what I'm talking about?"

Susan looked stunned. "Are you saying he did it with his mind? Like a scene out of *Carrie*?" she said, incredulous.

"What's Carrie?" David asked, confused.

Susan waved it away, "Never mind." She looked him in the eye, "But you're saying psychic powers, that sort of thing? There's no way it could have been something else? You sure he wasn't actually wearing some sort of body armour?"

David said quietly but fervently, "Something ripped that asp out of my hand and pinned me to the wall and Dass wasn't touching me. He didn't even move."

Susan stared into David's eyes for a moment, looking for confirmation. Then she flopped back in her chair. "Jesus," she said. And a moment later, "Jesus!"

Then she leaned forwards again. "You're absolutely…" she began.

"I'm sure," he said with finality, before she could finish. "I promise you, that's what happened. And Dass referred to Jan, he knew who he was. He said Jan was a stray and an exile, which means he's the same as Dass. They can both do this stuff. Whatever the two of them are, I don't think they're human."

Their food and drinks arrived a moment later and neither of them moved or acknowledged the waitress, who went away with a puzzled look on her face.

David picked up his cutlery and began to eat mechanically, as though he wasn't fully aware of what he was doing. Susan continued to stare, unfocussed, past his shoulder. Her blank expression indicated total absorption in whatever her mind was working on.

306   Robert Finn

When she focussed again she said, "Was he wearing tribute?" She rephrased, "Was he wearing a gold band?"

David said, "I don't know if it was gold, but yes, he was wearing a metal band around his head when I arrived. He took it off before he met the police." Susan absorbed this information without saying anything.

David added, "Actually, the two henchmen had their heads covered, so they might have been wearing them too."

Susan picked up her fork and began to eat. After a few moments her expression changed, as though something had occurred to her, as though a weight had been lifted.

"What are you thinking?" asked David, having noticed the change in her expression.

"That this is really good," she explained playfully, gesturing towards her plate with the fork she was holding.

"Any thoughts not related to food?" David asked witheringly.

Susan's expression was almost jubilant now. She was looking confident. She said, "Don't get irritated with me, but I want to tell you a silly little story." He didn't look convinced so she added, "Seeing as how you made me wait an hour after your cliff-hanger phone call."

He nodded, acknowledging her point and she began, "I read in the newspaper a long time ago about this guy who taught people to swim. He had a talent for it – frightened kids, nervous adults – he could help anyone. The reporter from the newspaper finished up the story by asking the instructor how often he himself liked to go swimming. And the answer was, 'I teach it, I don't know how to do it.'"

She looked at David expectantly. He looked back just as expectantly and said, "And? You'll have to give me more than that."

Susan was getting enthusiastic now. She said, "Don't you see? They're not aliens, they're just people, humans."

David still showed no sign that he knew what she was talking about.

She continued, "What an idiot I've been. I spend all day going through page after page of documents describing people able to do all the things we're talking about here. Then I put the papers back in the safe and come out and tell you that I have no idea what's going on. That's like…" she searched for an example, "a map-maker who can't find his way home from work. Or," she was grinning now, "an ornithologist who can't figure out why his milk bottle tops have little holes in them."

A hint of comprehension appeared on David's face. "Are you saying that all we need to do is treat the Teracus collection…" Susan couldn't wait for him to finish his sentence and did it for him, "as fact not fiction."

She threw up her hands in triumph. "Maybe this is what it feels like when you finally lose touch with reality. But let's just forget about sanity for a minute. Why don't we stop looking for the *real* reason behind all this madness and take it at face value? Jan, Dass and his merry men can do the stuff in the documents. And the Marker really can heal people, which is why they both want it. It's so simple."

She was eating quickly now, taking small bites and then talking around them. "God, I wonder if the longevity document is true. Jesus, that would explain why alchemy was so popular for hundreds of years." She wasn't really addressing David, just thinking aloud. "I must talk to Professor Shaw about this," she said. And then a frown appeared on her face, "Oh no, I can't."

David inquired, "Because he'll have you locked up?"

Susan nodded, "Right, exactly," she agreed, looking disappointed now. "Oh well," she shrugged. Then another thought occurred to her. "Shit," she said.

David asked, "What's up?"

Susan said, "You've just wrecked my post-doc. I can't pretend the collection's allegorical, knowing what I know. But I can hardly start writing about how magic really works. I'm screwed."

David had been watching her as she had her revelation and then thought her way through the implications. Now that she was looking dejected, he took it as his cue to take a turn at grumbling, "Yeah, and what am I supposed to do? Do I forget about it all? We agreed that whatever Dass was up to, we'd let him have the Marker back – and we'd let *him* handle Jan. But I can't just let him try to kill me and then forget about it." A moment later he said, "Only what other choices are there? Particularly given that he's probably capable of killing me with a wave of his hand." He brooded on that for a moment. "What else do you suppose he can do? Fly? Turn into a bat? Saw a woman in half?"

Susan wasn't sure. "Well," she said, "for the time being, I'm going to assume that Teracus knew what he was talking about. So I'm only going to trust documents in the collection – forget about all the other things I've read about magic. In which case I've got some work to do to answer that question. Believe it or not, I wasn't thinking along those lines when I first went through the collection."

She ate another couple of forkfuls of food while she considered. "You say Dass put some sort of shield around himself and then moved something without touching it. Jan seemed to be able to burn things as well. I've also read a document which refers to healing. I think these guys heal very quickly and they don't get sick."

David looked puzzled by that. "Well, if we're assuming this stuff is all true – and I have to say Dass hasn't left me much leeway there – then why would anyone care about the Marker? If they can heal themselves using a bit of ordinary gold wire then why fight each other for the Marker?"

Susan corrected David, "Tribute includes gold on each wrist as well as a band around the head. But you've got a good point. I think we've still got some mysteries to solve. Maybe I'm wrong and only the Marker can heal." Another thought occurred to her. "Imagine if you'd tackled Jan when he was wearing his headpiece. Or if I hadn't managed to knock it loose the first time I hit him."

David nodded, "I think it's safe to say we wouldn't be having this conversation. How could you ever stop someone like that? I think Jan let someone fire a gun at him, knowing they couldn't hurt him." Something else occurred to him. "God, imagine if they fought each other."

Susan waggled her knife and said, "Apparently there's a law against it. There's this whole scroll about how you can't attack magic with magic." She looked thoughtful, "Not that you'd imagine these guys would pay attention to the rules. Maybe something terrible happens if they try." She sighed. "You know, I'm going to have to reread every single word of those documents. I just wasn't thinking in the right way the first time around."

She paused a moment and blew out her breath, then she said, "So what do you want to do about Dass?"

David shrugged, "Even setting aside the fact that he's rich, powerful and probably indestructible – and I'm none of those things – I don't see what I *can* do. Even if he was a normal man, it would be difficult to get him arrested. Given that he isn't a normal man, it would just result in a few policemen getting killed even if I could persuade them to try it. I'm going to think about it, but I don't see any way forward."

Susan asked, "And what about Jan? Do you think he'll want to hush us up? It's a no-brainer that these guys rely on secrecy to survive. Obviously, if enough people knew what they were capable of, someone would find a way to take them down. You'd send a hundred guys and a tank or something. Their power is vastly more effective if no one knows they have it until it's too late. And – lucky for us – we're in on the secret. But if they're really serious about their privacy, won't they want to get rid of us?"

David thought about it. "Dass only knows about me, we reckon. He can imagine I'll cause trouble for him at work. I might even tell people he was going to bump me off. But he can guess what would happen if I accused him of having demonic powers without so much as a Polaroid of him shaking hands with Satan to back it up. Alive I'll spread some rumours that he's a crook, but won't be able to prove them. If I suddenly up and died, that would be my proof that he was out to get me – much good it would do me. He'd be better off leaving me alive and sounding like a looney."

Susan said, "And Jan?"

David said, "Wouldn't you think killing us would be low on his list of priorities? Not only is he on the run from the police, we can also be pretty sure Dass will have dispatched someone to find him. Dass knows the police won't be able to stop him, after all. In fact, there could be a small army of Dass's people after Jan – we don't really have any idea what Dass's resources are. It's only Jan we've got reason to think is a loner. He had surprise on his side when he stole the Marker, but now everyone's after him and he's on his own. I don't think he can afford grudges at the moment."

Susan didn't look totally convinced. "Hmmm," she said. "That's a lot of supposition. I can buy the idea that Dass is better off ignoring you – I doubt he has too much to worry about from 'some insurance guy', as my sister would call you." She reflected a moment and said, "But I haven't forgotten that five minutes ago you were telling me I was better off if Dass didn't know I was involved, and now you reckon there's nothing to worry about anyway." David gave her a weak grin. She concluded, "At any rate, it's Jan I'm not sure about. We really messed up his week."

David said, "We could always ask Dass for help."

Susan looked appalled, "Are you kidding?"

David shook his head. "Think about it," he said. "If he gave us a bodyguard he'd stand a better chance of finding Jan than if he just combs the streets – let Jan come to us and then grab him. It would definitely be in Dass's interest to keep us alive as bait."

"I understand all that," Susan said. "I just can't believe you'd go back to the guy who tried to kill you this morning and ask him for protection!" she said with some passion.

"Dessert?" a voice at Susan's shoulder enquired.

"Apple crumble and custard, please," said David, who'd seen the waitress approaching and checked the specials board while Susan was berating him.

Susan had been surprised by the interruption but recovered quickly. "Me too, but can I have ice cream instead of custard?"

The waitress smiled, "Sure. That's no problem," she said and left, taking their empty plates with her.

"Still not quite up to speed on the custard thing," Susan said uneasily. "Anyway, as regards our life expectancies, I have no idea where all that leaves us. Should we be running for our lives or is it all over? For that matter, have you just fired me?"

David said, "Well, I suppose this is the logical point to stop paying you. But I think this has gone beyond a job, don't you think? I'm hoping you'll keep talking to me even if you're not on the payroll. You're going to be burrowing into that collection regardless, so maybe you could keep me up to speed with whatever you find out? If you can learn a little bit more about these guys, maybe that'll set our minds at rest or perhaps it'll tell us how to protect ourselves. I stand by what I said, though. I think the way things are, Dass doesn't care about us and Jan's best bet is to move to Uruguay as quickly as possible and change his name."

Shortly after that, their desserts arrived and both of them tucked in.

Susan said, "Well give me a few days. You know what they say about paradigm shifts – they sort of invalidate all the things you thought you knew. I've got about seven years of thinking to re-evaluate." She finished another mouthful of crumble and said, "Obviously we should talk if anything happens, but otherwise I'll give you a call…" she petered out. She had one eye half closed as though either the ice cream was too cold or she was recalling something painful. "Of all the weeks for my sister to visit."

David said, "Listen, there's no rush. I don't think either of us is prepared to just let this go, but it's not as though there's anything we can actually do – apart from you re-evaluating the collection. Why don't you enjoy your sister's visit? Take advantage of the distraction and have a break from this do-or-die stuff. I'll still be waiting by the phone, full of curiosity, even if it takes you a month instead of a week to call." He looked her in the eye, "Though I'd rather see you sooner than that." He put his hand on her forearm, gave it a little squeeze.

"Yeah, I can't imagine going a month and not talking to you," she said. "Plus you're the only one I could talk to about all this." She was wrestling with her thoughts, conflicting emotions showing on her face. She took his hand. "About the hotel room, when I…" she said haltingly.

"Yeah, I'm sorry about that," David said, rushing in. "I misread… Well I don't know what I thought."

Susan said, "I want you to understand… I mean I don't think I did a very good job of explaining…"

David jumped in again, "Really, don't worry about it. You don't have to explain. If anything, after what we argued about…" He didn't go on.

Susan nodded. "Well, the main thing, I guess, is that we're still speaking to each other. Some time," she looked around at the diner, "not here, but sometime, we need to have a talk." She squeezed his hand and then let it go.

David's expression showed he really didn't think any more needed to be said, but he dipped his head solemnly and said, "OK."

She brightened, saying, "In the meantime, if you really don't want to go too long without seeing me you could come round to dinner, say this Friday, and meet my sister."

David smiled mischievously, "Why do I get the feeling that's not the generous offer the casual observer might think it was?"

Susan said, "You've got nothing to worry about. Dee's a charmer. You'll love her; everyone does. The vibe you're picking up is my lack of altruism in asking you. We just tend to get on each other's nerves after a few days and a little moral support and a change of pace would give me something to look forward to. Help a gal out and come?"

David smiled and said, "I'd love to."

CHAPTER 21

Six days later
Friday 25th April

The sun was low, but not yet setting, as David stood in front of the same lifeless townhouse where he'd been standing two minutes earlier. "This must be it," he muttered to himself.

He was in a tiny street in the City of London – not much more than two little terraces facing each other.

The street began as an unpromising single-lane cut-through between the headquarters of a bank and a shipping company. Thirty metres back and round a corner, the narrow lane opened out and there were the houses, three on either side, hidden from the world. There was just enough room to accommodate a fenced-off Electricity Board transformer before the road ended with the back wall of a seventeenth-century church.

Outside the first house on the left, David climbed the six steps up to a tall, windowless front door and pushed the doorbell. In the distance an electric bell rang. He waited.

He was wearing a navy jacket and trousers, and an open-necked shirt in dark red cotton. He was carrying a neat little package wrapped in gold paper, the ribbon inscribed with the name of a company renowned for its hand-made chocolates.

To the right of the front door was a bay window – its wooden shutters closed – behind very elegant wrought-iron bars. Beneath the window, the pavement stopped at the railing and he could see down into the one tiny window set into the basement wall.

He looked up again as the door opened. Standing on the top step, appraising him, was a slim woman dressed all in black, holding a crystal wine glass. She wore a short woollen wrap-skirt over long, darkly-stockinged legs; a merino sweater with a deep v-neck was tight around her trim waist. Her face, a paler, more delicate version of Susan's, had the same blue eyes, but her silky black hair was longer and fell almost straight to her collar-bone. She smiled at David with her dark-red lips and took a sip of red wine.

"Hi," David said, "Dee?"

Dee smiled down at him for a moment from the threshold, without replying. Her arms were twined together holding the wineglass near her mouth and she let the rim tap against her very white teeth a couple of times as though she were working something out. The light caught a tiny fleck of sky-blue sapphire above her right nostril.

A moment later, after David had begun to blush, her eyebrows flicked up for a split-second and she held out a hand. "Oh I'm sorry. You must be David," she said.

Her accent was polished New York City – melodious and a little husky at the same time.

They shook hands and Dee said, "Come in. Susan's in the kitchen." She glanced over her shoulder. "Let's get you a drink," she said, enunciating each word separately.

They stepped into a dim hallway, lots of dark wood on the walls and floors, and too few lights. The house smelled a little musty, but it wasn't unpleasant – a smell of age, but not neglect. To their left was a staircase and running to the right of it was a passageway leading to the back of the house and an open door, from which light and the sound of reggae were coming.

They followed the music.

Susan was cooking. As they came through the door, she was checking the contents of several big, old, aluminium saucepans that were bubbling away on a spotless cream-coloured cooker that looked like the latest in Fifties labour-saving appliances. Susan's face was pinker than usual and the steam had fixed a few strands of hair to her forehead. Her white silk blouse was sticking to her back.

Susan looked up as David came into the kitchen. She gave him a hassled smile which was abruptly terminated by an urgent hiss from the gas stove. A gulp of water had bubbled out of the front saucepan and dropped onto the flames of the gas ring with a crash of steam.

"Behold, the housewife of the future," Dee said in corny voiceover tones. David laughed. Dee went on, "With the latest space-age gadgets at her disposal, hubby's dinner is ready in a flash, leaving more time to gossip with the girls."

Dee held up a bottle of red wine for David to see. "Merlot?" she asked, continuing in a whisper, "Susan's got the keys to the cellar. In booze terms, we're millionaires."

David said, "Thanks," to Dee's offer and to Susan he said, "Can I do anything to help?"

Susan said, "I don't think…" but a loud crack from the oven interrupted her. Susan's face looked stricken as she hunted around for a cloth.

Dee winced, "Well. Now we know whether the dish is oven-proof or not."

Susan was swearing as she opened the oven door and peered inside.

Once more using her stage whisper, Dee said, "Why don't I show you round?" To Susan she called, "We'll leave you to it, Champ."

Dee handed David a glass of wine and took his arm. "You wanna see the wine vaults?" she asked.

* * *

Twenty minutes later, Susan yelled for them to come downstairs to eat. Dee had been showing David the bedrooms and the attic study from which it was possible to see a sliver of the dome of St Paul's Cathedral. Most of the time she had been telling David funny stories about her and Susan's childhood. They were still laughing as they came down the stairs.

Susan ushered them into the old-fashioned dining room at the back of the house. Two tiny chandeliers spread a listless mellow glow over the linen-covered table as though the electricity itself was from an earlier time. Candles were arranged between the place settings. The overall impression was an island of illumination twinkling at the centre of a room full of shadows.

David said, "It feels Christmasy," as he took his seat.

Dee and David sat, as Susan made a couple of quick runs to the kitchen fetching plates of food – chicken breasts in a red pepper sauce, green beans, carrots and cauliflower. Steam rose from the plates.

"I'm pretty sure I got all the china out of it," she said as she served the food.

David said, "This looks fabulous," as Susan dropped into her seat and motioned for them to start eating.

Dee said, amazed, "Wow, I haven't had cauliflower since Mom used to make it."

"I only gave you a tiny bit," Susan said reassuringly, "I know you don't like it that much."

David said, "This is excellent," after his first mouthful and Susan smiled appreciatively.

"You deserve a glass of wine, Sis. Jolly good show," Dee said, reaching for the bottle. She hesitated, "Hmm, are we allowed to have red wine with chicken? Isn't that a shocking *faux pas*?" She looked to David to provide the answer.

"Let's be peasants," he said raising his glass and toasting the ladies.

"I'm sorry the beans are a bit underdone. Just leave them," Susan said.

"Nonsense," David said warmly, "It's all lovely."

Dee looked up. "Remember when you cooked Thanksgiving Dinner?" she asked Susan, with a glance towards David.

Susan shrank a bit, looking embarrassed, "I was only twelve, Dee," she said quietly.

Dee quipped, "Nearly didn't make it to thirteen." She spread her hands dramatically, indicating newspaper headlines, and announced, "Family of Four in Salmonella Suicide Pact. Come to think of it, that was chicken too," Dee said, like a whodunit detective spotting an important clue. David laughed.

"Come on, Dee," Susan said, sounding a little bit tired.

Dee held up her hands in surrender. "Sorry. Never tease the cook; it's too easy for them to take their revenge. We'll talk about something else." She looked over at David, set her chin in her hands, and said breathlessly, "So, David, you're in insurance. That must be fascinating." Her eyes twinkled playfully as she said it.

David was amused and pretended to be puffed up with flattery as he said, "Oh, absolutely. It's glamorous, often dangerous work, but at least you feel truly alive. I'm so glad now that I decided not to go into space." He raised an eyebrow and said, "What about you? Didn't Susan say you deliver newspapers? That must be interesting work." Then he sat back, beaming, to see how she'd respond.

Now it was Dee's turn to smile and there was more than a little mischief in her expression. She said sarcastically, "Well, I'm stuck on the writing side at the moment, unfortunately. And, worse still, it's magazines, not newspapers. But I don't let it get me down. In a few years I'll be able to make the jump from fashion and entertainment into sports journalism, and then I'm hoping to get onto a declining local paper somewhere. From there it's just a matter of getting my name down for one of those little newsstands outside a subway station. Of course they prefer it if you drive a cab for a few years before they give you your own stand, but I sent the Commissioner of Outdoor Vending a box of fingerless gloves on his birthday and let's just say I'm quietly confident." Dee gave David a rather self-satisfied little pout, amused by her own wit.

David was grinning at Dee. He said, "Really? That's marvellous! Have you decided what you're going to hold the papers down with yet?" He made a flattening gesture, "A lot of people seem to think it has to be a lump of rock or half a roof tile maybe, but I've always leaned in favour of a good chunk of metal. You know, a bit off an old car, something like that."

Dee nodded seriously, but held up a finger, saying, "Don't forget New York winters; metal can get very cold to the touch until the cheap whisky kicks in. It's kind of premature to make a final decision, but lately I'm hearing some good things about composites." David laughed.

From her end of the table, Susan said, "There's more chicken if anyone wants it? David?"

David broke eye contact with Dee, and focussed on Susan for a moment, "Oh yes. That would be great, thanks," he said. Then he turned back to Dee and said, "Maybe that's OK in the States, but I don't think we're ready for anything too new-fangled over here. There's a lot of tradition. For instance, no London paper-seller worth his salt would shout anything in modern English. It might be the Evening Standard to you or me, but it's always going to be the..." he raised his voice, "'hipnee stannaaar' to a professional."

Dee said, "I guess you're right. There's sure a lot to learn. You want to know what's worrying me most, right now?" her face looking anxious, "getting the moustache right." She rested a finger just below her nose. "I've been letting this one grow for about eight months now and I'm nowhere with it." She held out her upper lip, the way a horse reaches for a sugar-lump, trying to show it to David.

He leaned across the table, squinting, and Dee stood up. Tilting her head back she tried to hold her lip forwards and at the same time talk, saying, "Shee? Shee?"

Susan came back in with David's replenished plate, set it down in front of him.

David shook his head, "I wouldn't worry. That's OK. Give it another couple of weeks."

Dee gave David a narrow-eyed look and then said to Susan, "He's feisty. I like that."

Dee and David were laughing with each other as Susan sat down. She glanced at both of them, looking a little left out.

After a moment, David noticed Susan's expression and put on a more serious face. Turning to Susan he said, "So what have you shown Dee while she's been here? The usual sights?"

Dee answered for her, saying, "We went shopping, which was cool, but we haven't done much sightseeing yet."

Susan sounded guilty as she explained, "Well, I've been pretty busy this week..."

Dee said, "Plus, Susie's not much more English than I am. We need a native guide."

David said, "Well, maybe I can help. I've lived in London for most of my life and while I haven't actually *been* to any of the famous sights, I think I've absorbed a fair amount of info. Maybe we could go to St Nelson's Square tomorrow, the three of us, and Buckingham Cathedral on Sunday? How does that sound?"

"See," Dee said sarcastically to Susan, "I told you you'd got the names all wrong. Listen to the expert," she said, pointing at David.

Susan looked awkward and said with reluctance, "I really need to work tomorrow. I've got to go into college."

David pointed out, "Susan, it's Saturday."

A flicker of annoyance crossed Susan's face as she said, "Well, there's some important stuff I'm working on at the moment." Her eyes were on David's as she said it.

Dee, undimmed in her enthusiasm, said to Susan, "Well *we* could go," indicating herself and David, "couldn't we?"

Susan looked at David who was keeping his expression neutral, obviously waiting for Susan to make the decision for him.

Dee nagged, "Can we, huh, can we?" She started to bounce a little and pout, "I'll do all my stupid chores first."

David shook his head slowly and, glancing sidelong at Susan, said, "Well, maybe we should wait until Susan has a bit more…"

But Susan interrupted, insisting, "You guys go. Maybe I'll join you later, when I get done."

Their plates were empty and Susan set about clearing the table. Dee got up to help.

David asked Susan, "Err, wouldn't you rather we made it another day?"

Dee complained, "She said go; let's go. It's no big deal. It's not like we're leaving Susie home alone. She's busy."

David continued to look at Susan, studying her expression for signs of disapproval. "What?" she said, exasperated, noticing his look, "Go. Have fun." Then more quietly, "I'll let you know what I find out."

David didn't look happy, but Dee was on to the next topic. As she took the used plates from Susan she said, "Dessert I bought myself. I even set it out to defrost without any help. Susan, you sit, I'll get this." And she bustled off towards the kitchen.

Susan sat back down. With the two of them left on their own, a silence welled up.

David broke it. "So how's the research going?" he asked, his voice neutral.

Susan replied, "Good. Well, kind of good. There's still a million questions, but I think I'm getting somewhere," a pause, "We should really have a talk before long."

David nodded and said, "Well, maybe I should tell Dee that I'm busy tomorrow." He sounded tentative.

"Jesus," Susan snapped, "give it a break, will you. I'm not your mother; you don't need my permission to do things. I thought we'd covered that."

David looked awkward, "I'm sorry, I just meant…"

Dee breezed back into the room. "You like cheesecake, right? What am I saying? Everyone likes cheesecake." She was oblivious to any tension between David and Susan. She asked Susan, "Big bit? Small bit?" An impressive cheesecake sat in front of her and she was waving a cake slice over it, demonstrating the range of sizes available.

Susan tore her gaze away from David. "I'm not really hungry, thanks," she said to Dee, with a shrug.

Dee frowned. "Impossible. Well, we'll come back to you. David?"

Dee's relentless good cheer gradually dispelled the concealed awkwardness of the other two. David was soon bantering with Dee again, though not quite as enthusiastically as before. Susan was still quiet, but she accepted a piece of cheesecake and then allowed herself to be gently teased by Dee when she asked for a second helping a few minutes later.

After that, Susan made coffee while Dee opened the doors of the sideboard to reveal an astonishing array of antique spirits and arcane liqueurs. They puzzled over the label of a large orange bottle with a twist in its neck. When Susan returned with a cafetière and cups, she was carrying David's chocolates under her arm. She held them up and said, "I found these."

David said, "Oh yeah, I thought I'd left them on the tube. I took a chance that you girls like chocolate." Susan and Dee gave him identical pitying looks.

Susan took a look at the bottle with the twisted neck and translated the key ingredient as violets. The bottle was returned to the cupboard promptly, as was a hexagonal green one with oriental script on the label. One whiff of the contents was enough to satisfy everyone it would be difficult, and perhaps dangerous, to swallow any.

David said, "See, it's probably intended for *cleaning* drinks cabinets with. That's why it's in there. It's an understandable mistake to make."

Dee said, "My guess is you wave a capful under the nose of anyone who's had a bit too much of the regular stuff."

Susan said, "And if that doesn't work you could probably embalm them with it – it's dual-action."

David chuckled and Dee said, "Susie, you made a funny. Does that mean you've forgiven me for bringing up Thanksgiving Dinner?" She realised what she'd said and corrected herself, "I mean for mentioning it. Obviously, we brought it up at the time."

David laughed loudly. Susan rolled her eyes, but looked amused. Dee said, "I'll take that as a yes."

The mood remained light as they pushed their chairs back from the table and continued to experiment with the contents of the sideboard.

Around eleven, David said he should get going, which triggered a discussion with Dee about plans for meeting up the following day.

David made another attempt to include Susan by suggesting that Dee should meet him late in the afternoon, which would give Susan most of the day to finish her work and perhaps join them. He arranged to meet Dee at the London Eye at 4pm and to take it from there.

As David walked back along the street, waving over his shoulder, Dee stood at the open door waving back, while Susan retreated inside. As David strolled towards the tube his expression was happy but thoughtful.

CHAPTER 22

A hundred metres from Alessandro Dass's front door stood a late Georgian house large enough to be called a mansion. It sat behind a high brick wall, which rose to flank broad, scrolled-iron gates and then dipped down again towards the far side of the property. The double gates (complete with intercom and closed-circuit camera) allowed those walking by to catch a quick glimpse of how the other half lived.

Currently, the lowest of the house's three magnificent storeys was caged in scaffolding. Thick polythene sheeting covered several windows, which were missing their frames.

In front of the house, on the sand and gravel drive, sat a skip. Two lines of duck-boards ran out from the front of the house, allowing workmen and their wheelbarrows to cross the lawn and reach the skip without damaging the grass.

The house itself was empty. The ground floor had been stripped down to plaster and floorboards – and in some places even the boards had been removed. The upper two storeys were still carpeted and papered, but no furniture remained. The doors leading to the upstairs parts of the house were sealed.

The roofline, which originally had run straight, in parallel with the road, had become more complex as the house had been added to. Now it included a number of geometric planes and angles where extensions met the original construction. In the dip between two of the roof's peaks, a man lay stretched out flat on his stomach looking down onto the street from complete concealment.

He was wearing lightweight Gore-Tex clothing and high-topped training shoes, all in dark colours. To his right lay an open backpack. A mobile phone, a pair of binoculars and a bottle of water rested on top of the pack. The handle of some long implement protruded from the bag's open top.

The mobile phone began to vibrate and the man snatched it up, swiftly inspecting the display before answering it. He said, amiably, "Good afternoon, Edward."

A voice – old but full of nervous agitation – said, "Yeah, yeah. Jan? Got something for you."

Jan said calmly, "Well done, Edward. What is it?"

Edward replied in his hurried, almost stuttering way, "Put that watch on exit points, like you asked. Got a flag on some airline tickets. Looks like your party. First class to Rome-Fiumicino on British Airways. Flight's tomorrow at 19:35. It's AZ209 on the boards." Edward paused a moment before asking, "Watcha gonna do with that? That info? Anything I need to know about?"

Jan replied in his measured tones, "Let's just say you'll probably want to clear away any signs of your interest in the man and his dealings. A lot of people will be asking questions about Mr Dass by the end of Saturday. It might be best if you had concealed your current interest by then."

Edward said, "Christ! What are you up to? Are you dropping me in it? Am I burned?" He was agitated, but still somewhat deferential.

Jan turned over onto his back, looked up at the sky and said warmly, "If there's any problem, Edward, I'm sure I've got enough time to pop round there and crush the life out of you. Just let me know if being well paid and continuing to breathe is distressing to you."

Edward was unable to speak for a few seconds. "No need. No need for that," he managed to say eventually. "It's just preparations. The more I know about what's going on, the more I can smooth the way at this end. Continue to be useful to you. If I'm in the know, that is. You can see that?"

Jan said soothingly, "Calm down, Edward. I'm sorry I said anything to upset you. After all," he chuckled jovially, "if I keep threatening your life, you'll probably conclude that I'm going to kill you whatever happens and then things really will get strained."

Edward was completely speechless now.

Jan said, reflectively, into the silence on the line, "No. It's probably best that you continue struggling to be useful to me. It helps both of us stay focussed."

Edward still made no response. The only sound from his end of the line was staccato breathing.

Something occurred to Jan and he asked, "Oh, you wouldn't happen to know which terminal that flight leaves from, would you?"

Edward sputtered "tuh" a few times.

Jan made a suggestion, "If you don't think you can get past the first syllable, can I ask you to skip over the word 'terminal' – ironic though it is – and try for the number itself?"

Edward remained silent. Then he managed to say "tuh" again.

Jan was full of patience as he enquired, "Or perhaps you were saying 'two'. *Do* B.A. fly out of terminal two these days?"

Edward gasped out, "Yes. Two. It's terminal two."

Jan was languidly surprised, "Well, well. It's a good job I asked, isn't it? There could have been a mix-up."

The line was still open. Jan said, "I think that's all for now, Edward. I'll call you if I want anything else. Take it easy, old man." He hung up.

Jan made another call. "Al, it's Jan."

Al was pleasantly surprised, "Jan? Good god, it's been a while – a long while. You after something?"

"Yes, and it's very short notice," Jan said.

"Well," Al said in a friendly way, "you tell me what you want and I'll see what I can do."

They chatted for a couple of minutes and Al read the list he'd been making back to Jan, "Stock M16, one off, under-slung with an M203 launcher, two 40 mil rounds supplied, plus a clip of 20 times M995 AP rounds."

Jan said, "That sounds like it. I need it tomorrow morning. Is that a problem?"

Al laughed, "It's just a shame you don't want five hundred of them. Technically it's all obsolete stuff – though it'll kill you just as dead. There's tons of it kicking around. Will any of it come under direct scrutiny?"

Jan replied, "Well, casings and slugs, of course. Is it a problem if the rifle *is* picked up?"

Al chuckled again, "Shouldn't be. You can get them mail-order in the States." Al paused a moment, "Listen, why isn't whatsisname calling this through for you? The kid? You haven't had a falling out with Mr Dass, have you?"

Jan sounded casual as he answered, "It's just quicker to do it myself. By the time I'd explained what I want... You know how it is."

Al said, "Fair enough. Aren't you getting a bit old for this lark, eh Jan? I know I am. My two lads handle most of it now. You know I'll be sixty next month?"

Jan sounded just a little impatient as he said, "No? Well, we'll have a proper natter once I've taken care of this bit of business."

Al said, "Right. I'm gassing on, aren't I? You sure you don't need a scope? Maybe a side-arm or a blade for this outing? You still got that gimmicky Jap thing?"

Jan considered a moment. "You know the way things have been going lately, you're probably right." He added a few more items to his shopping list and Al assured him that they'd be ready in the morning.

* * *

Hours later, after dark, a car pulled up in front of Dass's house. It was a huge, glossy black Mercedes 500SEL sitting low on its suspension.

The driver remained behind the wheel, with the car in gear, as a second man stepped out onto the street. He put his back to the wall of the house and slowly turned his head through one hundred and eighty degrees, taking in every detail of his surroundings. When he had completed his reconnaissance, he hammered twice on the front door, before resuming his vigilance. The front door was opened part way a moment later.

Dass stepped out of the rear of the car and crossed the pavement into the house, the heavy door opening at the last moment for him to enter. Only once Dass was inside did the driver turn off the engine and get out of the car. He locked the vehicle, pocketing the keys and he, and the man watching the street, disappeared into the house.

There was no movement outside for fifteen minutes.

Then, a man wearing dark trousers and boots and a light, ill-fitting sports jacket approached the house, preceded by a scruffy terrier on a lead. The dog leaned against its lead to sniff at the tyres of the Mercedes. The man paused and took a puff of his cigarette.

After a moment, he muttered, "Come on," to the dog and gave a half-hearted tug on the lead. The dog continued to investigate the back wheel of the limousine.

The man stepped across to the car, dropping to one knee and said to the dog, "That's enough, come on now." He reached out for the dog's collar (and swiftly attached something to the inside lip of the rear wheel-arch) before grasping the dog's collar and pulling it away from the car.

Having got the dog's attention, he set off back the way he'd come, the dog following without protest. After a few metres, he dropped the lit cigarette, half smoked, and ground it out with his toe.

He led the dog back up the darkened street and down a side turning. Fifty metres further along he dipped behind a hedge. Between the hedge and a sprawling hydrangea bush, a man lay motionless on his back. He was in his shirtsleeves, spread-eagled in the grass. The dog-walker slipped the loop of the dog's lead over the man's outstretched foot, lifting the leg a little to slide the leather strap beneath his calf. The foot twitched as he lifted it.

Laying on the ground beside the unconscious man was a black ski jacket. Slipping out of the sports jacket and dropping it over the supine figure's face, the dog-walker pulled on the ski jacket. Then he bent down to extract the wallet from the man's back pocket.

The man in the ski jacket emerged from behind the hedge and continued walking along the street, moving further away from Dass's house. A hundred metres later, he passed a rubbish bin, into which he dropped a nearly full packet of Dunhill cigarettes, a disposable lighter and the wallet.

* * *

THE NEXT DAY

At the very end of the afternoon, while it was still light, a filthy white Transit van, with a jagged and rusty rip in one of its side panels, broke down on a road bridge near Heathrow. The bridge spanned one of the main approaches to the airport and on the roadway ten metres below, traffic in three lanes continued to zip past, oblivious to the van's presence.

As the engine cut out, the van steered into the side of the road, coming to a halt halfway across the bridge. A moment later its hazard flashers came on.

The driver of the van, who was wearing heavy motorcycle leathers, got out and opened the bonnet. He stood and peered listlessly at the engine for a few moments, holding the hinged cover open with one latex-gloved hand. Then he secured the bonnet in its open position before climbing back behind the wheel and closing the door.

Lifting a copy of The Sun newspaper that lay on the passenger seat, he revealed a black box inlaid with various switches and dials. A gauge in the centre of the device was calibrated from 1 to 100%. The needle lay just below the 50% mark. The driver dropped the newspaper back in place.

Getting out of the van, he went round to the side door and, with a little bit of effort, managed to pull it open. Inside, a motorbike was anchored to the floor by thick straps which attached to loops in the corners of the grimy metal floorpan. He pulled the door most of the way closed behind him as he got in.

Immediately behind the front seats, a battered tool chest had been crudely welded into place. The driver fished a key from the pocket of his reinforced bikers jacket and unfastened the padlock which held the chest closed. He lifted the lid for a second and dropped the padlock inside.

He glanced at his watch and leaned over the passenger seat to check the hidden dial. The needle had climbed to 70%.

Next he unfastened the straps holding the motorbike in place, moved it up until the front wheel was almost against the rear doors of the van and setting it on its kickstand. He put the keys in the bike's ignition. Then he unfastened the rear doors of the van, but didn't push them open.

With the side door slightly ajar, there was a 5cm gap through which the traffic passing below could be seen. He peered out for a moment at the cars below, closing one eye and then the other, before sliding the door open another few centimetres.

He checked the device on the front seat again.

When the needle had climbed to 80%, the driver flipped open the top of the metal chest and took out a small metal canister and laid it on the floor just inside the door of the van. Next he removed a gold headband from its custom-made box and laid it next to the canister.

A long, slim, black tube, with a grip at one end, followed the headband. He slung it across his back, grip uppermost, using its integral strap.

Finally, he lifted out the rifle. He wrapped the sling around his left wrist and forearm and braced the butt against his shoulder. He flipped off both safety catches and sighted out through the gap in the door, keeping the tip of the muzzle just within the van.

He waited.

Several minutes passed and the traffic continued to flow. The sniper maintained his aim.

Finally, in the distance, a black Mercedes appeared. It was in the outside lane, moving swiftly towards the bridge.

The sniper reached behind him and turned the ignition key on the bike. The electric starter gave its rapid chirp as the engine skipped into life. The engine settled into a steady burble. The sniper returned his gaze to the road below. He took several deep breaths of fresh air through the gap in the side door and blew them out forcefully. Then he settled the rifle more comfortably into his shoulder and took aim at the approaching Mercedes.

The muzzle of the rifle gradually angled down as it followed the approach of the bulky limousine. He kept the weapon trained on the vehicle, until the driver's outline was visible behind the thick windscreen.

The car was now a hundred metres away as the sniper pulled the trigger. In the confines of the van, the sound was ear-splitting. The rifle cracked three times in rapid succession.

The first shot cratered the thick polycarbonate windscreen of the Mercedes without penetrating it. The second and third shots punched through, piercing the driver and slamming into the bodywork at the rear of the vehicle.

As soon as he had fired, the sniper slung the rifle over his shoulder and heaved the side door of the van open – the rusty runners on the door shrieked.

He jumped out onto the pavement and whipped the rifle up to his shoulder again, pointing it over the handrail and down into the traffic.

With a dead man at the wheel, the Mercedes swung across into the middle lane, shunting a Fiat Uno out of its way. The Fiat, in turn, was forced into the inside lane, where it narrowly avoided a black cab. The Fiat driver braked hard causing those behind him to do the same.

The sniper aimed his weapon at the swerving Mercedes and moved his hand to the grenade launcher slung beneath the rifle's barrel. He pulled the launcher's trigger.

A 40mm grenade leapt from the weapon and streaked down towards the driverless car. It struck the front bumper and exploded, lifting the front of the vehicle a metre in the air. The blast destroyed part of the engine and cancelled a considerable fraction of the vehicle's forward momentum.

The sniper pulled forwards on the grip of the grenade launcher, opening the barrel, and raised the muzzle. The remains of the spent round dropped to the concrete. Grabbing the metal canister from the floor of the van, he loaded it into the barrel of the launcher and pulled the grip back into place. Then he snatched up the gold band and jammed it onto his head. His eyelids flickered for a moment in concentration.

He took two rapid steps forwards and jumped over the handrail of the road bridge.

CHAPTER 23

THE NEXT DAY
SATURDAY 26TH APRIL

"So what are your parents like?" David asked.

They'd been talking about this and that – random subjects. He and Dee were standing in the queue for the London Eye, gradually shuffling forwards as each car descended and scooped away another party of tourists.

Dee put her head on one side and said, "Conventional, I guess. And kind of old-fashioned. Mom's always had her plans for both of us and Dad's always let her get on with it."

David said, "I suppose you and Susan don't see much of them these days?"

Dee had her hands in the pockets of her knee-length black wool coat. The late-afternoon breeze coming off the river was cool and she had pulled up her collar to keep her neck warm.

"Well, I'm in Manhattan, Susie's over here and they're in New Mexico," Dee said, then looked contrite and continued, "I shouldn't call her Susie, she hates it."

David said, "So it's just 'Susan' then? No nicknames or abbreviations allowed?"

Dee smiled at David and confessed, "Susan and I had a big fight about names once. She hates being called Susan and I hate being called Dorothy."

David began to react and caught the warning in Dee's raised eyebrow. He still sounded surprised when he asked, "You're Dorothy?"

Dee nodded and said, "Mmhmm. But no one calls me that. I don't know who came up with 'Dee', but it stuck – much to my relief. Somehow Susan stayed Susan."

David considered, "Sue? Susie? Ess? It's a tricky one."

Dee nodded, "But Susan being Susan, she likes to take it on the chin. She hates the name, but she doesn't let anyone try to dress it up or disguise it."

David said, "I quite like 'Susan'. The name."

Dee shrugged, "It's a good-girl's name and Susan was always a good girl. Mom was determined that…" she stopped, "You don't really want to know about this stuff," she said shaking her head.

David was nodding. "Really, I do," he assured her.

She gauged his sincerity for a moment and said, "OK. Background. Mom and Dad met in college. Dad was a geographer, still works for the U.S. Geological Survey. Mom was a journalist, worked on the college newspaper, got a job on a growed-up newspaper once she graduated. But then Dad asked her to marry him, she got pregnant and she hasn't worked full-time since. Susan was her chance to do all the things she was itching to do before marriage and kids happened. So Susan's had tutoring and extra classes and her pick of schools." Dee's voice held a note of frustration, which she now appeared to become aware of. Her voice softened as she said reflectively, "It can't have been very much fun for her, I guess. Lots of pressure."

David asked, "So what were you doing while Susan was being hot-housed?"

Dee bugged her eyes and held a shrug for a moment, "I dunno – watching TV? I was always hanging around with the neighbourhood kids, I think. Honing my people skills. We moved around too much for that to work out really well though."

David said cautiously, "Susan said – and I'm not making fun – Susan said you had an amazing job in New York. You managed that even though you didn't have all the pushing that Susan got."

Dee's introspective gloominess dispersed at the mention of New York and her voice filled with energy again as she said, "Well, what you have to understand is that at age eighteen, I'd had enough of life in the Midwest to last me until six weeks after the end of time. I took off. You could say I ran away from home, but I was eighteen, so really I just *left* home – though it felt more like a jailbreak. I went to Chicago, waitressed, temped, worked in clubs, met a guy. Met a *few* guys actually," she gave David a sly grin.

"One of those guys ran a club. He was, like, the King of New Stuff in Chicago. I don't mean the establishment things; I mean the underground – music, fashion – and art if it was subversive enough.

"I used to tag along, take some notes and then write it up in a newsletter – just a flyer really – telling the world what was hot, clueing the folks in. It started almost as a joke. I wrote it pretty ironically, like kind of a street-twist on a swanky society column.

"We'd give a few copies away at the club and they were always running out of them. It just kind of took off and we ended up distributing it all over. I got myself a cheap Mac and a ratty little office. I bumped up the page count and sold a little sub-culture ad-space. Long story short, after six months it got picked up and really did become a column in a city newspaper. Part of some youth-credibility makeover dreamed up by their PR wonks, no doubt, but no one else was doing anything real. It got me some exposure and I was offered an editorial job on a magazine in New York. I moved there about four years ago – where I lived happily ever after."

While Dee had been talking, they'd advanced almost to the head of the queue.

David said, "Wow. So your mum's pleased, I imagine? You're a journalist like she wanted to be. Given what you were saying about her living vicariously through you girls."

Dee gave David a 'yeah right' look. "Well even if I was the heir apparent, which I'm not, Mom was writing about foreign policy; I'm writing about how jeans are the new little black dress." She let the thought hang for a moment and then added, "But then they say parody is a form of flattery."

The next capsule was level with the walkway and people were disembarking. Once it was empty, Dee and David were moved up with a group of a dozen or so others and ushered into the pod.

Dee took David's arm, and said, "Listen, I forbid you to ask me any more questions about myself. You're stepping on my feminine mystique. Now hold on to me, heights scare the crap out of me."

"Why didn't you say?" David asked, following her into the car as it began to lift clear of the ground. It would gradually climb 130 metres into the air, laying London out around them.

Dee sat in the middle of the capsule, on the bench, while those around her pressed their noses to the full-height windows. Even from the bench, they had a great view and David pointed out various landmarks, freely mixing fact with fiction. "That's Battersea Power Station, where they used to generate the electricity for the Pink Floyd albums. And beyond," he pointed to the Crystal Palace radio mast, "you can just see the Eiffel Tower. Looks like the tide's out in the channel at the moment."

Dee hit him on the arm and said brightly, "I'm so lucky you're here. My flaky guide book has nothing like this level of, um, local colour." She smiled at him and he grinned back.

With gentle coaxing, David managed to get Dee to come to one of the windows. She gripped his solid forearm tightly throughout. She was frightened, but exhilarated, until an almost imperceptible movement of the capsule sent her scuttling back to the bench.

"This must be what Godzilla feels like," Dee said, as their part of the wheel reached the top of its rotation. "Help me pick out what I'm going to squash first."

Nearly half an hour passed before their capsule was once again level with the walkway. Susan still hadn't phoned, so when they were both back on the ground they talked about where to go next.

At Dee's insistence, they caught an open-topped bus which gave them a live commentary of London sights as it wound its way through the capital. Their guide had a tough-sounding cockney accent – like someone from a British gangster movie – and it made Dee laugh whenever he made an announcement. David imitated him, making additions to the commentary, but quietly so that only Dee could hear.

The guide said, "An' on yer left is the National Gallery where you can see many of the nation's favourite paintings."

"Some of which are worth a few bob," David said, sniffing, "if you can get 'em out without the bloke on the door seeing you."

The guide said, "An' this is Oxford Street, world-famous for its shopping. Oo knows, you might be able to pick up a bargain."

David added, "Speaking of which, if anyone wants a cheap camcorder, no questions asked, see me at the back of the bus."

As the bus finished its tour, Dee was giggling and shivering in equal parts. "Is it possible that this place is colder than Chicago?" she asked.

David said, "London can get as cold as it wants, from what I can tell. Two degrees in London beats minus fifteen in the Alps, I can vouch for that. Mind you, us locals tend to make sure a bus has got a roof on it before they get aboard."

They were strolling away from the bus stop now. Dee said through chattering teeth, "I've learned my lesson. Find me somewhere I can thaw out my icy tourist butt?"

David gave Dee an exaggerated wink and said, "Watch this." He stuck two fingers in his mouth and whistled loudly enough that people on the other side of the street looked round in surprise. At the same time he threw his other hand in the air. A black cab, which had just driven past, u-turned smartly in the middle of the street and came to a stop in front of them.

David said something to the driver and held the door for Dee. She was laughing as she said, "Impressive. You've just passed the practical section of the New York citizenship exam right there."

David hopped into the warm cab after Dee and slammed the door. She slid across the shiny and ancient black leather to make room for him. He tucked in next to her and confessed, "That must be, ooh, the ninth time I've done that. I've never had a taxi stop before."

Dee said, "So my nine predecessors were left on the sidewalk calling you an idiot, instead of snuggling up in the warm," she hugged his arm, "and sighing 'my hero'?"

"Pretty much," he said, cockily, then conceded, "I think it helps that it's not closing time and that you're not three drunk blokes holding up a fourth."

"That's one of my most endearing features," she said.

The cab was off and moving now, somehow threading its way through the slow-moving traffic.

David said, "So, let me ask you something. How come neither you or Susan seem to have boyfriends? Gipsy curse?"

Dee turned to him with a sharp look. "Who says I don't have a boyfriend?" she said haughtily, as though he were implying that she was unattractive.

"Of course you do," David said smoothly, "what was I thinking? So where is he at the moment?"

Dee looked at him curiously. David asked, "What did I say?"

"Nothing," Dee said. "I'll tell you later."

David looked intrigued but didn't pursue it. "Let me guess," he said, "you're seeing your boss who's ten years older than you. He's brilliant, but married."

Dee spluttered, "That witch! Blood is thicker than water, my ass. Susan's a dead woman."

David looked amazed, "You mean I'm right," he said, scratching his head.

Dee wasn't buying it; she gave him the evil eye and said, "You saying she didn't squeal?"

David assured her, "Susan tells me nothing." He made a zipping motion across his lips.

Dee looked grumpy but amused, "Well, score one for the psychic hotline. He's actually twenty years older than me, he's separated, in a complicated sort of way and he's my boss's boss. But he is brilliant. I mean it's ten parts doomed to one part future fairytale wedding, but it keeps me out of trouble for the time being." She wrinkled her forehead, "Depending on how you define trouble." She gave David another suspicious look and asked, "Susan said nothing?"

David shook his head emphatically.

Dee seemed to accept his denial and grumbled, "Oh shit, I'm a stereotype."

"Noo," David assured her, "I'm just good at that sort of thing. What else would a young, ambitious, hot-blooded women with high standards and no free time do?"

Dee asked, "A cliché?"

"Call it a tradition," he suggested. "So you're spoken for?" he asked, "It's just Susan who's the confirmed spinster?"

Dee gave him that curious look again as the cabby slid back the glass partition and called, "Here we are guv'nor," out of the corner of his mouth.

David caught Dee's strange expression and looked questioningly at her. She whispered, "I'll tell you inside."

They got out of the cab, David closing the door behind them and asking the cabby through the side-window, "How much is it?"

"Five pounds sixty, chief," the cabby said. David gave him a ten-pound note and told him to keep it.

The cabby said, "Much obliged." He lowered his voice, "This is for the smart pull-up isn't it? Reckon that might of cracked it for you," he said, nodding towards Dee.

David said nothing, just smiled sheepishly and glanced quickly over at Dee to see if she was listening. She seemed oblivious.

They descended into the sophisticated subterranean cosiness of Café des Amis du Vin. David ordered a bottle of Montepulciano and had them take the chill off it.

He said to Dee, "Call me a philistine, but we can't go drinking cold wine – it might give you chilblains. Gotta watch out for those Victorian ailments now you're in London."

They found a quiet table in the corner farthest from the door and David poured two large glasses of warm wine.

David looked like he was about to speak but Dee got there first, "So Susan was pretty mysterious about what you guys have been up to? She said she'd got that chunk taken out of her cheek when someone broke into her college. What's up with that?"

David said, "Yeah. Things got a bit hairy for a while. It's a long story and not a very believable one. I'm embarrassed to have dragged Susan into it all. I just didn't realise that she was in any danger until too late. Though, god knows, she doesn't exactly shy away from trouble."

He continued, "Anyway it all revolved around this stolen antique which is now back with its owner, so that should be that. There's just a few loose ends to tie up."

Dee said, "Sounds like you two had some close scrapes together."

"What's the American expression? Things were pretty *intense*." He nodded at his own words and said, "Susan's an amazing person. I hope we'll find a way to be friends once there's no, umm, work reason for us to see each other."

Dee agreed, almost sarcastically, "Yeah, friends. Let's hope, huh?"

David didn't get it. "What's up?" he said, quizzically, "I keep getting this feeling that I'm saying something that I shouldn't, but I don't know what it is."

Dee sighed slowly and let her shoulders drop. She didn't speak for a few moments and David waited patiently. Finally, she said, "You know, you're kind of attractive, David."

"Er, thanks," David said awkwardly.

"And I'm getting a bad feeling about us spending time together," Dee said.

David looked at her blankly.

Dee lifted her chin and asked him directly, "What exactly are we doing here?"

David was at a loss for an answer. He began to say something, but nothing coherent came out. Dee said, "OK. Try this. Have you got something going with Susan?"

David looked defensive. He shook his head. "No," he said defiantly, and then when Dee continued to say nothing, he added, "She isn't interested."

Dee raised one eyebrow and said, "So you thought you'd try me?"

David was flustered and a little bit annoyed. "Woah! Hang on a minute. I thought we were having a nice afternoon out. If something else has happened here, then I'm sorry, but I missed it," he said.

Dee continued to give David a challenging look for a moment longer and then let it dissipate. She began to look conciliatory. "Let's try this another way. When I asked Susan about you she got weird. All she'd say was that you were sweet. She told me how whenever she pretended to take offence at something, you'd practically fall over yourself to apologise. It made her laugh."

She checked that he was still following her and continued, "I tried a couple of times to tease you but you refused to be rattled. I was just wondering why Susan makes you nervous but I don't."

David still made no comment. Dee sipped her wine and said, "And you keep asking me about her. Maybe you're just being polite, right?"

David sat forwards. He said, "I don't see what you're getting at. OK, yes I think Susan's kind of fabulous. You're right. But she's pretty much let the air out of my tyres, if you know what I mean. There's nothing happening between her and me, and I'm trying to respect her wishes. She's busy today and her completely charming sister needs a tour guide. It's true, it feels more like she's doing me a favour, instead of the other way round, but it's what she wanted. I can't help it if I'm having the nicest day I've had for ages and maybe forgetting to hide the fact."

Dee looked at him impassively for a few seconds and then she gave him a very sexy smile. "It really is too bad you know. I could just about eat you up. But I think we're playing with fire here, whether you've realised it or not." She leant forward now and rested her elbows on the table. "So here's what you need to know, Sport. She's got a major thing for you. I'd put big bucks on it."

David's eyebrows went up and he leaned back. "I don't think so," he said cautiously.

Dee made a click with her tongue and said, "Yup. As soon as I realised how much you liked her, it suddenly gelled." Something else occurred to her then and she butted herself gently on the forehead with the palm of her hand. "God. I should have known something was up when I asked her about spending some time with you. If she'd shrugged and said 'whatever', that would have meant go ahead. But she practically insisted I hang out with you." She shook her head.

David said nothing. Dee went on, "Why this should be I don't know, but Susan doesn't trust a soul. Not me, not Mom and Dad, especially not guys. But for some reason I think she trusts *you*. Maybe it's something to do with all the cops and robbers stuff you two have been through together, but there's something different in the way she talks about you."

Dee gave a cynical laugh. "Knowing her, it'll be another ten years before she's sure about it, but I think deep-down she's already there. She told me you weren't her type and I took it at face value. Because, you know, it's her choice. She's a big girl. If you've seen her in any of her competitions you know she can take care of herself just fine. So why would she say she didn't like you if she did?"

David was enthralled and at the same time profoundly uneasy as he listened to Dee talk. He made no move to interrupt her.

She had a little more wine and continued, "Do you want to hear my theory? If she trusts you, that means she might actually find herself opening up to you. Now, there's never been any danger of that in her past relationships. It's like me and my married man, I guess – despite what we tell each other, there's no real risk of intimacy. But I think with you, maybe Susan's realised she's kind of vulnerable. I think she was pushing me towards you because she's a little bit scared."

David asked, "Scared of getting on too well with me?"

Dee nodded, "Scared that she's met someone who'll figure her out. Isn't everyone scared of that?"

"What's she got to hide?" David asked.

"Nothing," Dee replied, "as far as I know. But she's always been very private. This would be unknown territory for her."

David was trying to follow Dee's argument, "So if she's nervous about her and me, why would she be encouraging you to spend time with me?"

Dee drained her glass and poured herself some more wine. "My guess is that I'm supposed to steal you. Like I did to her once before," she said.

"That makes no sense," David said, confused.

"Sure it does," Dee replied. "People are always pushing others away just to see if they come back. It's a way of reassuring yourself that they care."

"So she's testing me?" David asked. "It's not that she doesn't like me?" He sounded as though he was doing his best to believe it but not having much success.

The wine had brought a bit of a flush to Dee's cheeks. She said, passionately, "Think about it. It adds up. She's nervous so she pushes you and me together. She tells herself it's so she can be sure of you, but it's really fear talking. If I steal you she has someone else to blame for the relationship going wrong, plus she's off the hook – her secrets are safe."

David had folded his arms. "Hmm," he said, noncommittally, "Well, it's one theory. How long have you known all this?"

Dee said, "I've just been putting it together since the taxi ride. I knew something was going on, but I didn't see what it was until I realised you had a thing for her."

David continued to be far from convinced by Dee's theory, but as they carried on talking, both of them would keep mentioning things that Susan had said or done which leant weight to Dee's interpretation of events.

The more David was swayed, the more he began to worry. Eventually he voiced his concern, "Do you think she sees this as a date?"

Dee shrugged.

David blew his breath out and looked dejected. He said, "It's been a while since I had such a fun day, Dee. You're really easy to spend time with and I was enjoying not thinking about where it might be leading. I suppose I should have known there'd be some terrible price to pay for giving my conscience the day off. I promised Susan that I wouldn't let her down. Do you think that's what I've just done?"

Dee thought about it. "I think you being here is how she gets out of the fix she's in. She might be pushing you away, but I'm sure that behind it all she's hoping that you'll come straight back again."

David was looking genuinely worried as he said, "Dee, I really don't want to disappoint her. I know this is putting you in the middle of something, and I know that's unfair on you, but I need your advice. Do you think by just being here I've blown it?"

Dee smiled sadly. "Well, I guess it depends on how today went. If I tell her you were polite but kind of frosty, then maybe you pass the test."

David looked hopeful. "Would you... Could you do that?" Then he said, "Wait, I don't want you to lie to her. There must be... What else could you say?"

Dee looked David in the eye. "How's this then?" she said with a sigh, "I tell her I had a great time and that you're a wonderful guy, but it's obvious to me that you're crazy about her."

* * *

Dee had continued to make light work of the wine. David had taken some time over his first glass and when he went to pour some more, there was only enough for half a refill. As David pointed out when he returned from the bar with a second bottle, it was starting to feel like they were old friends.

Neither of them were flirting, but that seemed to make the conversation somehow more intimate, in a platonic kind of way. Both of them seemed better able to relax now that there was no pressure to sparkle.

It was getting on for nine o'clock when Dee checked her phone. "I thought Susan might have called by now," she said. She'd had a good part of the second bottle by this stage and was beginning to speak with deliberate precision as the wine strengthened its hold. "I'm wondering if this thing's busted. I swiped Susan's charger but I don't know if it's working," she said, showing him the display on her phone. It was blank apart from a battery-level indicator with four of its five bars showing. There was no signal or network name.

David suddenly looked awkward. "Dee, we're underground. I completely forgot," he said.

Dee looked embarrassed, "Oops," she said, "Ahh, I don't suppose we'd have heard the ringing, even if she did prise herself out of a book to call us. We should she if see's… see if she's been trying to reach us."

David nodded and said, "We should probably call it a night anyway. We're not supposed to be having too much fun, remember?"

David left his wine and stood up to pull on his heavy leather jacket. Dee began to get her coat on as well. She leaned over and drained her glass before smacking her lips and announcing she was ready to go.

It had turned into a frosty night above ground. Dee shivered as soon as the chill air touched her skin.

David turned to her as they stood on the pavement outside the bar and said, "Dee, I really have had a lovely day. And thank you so much for helping rescue things with Susan. I just hope I haven't screwed it up already."

Dee smiled and said, "Fingers crossed. You can repay me by convincing Susan that I pick my own bridesmaid's dress." She muttered under her breath, "Sisters always get the cerise puff-sleeve bullshit."

David's and Dee's phones simultaneously began beeping and they grinned sheepishly at each other.

Dee was first to connect to her answerphone. It was a brief message. Dee looked puzzled. "And the prize for Girl of Mystery goes to Susan Milton. I wonder where she's planning on staying tonight." Dee was going to say more, but then she caught sight of David's face. A look of horror was spreading across his features as he listened to his own messages.

Dee's voice was filled with concern as she said, "What is it?"

David made a curt gesture for her to be quiet. He continued listening for a moment, his face becoming even more grave.

When it was finished he announced, "I've got to go." His voice was clipped, his throat tight with tension.

Dee demanded, "What is it?"

But all David would say, sounding distracted, was, "Dee, I have got to go. Right now."

"Tell me," she said angrily, grabbing his sleeve. It was clear that David was going to have to wrench her hand free or else explain.

"I think something's happened to Susan," he said.

CHAPTER 24

EARLIER THE SAME DAY
SATURDAY 26TH APRIL

S usan stood once again in the foyer of the London School of Antiquities. Above her, on a stepladder, was a man in blue overalls peering into a trapdoor in the ornate plaster ceiling. His assistant stood by and held the ladder with bovine patience. The only other person in the heavily marbled atrium was the security guard behind the main desk from whom she'd just signed out the keys to the Alexandrian room. According to the guard, no one else was working down there today.

As she waited for the lift, Susan was playing an answer-phone message on her mobile. "Hi Susan, it's David," the message began. "I just wanted to say thanks for last night and I hope you can make it later today. Anyway, it was lovely to…" she pushed a button on her phone cutting the recording off. "Message deleted. End of messages," an automated voice confirmed. She disconnected the call and dropped the phone back into her bag.

The ancient cage of the lift slowly descended a moment later. She wrestled the cantilevered doors open, then shut them behind her, riding down three floors in quiet contemplation, the occasional flicker of an unidentified emotion troubling her features.

When she got out of the lift, the basement was silent and deserted.

The fluorescents in the hallway blazed, but the doors of the various rooms leading off it were closed. She unlocked the Alexandrian room and turned a couple of the lights on.

At her usual workstation, she got her iBook out of her bag and pushed the power switch, attaching cables for power and network access while it went through its start-up routine. Then she wandered over to her locker. Even though the room was silent and empty, she glanced over her shoulder before putting the key in the padlock.

Once the louvred grey metal door was open, she lifted out a Tesco's shopping bag, tightly wrapped around an object about the size and heft of half a dozen sleeveless vinyl LPs.

Taking the bundle back to her workstation she unwrapped the bag, revealing a second bag underneath and a swaddling of bubble-wrap under that. Pausing a moment, she got up and went to the door. She peered out into the silent hallway.

According to the indicator above the lift doors, the cage was idling on the ground floor. Around her, the building was silent.

Closing the door, Susan locked it from the inside and went back to her desk. She finished unwrapping the bundle.

Inside was a plain gold band. A furrow was visible on one side of the band where she had struck it with the iron end of a window pole. She set it almost reverentially on the desk in front of her.

Then she took a jewellery case from her courier bag and laid it next to the circlet. The box was made from the same curious, hard, fuzzy, black material favoured by jewellers the world over. Prising open the snap-shut lid with its awkward spring, she revealed two gold bracelets pressed into the depression meant for one.

She removed them from their ruffled, white-silk nest and placed them on the desk. Inscribed around the inside circumference of one bracelet were the words, "To Susan, from Mom and Dad. We're so proud."

The inscription on the second read, "To Dorothy, with all our love, Mom and Dad."

Susan sat and stared for a while at the headband and the two bracelets. Her face was unreadable. Some powerful emotion was compressing her mouth and pulling her jaw muscles tight. The tip of her tongue emerged for a second, swiping moisture rapidly onto her dry lips. She absent-mindedly tried to hook her bottom lip with one of her canines, her eyes fixed all the while on the glittering haul in front of her.

Emerging suddenly from her reverie, she grabbed papers from her bag and began to spread them out on the desk. Then, she pulled the iBook towards her and opened Acrobat. A few moments later, an image of a document, handwritten in Latin, appeared on the display.

She flipped the top sheet of her legal pad over and began to make notes.

After a quarter of an hour she fetched a bulky Latin dictionary from her open locker.

For another hour, Susan shuffled and scrutinised the documents, periodically scribbling with rapid industry. Soon, sheets of paper had obscured the gold jewellery on her desktop. She kept returning her attention to one page in particular.

She created a new text document and, over the course of the next hour, she typed the following:

Lift your head out of the water and see the lay of the land correctly for the first time. Touch is the first of the senses to awaken. Touch and then feeling and seeing and hearing and the spirit of temperature and the permanence of air and the violent motions of things barely out of reach. Healthiness is one day a sense but comes first as an invisible companion/ friend.

In some there is a greater knowledge but it is [occlusive?]. Lesser knowledge is to have one foot in two countries/ lands; greater knowledge is to lift the back foot and to be an exile/wanderer from the country of one's birth. Greater knowledge is without effective power because it has not [got] the intention to use it any longer. It turns inward, but that is another matter.

Begin here with this [song?] and consider very well this drawing and think for a long time about what you wish to lay your unseen hand upon. It has been asserted by a lot of people that a knife [for eating?] is the most suitable object with which to start but perhaps what comes to mind first is simply what comes to hand first [correct idiom?].

Susan saved the file and pushed her laptop aside. She gathered her documents into a pile and transferred them to the next desk. Two pieces of laser-printed paper remained in front of her; they were reproductions of handwritten documents. One was decorated with a complex swirling pattern, roughly circular in shape. Parts of the pattern looked like details from Moorish tiles, other areas like Celtic knots. The ten-point-Arial title read 'Pattern 3 Ter-119G'.

The second paper had the title 'Nonsense rhyme? Ter-016L' printed on the top. Below the title were strings of handwritten letters in groups, certain sequences of syllables appearing repeatedly in different arrangements.

Susan fastened one bracelet on each of her wrists. Then she placed the gold band on her head. It fitted almost perfectly. Finally, from her bag she took a letter-opener. It was a slim bar of silver, without a guard or a covering over the handle – a gleaming metal pin, double-edged at one end and squared at the other. She laid it in the centre of the drawing and took several deep breaths. Then she began to read the poetry aloud. When she finished the page, she began again at the top.

She read it without pause, twenty times. Her voice was beginning to get a little croaky, but she continued.

After she had read it thirty-five times she hardly needed to glance at the paper and instead focussed on the knife and the pattern beneath it. She continued to repeat the poem, sounding the syllables quietly with her dry throat.

She had been speaking continually for one hour and fifty minutes when the knife rocked slightly, the tip bouncing once on the paper. "Shit," she said and stopped dead.

She stared at the knife for a while, her lips still. She had just pronounced the word 'pervolo' when the knife had stirred. She leaned in now and repeated it forcefully, "Pervolo, pervolo."

She dropped her head and sounded the 'per' syllable sharply several times, bringing her mouth close to the knife, allowing her breath to mist its surface. It didn't move. She blew directly on it, without trying to shape any particular syllable. Still no movement. She blew harder and the knife rocked slightly, as it had done before. The other sheet of paper slipped to the floor, disturbed by her breath. She retrieved it.

"Damn," she said wonderingly. She stood up and put her hands on her hips. She looked at the knife again and muttered, "Oh boy." Then she removed the jewellery she was wearing and laid it on the desk. She placed a few sheets of paper on top of it.

She went to the door and unlocked it, peering cautiously out into the corridor before opening it wide. No one was around.

Crossing to the coffee machine, she pressed the buttons for cold water. She drank two shiny beige plastic cups of icy water before entering the code for black coffee. She took the coffee back into the Alexandrian room, locking the door behind her.

She sat down at her desk, sipping the hot liquid. Setting the cup down, she winced a little and rubbed the back of her head. "Man," she said, as though she was in pain. She rotated one of her shoulders, then the other, and kneaded the back of her neck with one hand.

She sat, looking contemplative and taking delicate sips of coffee, one carmine-booted foot propped on the edge of her desk. When the cup was empty, she threw it in the bin. Then she gathered the bracelets and put them back in their box. The headband she once again double-wrapped and returned to her locker.

Then she spread out her papers and began reading and taking notes again.

An hour later, she took another break, this time making her way upstairs and outside into the daylight. She returned through the late afternoon chill with sandwiches, a Starbucks latte and a slice of carrot cake.

She ate while studying.

On the wall, behind her, hung an electric clock. The hands showed six o'clock by the time she had typed the following:

To begin is to take up the reins of a responsive beast of burden. Others have their hands resting on the reins also. They cannot contradict/silence your commands nor can they know what is said, but they will hear your voice if they listen. When you both walk dressed/adorned in [the clothes/covering of power?] it is as though you are walking nearby to your enemies but separated by a third of a third of a third of a parasang [5.6km/27=~200m] on a windless day.

Susan stopped writing for a moment and ran her fingers through her hair. Then she began to look concerned. She continued to scrutinise the document she was working on, periodically looking up to tap a phrase into her computer. Finally, she had written:

It is in this as in everything else that men undertake. There is a small amount of treasure/riches and it is guarded jealously. There is never love between those who have been awakened because the world is not big enough for everyone. In truth, to discover a neighbour is to discover a deadly enemy. The approach of a stranger is equivalent to a challenge. To overhear another is to listen to the voice of your conqueror. You will make him instead your prey if you think wisely. Contention without diplomacy is the natural order of things. For these reasons, do not sleep and never lie down comfortably. Be alert always and be ready to fight hard even in the quietest part of each night.

Susan was now frowning. She got up and went to her locker. From inside she took a second, smaller dictionary, bound in worn black leather, and returned to her seat with it. She began to fine-tune her translation. At the end of another hour she had made very few changes, but she had added the following lines to her document:

Fledglings are not found to be alive for long away from the nest. Only those with the protection of an ancient [school

for kings?] survive. The first utterance of the tiny bird is
very likely to bring the hawks towards it without fail. It
is the best moment to do away with one's future enemies.
Vigilance and quick action in this matter is the most
important thing. Listen always for new voices and then cut
across them angrily as quickly as you can.

Susan was chewing her lip again. She had wrapped one hand around
the other in front of her and was bouncing them up and down, repetitively,
subconsciously. As she stared at the document, she was rocking her head a
little in nervousness. "I don't like this," she muttered, "I don't like this."

She fired up Eudora on her laptop and scrolled through several e-mails
until she found the one she was looking for. It was from Bernie Lampwick.
She paged down through the text until she reached the following:

```
...albeit a rapid one, it seems to me to bear
a resemblance to passages from Il Principe.
Political treatises being all the rage at
the time, I wonder if this might not be an
allegorical piece in the same vein. Perhaps
it leans a little more towards Savonarola
than Machiavelli and the language is far more
obscure (perhaps the author was out of favour
at the time and masking his true meaning?),
but nevertheless I wonder if we might not have
here the work of a previously unknown 'Prophet
of Force'. As I noted in my doctoral thesis...
```

The sudden muffled sound of a drill, conveyed to her through the bones
of the building, made Susan jump. The workmen in the foyer had been
carrying a heavy, three-phase drill into the building as she had returned with
her lunch, but still the distant rattling grind of the masonry bit chewing its
way into a wall took her by surprise.

She forced her attention back to the e-mail and muttered, "What were
you thinking, Bernie? It's not about governing Florence; it's about magic."

She sat thinking for a little longer, nodding to herself. "It's a warning,"
she said softly, but decisively.

She flinched a second time, moments later, when the lift doors clattered open out in the hallway. For a moment she held her breath. Slow footsteps could be heard on the heavy vinyl floor outside the door – a gentle thump and squeak as each foot was placed then lifted. The door handle rattled as someone tried to open the door. Then a knock and a deep, serious voice saying, "Dr Milton. Hello?"

She sounded reasonably nonchalant as she called, "I won't be a minute. Who's that?" but her eyes were riveted on the door throughout.

"It is Oswald Olabayo, Dr Milton. I work for the security company employed by the college. I am making my rounds," a cultured voice said from the other side of the door.

Susan smiled and muttered to herself with relief, "Too goofy to fake." She unlocked the door to see a tall, elegant man with jet-black skin, wearing a baggy RAF-surplus blue jumper.

"Sorry," said Susan, "I'm a bit paranoid about security at the moment."

The guard smiled widely and said, "Of course Madam. We have to be vigilant. Is everything in order?"

"Yes. Thank you," she said, "Um, how often do you patrol down here?"

"Every hour I make my rounds, Doctor, as instructed," he said.

Susan didn't mention that whoever had the shift before him obviously operated according to a different set of instructions. She said, "Oh, OK then. See you in an hour."

"Yes, Madam," the guard said and turned his attention to the storeroom door.

Susan was still smiling as she returned to her chair. She took a couple of slow breaths. Her grin dropped away as her attention returned to her e-mail. A new message had appeared in her Inbox. The title read:

```
CustomNews.biz - Requested news alert
```

She opened the e-mail and read:

```
Susan Milton,

One of your pre-defined NewsAlert keywords -
"Dass" - occurs in at least one current news
```

```
story. Click on the link below to read the
news item(s).
```

```
www.CustomNews.biz/storyid=1447916
```

Susan clicked on the link and read the following:

```
Possible   terrorist   attack   near   Heathrow
Airport.

In the last hour…

A broad daylight attack on a chauffeured
limousine as it entered London's Heathrow
airport left three dead and motorists stunned.
Gunfire and an explosion disabled the limousine
while spectators looked on. A CustomNews
reporter investigating the incident uncovered
the fact that Alexandero Dass, a respected
Italian businessman, was the target of the
attack when he and his two associates failed
to arrive for a flight to Rome's Fiorentino
airport.
```

Susan read on, though there was little more to learn from the story –
beyond the author's lack of attention to detail. The article had no information
about the assailant, except to say that it appeared to be a man acting alone.
She tried several other online news services without turning up any new
facts.

Lifting the phone on her desk, she punched in her access code followed
by Dee's mobile number. It went straight through to her answer-phone.
"Dee," she said, "Susan. Listen, I might not make it back there tonight. I'll
call you in the morning to let you know what's going on." She hung up.

Glancing at her address book she punched another number. The tip of
her index finger was resting on David's name as her other hand pressed the
buttons. Again, she got an answerphone message.

She began to leave a message. "David," she said, "it's Susan. Listen, I
need to talk to you – right away. Dass is dead and I think it was Jan who did
it. Which means he could have the Marker again. That'd mean Teracus's

collection is his next priority. He blew Dass's car up in broad daylight, so I don't think he'd have any reservations about busting in here and wrecking the place to get what he wants. I think he's past caring about the mess he makes. You know there's no way security here would stop him and I can't even tell them what they're up against – they'd think I'd flipped. I'm thinking… what I think I might do… I think I need to move the collection. Now. Jan'll come here either way, but I don't want him to get this stuff. Whatever he's up to, it's nothing good."

She paused a minute and then said, "There's something else. I think I've miscalculated. I tried something… an experiment. I think I shouldn't have. I think maybe I've called attention to myself. There's a possibility Jan might come after me now. I'm going to…"

The door handle rattled. Susan froze. There had been no sound of anyone approaching but someone was right outside the door. It was forty minutes before the next security patrol was due.

There was a crash from above. Something heavy had struck the building. The impact rattled small objects all round the room.

"There's somebody here," Susan whispered, almost absent-mindedly, into the phone – her attention focussed on the door handle. Without glancing down, she ended the call. Someone was trying the door.

CHAPTER 25

THE SAME EVENING
SATURDAY 26TH APRIL

D ee was furious. And though her anger didn't seem to be intended for anyone in particular, David was getting the brunt of it, being the only available target.

They braked hard before taking a sharp corner and Dee snapped, "Should you even be driving? We had two bottles of wine, remember?" Her tone was openly hostile.

David was in nearly as bad a mood. "Right," he said, "and you drank them. I had two glasses in two hours. I've never felt more sober." He shot through a newly-red light and around a bus as it tried to pull out. Dee was bracing herself against the dashboard to avoid being thrown around.

"Well could you at least slow down please," she said, in some icy Manhattan dialect intended for rebuking the help. It didn't sound like a request.

"No I fucking well couldn't," David growled through gritted teeth.

That shut Dee up temporarily.

Outside the bar, she'd made it clear that she was sticking with David until they found out what was going on with her sister. So together they'd caught a cab to David's car. When they'd reached it, he'd bundled her in and before she even had her seatbelt done up they were racing through back streets constricted with parked cars, rocketing through gaps with only millimetres to spare. David had cut around any vehicle that slowed him down, intimidating oncoming drivers into giving way.

It was a couple of minutes after David's angry words to her that Dee ventured to speak again. They were now crossing the Euston Road heading south. Dee still sounded just as angry as she said, "I can't help it, OK? I don't deal well with this kind of situation. It makes me crazy." Her voice was thick from the wine she'd drunk earlier.

Even though her tone was far from conciliatory, her words seemed to affect David. His face softened and he reached across to squeeze Dee's hand without taking his eyes off the road. "I'm sorry I swore at you," he said. After a moment, he added, "When I panic I focus. It's not good for my manners."

Dee said nothing. David had slowed for a moment while he was speaking to Dee but he picked up the pace again now.

Another minute passed, the sudden pitch changes of the high-revving engine filling the car. David glanced over and saw a mascara-laden tear rolling down Dee's cheek.

He sounded both surprised and awkward as he said, "I really am sorry, Dee."

"I live in New York, remember? It's not the yelling," she sniffed, "I'm crying because I'm worried. I can't…" The last word was drawn out into the beginnings of a wail, cut short as she clamped her jaws together. Her shoulders bobbed in time to the puffing sound of her sobs – barely discernible over the straining engine.

Dee groaned loudly, a sound full of sorrow, and then slapped herself hard on the cheek a moment later. David looked shocked, "Hey, hey," he said soothingly, somewhat alarmed.

Dee sniffed viciously and said, "I'm OK, I'm OK," then added unhappily, "I can't believe I'm crying." She sniffed again and began hunting in her bag, eventually producing a pack of tissues. She blew her nose.

A moment later, they arrived at the School of Antiquities. David pulled up on the double yellow lines right outside, threw open the car door and ran in. Dee followed, scooping tears back up her face with her index finger as she bustled after him.

When she caught up with him, David was already in conversation with the guard behind the security desk. It took five minutes of talking at cross-purposes, before David managed to ascertain that there'd been no break-in – not this week at any rate – and to satisfactorily explain his interest. His initial demands for information had put the guard on the defensive. Only by starting again from the beginning, and forcing himself to be patient, had he made progress.

It turned out that the most excitement the School had seen that day was the accident which had shattered an area of the lustrous marble floor in the centre of the ornate entrance hall. The evidence was still there for David to see. A heavy, industrial drill lay at the heart of a web of cracked Italian marble, its cord like the slack tail of a crushed animal. A tall stepladder straddled its corpse.

The guard told them how he'd checked on Susan soon after he'd come on duty. Then, shortly after the workmen had dropped the drill, he had seen her hasten out of the building, seemingly late for a pressing appointment. She was heavily burdened with paperwork, and had flung her keys at him, in too much of a rush for even the most basic of pleasantries. "Besides…" he said, shaking his head sadly and indicating the cracked floor, which apparently occupied most of his thoughts at present.

A second guard had appeared in the foyer and heard the end of the conversation. He spoke now, "Dr Milton? I went to tell her the power was going off. She was a bundle of nerves – wouldn't open the door to start with. She usually like that, then?"

"No, she's not," David said.

He turned back to the first guard and said, "Thank you." And then added, "Excuse me," as he extracted his mobile phone and turned away to make the call. Dee had tried Susan's number twice since leaving the bar, but David made a third attempt. All he got was her answerphone.

Dee had left frantic messages at the end of both her calls and David evidently couldn't think of anything new to add; he hung up before Susan's recorded voice finished speaking.

The security guard offered to call David and Dee if he received any news or if he saw Susan. They both left their numbers with him, thanking him for his trouble.

They made their way slowly back to the car which was as yet undiscovered by late-shift traffic wardens or roving wheel-clampers.

"Dee," David said, once they were inside, "it sounds like she panicked for some reason and went to ground. If *we* don't know where she is, then no one else will either. If she thinks she might be in trouble, she'll be hiding somewhere. All we can do is wait to hear from her. She's probably cleverer than both of us put together; I'm sure she'll be alright."

Dee said nothing for a while. She looked awful. The worry, the inky tears and the dregs of alcohol in her system made her look years older than she had at the start of the evening.

"I think you should stop in a hotel tonight," David said, once they were both back in the car. "We'll go back to the Professor's place in the City and I'll run in and grab a few of your things and then we'll find you somewhere to stay."

Dee offered no resistance. The fight seemed to have gone out of her and she looked exhausted. She nodded, sadly, and sat quietly while David drove, hardly moving and saying nothing.

It took fifteen minutes to reach the house. David asked Dee for the keys and told her to sit in the driver's seat with the engine running. "If anything happens, just drive away. I'll sort myself out."

"I can't drive stick," she said, her voice tiny and hoarse.

David considered this for a second, and then offered, "Well, lock the doors while I'm in there and sound the horn if you need me. I'll come running," he said.

Getting out, he went round to the boot and opened it for a moment in order to retrieve the telescopic baton he'd carried with him when he'd visited Dass. He slipped it into his sleeve and slammed the boot, signalling to Dee to lock the doors.

Approaching the house, he looked for signs of life. It seemed as deserted as ever. The windows on the ground floor were still shuttered and no lights showed through the cracks.

He made his way up the steps and took a good look at the front door. The heavy-duty door lock seemed intact, its dull patina unmarked – no signs of uninvited entry.

Slipping the key in the door he pushed it open and stepped into the dark hallway. With the front door open, there was just enough light shining in from the street for him to make out the foot of the stairs. Quietly, he moved a potted fern so that it prevented the door from closing and then he made his way stealthily up the stairs.

The upper-storey windows weren't shuttered and the night, like all London nights, was far from pitch-black. Twice, distant noises caused him to stop abruptly, straining to hear more, but it was impossible to tell whether the sounds came from outside or not – or what might be making them.

He moved into the rear bedroom. The floor-length curtains lay open and through the sash window the branches of a plane tree were revealed, black in the faint orange light. The leaves were fidgeting sleepily in the evening breeze, stirring the shadows in the bedroom.

David grabbed Dee's toiletry bag, her cosmetics case and the partially unpacked cabin case which sat on the ottoman at the end of the bed. Thus laden, he retraced his steps, emerging from the house to find everything just as he had left it. Dee was sitting watching him from the car.

He put what he was carrying in the boot and had Dee wind the window down. "While we're here, I might as well grab everything. What else is there?" he asked.

"Two garment bags and whatever's scattered around the room," she said, after a moment's thought.

He nodded, had her wind the window back up, and headed once more into the darkened house.

He appeared two minutes later holding the two bags and a bulging duty-free carrier bag. With the edge of his foot, he pushed the plant pot aside and allowed the heavy door to swing closed.

David laid the bags on the back seat and hopped into the front, slipping in behind the wheel. He activated the central locking and moved away. He drove for a couple of minutes before speaking. "So have you got any ideas for where you could stay?"

"I've got a corporate account with Hilton," she said.

"Well, let's start with Park Lane then," David said with forced cheeriness.

* * *

A second ring on the bell was accompanied by a knock this time.

Banjo flung open the door ready to take aim. He was wearing a paisley silk dressing gown in a rich scarlet base tone and carrying a pump-action water pistol – the kind that looked like Disney's attempt at an assault rifle.

"What did I tell you?" he yelled, as the door opened. Then he stopped short as he caught sight of David standing on his bottom step.

"Did those kids put you up to this?" he asked David suspiciously. "Just tell me the truth and I won't be cross." The water-gun was no longer being aimed, but it was still held in casual readiness.

Banjo took a proper look at David, who appeared to have slept in his clothes. He hadn't shaved and his expression suggested a tired sort of pain.

Banjo said, "You look like my sister Doreen just after she had the twins." Shouldering the weapon, and with a single, darting glance down the street, Banjo retreated back inside, beckoning David to follow. "And what I said to her seems equally appropriate here: I'll stick the kettle on."

He led David through to the draughty Thirties-era kitchen, with its rickety, handmade cupboards and dark lino, now pimpled like the surface of a poppadom.

David slumped into a squeaky kitchen chair, while Banjo put a battered aluminium kettle on the gas hob. "You look all in, mate. You want some brekky?"

David shook his head, so Banjo concentrated on the tea. He bustled about, humming and occasionally stealing surreptitious glances at David. His piped scarlet slippers kept snagging rips in the lino, forcing him to shuffle like a geisha to keep them on.

A couple of minutes later, two mugs of tea were placed on the kitchen table. David's sat on a white patch the size of a soup plate, where the

Formica's gingham pattern had worn away, leaving not even a ghost.

As Banjo sat, he suddenly looked alarmed. "Oh god, it's not the Pope is it? Has something happened to him?"

David's slow smile brought to mind someone with a fish-hook in their upper lip, but it contained a tired twinkle of amusement too.

Seeing the smile, Banjo said, "I don't know the meaning of the phrase 'inappropriate humour', do I?"

They sat and smiled at each other for a moment, the smile of old friends. The morning sunlight creeping down the far wall glowed suddenly bright as a gap in the clouds opened up. For a second, the air was yellow and filled with floating dust like microcosmic snowflakes in a tiny tabletop world. The break in the cloud passed a few moments later, leaching away the colour, and Banjo shivered slightly in his dressing gown as the room dimmed.

"So, is it Susan?" he asked softly.

David nodded slowly and took a sip of his tea. He looked up from under a lowered brow. "Can I tell you what's been going on?" he asked, sounding suddenly hopeless.

"Course, mate," Banjo murmured warmly, "You can tell me anything."

"You might not believe me," David said, giving fair warning.

"You know me better than that," Banjo said. "This sounds like a good 'un."

They were on their third mug of tea by the time David had reached the events of that evening. Banjo appeared to be taking it all in his stride.

"What you told Dee," Banjo said, "that sounds right. Susan's done a bunk to be on the safe side. She's probably doing what you're doing; she's nipped round to see some old mate of hers until she gets over the collywobbles."

David rubbed the back of his neck and nodded slowly.

Banjo asked, "Where have you been since midnight then?"

David shrugged. "Here and there. I stopped in at Susan's work again, I sat in the car for a while, keeping an eye on the house she's staying in. And I, er, went round to both of that bloke Jan's addresses looking for signs of life. Oh yeah, and I stopped in at the Nick to see if they could tell me anything."

Banjo blew his breath out expressively. "I'd say that pretty much exhausts all the possibilities. You should probably just keep the mobile switched on and lay low yourself. That's about all you can do." He added, "Although a bath probably wouldn't be a bad idea sometime before you two lovebirds are reunited. Why don't you use my bathwater – and before you say anything it's still in the tank, I haven't used it yet – and then get a couple of hours kip. I won't let the phone out of my sight – guide's honour."

David nodded his thanks and then said, "You don't sound very surprised about the… more unlikely bits of my story."

Banjo arranged his sticky-up hair into a floppy Mohican, saying, "Any sufficiently advanced technology is indistinguishable from magic, as the man said. Granted, it's a bit too pat to expect the laws of physics to respond to human willpower. On the other hand, my mum phoned me last week from an aeroplane four miles above America. Seemed like science fiction to me." He shrugged. "People are always finding ways to make the universe do what they want. Where's technology heading if it's not working towards exactly the sorts of amazing things you've seen? What you're talking about, it sounds sort of like the ultimate Swiss Army knife." He flattened his hair back down and said, "Anyway, it's all ready for you up there. Towels are all fresh. I'll get the Presidential Suite sorted while you're soaking."

David made his way upstairs while Banjo went to hunt for fresh bed linen. Just as he reached the door of the bathroom it opened and out came a plump girl with perfect skin wearing only a pair of peach-coloured knickers. Her long red hair was flopped down over her heart-shaped face and she was forced to tip her head sideways to see who was standing in front of her.

"Hi," she said shyly and padded past David into one of the bedrooms. Before she disappeared, she yelled pleasantly, "Banjo, you big stud, where's my tea?" over her shoulder.

"Coming, Princess," came a distant reply from below.

With a look of surprise on his face David stepped into the bathroom and locked the door. With both taps full on, the old cast-iron bath began to fill rapidly, steam rising from the piping water into the cool air of the room.

David was up to his neck in hot water – and fast asleep – when Banjo knocked on the door and said, "I'm keeping an eye on your phone. The room's all ready. I'll call you in a couple of hours."

David managed to stay awake long enough to emerge from the bath, dry himself off, and scamper naked, carrying his clothes, into a bedroom with a fake American licence plate on the door which really did say 'The Presidential Suite' on it.

CHAPTER 26

"Tell me, dear girl, is there anything I might say or do that would persuade you that your embarrassment is quite unnecessary?" said Professor Shaw.

Susan continued to look ill at ease, saying, "I just couldn't think of anywhere else…"

The Professor broke in, "As you keep saying. And as I keep saying, you are very welcome here. These days, Saturday night feels much the way I remember wet Sunday afternoons as a small boy." His voice took on a gentle, patronising quality as he said, "I steel myself to wait until after the BBC's midnight news before I make myself a cup of camomile tea. It's a routine that just clamours to be interrupted, wouldn't you say?"

He left Susan sitting on the huge, sagging sofa and disappeared into the kitchen. His voice carried from there. "I'm also experiencing a long-forgotten sensation that might well prove to be chivalry. Give me a moment to work out where my housekeeper puts the cups for visitors and then let's get to the bottom of whatever's bothering you."

A few minutes later, they were sitting at opposite ends of the sofa sipping herbal tea which was still too hot to drink.

Susan launched into it. "Well," she began, "I've made the single biggest discovery in the history of our field. That's what we'll call the good news. The bad news is that I've just finished robbing the School of Antiquities, I'm probably going to need a new career – assuming I don't get arrested – I think someone is trying to kill me and if I tell you the story behind it all you'll think I've lost my mind and probably arrange to have me locked up for my own good. That's what I'm thinking of as the not-so-good news." This all came out in a rush. When she'd finished speaking, she looked up at the Professor to gauge his reaction.

"Do tell me if that tea's too hot," he said, "I can put a drop of cold in it. It's no bother."

Susan stared at him, waiting for him to say more.

"I'm terribly sorry," he said, "I suppose aplomb has become rather an indulgence of mine. Showing off really, but I like to think I can take an announcement such as yours at least as coolly as the next man." He took another tiny sip from his delicate china teacup and then set it back in its saucer. "I'm actually rather pleased that it's not a romantic setback that brings you here. I'd have done my best to sound sympathetic, I hope, but it's been the same old story since Adam was a lad. I was preparing myself to be a little disappointed in you." He slapped his thighs with both hands. "But instead you tell me that you're ruined, pursued, driven to crime and in possession of a tale you claim will defeat my best efforts to encompass it. I find my faith in you once again amply rewarded. And, in case it needs to be said, I will help in whatever way I can."

And so Susan told the Professor a similar story to the one David had told Banjo. Susan made more of the role played by the Teracus collection and rather less of the various violent encounters. The sequence in which the events were related was somewhat altered too, but when she had finished speaking she had covered approximately the same ground as David: a criminal with impossible abilities was intent on taking a mysterious artefact from another of his kind.

"Good god," the Professor said, rather sharply, at several points during Susan's narrative. When she finally sat back and picked up her cold tea, he said to her, "I'm very thankful you weren't killed while all that was taking place. Miraculously, you don't seem to have a scratch on you."

"I wouldn't say that, Professor. Thank god for concealer, is all I can say. I've got five stitches in the…" She stopped short. She'd run her hands over the back of her head, parting the hair with her fingertips as she spoke. Now she looked confused, continuing to probe.

"Indulge me a minute, Professor," she said, twisting round in her seat, "Will you tell me what you see here?" She held the end of her finger to a section of exposed scalp, the hair pulled to either side. "This is where I got hit."

Obligingly, the Professor came to stand over her and investigated. He said, "A little pinkness, the residual rubor of a wound perhaps. When did you say you were attacked?" the Professor asked as he retook his seat. Susan let her hair fall back.

She lifted her gaze vaguely skywards for a second while she calculated. "Ten days today. Actually I think I was supposed to have the stitches out a few days ago."

Professor Shaw nodded and said, "That's one of the problems with a blow to the head; it's a most inopportune moment to impart important medical advice. I worked in a London hospital during the last world war. I saw a lot of pretty young women too silly to wear their tin hats." He brought himself back to the present and said, "Perhaps you can tell me what it means, but I'd say that injury has been healing for at least four, more probably six weeks and there are no stitches in evidence."

Susan's face went blank and she confessed, almost blurting it out, "I used the headband my attacker left behind." She repeated, "This afternoon I tried to use it." She flared her nostrils and tipped her chin up as though the words were being pulled painfully from her. "I'm not sure, but I think," it seemed to be an effort to continue, but she managed it, "I think I made a letter-opener move just by concentrating on it. No, ignore that: I did; I'm positive about it."

"Can you…" the Professor hesitated. He wet his lips with the tip of his tongue. "Can you show me?"

Susan looked very uncomfortable, "I can't," she said, almost pleading.

"I know how this sounds, but I don't dare show you. I re-read one of my colleague's précis and realised he'd botched the translation. From what I can tell, it's a standing order amongst... amongst whoever these people are, to bump off any newcomers. It's a sort of reverse apprenticeship, whereby the old hands make sure there's no new talent coming through. They neutralise any potential challenges before they can find their feet."

"Adepts, my dear. You wondered what to call them. That's what I'd suggest. Those proficient in the *ars obscura*," he said. He added, sotto voce, and to himself, "Not the Latin for underpants as a pupil of mine once suggested."

Susan ignored his aside and said, "Well if I practice any of those concealed arts I'm apparently broadcasting the fact. Not my identity, from what I can tell, but my presence. I have no idea what range we're talking about or how close they have to be to sense me. But, having done the equivalent of lighting a beacon last night, I wanted to get the hell out of Dodge for the time being." She shivered, "It's a pretty creepy thought. Ears pricking up and heads turning, adepts everywhere suddenly tuned in to what I'm doing." She looked genuinely horrified.

Professor Shaw said swiftly, "Ahh, perhaps I should have encouraged you to venture out in your smalls, like that Jenkins woman in her dance attire. You might have got used to the universal attention by now." He pushed on, trying to distract her, "And incidentally, I believe our scheming has borne fruit. Your Mr Hartman has been seen in Ms Jenkins' company on a number of occasions since you decamped for the Big Smoke."

The Professor's attempts to change the subject seemed to have successfully derailed Susan's macabre train of thought. Her face had relaxed and she was shaking her head in disbelief, "That seems like a hundred years ago and another life. Remember when all I had to worry about was having a downmarket Don Juan for an assistant?"

The Professor cleared his throat and said, "You certainly do seem to have packed quite a bit into your time away, there's no denying it. But to return to our present predicament, what is it you thought I might do to help?"

"Well," Susan said, "receiving stolen goods, harbouring a fugitive and helping me unravel the secret of the ages were the top items on my list."

She reached across and squeezed his hand, receiving a raised eyebrow in response. She said, "I feel so much better than I did two hours ago, I can't tell you. Just talking to you makes me feel that maybe I haven't gone mad after all."

"You mean relative to present company?" he asked and Susan laughed. He eyed the bulging courier bag and the enormous flight case that Susan had arrived with and asked, mischievously, "So are you going to let me have a look at the swag then?"

"If you're ready for a life of crime," she said, nodding.

The Professor's living room included what must have once been a separate dining room – though now it was all one room. They cleared a heavy green cloth from the monumental mahogany dining table and began to spread Susan's stolen documents out. The originals were in plastic wallets, the reproductions paper-clipped to the outside.

Unable to resist, the Professor started exploring one of the document packs nearest him, becoming so absorbed that seconds later he seemed oblivious to Susan's presence.

Susan buried herself in another of the documents and the two of them sat quietly, the only sound the loud, wooden ticking of the mantle clock.

Some time later, Susan slipped into the kitchen and made them more tea – this time English Breakfast. The Professor received his cup and then a moment later seemed to remember himself and said, "Have I been away long? I really must beg your pardon; my manners are a disgrace. It's just that these documents, especially in light of what you've told me, make for the most extraordinary reading."

Having turned away from the collection to look at Susan, something seemed to occur to the Professor. He said, "I know you like to tease me over my fondness for gangster movies, but I should ask whether you think we are in any danger here. I can't seem to get very worked up at the thought for myself, but I really couldn't allow any harm to come to you. I could make a telephone call if you think we might need a, um, couple of heavies."

He went on to explain, "I tutored the son of a local policeman. A most unfortunate lad in respect of his medical difficulties, but scarcely a burden. Nonetheless, I'm assured that I have favours to call in if ever I need them."

Susan assured him that it was unnecessary. She came and sat down beside him. "Oh you would have been proud of my getaway, Professor," Susan said, "I got on a tube train and then got off again just before the doors closed. Then I travelled one stop down the line, got off and stood by the exit barriers pretending to look for my ticket until everyone who came up the stairs had passed me. Then I ran back down and jumped on a train heading the other way. Unless I'm bugged somehow then I'm sure no one knows where I am."

The Professor commented, "I really have no idea what's possible in that regard, although surely being underground must help. In my day the fugitive generally left a matchbook behind, often with an important phone number written on it. You were careful not to make that mistake, I trust."

Susan nodded. The Professor asked, "You've read nothing in these papers," he indicated the piles covering the table, "to suggest an arcane method of locating missing persons?"

Susan shrugged, "Some of these documents seem to suggest that anything's possible, but there's a consensus that abilities fall into two categories: a kind of working-set that David and I have seen evidence of and then the premium package – a kind of mystical guru version that's out of reach except to a few mad old hermits. The way it works seems very Zen: it looks like you can only have these extra powers if you're so disconnected from the world that you'd never use them in pursuit of a practical goal. I don't know if a mystic could track me, but there's no mention that the regular foot-soldiers have any way of doing so."

She added, "Originally I thought the higher-level abilities were just empty boasting, but given what I've already come to accept, it's probably best to keep an open mind."

After a moment of reflection, she went on to say, "Anyway, to answer your original question, I don't think I'm in any immediate danger. I came here with two problems. First, I alerted the locals back in London that there was a stranger in town – although I think I got away with that. I wasn't followed, so they can't know I'm here.

"My second problem is the collection. I think this guy Jan will be coming for it, but I don't believe he's got any way of knowing that I've moved it. I realise I'm totally dropping this in your lap, and it's a hell of a thing to ask, but I'm hoping you can help me figure my way out of this."

The Professor had just stood, as though he was about to head into the kitchen. He paused and acquired rather a calculating look, asking, "You don't think this vigorous young man, David, would be of more help?"

Susan looked down at the table. "It's complicated," she said. "And anyway, I couldn't get hold of him when I needed him, when I thought this madman was breathing down my neck. I need someone a little more trustworthy," she said.

"Ahh," the Professor said knowingly. Then he patted her affectionately on the shoulder and said, "A romantic setback after all, and no time to straighten it out. Your plate is certainly rather full." He nodded wisely and said, "But still, trying times can cement as easily as they divide."

Susan said nothing, lost as she was in her own thoughts. In the midst of her reverie she yawned and covered her mouth with her hand. After a couple of seconds she was still yawning and flapping her other hand to indicate that she was trying, unsuccessfully, to bring the yawn to an end.

The Professor chuckled at her display.

She said, "Boy, excuse me. Wow," having finally regained control of her mouth.

The Professor set off for the kitchen and the stairs beyond, saying, "I'd better turn down the covers in the guest bedroom. There's hot water and all the trappings of civilisation. You remember your way round?"

Susan made to reply and found herself yawning again. She shook her head, "You'd think I'd be used to adrenaline by now. I think I'm going to have to crash out pretty soon. I'll worry about all this in the morning." She gestured at the table.

Susan followed the Professor through the kitchen and up the stairs. She ducked into the bathroom while he attended to the guest room. When she emerged he was halfway down the stairs. He stopped and said to her, "Why don't I leave you to sleep in a little – unless you'd rather not?"

Susan's watch showed a quarter to one in the morning. "Could you call me at nine if I'm not up?" she said.

"Of course. Mrs Potter comes in at about eight to straighten things up. I'll see if I can't persuade her to lay on some breakfast. Sleep well, dear girl," he said.

"Thanks Professor," Susan said and wandered into her room. The bedside lamp was on, the bedspread was turned back from the pillow and a red light down near the valence indicated that an electric blanket was warming the bed's interior.

Susan undressed quickly, switched the blanket off and slid under the covers with a sigh. Her eyelids dipped for a second before lifting again just long enough for her to turn out the light.

CHAPTER 27

S usan sat eating bacon, scrambled eggs, sausage, fried bread, fried tomato and mushrooms. The Professor sat opposite her at the little kitchen table doing the same.

"My doctor estimates," the Professor said, holding up a section of sausage skewered on a fork, "that I can have one of these every two or three years with almost no ill effects. Although he suggests waiting six months before going swimming."

Susan took a swig of tea from a golden jubilee mug and asked, "Did you sleep at all last night Professor?"

"You know," he said, "you're quite welcome to call me Joseph or Joe. I don't suppose you will, but it seems to me that after tipping our entire profession on its ear you really shouldn't defer to me as though I'm the expert."

Susan said nothing. The Professor went on, "Well, whatever's most comfortable for you. But to answer your question, I might have nodded off in my chair for a couple of minutes, but most likely not. What sort of scholar would I be if I could receive those papers into my house, knowing what they contain, and then toddle off to bed? Besides which, sleeping these days is no more of a necessity than cleaning my spectacles – simply an aid to seeing things more clearly."

"So did you turn up anything earth-shattering?" Susan asked, "I mean besides the massive bombshells we already knew about, er, Joseph? Joe. Professor."

"I found a code," the Professor said nonchalantly, plainly rather pleased with himself, but attempting to conceal his excitement.

Susan was instantly avid. "Spill," she said, refusing to be teased.

The Professor said, "Your Dr Lampwick is falling down on the job. One of the documents in the collection makes use of an old merchant's cipher, one I happen to have come across before. I might have expected that the content of the document would have aroused some suspicion – being, as it is, a letter discussing chiefly the weather, the state of the roads and the health of an extended family with improbable names."

Susan looked slightly sheepish and said, "If it's the one I'm thinking of, Bernie had it classified as part of the personal correspondence of an earlier owner of the collection. I've been focussing on the documents that discuss magic directly and leaving the contextual pieces to him."

"Hmm," the Professor said, "well Dr Lampwick overlooked rather an interesting hidden message. The artefact you've been referring to as the Marker is discussed within. I believe I now know its function. But before I tell you, will you remind me of your working hypothesis?"

Susan looked dubious. "I'm not sure why you want to know, given that you've uncovered the truth, but I'll trust that you've got something nobler in mind than rubbing my nose in it." She collected her thoughts for a moment and said, "We know the Marker has something to do with healing and for a while I was convinced that this guy Jan was seriously sick."

The Professor broke in, "Excuse me, but why did you think that?"

Susan frowned, "Maybe I didn't mention it, but I saw these marks on him. They looked just like Kaposi's Sarcoma. I saw it when I did some volunteer work – working with addicts and homeless people. It's something you get if…"

The Professor interrupted again, "If AIDS has weakened your immune system. Of course," he said, as though it fitted perfectly. "No you didn't mention that, but you did mention you thought he was suffering from some terminal affliction. Given his extraordinary physical prowess, I wondered why."

They had finished eating and now they pushed their plates aside. On cue, Mrs Potter bustled into the room, collected the plates, refilled their mugs from a huge teapot covered in a crocheted cosy and bustled out again humming vibrantly all the while.

"Thank you Mrs Potter. A delicious breakfast," the Professor said to her departing back and then returned his attention to Susan. "And you are of course correct that Kaposi's is well-known for its tendency to follow in the wake of AIDS. Did you know also that it is also an affliction of the elderly? Old age weakens the immune system just as AIDS or certain medicines can. There is also a form common to equatorial Africa, if memory serves, which I assume is not germane here."

Susan looked surprised. "How do you know all this?" she asked.

The Professor smiled. "Consider that I've spent some part of each day for very nearly eighty years now reading and, for the most part, committing to memory. I was part way through training to be a doctor at the end of World War II. And though I realised it wasn't for me, I've never lost my interest in medicine."

Susan said, "Wow, I didn't know that. Your training would have been post-leeches, right?"

The Professor gave her a tart smile and she sniggered for a moment and then looked more serious, saying, "I'll shut up now. Don't let me distract you any more until you've told me what was in that code."

The Professor said, "Quite. According to the plain-text I extracted, it is alleged that the Marker does no less than restore the youth of those who know its secret. The passage describes passing into some sort of death-like trance, of what duration I'm unsure – but when it has run its course, the recipient is once more in their physical prime. The description makes it sound almost as though they emerge from a cocoon, but it's difficult to distinguish the figurative from the literal elements of the description."

Susan said, "Well I've got some direct experience that the practice of magic has immediate health benefits," then muttered, "even if it lowers your life expectancy in other ways." She went on, "I just couldn't figure out where the Marker came in." She stuck out her bottom lip as she put it all together in her mind, "So adepts get old, though maybe not as quickly as the rest of us, and when they do, they need the Marker to extend their life. So we're saying that Jan is actually an old man?"

"I believe he may be a few years my senior," the Professor said, "and I'll be eighty-three this June."

Both of them sat and considered this for a moment. Susan spoke first, "We should be having this discussion at midnight, in the flickering firelight. I can't sit here looking out the window at sparrows eating bacon-rind from the bird table and talk about immortality and ninety-year-olds who could sweep the board at the Olympics. I almost wish I still had my scars to remind me that this is real."

The Professor said, "I admit that while I believe what you've told me and what I've read since last night, it almost seems like a dream. It's like descriptions of the Big Bang – doubtless accurate, but difficult to reconcile with the view from a Clapham Omnibus."

Something else occurred to Susan. "Unless Jan's already used the Marker some time in the past, then he's a product of the twentieth century – which is certainly my impression – though I don't really know why I think that. Anyway, how old do you suppose Dass was?"

The Professor spread his hands, "We could speculate. In theory, I suppose he could be as old as the Marker, but you didn't describe him as Oriental in appearance and I doubt there were many Europeans in Qin dynasty China. The cipher I discovered dates from late sixteenth century Italy." He paused a moment, "Whoever wrote the message possessed the Marker at the time and I don't believe that person was Dass; I believe he was an Arab by birth. If we put the pieces together: Dass had yet to acquire the Marker when the message was written, and the message uses a code first invented around 1580." He summed up, "So, we could say that Dass probably didn't get the Marker until, let's pick a date, 1600 at the earliest. In order for him to make use of it immediately, he would have to have been born early in the previous century. I think we can tentatively assume that he was no more than five hundred years old."

Susan dropped back in her chair, obviously reeling with the idea. "No more than five hundred years old. Man, no wonder David found him imposing."

Susan considered for a moment longer and said, "And somehow, you're accepting all this?"

The Professor pursed his lips thoughtfully. "It is a fundamental shift in the order of things, I'll grant you. Perhaps I'm simply deluding myself that I believe it. But in a curious way, this makes much more sense than the world I've been living in all these years." He extended a hand, palm up, and said, "Take the persistence of alchemy as an illustration: how could it be so popular for so many hundreds of years without a single success?"

Susan looked excited, "Oh, alchemy, I've got a theory about that." She was almost wriggling in her seat. Seeing as how the Professor didn't object, she explained, "You know that the language alchemists use is always intentionally ambiguous, like using the same symbol for man, Mars and iron or for woman, Venus and copper, so that you can't tell whether you're reading astrology or chemistry?" She looked foolish for a second. "I'm being rhetorical, of course you know all that. Anyway, I was thinking about the way most alchemists seemed to believe you had to purify the body and the mind before you could move on to purifying base metal into gold – they felt those three things were linked. Well what if scholars have been confusing cause and effect? What if you have to purify the mind and the base metal before you can purify the body? Pure gold – in the form of tribute – plus certain mental exercises give you…" She pointed to the back of her head, "…a superhuman constitution. Look at Jan; he's ninety years old and he could hand Bruce Lee his ass." The Professor's eyebrows tipped back. Susan didn't pause for breath, "If that's what alchemy offered, that would explain a few things. It never made sense to me that alchemy was supposedly about making gold – because it was expensive and it never worked. What kind of ever-popular get-rich-quick scheme requires you to start off wealthy and then get poorer?"

The Professor had an approving look on his face. "Intriguing," he said, "You're thinking of the fabled Comte St Germain."

"And others," Susan said.

The Professor continued, "You see why it's surprisingly easy to accept what you've told me and the papers you've brought me? When a new idea re-opens so many previously exhausted avenues of enquiry, one can't help but feel that it's correct – how else could it be so fruitful?"

Susan was bubbling over with suggestions now. "Exactly. Think of the healing powers of The King's Touch – powerful men who wore gold bands around their heads for a living. For that matter, how do you suppose the idea of haloes became associated with people able to do the impossible?"

They were each occupied with their own ruminations for a moment and then the Professor composed his face, signalling a change of topic. "But tell me, my dear, what are your plans for the collection?" Susan immediately began to look tense. The Professor continued smoothly, saying, "Shall I take it off your hands?"

Susan's expression suggested she was experiencing two contradictory emotions. The Professor's offer plainly delighted and horrified her in equal parts. The inner conflict showed on her face for a few seconds before she said, "I need to do something with it. But it could be a death sentence for whoever looks after it. And it needs to be someone who understands the true risks Jan poses. If I'd left it at the School, they would have put it under lock and key, perhaps with a couple of guards, and Jan would have strolled in there and taken it. I could keep it, but I don't know where I'd go." She was starting to look panicked now, speaking more quickly, "I suppose I could go back to the States, try to get lost somewhere."

The Professor made a wafting gesture with his hands, meaning 'slow down'. He said, "My apologies for raising a subject that is both indelicately morbid and rather personal, but I assure you I have a relevant point: I wonder how long you imagine I might live."

Susan was taken by surprise. She appeared to have no answer.

The Professor said, "During my time at Princeton I had a friend, a fellow quite a bit older than myself, who was then in his eighty-fifth year. He used to say that he was living in 'bonus time'. One couldn't reasonably expect to live as long as he had, one could only hope. So it would hardly be a crime if one failed to make sensible, dutiful plans for how to spend those years. If one were lucky enough to reach such an age and find oneself in reasonable fettle, then it should be treated as a gift to do with as one pleased."

He looked up to see whether Susan was following him. Then the shadow of something crossed his face and he dropped his gaze from hers.

He said nothing for a few moments and some instinct prevented Susan from interrupting the silence. A weight now seemed to press upon the Professor and when he spoke at last, the heaviness had invaded his words too, "Despite my early interest in medicine, I don't relish my annual check-ups. My last such conversation with my physician was a particularly cheerless occasion."

He gave Susan a rather bleak smile and said, "He had one or two pieces of disappointing news for me, and precious little in the way of encouragement." He paused to see that she understood what he was implying.

He said, "It is not a matter of 'whether'; it is a matter of 'how soon'."

Susan's face had drained of colour as she listened to these words.

The Professor continued, his voice a little strained as though his throat were sore. "Perhaps you can see what I'm trying to say, but the essence of it is that I'd relish the prospect of spending more time with this collection. And should you-know-who come calling for it, I'm confident I can keep it out of his clutches whatever inducements he may offer. It seems, if my physician is to be trusted, that there is little he can threaten to deprive me of at this point. Whereas you, my dear, do have a future, a very promising one ahead of you, and we must do what we can to secure it."

A sudden tear rolled down Susan's face. Her lower lip refused to stay quite still and she stared at the Professor as though she had already lost him.

He did his best to seem untroubled as he said, "Think of it this way: in those documents are answers to questions I have wondered about since your grandmother was a girl. I can bring those answers tantalisingly close and at the same time help a friend in her hour of need – or I can opt for a few more months of the quiet life." He looked at her apologetically. "If you'll excuse my abominable self-flattery, I rather fancy ending a life of scholarship with something dimly reminiscent of heroism."

The old man's eyes were beginning to look red-rimmed and watery as he finished speaking. Susan was simply letting the teardrops roll down her cheeks.

The Professor stood, pushing his chair back, and crossed to the kettle. "I think that pot's a little stewed. What say we make some fresh?"

With her sixth sense for these things, Mrs Potter appeared in the room at that moment, saying, "I'll do that Professor, you sit yourself down with your guest." She spoke loudly, as though the Professor was a little hard of hearing, though he appeared to have no difficulty understanding Susan's softer tones.

Mrs Potter appeared not to notice Susan's distress. But as the Professor retook his seat, Mrs Potter placed a glass cake-stand – apparently produced from thin air – in front of Susan. It was layered with shortbread biscuits. "Try one. I make them myself. Lovely, if I do say so." Next to the cake stand was a tissue, which Susan quickly used to dry her face.

The Professor said to Susan, "We'll talk again later."

She nodded and then looked around her for something to occupy her attention, to distract her from her distress. "I should really phone my sister," she said, her voice a little thicker than usual. "And David is probably panicking. I told him I needed to see him urgently." She wandered into the living room to where her courier bag was hooked over the back of a dining chair. She pulled out her mobile phone and said, "Shit."

The Professor turned to his housekeeper and said, "I never hear language like that from you Mrs Potter. You're not repressing I hope."

"And neither shall you hear it," Mrs Potter said, her lips pursed. "My mum would never have tolerated it."

"A formidable woman by all accounts," the Professor agreed, offering a dubious smile. "Problem?" he asked Susan.

She said, "My battery is dead. I always keep it charged but my sister borrowed my charger. May I use your phone Professor?" She began to rummage in her bag for her address book.

"Of course. There's one in the hall," he said airily. Then moving close to where she was standing, he said, his voice low, "And remind me to tell you what I learned about combat between adepts."

Susan raised an eyebrow, as if to say 'go on', but didn't stop hunting in her bag.

"I rather think it's significant," he said, "though I have no idea of what. But apparently," he dropped his voice even lower, "one cannot use magic to attack a fellow adept."

Susan had her head almost inside her bag. Her muffled voice said, "Some sort of golden rule, right?"

"No, my dear, not a rule," he said, "It simply will not operate. No more, the text says, than if they attempted to use magic without their gold adornment."

Susan at last discovered her phone book and stepped out into the hall. The Professor had the look of someone about to deliver an amusing punch-line. "So you'll never guess how they resolve their disputes," he said expectantly.

Susan had the phone to her ear and was waiting for the call to connect. She was only giving his remarks half her attention. "Hmm?" she said absent-mindedly, "Does the defensive stuff still work?"

"It does," the Professor confirmed, still delighted with what he was going to impart.

"Well in that case, I suppose if they want to attack each other they must…" Susan only got that far. Her call was answered and she said, "David?"

CHAPTER 28

THAT SAME MORNING
SUNDAY 27TH APRIL

David and Banjo were drinking coffee, sitting in Banjo's workshop.

The room would originally have been a conservatory or a greenhouse in some previous chapter of the house's history. Whatever pale sunlight the day offered streamed unimpeded through the sloping glass roof. Scattered about the room were several pieces of furniture in various stages of repair. There were also large chunks of iron and glass, which might have been art or simply fire-damaged machinery, and there was a separate bench area for some sort of delicate metalworking.

The two of them sat on high stools, the kind intended for working at a bench, the tops of which had been reupholstered with layers of carpet. A convection heater blew warm air towards their feet.

Banjo said, "This has been a new lease of life for your job, I'll bet."

David nodded. "Well it's certainly been a bit more interesting lately," he said, wearing a poker face and restraining his smile, "what with one thing and another. A bit different from a couple of months ago."

"Yeah," Banjo acknowledged, "who'd have thought a month ago that you'd be prepared to risk your life for your company." There was an odd note in his voice.

David looked up. He took a moment to scrutinise Banjo's face before he said, cautiously, "Are you referring to my so-called death-wish?"

Banjo held up his hands. "I never said death-wish. I just thought you were getting what you might call dangerously bored. Remember, you were planning to bicycle through Cambodia and then hitchhike round Syria blindfold or something. Only now you can get your near-death kicks at work."

David looked as though he was becoming irritated. "Do we have to have this talk again, Banjo?"

Banjo held up a finger for a minute, as though he was about to speak. He held them both to silence for a few seconds and then said, in a very reasonable voice, "Tell me you haven't risked your life more than, ooh, say once a week since we last talked and I'll let it drop."

"You know I have," David said, sounding tired.

"Right. And I just want to know why. Surely there's no harm in telling me that," Banjo said, his voice still meticulously reasonable.

David went to speak, but found himself at a loss for words. Banjo didn't push him or appear impatient; he waited quietly for David to collect his thoughts.

When David finally spoke, he said, "Well, for want of a word that doesn't sound stupid when I say it, I'd say it was about destiny." He sounded a little defiant as he said the word, as though he almost expected to be challenged or laughed at. Banjo, however, was simply attentive.

David went on, "Like you said to me, we all believe in destiny. I'm sure most of us believe that the lives we lead will somehow match up with the sort of people we are. I don't suppose it's anything most people dwell on because it's not causing them a problem. They're nice quiet people living nice quiet lives. Their insides and their outsides match, if you know what I mean." He looked up. "Well mine don't," he said firmly.

"I don't think I'm meant to have a quiet life," he said, glancing at Banjo again, gauging his expression, "Of course I don't want to get myself killed, but when all this nonsense started I had a choice – I could see where it all led and take whatever risks came up or I could do the sensible thing and, basically, run away." He shrugged. "I knew I had to jump in." Then he nodded. "And you know what? It's the first time in I don't know how long that I've really felt like I was me." He pointed at his own chest.

He seemed to have finished, but Banjo said, "Go on."

David found he had more to say. "I think you know it was starting to get to me, the last year or so. So many things around me that I didn't care about and nothing for me to do that felt like it really mattered one way or the other." He nodded to Banjo, "And you were right that I was prepared to start taking risks – maybe even some stupid risks, I suppose – just to see if I could make something happen. But this is different." He emphasised the words, "This found me."

He went on, "I don't know if there's any such thing as destiny – maybe it's just that 'character is fate' thing and it's all in my head – but I'm telling you that this feels like what I'm supposed to be doing. Getting to the bottom of this thing, stopping this Jan bloke, doing whatever I have to do." He drew in a breath, "I don't want to sound like I've lost my marbles, but I'd rather come a cropper doing this than have fifty years living in suburbia and playing golf at the weekend."

David had been focussing inward as he spoke, and once the passion with which he'd spoken started to leave him he became more aware that Banjo had been watching him closely. He added, plainly looking for a laugh, "To summarise: frankly, I'm wasted on insurance."

Banjo didn't laugh. He ruminated on David's speech for a bit before finally announcing, "Yup, I can believe all that." He brightened as though David had passed some test or been forgiven some past offence.

Banjo said, "You know, within the bounds of following your destiny, and all that, do you think maybe you could try not to get yourself killed?" Another thought occurred to him, "And if you'd got any sense you'd start letting that Susan bird do some of your thinking for you." David appeared to be weighing the idea. Banjo continued, "I mean face it, she's a lot more clever than you are, isn't she?" As he said this, Banjo smiled as though he'd paid David a compliment.

A few moments later, David changed the subject, "So how are things with you and Melissa? Assuming that was Melissa whose boobs I was staring at."

"Oy," said Banjo, playfully, "get your own. No, she's fantastic, mate. I'm in that stage where you can't tell whether it's love or something a bit more shallow but equally as nice. I suppose I'll just have to see if it wears off. Be, um, really good if it didn't though."

Their chat seemed to have reached a natural conclusion. David was standing, ready to move back into the main body of the house. He'd picked up his mobile from the bench and was holding it, checking the display for the hundredth time.

Banjo stood too, saying, "Listen, is there anything you want me to do about all this cops and robbers stuff? I mean, just for the sake of argument, if Susan doesn't call in the next couple of hours, can I help you look for her? Or did you want to do something about the bad guy? I don't know what use I could be, but if anything occurs to you, the offer's there." Banjo managed to come extremely close to sounding nonchalant and unconcerned about the risks.

David shook his head appreciatively, saying, "It's handy for me if you're not involved; makes this sort of a secret bolt-hole. But thanks."

Then he put his arm round Banjo's shoulders and gave him a squeeze. "You're a good friend," David said, grinning.

"Get off," Banjo said, pretending to be uncomfortable with the contact. "Turning me all gay when I've got a bird upstairs."

David was smiling, about to say something, when a sound stopped him. His mobile was ringing. He glanced at the display. "Don't know the number," he said aloud.

Banjo gave a little flick of his head and point of his fingers, meaning, 'I'll leave you to it' and ducked out of the workshop into the hallway, pulling the door most of the way closed behind him.

Alone in the workshop, David answered the call, "Hello?"

"David, it's Susan," she sounded relieved to be speaking with him.

"Are you OK? Where are you?" he said, anxiously.

"I'm with my Professor in Cambridge. I'm fine," she said airily.

David frowned, uncertain. "That's great," he said, not sounding like he was too sure. "Why, um, why didn't you call?"

"I am calling," she said, her voice no longer quite so friendly.

David's concern had turned into something else. It seemed as though her breezy attitude had offended him. "I meant before now. I spent all of last night looking for you, because I thought you needed my help." It started as an explanation, but it was beginning to sound accusatory. "I've been frantic, waiting for you to call. I even staked out Jan's place in case he took you back there..."

"You did what?" she exploded.

He tried to be patient, "You left me a message saying that he was right outside your door."

"I did no such thing," she said, but a moment's doubt took some of the boldness from the statement. "After all we've been through, you still went to confront him?"

He sounded defensive as he said, "You tell me Jan's outside your door, then I hear nothing. What was I supposed to do? Have an early night?" This last was rather louder than the rest of the conversation. He got himself under slightly better control and said, "Listen, I don't want us to have an argument."

"I don't know that you get to decide that all by yourself," Susan said coldly. "But it doesn't surprise me that you'd think you could."

David had placed one hand on the bench beside him. He leaned on it heavily now, his mouth open, his cheeks flushed. "I..." was all he could manage.

Susan spoke. "This isn't..." She too was having trouble finishing her sentences. A moment later her voice seemed milder but it wasn't clear whether she was backing down or merely refusing to be drawn. "Come to Cambridge," she said, at last.

"Fine," David said, his voice full of some indeterminate emotion.

"I'll text you with the exact address," Susan said; her tone was definitely softer.

David's voice was merely stiff now, his sudden anger replaced with some sort of strained composure. "So I'll see you in a bit, then," he said, attempting to sound upbeat and missing by a mile.

They both hung up.

Banjo, who had in fact been listening at the door, which he'd held an inch ajar throughout the call, now pushed it open, apparently unconcerned about disguising his eavesdropping.

David didn't react. He looked as though he'd been hit in the stomach. Banjo put on an over-the-top American accent and blared, "What was *her* problem?" evidently not taking the spat seriously.

David's head was still dipped. He blew air through his fringe. He sounded lost as he said, "She obviously changed her mind about needing my help last night and didn't think it was worth a phone call." His tone was both hurt and slightly incredulous.

"Yeah, well, birds, eh?" Banjo said, not sounding as though he shared David's despair. "Why don't you chew on this," he waited until he had David's attention and then said, "What if she asked for your help, then you find out she doesn't want you to save her after all, but she hasn't changed her mind either? You with me?"

David looked up at Banjo. "I don't get it," he said vaguely, having only given it half his attention, the other half being reserved for brooding.

Banjo intoned slowly, "I said: what if she asked for your help, then you find out she doesn't want you to save her after all, but she hasn't changed her mind either?"

David was trying to make sense of what Banjo was saying.

While he stood there looking confused, Banjo added, "I may not be able to cast out my own planks..." With which cryptic comment he wandered out, muttering, "Woman like that, stands to reason."

* * *

David was already halfway up the M11, twenty minutes from Cambridge when his phoned beeped. The text message, from Susan's mobile, started with the words, "Had to buy new charger," followed by an address and instructions for finding it.

Once in the outskirts of the city, he had to pull over for a couple of minutes to scrutinise a road atlas, but locating the Professor's beautiful cottage just outside the town centre wasn't difficult. What *was* difficult was parking. Eventually, David drove into one of the large multi-storey car parks intended for shoppers and hiked back out to the Professor's street.

When he arrived, it was Susan who opened the door. She was wearing a trim, white, fleecy v-neck, with a pair of jeans and her red boots. She looked worried, her lower lip twisting uncertainly. He gazed at her guardedly as she stood on the top step. But before he could speak she came forwards and hugged him. He put his arms around her and returned the squeeze.

"David," she said, sounding relieved, her face pressed into his coat.

"Hi," he said, laughing uncertainly, the tension suddenly gone from his throat.

They separated and she said, "I'm sorry I gave you a hard time on the phone." She obviously had a couple of things to say before they moved from the doorstep to the cosy-looking interior.

He tipped his head on one side. "I think I started this one," he said, "I think I was doing that parental thing. I was so worried about you that the first thing I did when I realised you were safe was try to bite your head off." He looked her in the eye, "I really was worried. Your voicemail sounded pretty bad."

"And…?" she said, as though he'd forgotten to say 'please'.

He looked awkward as he realised what she meant. He smiled, almost shyly, and said, "And I'm sorry too."

She gave him another hug and led him into the living room.

"Ah," the Professor said exuberantly, "you've finished letting the last of the heat out. Good, good."

David smiled, but Susan looked concerned and said, "Let me get you a sweater, Professor."

The Professor waved his hand, gently dismissive, "It was sarcasm not hypothermia talking." He looked at David standing there, his bulk exaggerated in his chunky leather jacket. The Professor's expression was amiable but appraising.

David smiled politely, taking a couple of steps forwards and holding out his hand. "Hi, I'm David Braun."

They shook. The Professor said with a chuckle, "A weak handshake, I like that in a man."

David seemed unsure how to take the remark and the Professor explained, "Preserving my bones rather than demonstrating the doubtless formidable strength of your grip."

Then he said, "I'm Joseph Shaw, but most people call me by my nickname, 'Professor'," he glanced significantly at Susan. "Either are perfectly fine."

"Pleased to meet you, Joseph," David said, earning another delighted smile from the Professor.

"Susan?" the Professor asked, "Would you consider making us some tea if I give you my word that rheumatic knees, and not outdated views on gender roles, prompt my request?"

"Of course," Susan said sweetly, heading for the kitchen.

"I'll, um…" David said, pointing his finger, indicating that he intended to assist.

He joined Susan in the kitchen, leaving the Professor to sit in his customary armchair, apparently comfortably absorbed in his own thoughts.

Once out of the Professor's earshot, David said, "So have you spoken to Dee today?"

Susan gave him a look that was both indulgent and unimpressed. "You'd suck at poker," she said. She began to arrange the tea things on a tray.

David appeared confused, though it wasn't clear whether that appearance was genuine. "I meant whether she's OK," he said.

"*Oh*," Susan with exaggerated realisation, opening her mouth wide to make the sound. In other words she understood him, but didn't necessarily believe that's what he'd meant by his question.

"She's not happy," Susan said, "but she's not sure who to be pissed off with. She's going to stay put in that rather swanky hotel you took her to for the time being. She's got London to entertain her if she gets bored."

The kettle was close to boiling, the water rumbling.

"Good," David said and then realised that it wasn't necessarily good news, "I mean it's good that she's not more unhappy."

Susan seemed amused at his discomfiture. Sidelong, she gave him a fond look. She said, "She told me about your date." She turned to the kettle which had just clicked off.

David instantly registered concern. "Susan, you should know..." he began, sounding agitated. As he said it, he made some negating gesture with his hands to indicate that she might have got the wrong end of the stick. His hand bumped the edge of the tray as it overhung the worktop, rattling the cups and knocking one of them off the counter.

Susan saw David dislodge the cup. She turned and snatched it out of the air before it could shatter on the tiled floor. "David," she almost wailed, "for the millionth time, I'm teasing you. Dee told me what you guys talked about. She made you sound noble and chivalrous far beyond the bounds of credibility. But I get the message."

David was still staring in amazement at Susan's unbelievable swiftness and dexterity in rescuing the cup. He pulled himself back to the moment and realised what she was saying. A smile crept across his face. He said, "I know it's not what you want, but I can't help..." He got no further because Susan had placed one cool finger against his lips, silencing him. "Another time," she said.

They didn't speak again until they'd rejoined the Professor in the living room. Susan had found Mrs Potter's cache of shortbread biscuits, which she'd placed on a plate near David.

When each of them had their tea, the Professor spoke, "A colleague of mine told me about a wonderful new species of manager known as a facilitator." He looked from Susan to David. "Just savour the ugly newness of that word," he said with relish, addressing them both. "Seemingly, one is secretly still in charge, but without the need to take responsibility for any unpleasant outcomes and neither is one expected to actually do any of the work." He beamed at them, gauging their reaction. "In fact it's positively discouraged."

David looked confused, Susan was amused but patient, confident that the Professor was going somewhere with his remarks.

He continued, "It sounds just the thing for me. I thought I'd try it now, if you two are agreeable."

Taking their complete immobility as assent he became more serious, saying, "So what I'm thinking we need to do, before many more hours elapse, is the following: first, put the documents concerning the Marker somewhere safe. I know it goes against the spirit of facilitation, but I'd like to nominate myself for that job."

He checked for signs of dissent and then continued, "We'll also need to do something about the fact that the collection is now missing from the School of Antiquities. Before very long, someone is likely to point the finger at Susan – if for no other reason than that she's the one responsible." David glanced at Susan with alarm, but didn't speak.

The Professor went on, "Now, I'd like to volunteer to sort that one out as well; I have some influence there." He looked mildly troubled, "Oh dear, I seem to be making a hash of this facilitation business. No matter. Onward," he urged, holding a finger on high as though flourishing a standard. "Thirdly, we need to learn more about the predicament in which we are currently entangled. Many of the answers lie in the collection I believe. This being its new temporary home, I'd like to volunteer to handle that too," he looked positively disappointed as he continued, "though I suspect it rather puts the kibosh on my facilitating career."

He addressed them both as he said, "Finally, and perhaps most importantly, we need to do something about this fellow Jan and the fact that he will soon be vigorously casting about for the collection. We clearly cannot turn matters over to the usual temporal authorities, for the same reason one would not seek help from the Cats Protection League if one had cornered a wounded leopard. I think it's that last little matter that needs to occupy us now."

David cleared his throat. "I have some catching up to do," he said. "But I have to ask: Joseph, are you sure you want to get dragged into this? It's difficult enough to work out why I'm still involved and I was at least being paid to take an interest."

The Professor said, "Would it seem as if I were eluding the question if I asked Susan to set your mind at rest on that score once we're finished here? For the meantime, would you be prepared to take it on trust that I have my reasons and that I'm comfortable both that I can accept the risks and contribute to the endeavour?"

David didn't look as though he had any immediate objection. The

Professor glanced at Susan and said, "Perhaps you would tell David whichever parts of our discussion you think he would benefit from hearing."

Accepting this, David said, "OK, then." He looked from the Professor to Susan and said, "Now we are three." Then he asked, "Is there anything you two book-savvy types have learned that I need to know before I wade in with my suggestions?"

Susan and the Professor exchanged a glance. As though by telepathic consensus she began to explain the Professor's discovery of the Marker's true function and the light which it shed on Jan's motivations. She briefly touched on her own abortive foray into magic use, acknowledging that the full story was one of a list of things to tell him later. As she summarised a few of the other discussions she'd had with the Professor, the conversation began to broaden into a debate.

David cut into the amiable banter with a note of concern. He asked the other two, "Do you think Dass is really dead? Do these people die like normal folk or is he going to be coming back to haunt us?"

Susan tackled that question. "I think we've got a fairly good idea of what they're capable of. We don't know all the little nuances, but I'm pretty sure we've got the basics. And there's no coming back from the dead. The police found Dass's body. He even had a passport with him to help the identification along. I think he's gone."

That seemed to relieve some of David's concern. He moved onto his next worry. "I think it's probably difficult to feel in much danger in a place like this," he said looking up and gesturing around him at the sunny living room. "And it clearly doesn't help us if we panic. But on the other hand," he said, his voice taking on a note of urgency, "Jan could tear that door off its hinges at any second." Involuntarily, Susan glanced at the front door. "So here's another management notion." He paused. "Let's tackle the urgent stuff right now and get onto the other important things later." No one stirred. "So first: is the collection safe?"

The Professor nodded. "Would you like to know where it is?"

David said, "I don't think I need to. Not unless…" he faltered.

The Professor stepped in, diplomatically, to complete the sentence,

"Unless something happens to me."

The Professor lowered his voice. "Should you be, um, suddenly deprived of my involvement, you might wish to take a look at the particular copy of my doctoral thesis presently residing in the University Library. The last time I checked, it had not been requested since 1973. Starting on page 411 are some pencil notes – you'd be able to read the language, Susan. They hint at where I keep one or two items of value – which now includes the collection. Without that guidance, one would need to take this house down stone by stone to discover their hiding place."

David seemed about to speak, but doubt was evidently restraining him. The Professor gave him a wan smile of tissue-thin heartiness. "And I will keep my mouth shut whatever happens," he said simply – which seemed to answer David's unspoken question.

"Are there any other copies?" David asked.

"I trashed the network copy at the School, as well as their backups," Susan said, "and I brought the hard copies and the originals with me."

She went on, "There's also a digital copy on a CD," she pointed towards her bag. "I'm pretty sure I can make an encrypted copy of it, then I'll stick the unencrypted CD in the microwave."

David said, "Better write 'Dave's party mix' on it and keep it in a Discman, to be on the safe side." He sounded as though he approved of Susan's organisation.

The Professor muttered, "Just what I was going to say," evidently having no idea what David was talking about.

David glanced at him, explaining "My generation's way of hiding microfilm in with the holiday negatives."

Susan got up and fished the CD from her bag. Then she went into the kitchen and put it into the little portable stereo that sat on the window sill.

"Just for now," she said when she came back.

"OK," David said, "now how is Jan going to find us?"

There was a short pause and Susan said, "Through me. It'll be through me. He just has to figure out that the collection is missing and a bit about the circumstances and he'll know who took it." Susan added, "By the way, David, we don't think he has any special powers to help him find me, he'll have to do it the old-fashioned way."

David nodded, "So I think we need to vanish – Susan and me."

Susan said, "What, go on the run?"

"I think we had the right instinct when we headed for Brighton," he said. "We'll make for some destination that right now even we couldn't predict. Like you said, unless he's got us bugged, I don't see how he can find us."

"And then what?" Susan said.

David said, "And then, once you're safe, we take our time and make a proper plan."

CHAPTER 29

An hour after they'd decided to vanish, David and Susan were in David's car, driving. They'd agreed that one of them would come up with an initial plan and the other would modify it slightly – that way their next move would be unguessable – even to someone who knew a lot about both of them.

They acknowledged that it was a paranoid and faintly ridiculous idea, but neither of them wanted to veto it.

"OK. I've got family I never see who live south of Dublin," David said. "We get the ferry across from Holyhead, which gets us out of the country; it's the closest thing Britain's got to a back-door. The harbour and the boat are enclosed spaces with crowds, but before we get there we'll have plenty of time to double-check no one is following us." Then he added, "Sorry," as he realised how morbidly cloak-and-dagger he was sounding. Susan shrugged.

"OK," she said, "I like the ferry idea, but what's the one that goes to the southern tip of Ireland?"

"Fishguard to Rosslare," David said after a moment's thought.

"Right," Susan said, "We go that way and drive up from the South. Plus we only contact your relatives if we need something. It'll be like having local reserves we can call up if there's a problem – and in the meantime there's no risk they'll give our position away." She smiled glumly, "Now who's talking like a spy?"

"That's settled then," David said.

Susan let a couple of minutes pass and then asked him, "Why haven't you tried to talk me out of this little escapade? You made an attempt with the Professor. I mean I wouldn't listen, but you could always try."

"At this point," David said seriously, "I can't think of any way to prove to Jan that you're not involved. He'll still think you're part of this even if you and me agree you're not. If you go back to your old routine, I think he'll just, you know…" He couldn't think of a good way of finishing the sentence. "It won't get you off the hook with him," he said instead.

"Yeah," Susan said, sounding dejected, "I figured it was something like that."

"We could just give him the collection," David said suddenly, "that would probably do it."

The suggestion hung in the air, but neither of them seemed to want to comment on it.

A minute passed and Susan said, "I'll see about encrypting that CD. I downloaded some software that says it'll encode every block of data on a disk, I'm just not sure how to use it yet."

She hauled her bag over from the back seat and set her iBook up on her lap. For the next hour, she muttered to herself until, at last, she announced success.

"Wanna know what the secret password is?" she asked.

"OK," David said.

"It's Fuzzbundle Milton, all one word, with the zees as sevens and the 'o' as a zero," she said.

"Any particular reason?" David asked.

"Oh, it was my cat's name," Susan explained, "Though Mom refused to pay for all the letters to be engraved on her name tag, so she was just Fuzz to strangers." Susan looked off into the distance.

David turned to smile softly at Susan, saying nothing.

A moment later, Susan said, "What shall we do with this?" She held up the old, unencrypted CD.

"Have you got a plastic bag?" David asked.

Susan fished out the bag from the office-supplies shop where she'd bought blank disks and a phone charger. Stealing glances away from the motorway traffic, David took the CD from her, stuck his hand in the bag and folded the disk in two. It shattered with a snap into half a dozen jagged pieces and lots of smaller fragments.

"I don't know why," Susan said, "but I thought a CD-ROM would fold up."

"Maybe you're thinking of credit cards," David said.

Susan looked at the pieces in the bag. "You really would need to be very dedicated to put that back together." She held up one of the tiniest pieces, like a speck of glitter on her fingertip and waved it under David's nose. "Fiddly," she said, relishing the word.

She pulled some of the metallic backing away from the larger fragments, leaving clear plastic. Then she slapped her hands together to brush off the scraps of foil.

"And check this out," she said, showing him the new, encrypted disk. With a permanent marker, she'd written 'Rap compilation' on it and drawn some stars. "I figure if there's one thing a ninety-year-old guy won't be able to handle it's rap."

"Nice," said David, amused, "Good thinking." Then he said, "And it'll work even better if you encrypt a load of old rubbish and write 'Teracus Collection' on it, nice and neatly. In films, people always stop searching the instant they find something promising. So unless Hollywood have got so desperate for plot lines that they've started making things up, we'll be fine."

They both smiled. Once again a silence opened up, David concentrating on driving, Susan pondering.

Susan said after a while, "You know why I like the idea of a ferry crossing?"

"Because sorcerers can't cross open water?" David joked.

"Oh, hey, you know I think I get that now. I bet they don't like to."

She obviously wanted to share her theory, so David said, "Yeah?" encouragingly.

She launched into it, saying, "So, we know they can make this shield around them that will stop almost anything, even bullets I'm pretty sure. But what if you caught them on a boat and just sank it? There's nothing they could do. They'd drown just like anyone else. On land, an army might not be enough to stop them; at sea, one flaming arrow might be all you need."

David looked impressed.

"Anyway," Susan said, "that wasn't the reason I had in mind." She kept her voice neutral as she said, "I want to use the headband again."

Then she told David about her attempt to move the silver letter opener and her panic when she realised it might act like a beacon bringing her to the attention of Jan – and whoever else was out there. She said, "A few hours at sea is perfect. I mean what are the chances that the magical master race travel by car ferry? Same way I don't figure Dass owned a caravan." She grinned.

David looked over at her, taking in the grin. "You seem almost perky about this trip," David said, curious.

Susan grunted. "Well, I don't much like the alternatives. And I'm going through one of those dream-like periods where imminent death by supernatural means just doesn't seem like something I can get very worked up about. Real life doesn't feel very real at the moment. Maybe I'm just hungry." She looked sideways at the passing countryside, "You know what was really weird? I had a great time staying at the Professor's – in spite of everything. Having too many worries is almost like having none at all."

David said nothing for a while and then picked up an earlier thread. He said, "You know sorcery is still one of the so-called sins of the flesh according to the Catholic Church. Funny that they'd still include that in with licentiousness and gluttony."

For the next few hours, they chatted on and off. Sometimes Susan would tell David about something she'd read in the collection or discussed with the Professor; at other times they'd talk about inconsequential things, like wondering about the species of the birds they saw fanning their wings, hovering over the motorway's grass verges, ready to plunge down on whatever was scurrying below.

As they talked about birds of prey, David's attention drifted away. Seeing that she was losing his interest, Susan abandoned what she was saying and asked, "What's up?"

David returned to the moment, looking self-conscious and asking sheepishly, "How did Jan get down from that office window? It's not... He couldn't fly could he?"

Susan gave a polite smile, not laughing at him, acknowledging that it might *sound* ridiculous but it wasn't. She said, "I don't think so. There's no mention of any flying. Adepts can generate a sort of cushioning force that will hold part of their weight. So they can jump higher than normal people and a big drop will seem like a small one to them – but the force doesn't seem to be strong enough to lift them all by itself. They do seem to be able to generate something more powerful, but it's not a push, it's more like hitting something with a hammer. It's not the sort of thing you'd try to use on yourself."

David nodded, apparently relieved, "My friend Banjo said their powers sounded like the ultimate Swiss Army knife."

Susan considered this, finding that she agreed, "I guess they do. Or maybe like a set of outdoor gear that you don't have to lug around." She counted points off on her fingers, "There's a shield, there's something that seems to heat or cool, there's a means of getting down from a height, there's a first aid kit and there's a hammer." She looked suddenly thoughtful, "God, where do you think it comes from? Do you suppose anyone has ever tried to find out the source of these powers? There's nothing in the collection. And there's no way it's just a natural part of physics." She looked up at David to check, "Is there?" she asked.

David looked uncertain, "I don't see how. It's not the abilities themselves; they're exactly the sorts of things we used to do in physics class, but I don't believe the human brain would just happen to evolve as a remote control for the forces of nature." He shrugged, his train of thought losing momentum, "But can you even apply logic to something like this? I mean ordinary logic would tell you that the whole thing is impossible."

"Anyway," he said after a moment, "that list of powers is *it* you reckon? No unpleasant surprises?"

Susan said, "Too many of the documents agree – plus they fit with what we've seen. I think we've got the full list. Only the crazy mystics can do more and it sounds like no one's ever had any luck involving one of those guys in anything worldly – like chasing us, for instance."

David nodded, but made no reply, and once again they separated into their own private inner worlds, leaving the conversation to pass through another of its dry spells, dormant until some new idea occurred to one of them.

At one point, in the midst of a long silent stretch, David glanced over and saw tears running down Susan's face. She showed no other signs of distress and he said nothing. Ten minutes later, the tears were gone and she seemed in as good a mood as ever, volunteering her views about US freeways and how much better the diners were.

They stopped for petrol and sandwiches and then Susan settled down to doze through most of their trip across Wales. She finally woke up just as they arrived at the harbour. David was pulling in to buy tickets. A wide, low, glass-and-concrete building was directly in front of them as David edged into one of a long line of angled parking bays.

"Won't be long," he said. "Honk if you want me," he said cheerfully, indicating the horn control. Then he slipped off his seat belt and jumped out of the car.

From the passenger seat, Susan looked around her as David ran into the nearby building. It was early evening. The sun had already set and the wind had picked up. A few gulls were up late, fooling around in the unpredictable gusts.

A vast concrete apron extended behind them. Arcane paint marks, lighting poles, buried rails and snaking lines of cars decorated the immense expanse. Seemingly incongruous, the monstrous bulk of a ship lay behind it all, as though someone had built the vessel on the edge of a car park as some sort of tourist attraction. There was no sense of being near the sea.

When David came back, he jumped into the car quickly, the chill air buffeting the interior for the second or two that the door was open. He sniffed, the cold air having made his nose run. Susan had been sitting with her coat pulled over her, legs curled sideways in her seat. She sat up now to listen to him.

"Well," David said, "Our timing's spot on. The boats are running spectacularly late. The afternoon sailing hasn't left yet because the sea was too rough. They're loading it up now, though, and I got us one of the last three cabins."

He started the engine and pulled out of the parking bay to join the end of one of the enormous queues. Marshals, swaddled against the weather, waved and gestured, like some Eskimo dance troupe, lining the cars up as they approached the ship, acting according to some plan not obvious to the casual observer.

It took nearly an hour before David and Susan had left the Saab behind them among the tightly packed array of vehicles filling the cramped, permanent twilight of the car deck. They joined the throng, all climbing narrow metal staircases towards the well-lit passenger decks.

A few minutes later they'd left the mob behind them and found their cramped but cosy cabin. David shut the door behind them and then crossed the room to slump down on one of the two narrow beds. He rose again, momentarily, to pull off his boots and then stretched out once more, fully clothed, on the right-hand bunk.

Distant sounds and a vague sensation of shifting weight suggested that they'd got underway.

"You look beat," Susan said, turning out the main overhead light and switching on a small vanity light above a mirror. The tiny bulb was now the room's only illumination.

"I just need to close my eyes for a few minutes," he said in the gloom, his eyes already shut.

"Move over," she told him, before slipping onto the narrow bunk next to him, her shoulders pressing back against his chest until they were both arranged comfortably. He draped the flap of his heavy jacket over her, letting his arm rest along her side, his palm on her hip. After a minute she took his left hand, drew it under the coat and placed it tightly over her breast, her hand on top of his. "Sleep," she said.

* * *

When David woke up, he was alone on the bunk. Susan was sitting cross-legged on the floor, her back to him. Her head was dipped and in the dim light he couldn't quite see what she was doing. She still wore her jeans, but she had shed her fleecy top, stripping down to a white camisole and sports bra.

David turned around on the bunk, wriggling closer, moving around so that the light from the mirror's tiny lamp struck the gold headband Susan was wearing and picked out the drops of perspiration creeping down her face.

Looking at her uncovered shoulders, he could see the flare and tuck of compact muscles at the tops of each arm, the grooved bunching beneath the skin, as her posture shifted slightly. If Dee had the willowy proportions of a dancer, it was Susan who had a dancer's extraordinary muscle tone. And while her neat, delineated muscles hardly made her bulky, she would never look vulnerable or slight as Dee sometimes did.

He slid a little further down the bed until he could see over her shoulder.

She had set a little plastic disk on the floor just in front of her – a red, patterned circle a few finger-widths across, covered with a hard, transparent lid.

He looked closer. It was a cheap travel game, a little covered maze through which a tiny metal ball could be made to advance – if the disc were held in a steady hand and tilted skilfully enough.

As he watched, a bead of perspiration detached itself from Susan's hairline and ran down between her shoulder blades, following the smooth channel of her spine.

Pulling his eyes away from her damp skin, he looked back over her shoulder towards the plastic game.

The silver ball was making its way through the maze.

Susan's hands were folded in her lap and the game sat level on the cabin's motionless floor, in its own little circle of space, untouched. Nevertheless, the ball continued to make its way through the red plastic labyrinth of the puzzle.

He could hear Susan breathing – deeply and with effort.

Susan caught sight of David out of the corner of her eye and simultaneously the ball stopped moving. "Takes a lot of concentration," she said, through clamped teeth. Now the ball was stuck, despite her obvious effort. "Nah, I've lost it," she gasped, letting out her breath. She looked away from the puzzle and up at him.

"That's incredible," he said, looking at her with wonder.

"Yeah, I'm hoping to challenge Jan to a game of pinball in a couple of years time," she said, sarcastically.

She unfastened the top of a water bottle and took a long drink. When she'd finished gulping, she said, "Want some?" holding the bottle out to David.

"Thanks," he said, sitting back on the bunk and drinking.

"Man, it's sweaty work," she said, wiping her wet forehead with her hand. She looked up and caught David glancing at the shape her damp camisole made as it clung to her.

"You like?" she said playfully, in some mock-Eastern accent, striking a little pose with her hands. She raised an eyebrow suggestively, the corners of her mouth twitching up in amusement.

David laughed and nearly choked on the water he was trying to swallow. He coughed a couple of times, still amused. Susan rose gracefully to her feet.

Without warning, she moved to the bed and placed a hand on his shoulder. Before David realised what she was doing, she leaned down and pressed her mouth, still wet from the spring water, against his. She kissed him passionately for a couple of seconds, opening her lips and brushing the back of his neck lightly with her fingers. Then she broke away, looking fiercely elated and a little out of breath.

"That feels better, doesn't it?" she said, challengingly, looking him in the eye.

David seemed slightly stunned. "Did I miss something? Is magic some sort of aphrodisiac?" he asked, then added, "Not that I'm complaining. You can do that whenever you want." He stressed the last three words.

Susan smiled and considered her answer. "You know it might even be kind of a turn-on, I'll see how I feel next time," she replied.

Then she looked at him and said, "That," meaning the kiss, "was about something else, though." Then she said dreamily, "After all, we might be dead tomorrow." She spoke absent-mindedly as though she were reminiscing.

"Oh," David said, sounding deflated. "I can see how that thought would make you frisky," he said, meaning the opposite.

"You know what I mean," Susan said, focussing on him. "Why worry about the long-term stuff? It all seems a bit academic, right now. Why not take a few chances?"

"I suppose," David said, not sure whether to feel slightly insulted or not.

He sat up and swung his feet onto the floor. Then he reached for one of his boots.

It slid out of his reach.

He glanced sharply at Susan. A look of painful concentration had tightened her features and pulled her mouth open. The intensity slid away swiftly as she relaxed and she said, a little apologetically, "I just wanted to see if I could."

"You're starting to scare me," he said, half joking.

He pulled on his boots as she stretched. She was also working her jaw as though realising her teeth had been clenched together for too long.

There was a change in the sense of the boat's motion. "I think we're coming in to dock," Susan said, taking off the headband. She gave him a flirty peck on the cheek and ducked into the room's tiny bathroom, turning on the shower. "I'll just be a minute," she told him.

He rummaged in his pockets, pulling out various papers as she thumped about on the other side of the thin bulkhead. The muted patter of the shower sounded like heavy rain on a metal roof.

When she emerged, Susan was wearing the same clothes, but her drying hair was kinked and full and rather wild. "We're going to need to go clothes shopping again soon," she said, "else anyone with a sense of smell will know where I am."

She sat on the unused bunk opposite David, who was studying a free map he'd picked up when he bought the tickets. "Be quite a nice drive, if it wasn't the middle of the night," he said.

A beeping noise caught their attention. It took Susan a moment to realise it was her phone. She retrieved it from her bag and saw the voicemail symbol. "Hmm," she said thoughtfully and set about playing the message.

She had only listened to a couple of seconds of it when she snatched the phone from her ear, hit the button to play the recording from the beginning and plonked down beside David. She held the phone between them, their heads together, the tinny speaker loud enough that they could both hear the message.

The phone company's virtual-woman finished her preamble about the timing of the recording, then a man's voice spoke, his accent like an RAF captain from an old war film troubled by the turn the fighting was taking.

"I should think you can guess who this is," the voice began, pleasantly, but without enthusiasm.

Then, as though continuing a previous conversation, he said, "People talk about violence as though it were all much of a muchness. But surely, that makes a mockery of life. Of course there's opposition – given that we all want different things – and naturally that opposition can turn nasty. But it seems to me that there's a world of difference between honest combat and the idea of simply inflicting damage on a helpless prisoner."

A queasy charm warmed his voice now – charm of the kind found in chummy voice-overs for commercials selling funeral insurance. "Whereas torture," the voice announced, "is simply the province of anyone with a strong stomach and access to a toolbox." He sounded slightly put out, "No, it's a horrible thought, it really is – I can't see any satisfaction in something like that." He sighed and then the sigh turned to a drawn-out chuckle, "Listen to me go on – as though I hadn't butchered my way across half a continent." He sighed again, amused, and then cleared his throat, reluctantly getting down to business, "Anyway, what I called for was this: if you don't want your sister back one charred strip at a time, the thing to do is bring me the documents I want."

He finished amiably, "Call me on her portable phone at any time. I'm looking after it for her," he added.

Neither David nor Susan moved or spoke as the automated voice reeled off the various options for storing or deleting the message. The system was listing a second set of options it evidently reserved for those not tempted by the standard menu when Susan emerged from her clouded reverie to end the call.

CHAPTER 30

EARLY THE NEXT MORNING
MONDAY 28TH APRIL

The answerphone message shattered Susan's fey good humour. With her own life in danger, she had settled into some strategy for coping that allowed her to function almost normally. She had seemed to register the danger she was in without being paralysed by it. But the news of Dee's kidnapping pierced her composure, coming at her from a direction she was defenceless against.

Though she avoided many of the signs of panic – she wasn't shouting or crying – still, her focus had somehow been dislodged from the present, shifting away from her immediate surroundings to some inner purgatory. When David spoke to her, it was as though he were attempting, unsuccessfully, to break into another conversation, one that only she was hearing.

Her replies to his questions were sluggish and vague. She didn't look him in the eye or take note of his movements as he fidgeted around their tiny cabin.

At last, David stood and picked up his jacket, saying to her, "Stay here." She was sitting, hands in her lap, eyes distant, turned away from him on the opposite bunk. Had she heard him?

He came to stand above her and said, "I'm going to go and arrange for us to head straight back to England. It might take a while and I'll have to move the car." Her attitude didn't alter. He tried to get some sense that he had her attention by crouching in front of her, touching her hand, "So stay here," he said again with gentle emphasis. Her eyes wandered over him, not settling. She made some move of her head that might have been a nod or an indication that he should go. She didn't say anything, but it appeared that she was at least registering his words.

Leaving her caught up in the knot of her own thoughts, David left the cabin and fought his way down through the crush of passengers who were readying themselves to disembark. More than once he had to duck under a carelessly out-flung arm or ease his way sideways through a family absorbed in a corridor-wide squabble. The lights of the Irish harbour were sliding glacially past the dark, rain-beaten windows as he found the information desk.

The desk's harassed-looking steward was attempting to pacify a fierce woman passenger with flaming cheeks who was berating him in some shrill, contemptuous register. She stormed away as David arrived, leaving the steward twitching with defensiveness and unspent adrenaline.

Taking in the scene, and sizing up the steward's mood, David allowed his hurried stride to evaporate into a troubled hesitancy as he approached the desk. He composed his features in an approximation of Susan's distressed blankness.

When he stood in front of the fuming steward, he said in a halting monotone of helplessness, "I don't know what to do. Something awful has happened. I've just had a phone call. We need to get back to England." He looked down at his hands, never meeting the steward's eyes, copying Susan's attitude of shock.

The combination of David's tough-looking bulk and his unguarded, abject demeanour left a vacuum of authority into which the steward gladly stepped. He mustered a grave little smile and said calmly, authoritatively, "Tell me what's happened, sir. I'm sure we'll be able to work something out."

David made a struggle of telling his story, being scrupulously economical with the details, leaving Dee's predicament unspecified but open to interpretation as some sort of medical emergency. Having gleaned what he could, the steward took him to see the captain.

The conversation with the captain seemed to go more smoothly if David said little, limiting his contribution to one or two wild looks, and allowed the steward to intercede for him. The captain was as sure-handed and helpful when confronted with David's frayed nerves as the steward had been.

Having ascertained that David was at least composed enough to drive a car, the captain arranged that when David drove out of the hold he would be diverted from the normal exit route. He would instead wait in a reserved area adjacent to the ramp for a few minutes and then be allowed back onto the boat, the first car aboard for the return journey.

It took nearly an hour before everything was arranged for their trip back to Britain, the car had been moved and David could return to the cabin.

When he opened the door he saw that Susan seemed to have emerged from her morbid daydream. She appeared once again connected to her surroundings, looking up instantly, her face unreadable, as he entered the cabin.

He told her with an embarrassed look, "Well, I've just finished doing my 'Lassie with a bad paw' imitation. Thank god it seems to have worked. The Captain's trying to get back on schedule, so we should be underway in another hour. No way to get us back faster than that."

Susan nodded. She was wedged into the corner, on the bunk they'd shared, a pillow propped behind her, a pad and pen in her hands.

She returned her gaze to the pad and scribbled something, her concentration absorbed by the notes she was making.

David came to crouch next to her, kneeling by the bunk. He reached out and took her hand, lifting it gently away from the pad, wrapping his fingers around hers. She looked up slowly, her clear, blank eyes meeting his serious, examining gaze.

He told her, "I don't know what to say." He continued to hold her hand, her cool eyes resting on his as he searched her face, trying to read her.

He spoke again, his tone suddenly passionate as though some emotion had bubbled up inside him that he couldn't contain, "Don't worry, Susan.

Please don't worry. I'll find a way to get Dee back safely, I promise you I will. I don't care what I have to do. Just trust me; I'll find a way."

Susan's calmness, serene and almost eerie as it was, continued for a second or two after he finished speaking and then it began to come apart. A flush crept into her cheeks and the evenness of her smooth brow tightened into a lost-looking frown. As her expressionless poise disintegrated, her shoulders began to sag.

She took her hand out from within his grasp and laid her palm on top of his hand. She seemed choked with emotion.

"What?" he asked, sensing something, "What did I say?"

She reached up to stroke the back of her hand gently down his cheek. Her touch was delicate, full of care and somehow tragic. She said, "I know you would, David. I know you'd do your very best to save Dee and to save me – but I can't agree to that. I know you only want what's best for us, but do you see, I'll never forgive myself if I let you take over? I can't let go of this. I know what to do and you have to help me do it." Now she searched his eyes, which were beginning to cloud with confusion as he processed her words.

She said, "I've got a plan."

* * *

Ten minutes later they were sipping bitter coffee from white polystyrene cups. David had found someone to give them coffee and doughnuts from the staff restaurant. He had used the interruption to conceal the uncomfortable surprise and the sting of rejection written on his face at the way Susan had responded to his offer of help. She could see that he wanted to justify himself, to explain that he wasn't trying to take over, that she was doing him an injustice. But he didn't.

Susan watched him stifle the impulse to pull away from her, to withdraw. As he realised that Susan considered his guidance a luxury they couldn't afford, his hurt was evident in his face. And Susan's fond gaze almost gave way to tears as she saw him suppress his wounded pride. He had looked taken aback, almost affronted, as she spoke, as he felt their relationship shift, but she could see him willing that away, replacing it with the determined, receptive look she could see now in his eyes. It was obvious that he'd pushed past his instinctive, irritated reaction and accepted her lead.

He had come to sit on the edge of the bunk next to her, handing over one of the coffee cups, and asked, "So what's the plan?" his voice genuine, supportive.

She reached out, a trembling smile on her lips and touched his lower lip with the side of her thumb, gently. He looked bemused, but didn't question. She said, "One day I'll tell you why those words mean more to me than anything."

Then she nodded, as though settling something she had been inwardly debating, and addressed herself to his question.

"A flag of truce," she said. "I was trying to think of somewhere neutral we could meet – somewhere safe for an exchange. I was wracking my brains for something, anything, that an adept would respect enough to stop him double-crossing us."

He asked, "What did you come up with?"

"Nothing," she replied, "Nothing short of open warfare seems to deter them – the prospect of a fight big enough that the world would notice. So I decided to use that." She took a sip of her coffee and said, "I decided we needed an environment where Jan would have to deal with hundreds of people if he tried anything."

She tapped her pad, "I made a list of our requirements. We need somewhere very controlled, somewhere with crowds of people, somewhere with an escape route for us, a really good one – if possible, somewhere with dozens of heavily armed guards. Granted, that wouldn't stop him, but it would make life pretty difficult and hopefully give us a chance to get away. And ideally we want somewhere he couldn't bring tribute to, somewhere with metal detectors. You following me? This giving you any ideas?"

He shrugged. "A prison?" he suggested, unsure.

"An airport," she said, stressing the word. "Sure, Jan could fight his way past the armed police, but imagine the chaos. He'd never be able to control an environment like that. And he'll have to come through the metal detectors. We tell him no luggage and then we loiter near the entrance to see if he sets off the alarms as he comes through."

David said, "And what if he does? We can't go anywhere. They won't stop him carrying a gold band and a couple of bracelets with him; they won't think anything of it. Then he's free to come and find us."

Susan said, "Not if we figure out some way of destroying the collection before he can get to us, and we make sure he knows about it."

She looked down at her pad. At some point, while David had been out of the cabin, a single tear must have struck the paper. Now there was a dried wrinkle in the smooth paper where the droplet had obliterated part of a line of writing.

Susan's expression showed that some misplaced detail was still pricking her. "What's it called?" she said to herself, pressing a knuckle under the point of her chin. She looked up at David and explained, "A lot of the work I do is with archives. Storing documents properly and knowing a bit about the various kinds of paper is part of the job. I had a presentation from some guys once about some indestructible, acid-free paper they'd invented for use in archives. While they were there, I remember them telling me that they also sold some other stuff," she suddenly looked elated, "MDP, that was it! It dissolves in water very quickly – instantly, according to the brochure. It's kind of a novelty thing, like you could wrap bath salts in it and just throw a packet of it into your tub, no need to open it first."

David was wondering if he was following her, "So we'd print a copy of the collection on that stuff? Threaten to get it wet if anyone rushes us?"

Susan nodded, "Exactly. We can't very well set light to anything in the middle of a departure lounge and if we could it wouldn't be quick enough. But imagine we put the papers in a clear carrier bag, so he can see them, and hold an open bottle of Evian ready. It doesn't really look suspicious, but we only need a fraction of a second to destroy everything."

David was gradually getting up to speed. "So where do we get this paper?" he asked.

She gave him a pitying look and said, "We don't. All we do is tell Jan about it. He can easily verify it exists. I'll just print off some Pliny, or something, on regular paper, nice small print and maybe book-end it with some irrelevant bits of the real collection. It'll look fine until he gets a chance to study it, and thinking it's water-soluble should keep him honest."

David looked slightly shocked. "You're not going to give him the collection then? I just thought you'd... that you wouldn't want to risk..." he didn't finish that thought.

Susan said patiently, "The thing about this is that if we set it up right, so we can get away safely and he can't touch us, it works equally well whether we cheat him or not."

David didn't look convinced. Susan explained, "Let me put it another way. If we're honest with him, it doesn't guarantee he won't just kill us. And if we set it up so he *can't* just kill us, we might as well double-cross him." A fierce light twinkled in her eye as she declared, "There's no way I'm handing that bastard another century of life."

David was beginning to look horrified, "And what then, once we've double-crossed him? He's just going to come tearing after us as soon as he discovers he's been tricked."

Susan refused to be rattled. She said, "Well, I'm just thinking this through, I guess it's not set in stone, but I was assuming we'd make a run for it. The beauty of doing this in a departure lounge is that we book ourselves on one flight, he books himself on another – neither of us know where the other one's going – and assuming we don't accidentally pick the same destination, the next time we're out in the open again we could be anywhere. He won't know whether we got on a flight to China, Iceland or Ghana. I've already got somewhere in mind to stash Dee for a little while. I just have to persuade my dad to take my mom on one of his wilderness camping trips. You'd need to do the same for your family, of course."

She looked up expectantly at him and saw doubt written across his face. "Maybe it's easier for me," she said, "I'm not likely to be continuing my post-doc knowing what I know and I'm just a visitor to England – I don't have roots here. But there can't be too many people who could be used as leverage against you, can there?"

While she'd been speaking, David had been looking at her with growing impatience; now he threw up his hands, "Susan, this is insane. We can't go on the run, hide up a mountain somewhere. We can't just flee to the other side of the world. There must be another way."

She let him consider it himself for a little while and then said, "Either we give him what he wants, or we kill him or we run. You tell me what our other options are?" She looked him in the eye and said, "You think we should help him? Is that what you think?"

He looked awkward, far from convinced, but unable to think of an objection. She continued, "Think what he'd do with another hundred years. Trust me, he's not about to start doing charity work. We're the only thing standing in his way. If we help him, how are you going to feel, going back to your job, thinking about this for the next fifty years, knowing he's out there? That's even assuming he doesn't come after us. Face it: our old lives are over however this ends up." Her passion shifted to something like rage as she said, "God knows what he's done to Dee. He's not getting any help from me."

They sat in silence for a few seconds. Susan was breathing hard. She'd stirred up her adrenaline giving that speech and it had brought an angry flush to her neck and face.

David finished thinking it through. He gave Susan a lopsided and unhappy grin. He said, "One of these days I'm going to stop underestimating you, I really am." He nodded several times, jutting out his lower lip, "You're right – about all of it. You're absolutely right."

She leaned over to squeeze his shoulder, beginning to smile uncertainly back at him. He lifted her hand from his arm, captured it in both of his, held it to his lips and kissed it. "I would have got there soon enough, you know," he said, half joking.

"Sure," she said, nodding slowly, her smile growing warmer, "sure."

He still held her hand between his. He asked, "So now we've agreed that we're totally buggered whatever we do, what's next?"

Gently disengaging from him, she put her pad down and swung her legs onto the floor. "Breakfast, of course," she said, "We've got work to do."

CHAPTER 31

LATER THAT MORNING
MONDAY 28TH APRIL

S usan turned off the radio, which had only been a murmur anyway.
"If the last hundred years have taught him anything about people," she said, "I guarantee it's that they're afraid of him."

David took this in. "It still won't hurt to sell it a little," he said. "The dissolving paper thing is a bit too creative. And then insisting on an airport, it's too much. We sound like we're planning, like we're in control." He considered for a second. "I think you're right that he won't expect anyone to stand up to him, but we can't afford to make him suspicious." He drummed his fingers on the steering wheel. "Maybe we can make it sound like we chose the airport because we want to get rid of him. Tell him we want him to get straight on a plane and not bother us any more. Psychologically that sounds more like something a victim would say – it sounds like fear is doing most of our thinking."

They were back in the car, retracing the path they'd taken across Wales the previous day. The mid-morning sun was well and truly hidden behind the low cloud which hung over the fields to either side of the motorway.

"I like it," Susan said. Then she smiled. "You're really getting the hang of thinking like a loser. First your little wounded Lassie thing on the boat, now this."

"The Lassie thing was a new low," he said, "but I was thinking about helping you as I did it. See the effect you're having on me?"

"You realised it would work though," she said, "they might have told us to make a booking like everyone else."

David nodded formally, in lieu of taking a bow, and said, "Office politics – the great teacher. Until fairly recently, I always seemed to be the most junior person in any meeting. I've found you have to create an environment in which someone can see themselves saying 'yes'. A lot of times they won't agree if it feels like you're getting the best of them. Letting someone play the hero or the bully is often the key."

Susan looked impressed but there was comical distaste in her expression too. "Swear to only use your powers for good," she said, seriously.

David gave her a suspicious look. "What? You don't manipulate people? At all?"

Susan made a face, "No, I mainly just hammer away at them, being all earnest. The manipulation only comes in afterwards when I try to patch up the damage I've done and keep them talking to me."

David puckered his lips, weighing her words and then announced, "That's sort of admirable, not trying to control people. It's a scruple I don't think I can afford, but it's sort of noble. Like tapping someone on the shoulder before you take a swing at them." He added, "You wouldn't catch me doing that."

Susan snorted, amused in a disapproving sort of way.

David looked troubled as something new occurred to him. He said, "I still think we've got a hole in our plan. I don't think we've cracked the bit where we get Dee safely away afterwards. If she arrives in that departure lounge with Jan it means she'll have checked in with him – and that means he'll know her destination. We could buy her a ticket and leave it at the airport for her to pick up, but he's just going to be standing next to her. Once he knows where she's going, he can just tag along if he wants." He glanced over at her, "I wonder how many flights have sold all their first class or business class seats by check-in time? Not that many, I reckon.

He could just buy a last-minute seat on her flight and grab her again if he needed to. We wouldn't have achieved anything with all the cloak and dagger business."

Susan shoved him gently on the arm, "You're such a worrier; have a little faith," she said. She seemed amused.

"Susan," he said, "this is serious." As soon as he'd spoken, he knew he'd said the wrong thing.

Her face clouded over. "I know it's serious," she said, anger and irritation in her voice.

"Sorry, sorry," he said, "Of course you do. Of course."

She calmed herself and a few seconds later said, "I think the chances that Jan picked up Dee's passport are pretty slim. I mean why would he? So we buy three tickets for our flight. I get myself a black wig and make myself up to look like Dee. Then I check in as her, with all her luggage. Next, I ditch the wig, change my clothes, wait a half an hour and join a different check-in line, where I check-in as me. If anyone does recognise me the second time I can always say we're twins – the airline won't have Dee's date of birth, right? Given that we *are* sisters, I don't see how we're going to get caught out."

David was processing this. "But Jan also buys a ticket for Dee?" he asked.

"Right," Susan said, "You leave her passport with information once I'm done with it – you tell them you found it – and then Dee picks it up when she gets there – she just says she dropped it. That way Dee can be simultaneously checked in on two flights, only one of which Jan knows about. Her boarding card for the first flight gets her into the departure lounge, but then we switch to the second ticket once we've got her away from him."

David's expression was still pensive. "I'm just thinking about that second ticket. You pretend to be Dee in order to check in, but then that ticket goes in your pocket until it's time to get on the plane. That ticket never gets seen by security or passport control or any of those guys. So that ticket is skipping several steps. Will they let her on the flight if they've no record of her coming through departures?"

Susan shrugged, "I don't think they check that stuff. But even if they do, what are they going to accuse her of? We've got the real Dee, with her passport and ticket, ready to get on a flight. They can suspect her of teleporting into the departure lounge, but I think they still have to let her on the plane. They'll assume security screwed up."

David was nodding, looking tentatively convinced. "It works, doesn't it? And what about the other ticket, the one Jan buys? Won't that cause problems when Dee doesn't show up for that flight?"

Susan said, "Well, since there's no luggage in the hold, they'll just take off without her eventually. Maybe it'll cause some trouble down the line if they investigate, but I don't think they'll ever figure out what happened. No smuggler or terrorist is going to pull this trick because it doesn't really achieve anything. We booked someone on two flights and only used one of them. It's hardly worth making a fuss over."

"Yeah," David said, looking like he was finally convinced, "Yeah. I get it." He gave her a quick smile, "So where do you want to fly to?"

Susan looked out of the side window at the damp clouds brushing the tops of the hills, the misty air heavy with drizzle, soaking every part of the green land. "Somewhere warm," she said, then added, "with regular flights to the US so we can get Dee safely away."

They drove in silence for several minutes before Susan said cautiously, "Listen David, I want to do a little more practice."

David looked curious. "You mean…?" He flicked his eyes towards her bag on the back seat, where the headband and bracelets were stored.

Susan nodded. "Yeah." She volunteered, "I figure we're going eighty miles an hour, there's plenty of other cars on the road, so we're anonymous. If some adept registers me, what can he do about it? We're travelling better than a mile a minute. We'll be out of his territory before he knows what's happening. Plus, who lives right by the motorway? Like I say, I don't picture these guys slumming it."

David wasn't really following her argument; he simply waited for her to stop talking so that he could speak. He said, "This makes me very uneasy. You were messing about with that stuff on the way out *and* on the way back. Why do you need to do it again so soon?"

Susan glanced up at his expression, "What, you think this is like a drug or something?"

David was slightly agitated, "I don't know what it's like. But I'll tell you this: I don't think it's good for you. I'd like to believe there are some adepts out there who fight on the side of the angels, but realistically I doubt it. According to the stuff you've read, they're a pack of power-mad psychopaths." He looked at her, "Aren't they?"

Susan conceded, "But it's not the magic that makes them like that." She looked defensive as she realised how weak that sounded. "I really don't think it's the magic, David, I think it's who they are. Any power is like that. How many big-shot politicians do you think are still good people doing good work? Any power can corrupt you if you love it enough. But I don't. I don't want that sort of power at all."

David sounded almost pleading as he said, "Then why do you want to use that thing again? Why not leave it alone? If it's not addictive?"

Susan took a deep breath and spoke in a calmer voice, "Because I don't have time. Jan's had a hundred years and I've got a few days." She twisted round to face him. "Magic is the only thing we've got that might possibly slow him down, push him off course, surprise him a little. When he's got that power there's nothing you've learnt in your martial arts classes that could make him even break his stride. He could literally kill you with a wave of his hand and keep going. It wouldn't make any difference if you had a knife or a gun or half a dozen friends with you. He'd go right through you. This is the only thing that might slow him down."

An unpleasant thought was dawning on David. "You mean you'd bring your gold bands to the airport with you? You'd take him on?"

Susan gave nothing away in her expression. "If needs be," she said carefully, "I don't plan to. But if things go wrong, I need something that I can throw at him to buy a little bit of time."

David said, "You mean so that Dee and I can get away while you fight him?"

Neutrally, Susan acknowledged, "Just in case. In case it goes wrong. We need something."

Susan's words hung in the air for a minute and then she tried to lighten the mood. "What's that cheesy line? If you don't have a back-up plan then you don't have a plan."

David made an effort to smile despite his grim expression. He said, "I'm not happy about this, Susan."

"No," Susan said patiently, "I don't suppose you are."

Instead of reaching for her bag, Susan sat still. Minutes passed.

When Susan spoke again, enough time had passed that the mood between them had distilled into something else. "Do you ever get a phrase stuck in your head?" she asked distantly. "I've got one that keeps playing over and over at the moment."

David didn't speak, wondering whether Susan would go on. She did. "My Dad had an older brother. He's dead now. He was in Europe during the war – in France I think. He'd visit us sometimes when we were little kids." Susan's voice was dreamy, reminiscing, "He had this thing he said that became like a catchphrase with Dee and me for a while. He'd tell us what he was up to or sometimes he'd even tell us about the war, usually some harmless little thing. Then he'd say, 'Out of my depth and still functioning'. I can picture him saying it with a grin. Dee and I would copy it because it sounded so grown-up, like a joke we didn't understand. Out of my depth and still functioning."

She shook herself, trying to shrug it off and said, "That was a creepy kind of a Hallmark moment, wasn't it?" She avoided David's gaze for a moment.

David had been watching her closely as she spoke, stealing as much time away from the road as he could. Some aspect of her story had clearly touched him. Now he wanted to reciprocate, to tell her something, but he was struggling. "You…" he said and tried again, "You're just…" He had another go, "When I think of you I…"

And then instead of being serious they were both laughing. Susan said, "Eloquently put. You know, a lot of guys have trouble articulating their feelings, but you're just able to tap into this amazing ability to express yourself; I suppose you'd call it a gift."

"Ha ha," David said, in a mocking voice. "It's not easy. There aren't any bloke words for what I was trying to say." He was still laughing and looking self-conscious at the same time. "Anyway, you've ruined it now with your mickey-taking. That was my one attempt to reach out. I'll probably be emotionally closed off for life now."

Susan undid her seat-belt and twisted round so that she could reach over onto the back seat. Her fingertips were extended towards the strap of her bag. As she stretched, she needed to lean against David's shoulder. It brought her close enough that she could murmur in his ear, "I think I know what you were trying to say." Then she nipped his earlobe with her teeth.

"Ow!" he said, more surprised than pained. "Behave!"

"Yeah, yeah," she said, retrieving her bag.

Susan clipped the bracelets on, settled the gold band on her head. Then she fluffed her hair around the band to hide it from anyone peering into the car.

"I meant to ask: that's just ordinary gold?" David asked.

"Yup," Susan replied. "Now, shush."

He glanced over occasionally to see what she was doing, but beyond a look of concentration on Susan's face and the half-closed set of her eyes, there was no sign that anything was going on.

As before, a sheen of perspiration appeared on Susan's skin after a few minutes of effort.

Suddenly there was a screech of tyres as the Saab skidded. The rev counter plummeted and the car bucked as David twitched the wheel, fighting the skid. A horn blared from behind them.

David looked instantly charged with adrenaline, peering around at the other cars, looking for any clue to what had just happened.

"Shit," Susan said loudly, then, "Sorry. God, sorry. That was me. I lost it for a minute."

"What?" David demanded, then blew his breath out angrily, "Jesus. You did that?"

Susan looked awful, grimacing with embarrassment. "I'm so sorry. I'll stop now. There's nothing to worry about. It's over."

David breathed deeply for a few seconds, waiting for the adrenaline to dissipate, biting his tongue in the meantime.

Susan said meekly, "I'm making shields; I needed to practice them. I've been playing with the rain."

Now that his attention had been called to it, David focussed on the windscreen, noticing the lack of moisture on it, the dry screech of the wipers, despite the fact that the day was as wet as ever. Even as he noticed its absence, the rain started hissing onto the windscreen again, droplets once more driving into the glass.

"I must have touched the engine with one of the shields," Susan said. "I'm tired."

And sure enough she looked tired. She was breathing hard and the perspiration on her cheeks looked cold. Her eyelids trembled slightly.

"Don't worry about it," David said finally. "It just took me by surprise. We're still in one piece." He didn't sound enthusiastic but his anger was gone.

Susan took this opportunity to bring something up. Her voice was very quiet. "When we call him," she paused to let David figure out whom she was referring to, "can you do it?" she said, almost whispering.

David was caught slightly off guard, "Er, I suppose. If you want me to."

Susan nodded, "I've been thinking about it and I'm just not sure I could keep it together." Her voice wobbled a little. "If I don't think about what she's going through, how frightened she must be, then I'm sort of…" She puffed air for a moment, emotion not exertion disrupting her words. "Then I'm sort of alright," she finished at last, her voice straying higher and higher as she tried to keep from crying.

Having got the words out, she sobbed a couple of times now.

"Of course," David said, "Of course, I'll do whatever you want, but…" he paused. "I'll do it if you want me to, but don't decide yet. It might be better, given how you sound now, it might be better if it was you." He added softly, "He wouldn't suspect anything."

She looked up at him, through her tears, a hurt look on her face. "That's so calculating," she said, gulping back her tears.

David said nothing, just left her to struggle with her anguish.

So quietly he almost didn't hear her, she said, "You're right. I'll do it."

CHAPTER 32

<small>LATER THAT DAY
MONDAY 28TH APRIL</small>

They were back in London by the afternoon. Both of them were looking drained, Susan terribly so. They were both determined, however, that rest could wait – they had a number of things to organise first.

First they needed somewhere to stay. Neither of them had any confidence that their usual addresses were unknown to Jan. If he knew where Dee was staying, worse still if he had questioned Dee, he might know anything by now.

They opted for a hotel and David suggested that they stay at the one he had driven Dee to, the one she had been staying at when she was taken.

It was amazingly expensive, but they were going to need to get to Dee's belongings somehow and it would be a lot easier if they were staying in the same building.

Besides, as David pointed out, he had to accept that his life was going to change now. He'd been saving up to go travelling, in fact he had more than he really needed stashed away, so they might as well draw on those savings now. Because now he really was going travelling, albeit not in the way he'd imagined.

David checked in for both of them, requesting a twin room – there hadn't even been a discussion about taking separate rooms this time. Susan sat in one of the armchairs in the hotel's foyer reading a newspaper as David completed the transaction. She sat some distance away and gave no sign that she was with him. Once he had moved away from the desk, she put the paper down and strode up to the reception.

"Excuse me, my name is Dee Milton. I'm afraid I've lost my room key," she said to the man on the desk, exaggerating her American accent.

"Which room are you in, Madam?" he asked.

Breezing past the question, Susan said, "I'm over from New York, you see, and I'm just terribly jet-lagged. I can't keep anything straight." She pointed down at his computer terminal, "It's M-I-L-T-O-N. Dorothy, but I go by 'Dee'."

He tapped away at his terminal for a moment and then asked, "Do you have any identification, Ms Milton."

"Well, I do of course, but it's all in my room," she said smiling sweetly. "I can give you my home address or telephone number, any of that sort of thing."

"Yes, that would do," the man said. Susan reeled off Dee's details.

"I think I just locked the key in my room," she said, "If someone could let me in there that's probably all I need."

The receptionist gave his cool smile and beckoned over a young valet. He whispered something in his ear. The younger man came out from behind the counter and said to Susan, "If you'll just follow me, we'll get you sorted out." He led the way to the lifts.

Susan chatted away, as the young valet smiled politely, "Of course I wouldn't normally touch alcohol at lunchtime when I'm at home. I think it must be the jet-lag – so disorienting. Have you ever been jet-lagged?"

"No, Ma'am," he said. When they left the elevator, she blinked at her surroundings, making a show of being a little disoriented. She allowed him to lead the way to the room.

A minute later, Susan stood in the middle of room 319. The valet was hovering by the door. On one of the bedside tables she quickly located a paper packet containing a credit-card-style plastic key. It had obviously held two of them originally.

"There it is," she said, turning and holding up the key. "Thanks so much."

"Quite alright, Madam. Enjoy your stay," he said, retreating into the corridor and closing the door.

Susan had a quick glance round the room. There was little of interest to see; housekeeping had obviously tidied the room since it had last been used. It wasn't even clear which of the two standard-double beds Dee had used.

She picked up the phone, dialled zero and asked to be connected to David Braun's room. She spelled his name. A moment later it was ringing.

On the second ring, David answered.

Susan said, "I'm in room 319. Why don't you come down?"

"See you in a sec," he said, hanging up.

He was knocking at the door less than a minute later.

Between them they peered into drawers and slid back the doors to the hanging space. Susan snapped the light on in the bathroom and explored within.

"There's not much missing," she said. "Even her shoulder bag is here. It looks like she stepped out with just her phone and her pocketbook, and maybe a coat."

They spent a few minutes packing up Dee's things, returning her clothes to her suitcase and garment bags. On the writing desk Susan found a partly written postcard with the words 'Dear Mom and Dad' at the top, but nothing more. Reluctantly, Susan dropped the card into the wastebasket.

They carried her bags up two floors to their own room, which was almost identical to Dee's. Putting down the bags, David began to pace, obviously busy thinking.

Susan sat down on the far bed. She was rummaging through Dee's shoulder bag. "Well, at least we've got her passport," Susan said. "Unfortunately, mine's in Cambridge."

David looked like he wanted to groan at the news, but he didn't. He said, "Well, I suppose we've got quite a bit of travelling to do then. I need to pick up some stuff from my flat. It might be best to do all this tomorrow morning, before anyone's up. We can get a little bit of sleep and do our driving when there's no traffic."

Susan said, "Yeah. We still don't know if Jan's got any accomplices, whether he's got people watching the places we might visit."

David said, "Well, he's done his own dirty work up until now. If he was going to call in reinforcements, I think he'd have done it before this point. And he doesn't need to set traps for us any more; he's got Dee."

Susan said, "Even so…"

David finished for her, "Even so, we'll be careful. Early tomorrow morning is a good time for that. No one's alert at 4 a.m."

"Certainly not me," Susan agreed. "Oh and while we're at it, we need to drop into the Professor's place in the City too."

This time David did groan. "Of course," he said, "What about your parents' ranch in Idaho?"

"It's a house and it's in New Mexico and I think we can do without my prom dress and twelfth-grade yearbook for now," she said, mock-witheringly.

David nodded, "Oh, good," he said.

Despite the fact that they were joking with one another, there was a growing tension in the room. They had yet to contact Jan and the knowledge that the time for the call was approaching was beginning to affect them. Neither of them seemed ready to broach the subject yet.

David sat down at the writing desk. "I should call work," he said. "I need to tell them… something."

"Tell them you fell in love," Susan said, flopping down face first on the bed.

He pretended to consider this seriously, "I suppose it's not *that* far from the truth," he said.

Before Susan could make any sort of response he snatched up the phone and started dialling. He said to her, sounding business-like, "I think it's a good idea to sort of combine the truth in with what I tell them. It'll make it easier to keep the story straight later." He was holding the phone tucked under his chin listening to it ring. He added enigmatically, "I think you're about to get a promotion."

Just then the call was answered and David asked to speak to Reg Cottrell. When David was through to him, he started off by saying that he wasn't going to be coming in to the office for a while. Then he asked how things were going. From the way the conversation progressed, it was obvious that David's star had risen very high within the firm. He had rescued the business from ruin by retrieving Dass's property, despite the considerable risk to himself. He was also getting credit for urging the partners to dissolve Dass's account as swiftly as possible. David's prompting had resulted in a number of immediate changes being made – changes which would greatly reduce the firm's liability if Dass's estate found some basis for making a claim.

Reg assured him that a compassionate leave of absence would present no problem for someone of his good standing.

"It's my fiancée's family," David explained. On the bed, Susan twitched. "There's sort of a family crisis and I really want to help out. She's American and we may have to go over there."

David was silent while Reg responded. Susan was now sitting up on the bed watching him. David was saying, "Well, I haven't told that many people. We haven't set a date or anything."

Reg talked some more, then David said, "Well that's very kind of you Reg. Please express my thanks to the other partners too for being so understanding."

Another pause as Reg spoke. Then David said, "Well that certainly makes things easy for me. I'll call in a fortnight, then, let you know how it's all going. Thanks again."

He hung up. Turning to Susan, he said, "Wow. They're thinking of making me a partner. Reg practically insisted I take some leave. Sounds like we're *both* getting promotions."

Susan got up from the bed and came over to the writing desk. She slid down to sit on David's lap, hooking her arms around his neck. She put on her breathless Southern Belle accent. "And what about your poor little fi-an-cée?" She sang the three syllables.

David looked a little awkward, but put his arms around her too and said, "I thought if I told them I'd only just met you, then my running off round the world with you might sound strange. This way's easier if you end up having to talk to them for some reason."

She nuzzled his neck, "No proposal? No courtship? No *ring*?" she asked, teasingly.

"I'll tell you what," David said, "if we're still alive in a month's time, you can have anything you want – rings included."

Susan slid off his lap, pouting a little, "You're no fun any more," she sulked.

"I said you could have anything you wanted; what's not fun about that?" he asked.

"I liked it when I could tease you about stuff. You're supposed to wriggle more and blush. It's fun," she insisted.

He said, "Susan, I think maybe we're past that point. Compared with everything we've been through and all that's going on now, you can't expect a little teasing to even register."

"Oh well," she sighed, "I'll just have to think of a new game." She started to walk towards the bathroom. "We have been through a lot together," she conceded. Just before she disappeared through the doorway she said, thoughtfully, "Do you think we're ever going to have sex?"

Though she couldn't actually see David from the bathroom, her voice drifted back through the open door to reach him. "See? You can still squirm after all," she called.

* * *

They'd both laughed when Susan emerged from the bathroom, but it didn't last long. It was time to call Jan and any attempt at humour sounded false.

With the moment upon them, Susan's spirits plummeted. Her light-hearted, almost flippant façade only worked provided nothing reminded her of Dee and what she might be going through.

Unable to keep the thought from her mind any more, she tried to ask David what condition he thought they might get Dee back in – but she struggled to say the words. She wasn't able to frame the question in any way she could bear to utter.

From what she was able to get out, David guessed what she was driving at and gave her his opinion. He said that harming Dee at this point would get Jan nothing. In fact, from the point of view of being able to move freely with her, the less distressed she was the better. It only made sense for Jan to hurt her if he didn't feel he was getting full cooperation from them. Since their plan was to appear totally compliant, hurting Dee would only jeopardise that cooperation.

Susan wasn't wholly convinced, but his words obviously helped. She took a couple of minutes to compose herself and then picked up her mobile and dialled.

"Hello?" the cultured voice on the other end of the line said, "To whom do I have the pleasure of speaking?"

"It's Dee's sister," Susan said curtly.

His voice had an airy, theatrical quality as he said, "Ah, the elder Miss Milton. But look at the time. You really must have gone to ground if you've only just received my message. I wonder where you scurried off to. I was just beginning to think I'd have to raise the stakes."

"What have you done to Dee?" Susan said, "I want to talk to her."

Jan sounded less good humoured as he said, "Yes, well we'll get to that part in a minute. I'm sure you've watched enough television to have an inkling of the form here. We make our arrangements first, then you speak with your sister and we conclude with you making some empty threat about what you'll do to me if I put a scratch on her. Yes?"

Susan said nothing. Jan went on, "Silent agreement, I trust. Very good. Here's your first question: are you prepared to give me the documents I want?"

Susan hesitated a moment and said, "With some conditions."

"Ah, tut tut tut," Jan scolded, "We'll come on to the horse trading. Yes or no? I'm sure Dorothy here is hoping you'll say the right thing."

"Yes," Susan said, through tight lips.

"You're sure? Splendid. Dorothy is looking relieved. Now, have you got a pencil? I'll tell you what we're going to do."

"No," Susan said firmly.

"I beg your pardon? No, you haven't got a pencil?" Jan said.

"No, I don't want you to tell me your plan. I don't trust you," Susan said.

Jan sounded as though he was considering this, "I suppose trust is a rare commodity. Shall we ask Dorothy what she thinks you should do?"

Susan's breath caught in her throat and she bit her lip. "Just please listen to what I've got to say," she said.

There was a pause and then Jan said, "Alright. Tell me."

"You're not stupid," she said. "If I just bring you the collection, you have no reason to let me or Dee go. And you escaped when the police arrested you. We need to meet somewhere where you can't hurt us and then you have to agree to leave the country, straight afterwards."

"I see," Jan said. "But what choice do you have? Here is Dorothy, as frail a creature as I've ever seen. Think of what I can do to her if you don't cooperate. Just think." He sounded as though he were about to do something right that second.

Susan sounded frantic, "No, please don't. Don't hurt her. Just listen to me for a moment."

When Jan made no response, Susan said, "You want me to believe you'll let us go when you've got what you want, but now you're telling me how easy it would be to hurt my sister. You have to give me some reason to believe you won't just kill us both. If you don't, then you're not giving me a way to save her, you're offering me the chance to die with her." Susan was gasping as she talked, trying not to cry.

Again, Jan made no sound, but the line was still open. Susan said, "If you agree not to hurt her, if you agree to meet me somewhere where I might be safe, if you agree to leave the country as soon as you've got what you want, then I'll bring you the collection. But don't ask me to commit suicide when it won't even help Dee."

Jan said, "Tell me what you propose." He sounded angry and dangerous.

Susan said, patiently, "We meet at an airport – in the departure lounge. You come without any hand luggage and I'll watch you walk through the metal detectors. So no gadgets or weapons." This had been one of the things

Susan and David had agreed. Susan would show no sign that she believed in magic. She would also make no mention of David. She went on, "I'll print a copy of the collection and have it ready for you. If you try to take it from me or you don't bring Dee, I'll destroy it. I'll use water-soluble paper, so you might want to be careful how you handle it."

"Go on," Jan said, sounding good humoured, almost amused, once again.

"Once we've made our exchange, I'll take Dee with me and we'll get on a plane. You get on yours and you don't come back; you let us get on with our lives," she paused a moment. "You'll need to buy Dee a ticket and you'll need her passport, which I'll leave at the information desk."

"Very good," Jan chuckled. "Am I allowed to make a suggestion? I take your point; if I want you to risk your neck then I need to offer you a little reassurance. I could give you my word that all I want is the collection, but I can see you might not be swayed." Jan cleared his throat. "So why don't I make it easy for you. I'll stay away completely. I'll send someone harmless, my little friend Sati. She's about nineteen, skinny as a beanpole. She'd come up to Dorothy's shoulder. I'll tell her to wear something impractical for concealing weapons."

Susan was stuck for something to say. He continued, "I'll still leave the country. That fits very nicely with my plans, but little Sati I think, needs to remain behind. How about you and her take domestic flights? It's easier for you both to get home; you can get a train if you don't want to fly and it means we don't have to muck about with passports. She'll take a longer flight, let's say Aberdeen, and you can have your pick of the shorter trips. How does that suit you?"

"I…" Susan wasn't sure, "I suppose so," she said, sceptically.

"It's everything you were asking for and more besides. I have one or two things to do tomorrow," he coughed and cleared his throat again, "but Wednesday should give us time to arrange things."

Susan said, "And you won't even be there?"

Jan replied, "Nowhere near. I would expect you to destroy the collection if you come to believe otherwise, but I won't be nearby, I promise you. Good enough?"

Susan hesitated for a few seconds and then simply said, "Yes."

Jan said, "Well, shall we say 2pm at Gatwick North Terminal? And I expect you'll want a few words with your sister. Now don't be alarmed, but it's better all round if she remembers as little of this ordeal as possible. For that reason, you may detect the effects of Valium when you speak with her. I'm sure you wouldn't wish her to be frantic."

There was a pause and then Dee's voice said, "Hello?" She sounded groggy.

Susan's hand flew to her mouth. "Dee, it's Susan. Don't worry about anything, we're going to take care of everything."

"Susie? It's really you?" Dee said, slurring her words.

Susan said, "It's Susan, Dee. Dee, are you OK? Are you alright?"

Dee said, "Oh yeah." She sounded confused. "Maybe a little sleepy."

Then Jan came back on the line. "Let me know if there's anything else I can do for you." Then he hung up.

Susan set the phone down and turned to David, her eyes bright with tears. When she finally spoke, she said, "I think Dee's alright and I think he's going to let us have her back."

David came over and wrapped his arms around Susan and they sat that way, not moving, for a long time.

CHAPTER 33

Two days later
Wednesday 30th April

"I think I can see her," Susan said.

A glass wall separated the shops and seating of the departure lounge from the security area. Susan and David were standing looking through the glass at the three lines of people who were shuffling towards them – each line making its way toward a metal-detector arch. Adjacent to each arch stood an x-ray machine.

The woman Susan had been staring at turned to talk to a friend, revealing her features for the first time. She was laughing as she turned. It wasn't Dee.

David said, "Do you know what I like about going to the dentist's?"

Susan turned to look at him momentarily, grateful for the distraction, but sceptical about this particular remark. "You like going to the dentist's?"

"How long have you been in Britain? It's sarcasm. I hate going to the dentist's." He shrugged his shoulders in a caricature of tough posturing and said, "As you can imagine, I don't care that much about the pain, but I'm not too enthusiastic about the feeling of powerlessness. Not appealing." He went on, "Anyway, the bit that always amuses me is when they take a dental x-ray and everyone runs out of the room to hide. I mean it's perfectly safe for me, but they still scatter like, er, rabbits," he said, looking unsure about his choice of simile.

Susan's eyes were flicking from person to person, scanning the crowds entering the security area. She paused for a brief moment, considering David's words, and said, "I think it's the fact that you get two zaps a year and they'd get twenty a day."

"I know," David said, lazily, "So how do you think these guys feel?" David indicated the nearest operator of the x-ray machine. "Spending all day sitting nine inches from a continuously operating x-ray source powerful enough to see the inside of a metal briefcase."

Susan snorted but didn't reply.

A moment later, she said, "It's her."

David had been checking a different queue. Now he followed Susan's gaze and picked out a tall, slim girl with dark hair just entering the security area: Dee. She was wearing a black mohair jumper and white jeans which Susan could see even from this distance were filthy. Dee seemed unsteady on her feet and her arm was looped through the arm of another girl several inches shorter than her.

The smaller girl had olive skin and black hair. Her features might have originated in India, though her attire certainly hadn't. She was wearing skin-tight purple trousers in tissue-thin rayon, silver boots and a stretchy pink t-shirt too small even for her slight frame. The t-shirt said 'Babe' across the front in silver glitter. It was a cheap and cheerful party outfit worn by a girl young enough and attractive enough to make it seem fun – except it looked uncomfortably out of place here – especially when contrasted with the girl's drawn expression. The dark smudges under her eyes suggested anything but a fun-loving existence. They gave her the appearance of someone almost sick with worry.

As they watched, the Asian girl jerked Dee forward, moving her several steps closer to the x-ray machine. Despite Dee's drugged and scruffy appearance, she still looked healthier than the girl holding her arm.

David said wonderingly, "She can't be an adept, can she?"

Susan also sounded surprised, "Less adept, more addict, I'd say. She reminds me of some of the girls I saw at the shelter when I was volunteering. She looks kind of like a hooker – and not a very successful one."

David was beginning to register disgust as he stared at the girl who was dragging Dee towards them. His voice was free of any humour as he said, "I see what he meant: she's not hiding any weapons."

"Well," Susan said, "we should probably still be on our guard. We'll wait until they're through the metal detectors and then drop back a bit."

Dee and then her minder passed through the arch of the metal detector without triggering the alarm. They had no hand luggage beyond their mobiles and Dee's small purse.

Susan said to David, "You probably shouldn't risk her seeing us together."

David nodded and moved away to stand by one of the public telephones. He picked up the receiver and began muttering indistinct nonsense as though in the middle of a call. His sidelong glance alternated between Susan and the two girls approaching her.

Susan had her carrier bag in one hand and an open bottle of mineral water in the other. Inside the bag, a sheaf of white, laser-printed paper was visible through the transparent sides. She stood stiffly in the centre of the departure lounge, more or less in the path of those emerging from the security area.

Dee spotted Susan and reacted with a bleary smile, but in slow motion, as though she was too drunk to know quite what was happening. Susan's face was a rigid mask.

"You're Sati," Susan said to the Asian girl.

The girl's tense face wrinkled in disgust at Susan's words. "No, I'm Priya. That's what he calls me, though. It's some sort of joke," she said, almost spitting the words out in her tired London whine.

Susan looked at Dee and then back to the girl. "You haven't hurt her?" Susan asked.

"I haven't hurt anybody," she said and sighed deeply – an involuntary sound she didn't appear to realise she was making.

"You don't work for Jan?" Susan asked, tentatively.

The girl gave a joyless laugh. "You've got some papers to give me," she said, "I'm not to come back without them."

Susan looked unsure. The beginnings of concern for the girl crept into her voice, "Is he threatening you?" she asked.

"What do you think?" the girl said angrily, as though the words were exhausting the last of her energy. She held out her hand.

Susan looked at her for a moment, confused, as though she were being asked to shake hands, and then she realised the meaning of the gesture and placed the plastic bag in the outstretched hand.

Grasping the bag, the girl gave Dee a little shove in Susan's direction. Dee tottered forward a couple of steps into Susan's arms.

Through clenched teeth, Priya said, "Hope your sister's alright." Then she turned and walked away before Susan could say anything more.

When Priya had disappeared, David came forwards and helped get Dee to one of the nearby seats. He said, "No one appeared to be watching you. It was just the girl."

They sat together, Susan stroking Dee's hair. Dee's head was resting on Susan's shoulder, her eyelids drooping. Susan said, "That girl seems like just as much of a victim as we are. God knows what he's holding over her."

David looked down at Dee, taking in her slack features and dirty clothes. "How is she?" he asked.

Susan lifted Dee's head and looked into her eyes. Dee smiled lopsidedly back at Susan. "Doped to the gills, but she doesn't seem to have a scratch on her. If it's just Valium, it should wear off in a few hours." Susan wrapped her arms around Dee, squeezing her gratefully, rocking them both slightly as she did so. Dee didn't resist.

After a few moments, Susan said, "Help me get her to the gate." Her face showed that she was holding back any sense of relief for the time being. Her features were set in the same slight frown she had worn for the last hour.

* * *

An hour and a half later, they were in the air. Dee was by the window, still drowsy and not quite up to speaking, but she was nowhere near as listless and groggy as she had been. Susan sat in the middle, with David taking the aisle seat.

Just as the seat belt signs went off, Susan turned to David and said, "What am I missing? Have we done it? Have we got away with it?"

David said, "You've been holding your breath for about two hours now, haven't you?"

She gave him a nervous smile. "Uhuh," she agreed.

"Well," David said, "You, me and Dee all seem to be in one piece. It's looking pretty hopeful, I think."

Susan said, "You think it's safe for me to let my breath out?"

He reached across and took her hand. He nodded.

"Thanks," she said. "I want you to know I realise it wasn't easy for you to let me plan all this and for you to just follow my lead, and I really appreciate the fact that you did it despite how difficult it was."

David took in her little speech. "You thought it all through, you came up with a great plan," David said by way of explanation, "at *least* as good as anything I would have thought of. I…" he hesitated.

"What?" she said, smiling, encouraging him to continue.

"It's just that I was hoping we could talk about this stuff," he said.

"About what? I can't think of anything to say except 'thank you'," she said.

David said carefully, "I mean about why it was… an issue in the first place. You know, the trust thing?" He paused, "I know it's not the best time, but it's as good a moment as we've had for a long while and I need to talk about this sooner rather than later."

Susan looked uncomfortable but she didn't try to stop him talking.

He drew in his breath and said, "Susan, I can see that you've got some feelings for me, whatever you say. And I, um, well I hope you know how I feel about you, how much I care about you." He smiled. "I just want to… to settle all this… whatever-it-is that's in the way – whatever it is that's not right between us." He came finally to the point, "I'm hoping you might have got to the point where you feel you can trust me."

Susan looked awkward, shifting in her seat and considering her words before saying, "It's not quite as simple as that," she said.

"Sure. OK," he accepted, "But that's why I want to talk about it."

Susan said, "You really want to do this?" She didn't sound angry; she sounded like she was hoping that he'd say 'no'.

David said softly, "Don't you think I've done enough, shown that I'm prepared to risk enough, that I deserve to know?" He said it gently, but the challenge in his words was still evident.

Susan said, "Alright. If you're sure you want to have this conversation." She was gathering herself to speak, obviously not relishing it, but pushing ahead before her resolve weakened. "It's not so much about whether I trust you or not; it's that you don't trust me – at least not in the one way that I need you to."

Her voice became tender. "I don't blame you for that; it's just how you're made. But ever since I met you it's been obvious to me how you think. It's just not part of your nature to let someone else tell you how to make your decisions – to let them know what's really going on in your head. You can do it if you try, but it's an effort and every time you're put under pressure, you go back to what you know: thinking and acting on your own – looking out for other people, but not consulting them first."

She laid a hand on his arm, "You can see I'm not criticising you, can't you? It's just who you are. Just like it's the way I'm made that I can't handle it. I bet there are a million girls who would love you to take care of them, to take over, but I'm not one of them. I can't be."

David tried to reply, "I don't... I haven't really..." But he couldn't finish the sentence.

Susan said, "That's why I got so angry every time you ran off by yourself without talking to me. I mean yes you were being irresponsible some of the time too, but it got to me because it was rubbing my nose in the fact that I had two choices and both of them were lousy: I could let you sweep me off my feet or I could push you away. What I couldn't have – and what I need – is a proper partnership. I don't need saving, not if it means surrendering, letting go of who I am. That's what my mother did – and it didn't work. She let my father take over and it made her miserable. It was the only way she could be with him, but it wasn't right. When I look at what it did to her, I realise that I'd rather be on my own." She was close to tears as she spoke those last words.

David was struggling to frame his reply. He wanted to dispel what she'd said, to disprove it. "That's not true," he said. "I mean it's true I've been like that in the past, but it's not set in stone. I have more respect for you than anyone else I know and I let you do your thing when it came to getting Dee back, didn't I? Not a word of complaint."

Susan nodded, "And it nearly killed you," she said, "I could see that. Which is why I'm so grateful you did it anyway."

David said, "You're wrong, Susan. OK, it ruffled my feathers a bit, and I suppose you're right, I have never placed myself in someone else's hands like that before. You've read me correctly: I don't like letting someone else into my thoughts. But it's different with you. I trust you. That first time might have been difficult, but I'd do it again. You don't need to give in to me. You don't need to change. I like you as you are." He stopped talking, suddenly looking vulnerable, uncomfortable and then he pushed on, his voice sounding strange as he said, "Or to be a bit more accurate, I love you as you are."

Now Susan was crying – gently, not hurt, but too moved not to cry. She sniffed and said, "I want to believe that. I want to believe it more than anything. I'm doing my best, but you have to understand who I am." She looked over at Dee who was stirring in her sleep, shifting about in her seat. Susan lowered her voice, "When we were growing up, all my parents did was push me. They were only happy when I was achieving something. Dee... God, Dee just had to be, to exist, that was enough. Wherever she went, she made friends. She didn't have to do anything, she was just herself and people responded. I've never been like that. Unless I'm pushing myself I'm not happy, I don't feel happy with myself, I don't feel... lovable. I'm not sure I *am* that lovable unless I'm busy doing something I do well. I'm not someone people just adore because of who I am. If I'm special in any way it's because of what I'm capable of. Which is why I can't follow in my mother's footsteps. I often wish I was like Dee, but I'm not."

Susan stopped speaking, letting her words sink in. After a moment she realised she could hear something from the seat beside her. She pivoted round to see that Dee was awake and she was laughing. It was quiet laughter, but nonetheless it was deep – slow belly-laughs which shook her whole body.

"Dee," Susan said, concerned, "are you OK?"

Dee continued to laugh for a minute and then said, "Four years and eighty-eight grand." She laughed some more, apparently helpless to stop herself.

David and Susan watched her, confused – relieved that she was awake and talking, but disconcerted by her behaviour.

Getting herself under control, Dee said, "I went to a therapist every week for four years to talk about exactly how charming and lovable I felt. How many hours is that? I don't know. But never once did it occur to me that I was the lucky one."

She sat up straight now and twisted to talk to Susan. "You're right, Mom and Dad never gave me a hard time; they didn't bitch at me about my grades, they didn't nag me if I wasn't learning new things, if I wasn't getting picked for school teams. In fact, they didn't really complain about anything, whatever I did, however late I stayed out or whoever I stayed out with. Towards the end, just before I left home, I was determined to get them to notice me, to get their attention away from you for just one second. And you know what? I couldn't. So I left. I left them with their one perfect daughter, the one they cared about."

Dee started laughing again and then said, "And guess what? You felt unloved too. The one who got every second of Mom's attention every day of every week; you felt unloved too."

Susan looked shocked, "I never knew," she said.

Dee shrugged, "Well I guess it's not everyday chit-chat. 'You feel unloved? Hey, me too Sis.'" She paused a moment and said, "I went to see Mom about it last year. My therapist thought it would be good for me. And maybe it was. It doesn't change how I feel about me, but it stopped me resenting Mom." She had Susan's total attention now. She went on, "You know what she told me? She sat me down, like I was a kid again, and said, 'But Dorothy, honey, your father and I decided not to treat you the same because you weren't the same.' Mom said, 'I grew up trying to be a good daughter just like your father tried to be a good son. It didn't matter who we wanted to be, we were expected to behave a certain way and we were treated a certain way. Your father and I promised ourselves we wouldn't put you and Susan through that. We'd acknowledge that you and your sister are individuals, with your own personalities and strengths and we'd encourage those strengths, not stifle them by trying to get you to conform. We never pushed you the way we pushed Susan because we could see that you already had all you needed to make it in the world. Susan we worried wouldn't get there without a push and if she didn't reach her potential we knew she'd be miserable.'"

Susan was sniffling again, "She said all that?"

Dee nodded, "I can't promise I've got every word right, but it's close. Even if I wasn't a journalist, I'd remember that conversation."

Susan said, "I always figured she was trying to live through me, do all the stuff she'd always regretted not doing."

Dee said, "Who knows? But I can tell you what she believes, because I could see in her eyes that she meant what she was telling me. She believes she pushed you because she knew how it felt not to be stretched, to fall short of what she could have been and she was determined to spare you that pain."

Susan was crying now and it was setting Dee off. Susan turned and wrapped her arms around Dee and Dee did the same.

"Jesus," David said, pretending to be disgusted. "We're in Britain now. You're not in the land of the spontaneous group-hug anymore."

"Shut up," Susan sniffed, separating her right arm from Dee and reaching over to grab David. She pulled him to her so that the three of them were pressed together.

They stayed that way for nearly a minute with Dee and Susan alternately sniffing and sobbing quietly, almost happily. After a moment, David stopped resisting. The clinch was only broken when a stewardess stopped at their aisle and asked if everything was alright.

David separated himself from the huddle and said, "Family celebration," indicating the two tearful girls, still hugging. "You wouldn't have any champagne, would you?"

"Certainly sir, I'll see what we've got," the stewardess said, bustling away.

"None for me," Dee said, letting go of Susan and clutching her head. "I feel worse than the morning after my twenty-first. You guys celebrate my safe return for me. And maybe when you're done, you can tell me what's been going on while I've been on my little pharmaceutical vacation. Nothing about the last few days makes any sense and oh my god," Susan and David both looked round to see what had alarmed Dee. She was looking down at her grubby white jeans, "What the hell am I wearing?" she said.

CHAPTER 34

S usan and Dee were hugging again as they stood to one side of the security gate at Manchester Airport. Passing them were a steady stream of people making their way through to international departures. David stood next to the two girls, one of his hands resting on Dee's shoulder, his foot on the edge of their luggage trolley.

Susan said, "I don't think it'll be for long, Dee. It's your choice, but Lincoln and Petey will take good care of you if you let them. They mainly work relocating women with abusive husbands, so this isn't too much of a stretch for their professional skills. Anyway, they're funny guys, tough as shoe-leather and they know how to make people feel safe." She gave Dee a final squeeze. "And I promise I'll let you know the instant we can all get back to normal."

Dee nodded, "How will I recognise them when I get to Newark?"

Susan laughed, "You'll recognise them. Big white guy, medium-sized black guy – they'll be arguing. Ask information to page the Zorro Brothers if you have any problems. That's what they called themselves when we used to work together."

Dee laughed, "Oh right, because you were…"

Susan finished the sentence for her, "Zorro's little sister. Exactly." She was laughing too.

Then Dee became serious and hugged Susan one last time, "You be careful." She looked over to David, "You both be careful. Whatever it is you're caught up in, I hope it gets sorted out soon. When the craziness is over, maybe you can both come visit. I'm betting you'll need a vacation before much longer. I know I will."

"Take care, Dee," David said, leaning over to kiss her on the cheek.

Dee picked up her carrier bag – it held magazines and various goodies for the flight – and walked away from them. She was wearing the clothes she'd bought in one of the airport's shops after they'd landed; her previous outfit had gone straight into the store's rubbish bin.

With much waving and blowing of kisses back at Susan, Dee presented her boarding card to the woman on the security desk and disappeared in the direction of the departure lounge.

Once Dee was out of sight, Susan said, "I hope there *is* a point where we can get back to normal. I just want to get her safe first, then I'll worry about what happens if we're still in this position a month from now."

David said, "I can't see it taking that long. Between you and me, we'll come up with a way out of this before then." As he spoke, he slipped an arm around her waist and she leaned in to him, relaxing.

David pointed to a row of seats nearby, "Can we sit down for a couple of minutes? I'm knackered." Then he added, "What was the Zorro thing about? I didn't follow."

Susan said, "Come on, you must know Zorro? They got that show over here didn't they? Fighting for justice et cetera?" She made a sweep with her hand, whipping out the letter 'Z' in the air.

David said, "Yeah, yeah. I know who Zorro is. How does that link to you?"

She stopped dead, turning to face him, slightly puzzled. "Did we never get around to this conversation?" She frowned, "I guess we didn't," she shrugged. "Well, that's what I do when I'm not being a history nerd: I fence. In fact…" she said, adopting a swagger for a moment, "when I was a teenager I was told I might go all the way, might end up on the Olympic team." She made a face, "It didn't work out because of us moving around so much with Dad's work, but I was on track for a while. Anyway, when I was about twelve and I first got the fencing bug, I used to pester everyone, wanting to know if Zorro ever had a little sister. I think I was hoping for a role model I could identify with – ideally one who wore braces. I don't actually remember it, but it's one of those family stories that's now passed into legend." She gave him a silly sort of grin and shrugged.

Then she turned serious for a second, adding, "That's what pushed me into practicing with Jan's tribute. I figured if adepts fight with blades, it's only the magic side of things that would put me at a disadvantage. I mean, if I can learn to make a shield the way they do, I might actually stand a chance against one of them."

David was looking confused. "Blades? I'm not following."

Susan looked shocked, "Jesus. Didn't we talk about this either? I know the Professor and I had a really long chat about it. Shit. Sorry. It's been a hectic week," she said, looking embarrassed. She explained, "Adepts can't use magic to attack each other, right?"

"Yeah," David nodded, slightly impatient, "I got that bit."

Susan squeezed his arm, meaning 'sorry', and said, "So they have to find some other way to hurt each other. But the thing is, an adept can just wrap a shield right round himself and he's safe – so you can't force anyone to fight if they don't want to. The problem is that with a complete shield in place you can't move – it's a bit like being inside a block of ice – you're protected, but you're kind of trapped too. So if you want to remain mobile, or you want to be able to lash out at the other guy, you can only make a partial shield – one with gaps in it – gaps you can stick a sword through. That's how they fight." She acknowledged, "I mean I'm sure they prefer to kill their enemies while they're asleep in their beds, but if that fails they use swords."

David asked, "Not guns?"

Susan shook her head, "Think about it," she said, helping David push the trolley towards the nearby seating, "You want to fight someone and you've both got guns, so you both create big shields. Obviously you're only going to let your shield down at the instant you fire. But then the other guy's shield stops your bullet. So you both need to fire at the same time, like in a duel, because that's the only time both shields are down. If it works you're both dead, and if someone's timing is off you're both alive – and either way it sucks. But swords can be used defensively; even with quite small shields you're not totally exposed because you're using your blade to defend yourself. In those kind of fights, most of the damage gets done with ripostes. You let the other guy's sword through and then turn your defence into a counter-attack, because that's the moment you know where the gap in the other guy's shield is."

David asked, "If you can make a shield at will, how does anyone ever get hit?"

Susan, "Because it's not fast like moving your arm, it's slower, like moving something heavy. You can move or change a shield like this," she swept her arms around a little, like she was dancing, "But not like this," she executed a little lunge-parry-riposte at startling speed. A nearby child tugged its mother's arm, pointing at Susan, but by the time the mother looked round there was nothing to see.

They sat down, "That's…" David said, obviously wondering what it was, "pretty amazing," he concluded.

"Yeah," Susan said, "Isn't it? Even if I'm kind of amateurish when it comes to creating a shield, just wearing tribute and maintaining minimum concentration will stop another adept using magic on me. So I just need to trust to my mad fencing skills. I reckon a crappy adept who was good with a sword could take someone whose abilities were the other way round."

David volunteered, "Well, I've done a certain amount of kendo."

"Hmm," Susan said, unconvinced, "That's mainly a slicing weapon. It's gonna be tricky to slice, because the blade covers so much territory; you're likely to catch the other guy's shield wherever it is. You really want a thrusting weapon, like a rapier. You follow back along the other guy's line with your riposte." She thought for a moment, "I guess if the other guy had a slicing weapon too it might work, because he'd need to pretty much dispense with his shield in order to swing it. But unless you get to choose the other guy's weapon for him, I wouldn't try it."

David looked irritated, "Nearly fifteen years of martial arts and none of it is any use."

Susan said, "Well, it hasn't exactly been wasted. With your speed and strength and balance, you'd learn to fence in half the time it would take any normal mortal."

She gave him a twinkly smile and added, "So you'd only need eight years to get as good as me," she pointed to the people around her, "instead of twice that for everyone else."

David gave her a sarcastic smile.

Susan leaned on him, snuggling into his jacket and said, "I'm sorry I hadn't told you all that stuff. Especially after my big speech about you not including me when you're busy devising your grand schemes."

He enfolded her with his arms. "Well, I know now," he said, and then added more graciously, "And you intended to tell me; that's the difference. It's just that the world's been wall-to-wall mental lately."

She buried her face in his collar, pressing the tip of her nose against his neck. "You forgive me then?" she asked, indistinctly.

"Mmm," he agreed. "Not only are you forgiven, but I'm going to find a way to prove that you're officially part of the inner circle, when it comes to planning my life. That's a promise."

She sighed against his neck – happy and exhausted at the same time. "OK," she said sleepily.

A few moments later, David's mind had wandered sufficiently for him to say, "When they decided to make these seats from sheet steel, do you think they were worried that too much comfort would tempt people to sit here all day and they'd miss their flights?"

Susan shifted slightly and mumbled, "They are kind of brutal."

He said, "The design brief was obviously 'whatever else, make sure their arses want to leave the country'."

Susan gave a muffled giggle and then lifted her head, sitting upright in her seat. "I'm going to find a bathroom and then get us some coffee. Watch my bag will you?" she said.

"Yup," he replied. He glanced up at a digital display showing the time. "They'll probably let us check in soon."

She nodded. "Why don't you give the Professor a call, let him know how we're getting on. I'll have a word with him when I get back." She gave him a rapid peck on the cheek and then stood up. She glanced around, orienting herself and then set off.

David sat for a few minutes, lost in his own thoughts, before he pulled his mobile out of his jacket pocket and paged through the phone's memory looking for the Professor's number.

A few moments later it was ringing. "Cambridge 2616," the Professor said.

"Professor Shaw – Joseph – it's David."

The Professor sounded delighted, "David. What news from the front?"

David smiled, "So far, so good. Dee's boarding her plane about now, Susan's just off getting some coffee and I'm sitting around doing nothing. Things seem to be looking up."

"I'm delighted. I gathered from your tone that the news was good." The Professor's voice took on a note of concern as he said, "Susan's sister: how is she faring?"

"Better than I really dared hope," David said, gravely. "Physically she's fine, though a bit groggy. He kept her tranquillised, which probably made it a lot easier on her. I'm sure it wasn't his intention, but the whole thing seems like a dream to her. She knows she was kidnapped and taken somewhere, but by the time it had sunk in, she was chock-full of Valium. Could have been a lot worse."

"Still, the poor girl," the Professor said, "One can only imagine."

David went on to say, "You should have seen the girl escorting Dee; she's obviously being coerced into helping."

A moment later he picked up his original thread, "No, it all went perfectly. The only slight disappointment, if you can find fault in such a lucky escape, is that Dee can't tell us much about Jan. She doesn't know where she was taken even. The only thing she could say was that she overheard the tail-end of a phone-call as Jan was coming in to check on her. She heard him mention Section Five. It means nothing to us; we wondered if you'd heard of it. I assume it's some sort of… er, what's the male equivalent of coven?"

The Professor answered mechanically, as though his thoughts were elsewhere, "A coven is a collection of witches, who may be of either gender," he stated, but there was a note of alarm in his voice as he went on to say, "Section Five is not a coven, however. At least not the Section Five that I'm familiar with."

David asked, "Well, what is it then?"

The Professor said, rather gravely, "It's an old name for MI5. It's the domestic intelligence service."

David didn't know what to make of this news. "Why would he be talking to MI5?" David looked thoughtful, "Although it does make you wonder what they know. Do you suppose the government is aware of adepts?"

Instead of answering, the Professor asked, "Did Dorothy overhear the context in which the name was mentioned?"

David rubbed a hand across his forehead in a gesture of weariness. He said, "Sort of. She thought she heard him say, 'You're supposed to be Section Five, you tell me.' Though she wasn't too sure about it."

"David, this is a concern," the Professor said. "When I discussed recent events with Susan, we concluded that Jan operated alone, at least in terms of what you might call 'field operations'. We've seen no sign that he has willing foot soldiers he can call upon. But on the other hand, we thought it likely that he had contacts he *could* go to for information or perhaps equipment. We had tentatively ruled out contacts within the police force, because he seemed to be in the dark regarding the investigation into the Marker's theft. Yet somehow he was able to locate Dorothy. And his information on Dass's travel plans were spot on too. The latter could be explained by the existence of a secret ally within Dass's organisation. Dorothy's whereabouts, however, would have required a different sort of informant."

David asked, "Was he tracking her credit card? Might someone be passing him that sort of information?" Then he muttered to himself, "Though he didn't seem to be able to track Susan's or mine."

The Professor obviously had a different thought in mind. He asked, "Do you know if Dorothy had made recent travel plans? MI5 routinely keep an eye on who's entering or leaving the country."

David said, "I don't know how far she'd progressed with them, but she was making arrangements to return home just before she was snatched." He was beginning to sound very worried as he said, "You think he might have traced her through a plane ticket? Oh my god." David was on his feet now looking around him.

As David anxiously scanned the throng of people in the terminal, looking for Susan's face, the Professor was saying, "MI5 would certainly keep track of flight bookings. It wouldn't be uncommon for them to search for particular surnames. From what little my sister used to say on the subject, it seems that sort of information is freely available to the department. Advances in computerisation and the current paranoia over air travel will have made it even more common."

David was moving towards where he'd seen Susan last. He said, "Susan reckoned Jan came around to our plan quite suddenly. We assumed we'd manipulated him into it. Stupid! It was probably the mention of airports that got him interested." He glanced back at their luggage, sitting abandoned now.

Unsure what to do, he strode back towards the trolley, to where they'd been sitting, and stood up on the seat. His eyes urgently searched the crowd, flitting from one stranger to another, looking for that one familiar face.

The phone was still to his ear, "He suggested we take a domestic flight; he said it was easier for all of us because it was a shorter round trip. We agreed because we didn't want him to know we were planning to leave the country. He also volunteered to send someone harmless instead of coming himself, which sounded great." David's voice was tight with tension. "But that would have left him free to come up here ahead of us."

The Professor had already thought it through. Quietly, and without optimism in his voice, he asked, "You are trying to locate Susan, yes?"

David was still searching, "I can't see her anywhere," he said, sounding wretched. He looked up at the time on the digital display; she had been gone fifteen minutes. He was still thinking aloud as he spoke to the Professor, "He even volunteered to take the farthest location for his assistant. He wanted to make sure we chose somewhere nearby."

The Professor said, quietly, "I'm rather afraid that once he discovered your destination, he intended to drive there."

David's eyes had stopped roving across the crowd. They weren't focussed on anything now. David had arrived at the same conclusion. He said, "Because if he had someone with him for the return journey, someone travelling against their will, he couldn't take them on a plane."

"Quite so," the Professor gently concurred. He said calmly, "David? I'm going to be going on a trip shortly and I need to share a few of the details with you. Why don't I leave you to look for Susan now and perhaps you'd be kind enough to telephone me back once your search is completed."

"Right," David said and hung up.

He almost seemed to be in shock. He climbed down slowly from the seat he'd been standing on, his movements tentative. Then he put the phone away, taking several attempts before he found his pocket. Then he shook his head sharply, focussing on his surroundings.

David turned to the middle-aged couple who had just sat down several seats along from him and said, "You couldn't keep an eye on my bags for a moment, could you?"

They looked uncomfortable and it was obvious that they were going to say 'no'. David said, pleadingly, "Just a couple of minutes. I'll be right back."

"You shouldn't really even ask me that," the woman said, "Don't you watch the news?"

David turned away from them. He looked at the luggage. Out of the corner of his eye, he could see the couple watching him. If he left now they'd alert the police.

Then something occurred to him. He grabbed Susan's bag from where she'd been sitting and sat down with it on his lap. He rooted through the contents. No phone.

Fishing out his own mobile, he brought up Susan's number and pushed the green button. Holding it to his ear he could hear it begin to ring. Four times it rang, then five.

Finally it was answered. Background noise: a car? A man's cultured voice said, "Interesting. So you're working together." He took a breath, "First things first: if you were very swift you might be able have the roads blocked, but I think we both know it wouldn't stop me and it wouldn't get you Ms Milton back in anything like one piece."

David couldn't seem to find his voice.

Jan continued speaking, "I don't hold a grudge," he paused to cough unpleasantly, "in fact I find your deception rather endearing. You must have been so proud of yourselves." His tone grew colder, "On the other hand, of course, you must realise that your credit has run out. I won't be listening to any more ingenious suggestions you might wish to make. You will simply do as you're told this time."

David's mind was racing. He licked his lips and found himself holding his breath as he struggled to take in this horrifying development.

"Hello?" Jan said, "You know, it would help us get this all sorted out if you'd be so kind as to speak when you're spoken to."

"Sorry," David said, without thinking. He hesitated a moment longer, his expression one of frantic concentration. Then he said, "I'm ready to do whatever you want, no argument, but there's something you need to know: Susan's sick. She has," he cleared his throat to disguise a moment's hesitation, "she's got liver cancer. She can't handle you drugging her like you did Dee – it could kill her." He gave Jan a second to consider this and said, "I know she'd do anything to stop you getting those papers, but you must promise me you'll ignore her if she suggests you drug her. Whatever those papers are, they're not worth her life. All I care about is keeping Susan safe. Look after her and you can have whatever you want." He sounded desperate, as though he could hardly think straight for the worry.

"Well, that's all very heart-warming, particularly the touching faith you have in my promises." Jan's voice was muffled for a moment, suggesting he was moving around, "She certainly looks healthy enough to me," he said after a moment, "but I've learned that looks can be deceptive. At any rate, I like your attitude. Do just as you're told and you'll have her back in no time. Simple obedience, no conditions."

David said, "No conditions from me, just prove to me that she's fit and well before we meet and I'll turn over the papers." His voice was closer to the tone he used when talking with Banjo – less cultured, less the voice of someone used to being in charge.

Jan said sharply, "No conditions except that one, you mean." But then he softened, "Which I can live with. It is traditional, after all." His voice took on a business-like quality, he was instructing David, talking down to him, "This level of obedience is good. But don't do any more thinking; don't get sneaky. I don't want you wasting your time coming up with some ingenious…" he broke off for a second, coughing again, "some ingenious little scheme that will get you killed. We'll meet tomorrow, when I say we'll meet, at a place of my choosing. You'll bring the papers and I'll bring your girlfriend. When you get there, you wait outside and phone me to say that you've arrived. I let you speak to her. If we're both happy with how that goes, you come inside and we perform the exchange. It'll be somewhere in Central London, so make sure you're in the vicinity by then. Anything you want to add?"

David said nothing.

Jan concluded, "Good boy," and hung up.

CHAPTER 35

THAT SAME AFTERNOON
WEDNESDAY 30TH APRIL

D avid called the Professor back a few minutes after his call to Jan. It had taken him a little while to compose himself before he was ready to talk to anyone.

The Professor answered the call immediately, saying, "Has he taken her?" the question coming without preamble.

"He's got her," David confirmed, the weight of the world in his voice.

A leaden silence lay between them. David eventually broke the spell by telling the Professor about his conversation with Jan and what he thought Jan's responses implied. David had formulated the beginnings of a plan while he had been talking to Jan, but – as he confessed to the Professor – there were huge holes in it.

He shared the few details he had worked out. "I want him to think that I'm reasonably brave and reasonably stupid. And macho wouldn't hurt either."

"Good, good," the Professor said encouragingly, "It seems to me you've been using your head in some dreadfully unsettling circumstances." The Professor's voice was full of grave energy.

David gave a weak smile and said, "I appreciate the moral support, Joseph. In case you were wondering, I am coping. Unfortunately I'm going to need to do a lot more than just cope."

He added, "I think the way to stay sane is just to think about nothing else except getting Susan back." David paused for a few moments and said, "The thing that's really giving me trouble is what to do about the collection. I don't suppose Susan would want me to let Jan anywhere near it, but I can't see any chance of getting her away from him unless I let him have what he wants."

The Professor said cautiously, "It seems to me that you're in an almost impossible situation. And I won't presume to tell you the best way to resolve it. You know as well as I do that if Jan is able to rejuvenate himself he will continue to ruin lives for as long as he walks this earth." He paused for emphasis and said, "But there have always been wicked men like him in the world – and you surely didn't make them the way they are."

David said nothing and the Professor tentatively offered a few more words. "I don't know if philosophy is appropriate at such a moment, but it seems to me that your dilemma is not an entirely new one. Many doctors have been asked to extend the life of a murderer or a tyrant and many have done so without qualms – and without the unbearable ultimatum you are confronted with." He took a deep breath, "Whatever you choose, you may end up beset by guilt – I would simply suggest that you choose whichever burden you think you will be most able to carry. That is all you can do: think about what you are best able to live with." He concluded, "You will certainly be in my thoughts."

David didn't respond. It wasn't clear how many of the Professor's words he had taken in or whether they had helped. The Professor didn't attempt to say more.

So their talk moved on to other matters. Before the original plan came unglued, David and Susan had been planning to travel on from Manchester to Spain. That thought abandoned, David was now planning to return to Gatwick as soon as he was able. He arranged to drive up to Cambridge later that evening and drop in on the Professor, with the aim of collecting a few of the things he would need the next day – the collection included.

Next David asked, "Do you happen to know the whereabouts of a good, modern chandler?"

Once the inevitable question had been resolved of how David came to be interested in such a thing, the Professor suggested a firm he had once used, many years before, and who he believed were still trading – though he could offer no reassurance that they had moved with the times.

Another thought occurred to David, "I've got a lot of planning to do. You haven't discovered anything I should know about – no new powers? Jan's got no tricks up his sleeve so far as you know?"

The Professor replied, "There can be no absolute guarantees. But the collection is remarkably consistent on the matter. I have Susan's translation here. Just give me a moment…" The Professor could be heard rustling papers. Then he came back on the line, "Here we are. Let me summarise it for you."

David listened in silence. The Professor said after a moment, "Some form of clairvoyance. The ability to heat or to cool. The ability to make what Susan refers to as a shield. A pushing force and a shattering force. And a healing ability which they can learn to influence. That, and the fact that magic protects against magic. It's a formidable list, I'll admit, but it hasn't stopped many of their kind meeting sticky ends at the hands of ordinary citizens over the years."

David didn't reply, he was biting his lip and considering the Professor's words. After a few seconds of silence he brought himself back to the present and asked, as heartily as he could, "So what's this about a trip; when are you setting off?"

The Professor replied, "I thought it might be a good idea to make myself scarce and to spend a few weeks down in Cornwall. I will probably set off first thing in the morning. If all goes well, you will still be able to contact me. When Susan was staying with me, she suggested I might like to enter the twenty-first century – or at least make use of its technology. She had some specific suggestions and I have taken her advice. I now have a brand new laptop computer and a mobile telephone."

The Professor continued, "One of my very capable students is travelling down with me; she believes that a fortnight of diligent effort on her part, though not sufficient to turn me into what she calls a 'hacker', may suffice to impart a few of the basics. When you retrieve Susan, you can tell her my student is also helping me with PGP; she'll know what I mean."

David took down the Professor's new mobile phone number and his e-mail address and agreed to call as soon as he'd had any more contact with Jan. Then they said goodbye.

David was back at Gatwick by early evening. The next leg of the journey, from the airport to where his car was parked near Banjo's house, took longer than the trip from Manchester. He loaded his and Susan's luggage into the car, for want of anywhere better to stow it, and set off for Cambridge.

When he eventually arrived, the Professor welcomed him warmly. The two of them talked late into the night and it was nearly three o'clock by the time David had made his way home and closed the front door of his flat behind him.

The Professor had wondered about the wisdom of David returning to his own home. But David felt, with an exchange planned for the next day, there was little point in Jan coming for him now. Whatever the validity of that reasoning, each time David woke up with a start in his own bed, he found himself alone and unharmed.

David had come away from the Professor's with the paper originals of the collection, while the Professor now had the encrypted disc – and a mental note of the password. The papers were still there when paranoia got the better of David and he checked their hiding place at eight o'clock the next morning.

By half eight, he was on a bus heading into town to visit the chandler the Professor had mentioned.

By one in the afternoon he had ticked off all the items on his rather exotic shopping list. It was as he was walking back to his flat from the bus stop that his mobile rang. It was Susan's number.

"Yes," David said, answering the call, his tone as neutral as he could make it.

"Got a pen?" Jan's voice said, sounding jaunty.

David grabbed a pen from his pocket and snatched a receipt from one of his shopping bags. "Go ahead," he said.

"The priory church of Saint Bartholomew the Great," Jan said. "It's between Bart's Hospital and Smithfield Market. Be there at two-thirty this coming morning. Don't arrive early and don't bring anything with you except your phone and the collection. Call me on this number before coming through the door. Got all that?" Jan said, "I don't want any mistakes."

"I've got it," David said, his voice tight.

"And make sure you bring the real collection," Jan said, "I'll be giving you a little test before you're allowed in."

"OK," David said, sounding resigned.

"Chin up," Jan said, "It's nearly over." He hung up.

David grabbed his purchases and walked quickly back to his flat. Half an hour later, he was trotting back the other way again, a full-sized hiking rucksack slung over his shoulder.

CHAPTER 36

THE NEXT NIGHT
EARLY FRIDAY 1ST MAY

The church lay just outside London's old City walls, wedged into a corner where the normal rules of archaeology had lapsed. The new hadn't covered the old here, it had simply crowded it to one side.

The ancient church seemed to be set almost in the garden of a block of post-War council flats. The path to the main door of the church cut across the grass, but in a channel – being several feet lower than the much newer lawn around it. The buildings on either side loomed so close and so high that the church – despite its solid, Norman bulk – was almost hidden away until one was upon it.

At this time of night, all the lights inside the council flats were extinguished – only those on the outside walkways were still lit. The nearby market was silent and David encountered no one else as he walked up from the bay where he'd parked his car.

As he made his way along the path, the ground rose steadily around him until he stood just outside the church. He was carrying his phone in his right hand, a heavy flight case in his left. He was wearing a lightweight sweater and no jacket: an outfit ostentatiously devoid of good hiding places, unlikely to antagonise Susan's captor.

Pausing a few metres from the darkened vestibule, David set the case down for a second and dialled Susan's number. "I'm here," he said, when it was answered.

"Read me something from the collection," Jan instructed him.

"What?" David replied.

"Take a piece of paper out of the collection," Jan said in his lecturing, schoolmaster voice, "and read something to me from it."

David opened the flight case, lifted out one of the clear wallets and began to read a passage in Latin.

"Enough," Jan said, as though David's pronunciation offended him, "We're ready for you." There was a pause, some muffled words, and then Susan was saying tentatively, "David, it's me." Her tone was uncertain, but her voice was clear and strong – and she still sounded like Susan. Whatever her physical condition, in some important, fundamental sense she was unharmed.

Hearing her voice, David found himself imploring her, "Don't worry, Susan, don't worry."

Then it was Jan's voice again, saying, "Yes, yes," impatiently, cutting into David's reassurances. "Alive and well, as promised. Now, please join us," he said.

David ended the call and slid the phone into the pocket of his jeans. He pulled open the heavy oak door of the vestibule, letting it bang closed behind him, and crossed the flagstone floor, passing through the inner door and into the space beyond.

Inside, the church was like a great geode: enclosed and encrusted, dark and glittering, full of jutting pillars and cramped geometric niches – the high, vaulted centre was like the hollow at its mineral core.

Above the entrance, spreading up the back wall, was an elaborate church-organ surrounding a pulpit. Its chambered wooden mass now plugged the blunt stone end of the ancient chapel like a wasps' nest.

At the heart of the church lay a stone font flanked on all sides by rows of low pews. At the edges of its mosaic floor, walls of stacked stone arches rose three tiers high to support the roof's shadowed spars. Beyond the pillars of the lowest tier, a cloistered path encircled the whole expanse, leading back to the entrance.

As David stepped out of the cloisters and entered the high-ceilinged space, he saw Jan and Susan standing at its centre. Susan was leaning heavily against the blocky, limestone font.

What light there was came from flickering clusters of votive tapers and from a dozen or more heavy candles, thick as artillery shells, held in tall metal standards.

As Jan turned to face him, David could see that his appearance was altered. An ink-like stain had spread across his neck and the bottom of one cheek, black like an unhealed bruise. And yet this was not the damage David had seen the last time the two met; this was some new corruption. One side of Jan's neck now bulged as though something were forming within.

Despite these signs of unchecked morbidity, his movements were agile and fluid, and a new gold circlet glinted on his forehead.

David's gaze shifted to Susan. She was still leaning on the font, but now he could see that this was not through weariness; she was tied to it. Two ropes were wrapped around its solid base. One extended a metre out from the stonework to loop around her ankles, binding them; the other was fastened to the central chain of a pair of chrome handcuffs which secured her wrists.

Physically, she seemed unharmed. She looked tired and tense at the same time and she returned David's gaze anxiously, searching his face as though she hoped to learn something important.

The font she was anchored to lay at the meeting point of two aisles, which ran at right angles to each other, cutting through the rows of pews. One path stretched the length of the central space, following the line of the roof, the other spanned its much narrower middle. Together they formed a slender cross with Susan at its heart.

David began the walk down the longer aisle towards the two figures. Jan waited for him, watching every step intently.

When he was still fifteen metres from Jan, he stopped and set the case down. Then, releasing its catches, he flipped the top open and stepped back. He moved to one side, retreating between the pews, leaving the case sitting by itself in the aisle.

"Where are you going?" Jan demanded, testily, as David withdrew.

"There's your papers," David announced, pointing to the case, as though it was an explanation. He lowered himself onto a pew. He was leaning back, drawing away from Jan as though he were cringing.

Jan sighed, as though exasperated from dealing with an imbecile. He strode down the long aisle towards the case, his footsteps sounding loud in the empty church. He warned, "If you've booby-trapped that case, I can still kill her from here."

Jan stopped just short of the case and beckoned. Obligingly, it tipped onto its side and a sheaf of plastic wallets slithered out onto the stone floor. He bent down and picked up a handful of the nearest ones. As he did so, his spine curved and the compact, guard-less sword strapped diagonally across his back stood out in silhouette. Gold flashed at his temple.

He flipped through a couple of folders, attempting to keep one eye on David and occasionally glancing back towards Susan, who remained tethered and immobile a dozen metres behind him.

Jan read for a moment, unmoving, intent upon a particular document, and when he glanced up, David was nowhere to be seen.

"You," he growled, "Come out." His right hand moved instinctively toward his sword, which lay snug across his back, the top of its grip just level with his shoulder.

Suddenly David leapt to his feet and began running. He had been momentarily concealed beneath one of the benches and now he'd broken cover, racing away from Jan, round towards the shorter, transverse aisle which would lead him to the font.

Before he disappeared from sight, his hands had been empty; now he was carrying weapons, a sword in each hand. Something else was different too; a double-loop of gold chain was wrapped around his temples.

Jan dropped the papers and turned, his inhuman senses suddenly revealing the presence of a second adept. For a moment, it didn't occur to him that it could be David. His eyes flicked instead towards the entrance (David temporarily forgotten) as he reacted to the new threat.

An instant later his gaze returned to David, registering at last the glint of gold.

Now Jan sprinted back the way he'd come, whipping his sword from its sheath and yelling something incoherent.

David reached the font first. In his left hand, he was also holding a black velvet bag. He opened his fist, throwing the bag and one of the swords at Susan's feet. Now that he had a hand free, he grabbed the scabbard of the other sword and pulled it loose. The blade he revealed was long, perfect and slightly curved: a Japanese sword, a katana. It had a single, exceptionally keen edge which ran the length of the blade's outer sweep.

A moment later, Jan reached the font, striking at David in a cutting attack which caused their swords to collide.

David was able to deflect the blow. He retaliated by bringing his blade slicing up towards Jan's exposed middle, the bright tip arcing towards the other man's stomach.

But the lethal edge never reached flesh; an invisible barrier turned the assault aside. Jan sprang back.

David now stood between Jan and the font. While his concentration held, Jan would not be able to attack him directly with magic. He shuffled backwards, making sure he was close enough to Susan that she too would be protected.

"The bag," David said urgently, twisting his head slightly to talk to Susan. All the while he kept the point of his sword aimed at Jan's face, his blade held out in front of him in a two-handed grip.

Jan faced him in a very different stance. He was standing sideways-on to David, his blade extended one-handed, reminiscent of a traditional fencer, except that his left hand was down by his hip, not held up in the air.

Jan's sword was a peculiar hybrid. It was narrow and straight, with a sharpened tip, a little like a fencing foil, though not so slender – but the blade was flatter and both edges had been ground to razor brightness. It could thrust as well as slice.

As David and Jan faced each other, eyes locked and swords ready, Susan did as instructed. Severely hampered by her bonds, she tipped the contents of the bag onto the floor. Jan's old headband and two more heavy gold bracelets, like the ones on David's wrists, tumbled out. She ignored the bracelets – she was still wearing her own – but she grabbed the headband

and pressed it quickly onto her head.

Susan's eyelids flickered for a moment as she concentrated.

While Susan had been retrieving the headband, Jan had taken several steps to his left, circling around them both. Now he lunged, not aiming at David – instead intent upon Susan. David jumped forwards, bringing his blade down to deflect Jan's.

As Jan's blade was beaten down, his eyes flicked towards David, who had been his target all along. He allowed his blade to be carried downwards, and as he did so he let the tip drop, disengaging his sword from David's, but leaving David committed to the movement, a victim of his own momentum.

Once Jan's blade was free he swiftly reversed its direction, bringing it back across David's extended body, the tip scoring a channel in the meat of David's left shoulder, the point catching for a moment in his muscle before tearing free.

David gasped, and then recovered himself. He moved round to place himself once more between Jan and Susan.

Jan snapped, "Where is your shield, boy? Do you even know what you're doing?"

By way of an answer, David stepped forwards, cutting twice at Jan, once at his head, the second time at his waist. But as if to underline Jan's question, both blows were deflected by unseen barriers.

Susan whispered to David, "I can make a shield, you don't need to protect me, but I can't break these handcuffs; I don't know how." She sounded desperate.

Jan ignored, or failed to hear, the whispers. He said, "Also: interesting choice of weapon." His tone was mocking.

"Folded Japanese steel," David replied, through clenched teeth. "The finest swords ever made; they can cut right through an opponent's blade."

Jan looked contemptuous. He said, "Fascinating schoolboy hyperbole. But did no one ever tell you that they're useless when fighting the Awakened?"

David moved a little to one side of Susan, stepping slightly away from the font, giving himself room to fight.

"Funnily enough, it did come up," David said, trying to sound conversational. "Hopefully, Susan has a little more faith in my judgement than you do." He glanced meaningfully at her. She frowned, puzzled, searching for the meaning in his words.

They were now in a triangle, equally spaced from one another. David and Jan maintained eye contact, the tips of their blades almost touching. Susan looked from one man to the other.

David said, "She advised me to get a sword like hers." Behind him Susan had picked up her weapon – a long, straight blade, elaborate guard, a needle-sharp point, but no edge. She had unsheathed it, but with her hands cuffed, her grip was awkward.

David continued, "Of course a weapon like that," he nodded towards Susan's sword, "also has its disadvantages." He explained, "You can't cut with it."

Jan looked disdainful for a moment, evidently convinced that David was rambling. A moment later he lunged at David's mid-section, beating David's blade aside, demonstrating the use of a thrusting weapon. David was unable to parry in time, but jumped back quickly enough that the thrust missed him.

David took a second to recover, adjusting his stance. Behind him, a look of comprehension blossomed on Susan's face. She switched her sword to her left hand, holding it out of the way, and leant on the font, her fists out in front of her.

David said, "Think what a fool I'd have felt if I'd put a knife in that bag and then discovered you'd used handcuffs." He raised his sword above his head and Jan instantly shifted his weight back, ready to retreat. Then David pivoted towards Susan.

Susan spread her hands, stretching the chain of the handcuffs taut across the flat stone top of the font. David's blade whipped down, aiming for the centre of the chain.

Jan, momentarily wrong-footed, realised what David was doing and braced his back foot, trying to turn his retreat into a lunge.

David's blade flashed down and buried itself in the top of the font, parting the chain at its left-most link, dangerously close to Susan's hand, the blow landing just as Jan leapt forwards.

David tugged the sword free and jumped back, but not quickly enough to stop Jan's blade reaching him. The tip pierced his side, sliding in below his rib cage, a hand's width of blade entering his flesh.

David sprawled, falling away from Jan. A gasp was pulled from him as he collapsed.

Susan, her wrists no longer joined, whipped her sword around in her left hand, the tip scoring a track across the side of Jan's head, which caused him to duck and scuttle to one side, taken by surprise.

Once again, they were spread out in a line. Now Jan was on one side of Susan, David on the other. But whereas Jan was tentatively smearing the blood from his head-wound around his cheek as he tried to inspect the damage, David was still on the ground.

Susan stood between them, sword held expertly in her right hand – but her legs were still tied, the rope wound tightly around her ankles, keeping her from adopting a fencer's stance or taking a full step.

David scrambled to his feet, his left arm clasped across his torso, immobilising his torn muscles as much as possible. His right hand held his sword, the tip waving unsteadily in Jan's direction, bobbing and dipping as David struggled to stand up straight.

Jan stood regarding him. He grunted, as if to say he didn't consider David much of a challenge. Then he began moving round towards his injured opponent, keeping well clear of Susan.

As he passed her she lunged at him, her sword pushed out to its furthest extent, but it wasn't enough to reach him. He gave her a sneering look as her sword-tip jabbed the empty space to his right.

"I should think you're regretting you didn't put a knife in that bag after all," Jan said, an unpleasant smile on his face.

David twitched a couple of times in what might have been pained laughter. "Yeah," he conceded, "cuffs *and* rope. You think of these things afterwards and you could kick yourself."

Jan approached him, moving to his right so that for a third time they were all in a line. This time Jan was in the middle, his back turned towards Susan, who was just too far away to reach him.

"Well, what now?" Jan said, "She can't get free. You seem unable to defend yourself. And your nonexistent grasp of the arts is stretched to its limit in simply preventing me crushing your heart from over here. Is there any more to your brilliant plan? Or does it end with you bleeding to death, leaving me with the collection, and your girlfriend tied to the spot ready for me to kill at my leisure?" When David didn't answer immediately, Jan prompted him with a mild, "Hmmm?"

David nodded. "I'd got one or two other ideas," he said, "but this isn't quite the right time."

Just audible over David's hoarse breathing was the drip-drip sound of droplets of blood falling from the fingers of his left hand and splashing to the hard stone floor.

"No," Jan said, sourly, "I don't suppose it is."

Looking down at David's wound, and the blood leaking from his side, he added helpfully, "If only you had a week, you could probably heal that. Let's see what you manage to accomplish in the five minutes before I kill you." He took a step forwards, beginning to crowd his adversary.

David staggered for a moment. He tried to say something but a sudden twinge of pain made him catch his breath.

He tried again. "I had this big dilemma," he said, trying to keep his sword from dipping. "Do I let a shit like you rampage around, screwing up people's lives for another hundred years or do I risk getting the woman I'd do anything for killed because I decide to get in your way?"

While the two of them had been circling, Susan had been picking at the knot that secured her to the font. It was pulled impossibly tight. There was no way she would be able to loosen it using just her nails and a sword with no edge. She stretched out towards the nearest of the hefty candlesticks but it was considerably beyond her reach. She closed her eyes and concentrated hard, but the weighty brass holder scarcely rocked on its broad base.

"It's a tricky one," David was saying.

He took a few steps to his right, focussing hard, beginning to look more purposeful. Jan responded, circling in counterpoint, his expression indulgent, as though he had all the time in the world and was prepared to delay killing David until he'd learned anything of interest his victim might have left to say. His diseased features registered confidence.

Circling, David almost tripped. He righted himself, ignoring the stumble and said, "A friend of mine told me I should choose whichever option I'd be best able to live with. So I thought about it last night. Which would be the biggest burden?" He twitched with painful laughter again and Jan looked at him quizzically.

Finally David said, "Then I realised something." He moved to his right a few steps and then to his left, pulling himself upright as he did so. Then he darted to the left pushing forwards, Jan's sword moving instantly to block him. He pulled back.

"I realised that I really don't need to worry about it," David said, his voice growing triumphant, "Because there's no way I'm going to get out of this alive."

As he said it, he dipped to the right, slashing at Jan, who raised his blade to parry and was forced, by the energy of the attack, to take a step back.

Susan hopped as far away from the font as the rope would allow, stretching it as taut as she could. David slashed a second time at Jan, his sword glancing off the shield Jan was projecting, then he extended his blade lunging at full stretch to hack at Susan's tether.

Jan had been pressed back for a moment, but he had recovered again before David had completed his manoeuvre. David had created an opening through which he could push forwards, but there was nothing to prevent a counter-attack. As David lunged, he left himself completely open to Jan's retaliation.

For a split-second Jan's face registered surprise that David would risk something so reckless. Then, as quickly as it had come, his surprise evaporated and his jaw tightened with anger. As David's sword swept down, severing all but a single strand of Susan's rope, Jan stepped forwards, switching to a two-handed grip and brought his blade flashing down, the edge catching David's wrist, cutting deep into his flesh, splitting the ulna and stopping just short of severing the hand.

For the second time, David fell sprawling to the ground. This time his sword tumbled from his ruined hand.

Susan jumped back, whipping the rope tight and snapping its last few intact fibres; the loops around her ankles came uncoiled. Freed, she launched a flurry of attacks at Jan, almost knocking his blade from his hand and causing him to flinch even as his shield deflected the more violent of her thrusts.

Jan was beaten back, forced to step away from David's body. He adjusted his stance a little, obviously withdrawing his shield slightly to give his blade more room, and engaged Susan, relying on his swordplay to blunt her assaults. Confident and capable as he was, he couldn't help being pushed backwards and their conflict edged down the long aisle of the church, moving further from the entrance.

"Maybe I was too hasty in what I said to the boy," Jan said, breathing hard. He dipped his head towards David's prone form, "I couldn't have done *that* without an edged weapon." Susan looked at him with disgust, her lip curling back from her teeth.

She said nothing. She was in a rage, all her furious concentration channelled into the overlapping barrage of attacks she hurled at him, her shield shifting neatly to ward off his counter-attacks.

On the ground, David was stirring. He was protected from Jan's invisible attacks only so long as his concentration endured. Susan and Jan would both be able to sense it if he faltered. Susan stole a glance in his direction. "Focus, David," she called.

David didn't reply, but he began to crawl away from the font and into the relative safety of the pews, dragging his sword in his left hand.

"He'll drop his guard soon enough and I'll put him out of his misery," Jan assured her.

She took advantage of his remark to press the attack. He snatched his hand back from her darting blade. He said, "It's lucky for you that you can fence."

Susan shrugged. Her tone extremely clipped, she said, "We'd have just found some other way to stop you."

"Of course, this is not exactly fencing," Jan said, ignoring Susan's remark. "That nonsense they teach these days with their springy toy-swords. And awarding points for a tap that would get you gutted a split-second later if you tried it in an alley fight."

"Oh, please," Susan said, sweeping her blade up for a second so that Jan could see it. Far from being a light, modern design, she showed him a heavy, traditional rapier with a rigid blade. She began to push him back even harder, saying, "Given what I do, did you think I'd only learn the modern stuff?"

As she said this, she was able to run the shaft of her blade along Jan's sword, pressing him slightly off target, so that the brutal lunge he unleashed passed harmlessly to her right, while her own point bit into the muscle across his rib-cage.

Though the thrust struck a rib and failed to penetrate, it gouged a furrow along his side, which instantly welled with blood. The dark, synthetic material of his long-sleeved top was now ripped, exposing the wound.

Jan yelled in pain and launched a counter-attack at Susan's head, slicing instead of thrusting with his blade in an attempt to catch her off guard. It was too slow; she easily withdrew ahead of the advancing weapon, her shield stopping the attack dead.

Jan jumped back and dipped around the other side of a wooden lectern, placing it between them.

Several metres back, behind Susan, David had crawled in amongst the rows of seats. He was beneath the same bench he had hidden under earlier. In his weakened state, he seemed to be struggling with something.

Jan dropped back a little further from the lectern, but each time Susan made a move to circle around the obstacle in order to close with him, he darted in the opposite direction, keeping it between them. Susan retreated slightly hoping to be able to make a dash to one side.

Though Jan's expression was pained, his voice was still steady as he said, "Whatever you've been taught, the rules are different here." He took another step backwards, as though he was about to run one way or the other. Susan dropped back too, opening the distance between them, so that the lectern wouldn't obstruct her if she had to sprint after Jan.

"For instance," Jan said, breathing hard, "defensive cover needs to be kept close to you," he nodded towards the lectern which sat in the open space between them, "or it becomes a target," he concluded and then his eyelids flickered. The wooden lectern exploded, breaking into several large pieces, one of which struck Susan in the chest, hurling her backwards to sprawl amongst the pews.

Now, for the first time, Jan and Susan were more than a couple of metres apart. This was David's cue to haul himself, struggling, to his feet. He had something grasped in his left hand – his right hung uselessly at his side.

Jan caught the movement and stared defiantly at him. He opened his arms wide, inviting attack from David, the air almost seeming to stiffen as he adjusted his shield. "Whatever that is, boy, it won't be enough."

David was holding what looked like a whisky bottle. He banged its base on the pew beside him and then hurled it, as best as he could, towards Jan.

To the side of the whisky bottle had been taped an upside-down marine flare. With its cap twisted to arm it, the flare needed only the sharp rap on the bench that David had given it to ignite the chemicals within. A blinding red glare hissed into life, lighting up the bottle as it flew through the air, smoke pouring from the blazing tube.

The bottle struck Jan's shield and was repelled. It dropped to shatter on the flagstones, the angry, bass whump of ignited petrol suddenly illuminating the entire church. At the heart of the spreading flames, Jan's shield had created a little bubble of protection, through which the fire could not pass.

But a second later, the burning liquid had seeped under the lower rim of his defensive barrier and begun to burn within the bubble.

For a moment, the bubble remained – a smaller fire within, screened off from the greater conflagration – and then Jan screamed and the bubble disappeared. For several seconds, Jan was lost within the flames.

Susan lay beyond the reach of the fire. She pulled herself painfully to her feet and retrieved her sword. Then she began to move closer to the burning fuel, attempting to get a look at Jan. At the same time David fell back, to lay helpless between two rows of seats, for the time being unable to move.

As Susan approached the blaze, the flames abruptly dipped. The fire was beginning to die down, despite the fact that unburned petrol still washed across the flagstones. Within the waning flames, Jan rose from the ground to stand, sword in hand, his scorched features a mask of concentration.

The temperature around him plummeted, the flames dying down further and the air taking on a curious crystalline quality as it chilled. A few seconds later, the last licks of flame sputtered out and the burning flare was suddenly extinguished. Above him a dust of ice crystals was spiralling down from the freezing air, glittering and catching the light as they fell, to lay amongst the hard frost at Jan's feet. The breath steamed from his mouth as he gasped air into his scorched lungs.

Jan's shirt was partly fused to his chest now and huge ragged gaps had been opened by the fire, beneath which his dusky skin was charred and tight. His hair had shrivelled exposing patches of soot-blackened scalp. The skin of his face was pulled back from his teeth, giving him a permanent snarl.

Susan took a step towards him, raising her sword. As she did so, she glanced across at David. A look of panic crossed her face. "I can't sense you, David," she yelled, "Concentrate!"

Jan attempted to speak, but no sound emerged except a dry wheeze. He coughed, curiously abrupt and rapid, like an animal, an unpleasant swallowing sound accompanying the effort. He tried again to speak, "Shouldn't be long before I can pick him off," he said, his voice a brittle whisper, his whistling breath distorting his words.

"David," Susan called again, urgently, "You need to stay awake or he can attack you."

There was no reply. She glanced rapidly over to where David lay. Looking up, she saw that Jan was directing a look of focussed intensity in David's direction.

Before Jan could muster any sort of attack, Susan launched herself at him. His sword rose unsteadily to divert her first thrust, but she slipped around his blade to inflict a long, shallow wound on his blackened forearm.

He hardly seemed to notice the damage. He withdrew a little, gathering his shield and attempting to keep Susan at bay. His eyes flicked once again towards David.

In desperation, Susan jumped back and turned to face David too. Her eyelids dipped, allowing her eyes to close completely for a second. With a crash, a split appeared in the row of pews behind David's position and a handful of splinters exploded into the air.

"David!" Susan screamed and turned back just in time to deflect Jan's lunge. She wasn't quite quick enough and the tip of his sword plunged into the muscle of her thigh. She sucked in her breath convulsively as the damage registered. It was a clean puncture and, though deep, had not badly torn the muscle. She could still stand, though her leg trembled a little as she did so.

"David," she called again, no longer shouting.

"I'm here," he said groggily. She shuffled rapidly backwards and risked a look in his direction. "I'm here," he repeated, even more weakly.

He attempted to pull himself up onto the nearest pew, succeeding on the second try. His useless right hand lay in his lap and his jeans were stained black with blood. His left hand loosely gripped his sword, though its tip rested on the pew in front. His eyelids drooped even as she watched.

Wrestling her attention back towards Jan, she began to circle him, batting the tip of his blade away repeatedly, but not closing sufficiently to give him an opening. She allowed him no respite and pressed him so hard that he had no chance to think of anything but his own defence.

Gradually she turned him around so that his back was to David. Now she began to attack in earnest. She tied up his blade and leapt past it, time and time again, nicking his flesh and twice missing him by millimetres with thrusts that would have skewered him. Steadily she forced him to retreat, approaching the pew where David had propped himself, sword in hand.

Jan was increasingly unsteady on his feet. His reactions were slowing and he was barely able to maintain an adequate defence. Against his will he was being inched backwards towards an armed enemy.

And at last, Jan's exposed back was within reach of David's sword. But David seemed to be in trouble. He struggled to lift the weapon and it nearly slipped from his grasp. Susan pushed Jan a step further back and still David couldn't attack.

At last, with a frantic flurry of attacks she sent Jan's blade twisting from his grip to whirl away into the darkened rows of seats.

"David," Susan hissed as she moved in for the kill. But David's face showed only an apologetic smile, drained of all energy. The sword dropped from his left hand and his eyes closed.

Jan sprang back, jumping over David's legs and snatched up his opponent's fallen sword. A moment later, he had its tip pressed into the flesh over David's heart, his hands gripping the hilt ready to drive it home.

Susan hesitated.

Jan made his strange gulping swallow and said, "You decide."

Susan was clearly gauging the distance she would have to cover to disable Jan. There was no way she could move quickly enough to stop him dropping his weight onto the blade.

Susan let the tip of her sword dip until eventually it rested on the floor. She stood there panting, looking at Jan as defeat crept at last into her expression.

"The sword," Jan said, jerking his head to one side.

She cast her weapon aside.

"And my band," he said, nodding towards the circle of gold around her temples.

She lifted the headband free and tossed it after the sword.

"If I were you," he said, "I'd have kept fighting." He lifted the gold chain from around David's lolling head and threw it to one side. "Surrendering won't save you," he said, patiently, his voice rattling as though something inside were trying to tear free, "Though I suppose it means you won't have to watch him die."

He lifted the sword from David's chest and brought it to his side. Then he took a breath and closed his eyes for a second. Susan was hurled backwards to tumble among the seats on the other side of the aisle. She lay where she fell – conscious, but stunned.

"If it's any consolation," Jan said, "I wouldn't have let you live however this had turned out."

He raised the sword and advanced on her.

A banging door distracted him.

From over by the entrance, a woman's voice said, "You'll give us a bad name, Jan."

Walking down the aisle was a very tall, blonde woman with pale Scandinavian skin. She was immaculately dressed in a tailored grey wool suit with a faint white pin-stripe. In her elegant hand she carried a rapier with an elaborate basket hilt. She gripped it carelessly as though she were holding it for a friend.

Jan's head whipped round to look at her. For a second, with his bared teeth and wild expression he seemed feral, cornered. "How did you find me, Karst?" he demanded.

"Some old man," she said pleasantly, "presumably a friend of whoever you're busy torturing at the moment."

Jan was backing away now. He seemed to have forgotten all about Susan. He was retreating towards where he'd last seen his own sword.

Karst was taking in the scorched stone floor, the splintered lectern, the bodies and the blood. She tutted.

She jumped up to walk gracefully along the seats rather than between them. She was making for the open flight case which lay abandoned at the end of that row of pews.

When she reached it, she glanced at the scattered papers and began to pick them up. "I think the old man lied. He threatened to share this collection with the world if we didn't help. It looks like that was never in his power."

Then she shrugged agreeably, "Oh well," she said, "I suppose I promised to come straight here instead of spending a pointless hour searching your lair." She dropped the collected papers into the case and fastened its lid.

She turned now to face Jan and began to advance upon him purposefully. He had found his sword and swapped it for David's, but he was still backing fearfully away from Karst, his recovered blade evidently giving him little comfort.

"Tell me where the Marker is," Karst said, icily, "and we'll come to an arrangement which doesn't involve me spitting you like the roast you now resemble."

Jan was shaking his head and retreating.

"You need all the friends you can get," Karst said, patronisingly. "This is a chance to get in my good books. Where's the Marker?"

"Nowhere you'll think to look, Karst," Jan said with all the defiance he could muster.

She held up her left hand and inspected its unblemished skin for a moment. "I should say I have another seventy years before I need it again." She was almost upon him now. "In that time I think I can find it without you."

Her sword flashed out towards him. He blocked it at the last possible moment only to find that she had already countered. He attempted to beat her thrust aside, but even as he began to move, she had flicked her blade a third time, so fast it was like watching a film from which frames were missing. She landed two quick blows, her sword leaping out to sting him as though of its own accord. And then with a final, effortless reverse she broke his sword just above the grip.

The silver blur whirled, to stop, tip first, pressing into his windpipe. "Those two," she said, indicating with her eyes Susan and David, "both victims or is one of them an accomplice?"

Jan said, "The girl is with me."

Karst said, "Hmm," as though she would think about it. Then she placed the point of her sword under Jan's chin and ran it diagonally up into his skull. As he crumpled, she slid the blade free and flicked its tip to remove the blood. Jan's body dropped like a sack of grain.

She left his corpse where it lay and walked across to stand over Susan, who was cradling her broken arm, still sitting where she had fallen. She looked up at the other woman with frightened eyes.

Karst reached out with the tip of her sword and ran it gently up the side of Susan's head as though probing for anything solid concealed within her hair. Then she peered behind Susan, glancing at her wrists which were now bare.

"Forget this happened," Karst said, with what might have been a smile. She wandered for a moment over to where David lay in a spreading pool of his own blood. She gave him only the briefest of glances before transferring her attention to a display table set against one wall of the church. The white tablecloth beneath the display was plastic, textured to look like cloth. With her left hand, she whipped it from the table, scattering leaflets and a bookstand.

Then she strode back to Jan, spread the tablecloth on the floor and rolled his body onto it with one neat suede boot-tip.

She wrapped him in the cloth and then, apparently without effort, she hoisted Jan's shrouded body onto her shoulder and walked back to collect the case. Dipping at the knee, she grabbed its handle in her left hand, her sword still in her right and strode back to the entrance. With a bang, the door closed behind her and she was gone.

Susan struggled to her feet and limped, as quickly as she was able, over to where David's body lay. She fumbled the phone from his pocket, one-handed, and dialled.

CHAPTER 37

To: **Dee_Milton@AtlanticMagazines.com**
From: **Zorro_Lil_Sis@hotmail.com**
Dee,

It's very sweet of you to say it, but I'm sure any big sister would have done the same. And of course I keep thinking that you'd have never got mixed up in all this in the first place except for me. But anyway, thanks. I'm proud of you too.

First order of business is to get this encryption thing set up. David's got it working for his e-mails so we can't let him show us up. There are definitely a few things I don't want the guys in your IT department reading. I'll send you a couple of links to help you figure it out.

So anyway, I think Mom and Dad can stop worrying about us. If we can survive this sort of stuff, their parenting can't have been too disastrous. I'm planning to give them a call in a few days, so we'd better get our stories straight – I don't think they're ready for the R-rated version.

And oh my god, I can't believe you're seeing Petey. Not that I should be surprised. He's kind of a prince, when you get to know him – as I guess you've found out. Unfortunately for you, dating him will mean letting Lincoln crash at your place and raid your refrigerator. Which is a little like trying to keep a rhino as a pet. It's definitely going to put a dent in your grocery bill.

It's weird that you might not have met Petey if this whole thing had never happened. I know that doesn't make it OK – it must have been truly awful for you – but I look at David and I wonder whether we'd ever have got together under normal circumstances. After what we've been through, I can't imagine not trusting him – or wasting time worrying that he doesn't love me. I mean he was prepared to go down fighting if it meant I'd be alright. Beats flowers any day.

So I suppose I'm just saying there are one or two consolations in all this. Plus, Petey can really get you plugged into 'the street' (is that the term?) like you were in Chicago. He can get you into clubs whose existence you had never previously suspected. Just don't wear your good shoes.

Do you think Dad will say something stupid when he finds out you've got a black boyfriend? I really hope he's found his way out of the Fifties by now. I know it won't even register with Mom. And just in case you're wondering, I never had a thing with either him or Lincoln. In fact when I met them, I assumed they were going out with each other. Don't tell them I said that.

Anyway, we're staying out here for a while. Neither David or I are in any hurry to get home – wherever that is. We're going to get David's pal Banjo (must find out his real name – I assume he wasn't christened Banjo) and his girlfriend out here. Maybe you and the Pete-ster can come too. I'm afraid there's absolutely nothing to do here, but for once I'm guessing you might be able to cope with that. The flights are my treat, by the way – I'll explain more once we're using our secret decoder rings. Anyway, keep in touch.

Your lovable sister,

Susan   x

p.s. If you and Petey come you'd better invite Lincoln. He'll pine and wreck the furniture if you leave him on his own.

To: WorldOfBanjo@hotmail.com
From: SecretSquirrel@EuroMail.com
Encryption: PGP 8.0.2 Freeware for Macintosh

Banjo,

I'm glad to hear that Melissa is still under the delusion that you are somehow a catch (!). Long may it last.

I'm told you came to visit me while I was laid up, but I'm afraid I can't have been much company. I was still away with the fairies. By the time I knew what was going on, Susan had decided to kidnap me.

And, I finally worked out what you were on about with that little Zen riddle of yours about Susan wanting my help. It looks like I twigged it just in time – though I did cut it a bit fine.

I don't think Susan can really ask for more proof that I'm prepared to share the big decisions with her than the fact that I planned a rescue attempt for her where she had to take over halfway through. Some people might call it half-baked, but I thought: get her on her feet and give her a free hand and she'd find a way to sort the whole mess out. And sure enough, she kicked his arse.

If I hadn't fainted (and feel free to keep that

fact under your hat) I think she'd have finished it right then. Though I'm sort of glad for her sake that she didn't have that on her conscience. Not that he didn't have it coming, but I suspect it would screw you up a bit anyway.

When it came down to it, it wasn't as difficult as I thought, trusting her. I think it helps if you find the right person. Or maybe I was ready. Who knows.

Anyway, after saddling her with half the rescue, Susan'll probably start complaining that I don't take responsibility next.

Nah, I'm only joking. She's been a saint, looking after me. She pulled me out of that hospital when I was still in a pretty bad way. They hadn't even finished explaining that my hand was buggered for good, though they'd told Susan. You could see that they thought she was mental, dragging me out of there while I was still at death's door - but with my agreement they couldn't stop her. And of course she had a slightly more effective remedy in mind.

The next problem was getting me on an aeroplane while I was half-dead. In fact, her broken arm wasn't sorted then either - she was adamant that she wanted to get us somewhere safe and quiet before we started any of that occult healing malarkey. The flight to Athens was actually pretty funny, in a macabre sort of way. My stitches started coming undone halfway through the flight and we were sure we were going to get stopped coming through customs for bleeding on their floor. Then they'd have wanted an explanation of what Susan was carrying around in her bag (more about that in a minute). We made it though.

Anyway, I have to say this island is paradise. There's about thirty people living here. There are two bars and two restaurants, both down by the jetty where visiting boats can tie up. Then there's a church – but no priest – and a few houses. We're up the top of the hill with the most amazing view of the sea.

I can see Susan from the window as I'm typing this. She's got her olive tree to sit under and a book – no goat unfortunately – but I don't regard that as any great loss. And I'm actually typing this two-handed after only a fortnight. You should have seen the state of my wrist when we took the bandages off. It was enough to turn you vegetarian for life. What a mess! Now I've just got a few odd-shaped lumps around the wound and a lot of new pink skin. Still looks weird, but it works OK and it doesn't even hurt! The hole in my side is nearly fixed too.

It took a couple of days to work out how to do the healing trance thing. Just using the mojo makes you heal fast, but there's an accelerated healing thing you can do if you know what you're about and you're in a hurry.

In fact, according to Susan, that's what Jan was doing all evening before I went to meet him for the exchange. Apparently, he was having to spend hours healing himself everyday, but it was obviously a losing battle. Maybe he was a lot older than we thought. Or maybe it was genetic – perhaps if he'd led a normal life he'd have been dead by forty.

Anyway, if he hadn't told me well in advance where he wanted to meet, I would have been stuffed. I wouldn't have been able to hide anything there (though god knows, that was a job and a half persuading them it wasn't a bomb or drugs or something). But he needed to spend a few hours in his trance, getting ready for the meeting, so he made the call early. It's amazing how the little details can make such a big difference. If he'd left the call to the last minute, I might not be here now. (Though I still wouldn't be without the Professor's intervention of course.) Or maybe it didn't all hinge on that call. Like Susan says, maybe we'd have just found another way.

Also, I've got to apologise for siccing/sicking (? that thing you do with attack dogs anyway) Hammond on you. I just needed a name and address in the UK that I could give him in case he wanted to contact us. I know he's a bit of a knob, but we'd still be sorting things out if he hadn't got involved. It helped that Dass was Italian because Hammond instantly thought Mafia (do they still exist?). And Susan was able to tell him a story that had a surprising number of real facts in it. We left out Dee's kidnapping because he hates DIY crime-fighting, but we told him about Susan being taken and the ransom being the collection. Plus she explained away the fact I didn't involve him by saying he'd warned me not to contact the police. Then when she got to the bit about someone from Jan's old firm turning up to bump him off, she said you could hear Hammond muttering, 'gangland-style killing' like he was almost excited. He seemed to consider the swords just a part of the ransom that the 'hit man' had missed, which helped. Don't worry though, you don't need to get all this straight. He knows you weren't a witness to any of it. I just thought you'd want to know. He even helped me get my car back from wherever they'd towed it to without me having to pay a button for it. Result. Susan says the keys are in the hall drawer, so help yourself if you want to.

Well, I think that's enough for today. Except I did threaten to tell you about Susan's bag. I don't know if Jan believed my little lie about Susan being sick or he just didn't feel the need to keep her drugged up - whatever it was, she was in much better condition to spy on him than Dee was. She still doesn't know where he stashed the Marker, but she did spot one of his hidey-holes - one that Karst missed. Susan, gutsy (insane?) woman that she

is, went back there while I was having fun being
operated on and she swiped the goodies. She found a
quite staggering amount of cash, mainly in dollars,
and a kind of notebook or diary. I can't read a word
of it, but Susan's working her way through it and
she thinks there might be all sorts of interesting
info in there. She even found a bit where Jan was
complaining that no one wears hats any more. But
it's true: we don't seem to trust people who cover
their heads. Makes sense.

The bottom-line there is that I'm probably a good
bet if you need a sub. It certainly means Susan and
I don't need to worry about working for a living
for a little while. (You'll be pleased to know
that my bosses are holding my job until I'm well –
though I can't see myself going back.)

Anyway, I'm sure I don't have to say to be a bit
cautious with this e-mail. As I understand it, the
encryption is pretty unbreakable stuff, but don't
let Melissa read it over your shoulder, she might
start to worry about you.

Have one on me,

David

p.s. Hurry up and book some flights out here. I want
to see what the fierce Greek sun does to your soft
albino skin.

To: SecretSquirrel@EuroMail.com
From: jhs1192@cam.ac.uk
Encryption: PGP 8.0 Freeware for Windows

Dear Susan and David,

Assuming you crack the code and I've done everything correctly, you'll be reading this sitting in the sunshine somewhere in the Aegean. Imagine that! It'll be talking pictures next.

But enough levity, I'll press straight on with the apologies and grovelling. I hope it's clear to both of you that I didn't intend to take away your right to choose your own destinies. I know you haven't accused me of such, but you may nonetheless be thinking it. I ask you to believe I wished only to help.

I gave David a certain piece of advice – having of course prefaced my remarks with an assurance that I would never presume to offer direction (but I suppose hypocrisy is the least of my crimes). No sooner had I spoken than irony struck; I succumbed to my own words. When I contemplated David's options it seemed to me that – whichever path he chose – he would soon carry a heavier burden of guilt than any young man should have to bear.

And really the decision was never in doubt. David would of course choose to save your life, Susan, if it were in his power to do so. I realised that if I were happy to transfer the burden to my own shoulders, it opened up the possibility of sending you a little help. By communicating your predicament to Dass's surviving associates I believed I was sealing the fate of both the collection and the Marker: they would once more be the instruments of wickedness. But I decided to press on anyway.

I am delighted beyond words that the Marker has not been found. The collection is no great loss, considering that we retain our own copy and the knowledge it contained must largely have been known to Dass's erstwhile associates already.

At any rate, I determined that giving up the Marker might well be the price that would purchase your lives. And I felt I could live with the thought of aiding the enemy for whatever time I have left. It also seemed clear to me that David would <u>not</u> be prepared to grasp at that particular, desperate straw for fear, Susan, that it would seem like he was betraying you. You had after all made it plain that you intended to deny these people their precious treasure. I would rather you lived, even if it ended our friendship to arrange it – but surely David could not go against your heartfelt wishes quite so easily. It was a decision I felt only I could take.

I hope you'll forgive me a hopelessly melodramatic image – perhaps my monstrous vanity will even amuse you – but the situation put me in mind of throwing myself on a grenade, but in a karmic sense if you take my meaning. Ridiculous, mawkish bravado, I know, but irresistible nonetheless. I like to think that whoever one day writes my obituary, they will now have more material to work with than just the phrase 'diligent scholar'.

I let those I contacted believe that you were, both of you, held ransom pending delivery of the collection. I promised them that I would not make its contents public on condition that they remove Jan from the picture and let you two innocents go free. As I understand it, they cleaved to their word with a lack of integrity matched only by my own – an occupational hazard, perhaps, when liars treat with villains.

I wonder now if, despite all the many dangers you

both faced, the moment when Karst deliberated over your fates was not as perilous as any. Had she caught a glimpse of gold upon either of your fallen forms it might have sealed your fate. Yet, a little quick thinking on your part, Susan, completed the job Jan started when he disarmed you – and so, despite himself, he helped to save you from Karst. If between you (Susan) and Jan you had failed to conceal all that gold jewellery, might she not have dispatched you both simply to err on the side of caution. Then again, it occurs to me that she saw Susan as a protégé. Consider: I have found no mention of women adepts anywhere in the collection. Ah, but we needn't dwell on these things. Not now that the sun is shining (where you are at least) and all is well.

So rather than ramble on all day, I'll save the rest of my idle thoughts for the next instalment. I'm going for a walk along the head in a moment – the sea air agrees with me, or at least I imagine it does, which is nearly the same thing. Today I have the heart of a lion.

Of course, perhaps my improving health has nothing to do with the sea. It could be the change of pace or some subtle but important alteration in my diet. It could even be those very interesting meditation techniques I've been studying in the collection. (If my dear, departed sister could see me decked out in her jewellery I think she'd despair for me.)

Which leads me to my parting thought. When you have both mended and taken some time for yourselves – I am thinking in terms of months, after all you have been through – once you feel you have recovered, we'll have to give some thought to what we want to do about all this. There are things here that perhaps the world at large should know.

At any rate, I think I can safely say I'll still be in the land of the living when you feel it's time, so don't hurry back on my account. And I'm sure Susan will want to know that I believe I've found another code in the collection and the contents are rather disturbing. Naturally, they are three hundred years old, so disturbing or not, they can wait until Autumn (though whether Susan's curiosity, now doubtless piqued, can also wait we'll have to see).

I'm going now to see if I can locate an ice cube. Can you believe it; I have a new tooth coming through!

Yours with all possible best wishes,

Joseph Shaw

The End

Snowbooks

Adept Copyright © Robert Finn 2004
Underlife Copyright © Robert Finn 2008

Proudly published in Great Britain by
Snowbooks Ltd.
120 Pentonville Road
London N1 9JN
www.snowbooks.com
Printed and bound by J. H. Haynes & Co. Ltd., Sparkford

A CIP catalogue record for this book
is available from the British Library

ISBN 978-1-905-00592-5

www.snowbooks.com/RobertFinn